Derek Wilson is a leading writer of popular history, biography and fiction. He has over thirty titles to his credit, including the internationally acclaimed *Rothschild: A Story of Wealth and Power* and *The Astors: Landscape with Millionaires*. After graduating from Cambridge he spent several years travelling the world, working by turns as teacher, antique dealer, magazine editor and radio presenter, and he still writes documentaries and radio plays as well as serving as an Anglican lay reader. Since their three children grew up, Derek Wilson and his wife have divided their time between homes on Exmoor and in Normandy. Also available from Headline, *The Triarchs* is his first novel featuring Tim Lacy, and a third, *The Hellfire Papers*, will follow shortly.

Also by Derek Wilson

FICTION
Feast in the Morning
A Time to Lose
The Bear's Whelp
Bear Rampant
The Triarchs

NON-FICTION
A Tudor Tapestry
White Gold – The Story of African Ivory
The World Encompassed – Drake's Voyage 1577–80
England in the Age of Thomas More
The Tower 1078–1978
Sweet Robin – Robert Dudley Earl of Leicester
Rothschild: A Story of Wealth and Power
The Circumnavigators
The Astors 1763–1992: Landscape with Millionaires

The Dresden Text

Derek Wilson

HEADLINE

First published in 1994
by HEADLINE BOOK PUBLISHING

First published in paperback in 1995
by HEADLINE BOOK PUBLISHING

10 9 8 7 6 5 4 3 2 1

ISBN 0 7472 4427 8

Typeset by
Letterpart Limited, Reigate, Surrey

Printed and bound in Great Britain by
Cox & Wyman Ltd, Reading, Berks.

HEADLINE BOOK PUBLISHING
A division of Hodder Headline PLC
338 Euston Road
London NW1 3BH

'The old order changeth, yielding place to new,
And God fulfills himself in many ways,
Lest one good custom should corrupt the world.'

Tennyson – The Passing of Arthur

PART I

THE RIDER ON A WHITE HORSE

Then I saw the heaven opened, and there was a white horse. Its rider is called Faithful and True; it is with justice that he judges and fights his battles.

The Revelation of John the Divine 19:11

Prologue I

The television screen flicked instantly from blank grey to an interior scene depicted in clear detail. Elevated view, wide angle. It showed a small, empty vestibule. On the left was a glazed street entrance. On the right, a receptionist's desk and behind it two office doors. No sign of life.

Then an indistinct figure appeared outside. Moments later one of the office doors opened and a man in the dark uniform of a security guard emerged. He crossed to the front door. He called through the glass. He peered at something pressed to the pane by the visitor. Hesitated. Then took a bunch of keys from a top pocket of his blouson jacket. With one he opened a bottom drawer of the desk and pressed the first of a row of switches. He returned to the door and, using three more keys, opened it.

The figure that stepped into the foyer was a policeman. Rain dripped from the peak of his cap. After a brief exchange the security man turned, leading the way into the premises. Immediately, the policeman drew a gun from inside his topcoat. It had a long barrel. He pointed it at the guard's neck. The weapon recoiled three times and the victim fell forward, bounced from the desk and collapsed to the floor. The policeman walked round him and disappeared out of shot to the right.

Tim Lacy pressed the rewind button, then started the tape again. For the fifteenth time he watched the murder of his friend.

Prologue II

Black and white velvet. The night and the snow. A full moon drifting between opal clouds illumined the upward-tilted fields between the river and the forest edge, now submitting to the silent application of winter. It confused the monastery into blocks of solid shadow and insubstantial patches of brick. The buildings, sprawled beside the wide expanse of water, slept within the security of their protective ramparts. Their inmates slept. The fields slept beneath the deepening comfort of white fur. The river, too, seemed to sleep: the dull gleam of its monochrome surface betraying no motion.

The crash of massive doors violently thrown open split the stillness. Four horsemen emerged from the blackness of the main gateway. Cantering up the slope they went, the thud of hooves muffled by the snow. Only at the brow of the hill, where the impenetrable pines began, did they rein in.

No words passed between the four hooded men. Three watched as their leader brought something heavy out from the thick folds of his travelling cloak. He spread it on the horse's mane and the moonlight glowed on gold leaf, on vivid splashes of blue and crimson. He divided it into four parts. One he tucked back inside his cloak. The others he distributed. He raised a hand in salute, wheeled his horse and cantered southwards along the forest fringe. The others turned to the north-west and spurred away into the darkness. None cast a backward glance at the monastery.

Flickering yellow light now streaked the snow between the buildings. Somewhere there was the crash of a collapsing roof and a shaft of flame arrowed upwards into the night. Across the snow-subdued landscape came the urgent, agitated clanging of a deep-toned bell.

Chapter 1

Tim Lacy did not like New York. He did not like private views. And he did not like having to be polite to clients in whom ignorance and arrogance jostled for supremacy. He turned a well-trained smile on the young man before him and raised his voice above the chatter in the stuffy, crowded gallery.

'Good turn-out, Rob.'

Robin Brand fingered his Harvard tie and looked around the Manhattan smart set with a smirk of self-satisfaction. 'Yeah. I can't wait to find my dad and tell him "I told you so". The old buzzard was convinced no one would come to a view just before Christmas. "Anyone who matters will be either out of town or panicking over last minute shopping," he said. Yeah, well, just take a look.' He waved his glass of white wine towards the fashionable multitude. 'The arts editors of the *Tribune* and the *Times* are both here, along with all the little guys. And several top collectors – Senator and Mrs Gracewell, Abe Karnheit. And, of course, all the big dealers, come to look at the new boy on the block. The old man's going to eat his words and I'm going to be holding the spoon.'

'Don't be too hard on him. He did put up the money.' Tim liked Constantin Brand. The old man had run the best

7

modern art gallery on Fifth Avenue since long before he could remember. His impeccable discernment and clever business methods had, over the years, launched a dozen painters and sculptors who were now household names. It was because of Constantin that Tim had agreed to install the security systems in Robin Brand's new gallery. 'You are the best,' Constantin had said, clasping Tim in a bear hug. 'And I want only the best for my Robin.' Useless and, perhaps, unnecessarily cruel to tell the old emigré that the 'all-American' son he was so proud of would almost certainly turn out to be his greatest failure. Fresh out of college, Robin Brand thought he knew all there was to know about the complex international art and antiquities market. Tim watched the petulant frown crease the face of this boy, little more than half his own age, and was suddenly glad that he had not had a rich father to back his career. Everything Tim Lacy had learned had been learned the hard way.

'Peanuts! In a couple of years this place will be turning over millions.'

Tim vetoed the retort that sprang to his mind. He said, 'I'll drink to that,' and raised his glass.

Rob Brand's lips registered something between a smile and a sneer. 'You don't believe me, do you? Well, you just carry on with your – *expensive* – security business and watch this space. Judy, hi! Glad you could make it.'

A thirtyish brunette swathed in designer silk drifted up and offered her cheek. 'Bruno and I are *en route* for the Carnegie concert. We just had to drop by and see your collection. Rob, however did you manage to find so many beautiful things . . .?'

Thankfully, Tim detached himself and slithered through the crowd.

'Making good your escape?'

'Gerda!' Tim smiled his genuine pleasure at the tall blonde who held her hand out to him. 'You're a long way from Geneva.'

'Walter and I came over for the Sotheby's Renaissance sale a couple of days ago. We had to stay on for today's opening. It's called keeping an eye on the competition.' She spoke excellent English but with a heavy Teutonic accent.

Tim laughed. 'Competition? In a millennium from now, when Rob Brand knows as much about medieval art and antiquities as you do, then you can start worrying about competition.'

'Do I detect a *frisson* of disapproval? I don't care much for Brand *fils* either, but he has put on a very good show. Getting together this loan collection of illuminated manuscripts was quite an inspiration, you must admit.'

Tim nodded. He gazed around the exquisitely-arranged display. Spaced around the walls in glass-fronted alcoves were fifteen glowing examples of medieval monastic penmanship. Rob Brand, trading on his father's connections in two continents but distancing himself as far as possible from the old man's sphere of expertise, had decided to go in for rare pre-1500 artefacts. He had decorated his suite of display rooms in Walt Disney Gothic – all arches and imitation stonework. His greatest coup had been to persuade private collectors and museum curators to lend some of their prized possessions for his highly-publicised opening. There were psalters, Bibles, books of hours and glittering fragments from once-great volumes, sundered by time.

'They add tone, don't they?'

'Yes, Gerda, they certainly add tone.'

The proximity of these masterpieces to Brand's own stock of medieval carvings, pottery, ivories, tapestries and paintings had enabled him to add twenty per cent or more to the price of every item. As an exercise in hype, Tim grudgingly had to award it full marks.

'I assume it's this very valuable collection that brings Tim Lacy here with his bag of tricks?' Gerda Frankl arched a plucked eyebrow. 'Have you been setting Master Brand up with hidden cameras, infra-red beams, pressure pads and sundry computerised gadgetry?'

'The owners had to be satisfied that their precious manuscripts were safe.'

'The name Lacy is a good enough guarantee for any guardian of private or public treasures today.'

'It's good of you to say so.'

Gerda pouted. 'Don't be coy, Tim Lacy. With so many unscrupulous and clever thieves about and highly-paid gangs stealing to order, we depend on your – *unconventional* – brand of security. Look at the Liège Psalter over there. There's only one man living into whose custody Van Helgen would have entrusted that. Hello, Oscar.'

They had been joined by a stout, lumbering man with ample, ruddy features. 'Rubicund' was the word which came to Tim's mind whenever he bumped into Oscar König.

He nodded in response to the German's greeting. 'The world and his wife seem to be gathered for Robin Brand's little soirée.'

Oscar pulled a large, patterned handkerchief from his breast pocket and wiped moisture from his brow. 'I spend as much time in New York as Berlin nowadays – though why, heaven knows. The American way of life – pah! You know why so few Americans go to hell, Gerda?'

'Tell me, Oscar.'

'Because it's too damned cold for them. I'm getting out of here – too stuffy.'

Tim nodded. 'I'm going to cut and run soon.'

'Good, good. You can join me for dinner.'

'I'm afraid not, Oscar. I have a couple of bits of shopping to do, followed by an early night. I'm booked on the first London flight tomorrow.'

The big man shrugged. 'Next time, then. Remember me to your lovely wife.' He cut a swathe through the crowd. After five paces he stopped, half turned and waved. 'Happy Christmas!' he bellowed, then blundered away towards the street door.

Gerda gazed after him thoughtfully. 'Odd to see Oscar here. This is scarcely his line of country.'

The Berlin dealer, as they both knew, specialised in the Russian icons and religious artefacts which flowed through the no-longer-divided city. Most of them were stolen from remote country churches and smuggled westwards by truck drivers, diplomats and other paid couriers. There was no doubt in Tim's mind that König was hand-in-glove with a Moscow crime syndicate.

Tim drained his glass and handed it to a passing wait-ress. 'Perhaps he's broadening his scope – in case things get difficult in his present line of business.'

The elegant Gerda emitted a surprisingly deep, throaty chuckle. 'Yes, things could get even hotter for our friend if he's not very careful.' She held out her hand. 'So you're hurrying back home for a typical soggy English Christmas – plum pudding and indigestion by the fire. Well, I won't keep you.' Her grip was very masculine. 'Till we meet again, Tim.'

'Goodbye, Gerda. Compliments of the season to you and Walter.'

Tim checked his watch and wondered if there was anyone else among the throng of people who were here to be seen who was worth seeing. Then, he noticed the unmistakable, bizarre figure of Arthur Meredith, beckoning to him over the heads of the crowd. Six-foot-four, thin to the point of emaciation, clad in black and sporting exuberant facial whiskers, he looked like a Victorian undertaker. As Tim joined him he pointed at the fifteenth-century book of hours he had been studying intently.

'Fantastic, just fantastic. Isn't that fantastic?' He spoke American with an English accent. 'What wouldn't I give to have something like that in my little collection?'

Tim smiled. 'As I remember, you have a couple of examples of French work which run this pretty close.' He recalled his visit to Meredith's Frankfurt home a few months before: the modern, architect-designed house; the expanses of white wall which showed off the exquisite Italian Renaissance furniture; the library which housed this strange man's treasured accumulation of early manuscripts.

Meredith sighed deeply, unable to avert his eyes from the illuminated display. 'But collecting is all about the quest for elusive perfection and the unfulfillable desire to possess it. It's a disease. You're not a collector, are you, Tim?'

'No, I just try to help collectors hang on to what they've got.'

'A sort of unofficial policeman?'

'Policeman? No, I try to prevent crime, not solve it.'

'Well, anyway, don't ever let yourself get bitten by the

bug.' He looked doleful – an effect enhanced by the bushy side whiskers.

'Are you over here long this visit, Arthur?'

The tall man flapped his long, seemingly uncoordinated arms. 'I spend all my time travelling. The other day someone asked me where I live. I told him "At thirty-five thousand feet somewhere over the Atlantic." Still, it has its occasional compensations. There are some wonderful pieces here that I've never seen. This one is a gem.' He nodded towards the case. 'Tell me, if such a book came onto the market, what do you think I could expect to pay?'

'You know the market in early manuscripts better than I do.'

'Yes, but I'm interested in your opinion, Tim. Humour me. Say, "Arthur, you can expect to pay X for such a book." '

Tim laughed. 'OK, Arthur, I guess you can expect to pay a million for a book like this.'

'Dollars?'

'Pounds!'

'Yes, I suppose you're right. Ah, well.' He took out a gold hunter from his waistcoat pocket and flicked it open.

'Goodness, can that really be right? What time do you have, Tim?'

Tim checked his wrist watch. 'It's about 6.30.'

'I must go. So long, Tim. Look me up next time you're in the Fatherland.' He swayed his way agitatedly through the crowd.

Tim had brief words with a couple of other acquaintances. Then he, too, eased his way to the door. On the right were two offices. The spacious one, with 'Robin Brand' on the door in gilt Gothic, he ignored. The purely functional secretary's room was doubling as a cloakroom

13

and Tim collected his topcoat from a pile on the desk. He opened the connecting door to another office at the rear which was little more than a cubicle.

'I'm just off, Mike. Everything OK?'

The small, middle-aged man swivelled his chair around so that he was no longer facing the three TV screens. 'Right as rain, Major.' There was something refreshingly normal about the grinning, bald Yorkshireman. He was genuine, straightforward, unpretentious – unlike the clientele milling about in the gallery oohing and ahing over the exhibits while eyeing each other shrewdly and, above all, trying to impress each other with their knowledge and their wealth. Tim and Mike went back a long way. 'Sergeant Thomson, MK', as he then was, had served under Tim in the SAS and had been one of the first to sign up with Lacy Security in its tentative beginnings, seven and a half years before.

Tim closed the door behind him. 'You ought to know that we're not altogether flavour of the month with our young client.'

'That's all right, Major. I'm none too struck on him.'

Tim laughed. 'He's a pretentious twit, Mike, but he is our client. So keep that northern frankness of yours under control. And don't get drawn into any arguments about equipment or money. Mr Brand is convinced that we're overcharging him.'

Mike snorted. 'We've cut every corner we can, and one or two we shouldn't have.'

'I know. And Mr Brand knows. I've told him that this,' he waved a hand at the command panel beneath the bank of monitors, 'isn't up to our usual standard.'

'If he thinks security's an unnecessary luxury, he'll learn the hard way. Folk like him are such know-alls until something goes wrong. Then . . .'

'Just you make sure nothing does go wrong.'

'Don't worry, Major. Just leave it to me. You get back to the bosom of your family and have a lovely Christmas.'

'I'm sorry you and George are going to be stuck here over the holiday.'

'Well, I'm not sorry.' The older man winked. 'Best alibi I've had in years. We're due to go to the wife's brother and sister-in-law. We do it every other year. God knows why. It never works. Me and Reg are like oil and water. Well, this year I've got the perfect let-out. How about you, Major? Christmas at home?'

'Yes, it'll be very quiet. Last year we came over to Maine to be with Catherine's parents. But that was before the baby arrived. Now that she's a mother Catherine's got a home-building fixation. So we've got to have the works – turkey, tree, mince pies, crackers . . . the lot.'

'Quite right, too. Oh, your mentioning the baby reminded me.' He took a gift-wrapped package from the pocket of his blue uniform jacket. 'Something for young Toot.'

'Toot' was the nickname of Tim's son. When he had been christened 'Timothy Younger Lacy', his maternal grandfather, a Bible-loving Presbyterian, had immediately dubbed him '2 Timothy', and this had been progressively shortened to 'Tootim' and 'Toot'.

'Mike, that's very kind of you.'

'It's nothing much.' Mike covered his embarrassment with a gruff command. 'Now then, away with you and don't forget to wish Mrs Lacy all the best from me and George.'

Tim emerged onto 43rd Street, turned into neon-spangled Fifth Avenue where the hordes of shuffling shoppers were illuminated by the light from overstuffed store windows, ran the gauntlet of charity-can-rattling Santa Clauses and found the shop he was looking for. It sold original paintings on acetate from animated cartoon studios. He bought a couple of Bugs Bunny designs for Toot's Christmas present. They would look bright on the nursery walls and their value would increase with the passage of the years.

He decided to take a cab the short distance to the St Regis Hotel. He dined in his room, ordered an early call, went to bed at 10.30, drifted into oblivion with pleasant thoughts of homecoming filling his mind, and slept the sleep of the just.

In the morning he phoned Catherine to tell her that he was on schedule. 'Back about midnight, Darling. Don't wait up.' He knew she would.

'You'd better have plenty of energy left,' his wife said. 'No time for jet lag. It's Christmas Eve tomorrow and you drew the short straw for trimming the tree. And you haven't forgotten that half the county's coming for drinks in the evening?'

Tim grinned. 'You certainly enjoy playing the English squiress.'

'English, nothing!' Catherine protested. 'It's pure New World hospitality. Anyway, I have to run. I've a list of things to do as long as your arm. See you soon.'

Tim spent most of the cab ride to Kennedy Airport reflecting on how lucky he was. It was eighteen months since he had brought a tall, blonde, twenty-nine-year-old American bride back to his new Wiltshire home. Not that Farrans Court was new; far from it. Part of its stolid façade was already old when the Wars of the Roses were raging. Successive owners had added their own contributions to its sprawl. Fire and 'restorers' had lopped bits off. After the changes and chances of history the Farrans Court of the late twentieth century was a medieval-Tudor house crouched in a shallow hollow near Marlborough. To the Lacys it was home and office, business and pleasure, a practical centre for their commercial activities and a piece of English heritage to care for and be proud of. Above all it was a place to love. Catherine and Tim loved it very much. It was also fiendishly expensive to maintain, which was why it had to pay for itself. As well as being the nerve centre of the security firm, Farrans was run as a gallery-cum-hotel where young artists could display their work and meet dealers, critics and collectors. The arts centre was Catherine's business and she ran it with efficiency, charm and flair. It kept her busy, which was as well, since Tim's work often took him abroad. Farrans. Catherine. Toot. They were the sheet anchors of Tim's Flying Dutchman restlessness. Anchors which, until a couple of years ago, he had despaired of ever finding. Yes, at thirty-eight he was certainly a very lucky man. In vain he looked around the cab interior for a wooden surface to touch.

He timed his arrival at the airport to ensure minimum delay, checked in and declared only a single piece of hand luggage. He had long-since perfected the art of packing one case with all his necessities so as to avoid hanging around in baggage halls or having his belongings carried to wrong destinations half a world away. He went straight to the departure lounge.

His flight had just been called when he was aware of his name being announced on the loudspeaker.

'Would Mr Timothy Lacy, passenger for London, come to the information desk, please?'

The stewardess smiled and handed him a telephone.

'Hello, Tim Lacy here.'

'Mr Lacy, glad I caught you.' A man's voice – brisk, official, colourless. 'Lieutenant Freeman, New York Police Department. I'm speaking from the Brand Gallery on 43rd.'

Tim felt a sudden lead weight of foreboding in his stomach. 'Trouble?'

'You could say. There was a break-in here last night. I believe your company handles the security arrangements.'

'Yes, but—'

'I'd be grateful if you could get over here. There are one or two questions . . .'

'Is that really necessary, Lieutenant? I want to get home for Christmas.'

'Yeah, me too. Stay in the terminal building. I'll have a squad car pick you up.'

Tim tried again. 'There are two of my men on the spot there. I'm sure they can tell you everything you want to know.'

'I doubt that, sir. There was some shooting. The duty security guard . . .' he paused – consulting his notes, Tim assumed – '. . . a Mr Michael Kevin Thomson, was killed.'

Chapter 2

'So much for your goddamned security systems!' Robin Brand pounced before Tim had taken two paces inside the door. Gone was the suave image of the previous evening – the Italian suit, the silk shirt and college tie. The proprietor barred his way, clad in jeans, sneakers, and a cashmere sweater, quivering with rage, indignation and fear. 'I only hired you because my father recommended you. And what happens? I get turned over the first night. Jeez! I'll be a laughing stock and it's your f—'

'Mr Lacy?' Tim was rescued by a balding, moustached man in his mid-forties. 'Al Freeman, NYPD. Sorry to mess up your plans, sir. Would you come through into the office, please?' The policeman was more brusque with Rob Brand. 'Sir, would you please go with this officer and check the stock one more time? We need to be absolutely certain that only the one item is missing.'

'But, Lieutenant, I already told you . . .'

'Sir, we have to be sure.'

Brand stamped off, muttering furiously. Tim preceded Freeman into the security office. The first thing he saw was the solid form of George Martin, immaculate in blue suit with the 'Lacy' flashes on the lapels.

'George, I'm sorry about all this.' Martin had known

19

Mike Thomson even longer than Tim had. Tim knew what
the ex-Marine sergeant was feeling. Knew also that Martin
would not let any trace of his emotions show.

'Good of you to come back, Major. This is a nasty
business. I just wish I'd been here. If I'd been twenty
minutes early reporting for my shift, I'd have caught the
bastard. Then it would have been his body in the morgue,
not Mike's.'

Tim shook his head firmly. 'Don't even think about
blaming yourself, George. What time did it happen?'

Freeman interrupted. 'Can we get down to business, Mr
Lacy? I don't want to hold you up any more than I have
to.'

He dragged a chair up to the small table and motioned
to the others to be seated. 'Thanks to your excellent
equipment, we can watch the whole thing. Your man here
has sorted out the tapes from the various cameras. I've
already run them through a couple of times. Now, I'd like
you to take a look, see if there's anything you can tell me
about the killer.'

'Anything I can tell you?'

'Just watch.' Freeman firmly brushed aside the question.
To George Martin he said, 'Play it again, Sam.'

The right-hand console flickered, then threw up a black
and white image. Fascinated and horrified, Tim watched
the last moments of Mike Thomson's life captured for
posterity. Captured and timed – beginning, as indicated in
the right-hand bottom corner of the screen, at 02.35.09.

The security guard came into shot walking towards the
glass front door of the gallery. A figure on the outside
could be dimly seen, gesticulating. Mike peered closely at
something in the visitor's hand.

Freeman explained, 'There's a police patrolman at the

door. He wants to come in and your man is very properly demanding to see his ID.'

Mike walked over to the desk and opened a low drawer. 'He's switching off the door alarm,' George said.

Mike returned to the door with his bunch of keys, and unlocked it. Freeman said, 'Watch this bit closely.' Mike stood for some seconds in the open doorway. Then he stepped back and the policeman, in cap and overcoat, took a couple of paces inside the gallery. Mike said something and the man nodded. Mike turned, leading the way back into the gallery. The visitor closed the street door. He pulled a silenced automatic from inside his topcoat. He shot Mike in the back, three times.

There was something surreal about the dumbshow assassination – the soundless recoil of the gun, the puppet-like jerk of Mike's body, arms flung wide, its slow-motion toppling first to the desk, then to the marble floor without any noise. Tim was mesmerised. Feelings numbed.

He saw the 'policeman' walk round the body and out of shot. Then the screen blacked out as George switched to the second console and a different tape. It showed the centre room of the gallery from a high angle. The murderer entered, stage right. He paused, looking at a piece of paper, then crossed to one of the glazed alcoves which housed the loan exhibits. He read the display label, checked his note again, then set to work – swiftly and efficiently. From his pocket he took a small quantity of plastic explosive and applied it to the lock. He attached two wires and backed out of sight. Seconds later, a silent explosion set the toughened glass door gaping. No sharp splinters. No mess. No risk of damage to the contents. Lock blasted cleanly from the wall.

The third act of the drama was the briefest. The assassin

reappeared, removed the item from the case, slipped it inside a plastic shopping bag, and left with firm, unhurried steps.

'Show over!' George pointed his remote control at the screen and the image faded.

Freeman stared across the table. 'What do you make of that?'

Tim was still having difficulty interlocking thoughts and feelings. It was hard to register that he had just watched the cold-blooded murder of an old friend. The only words that came were stunned, unconnected units of sound. 'Professional. Ruthless. Pointlessly ruthless.'

Freeman rubbed his tired eyes. Tim realised for the first time that, as case officer, he must have been here five or six hours already. 'Pointless?' The lieutenant shook his head. 'That's not the way I see it. This was planned, down to the last detail.'

'Even the killing?'

'Yeah, even the killing. Did you notice anything about that bogus cop? He never said a word. He made signs through the door. When your man asked questions, he just nodded, perhaps grunted.'

'So?'

'If he'd opened his mouth, your man might have been suspicious.'

Tim frowned.

'Not convinced? OK, let's try another angle. I don't know this bastard. I don't recognise him or his *modus operandi*. I've been in the department twenty-six years, most of them right here in this precinct. In all that time I've never come across a crime with the same brand image as this one. We'll run all the data through our computers, but I've got ten dollars says this is no home-grown homicide.

This killer was brought in from out of state to do a specific job.'

Tim nodded. 'I go along with that. This has all the marks of a contract theft. Someone wanted a specific item stolen, and they paid a professional to steal it.'

'Right. Now, you've been involved with security in the international art market for a long time. Did you ever see this pattern before? Like I really think this guy's a foreigner. Not just from out of state; brought in from abroad.'

'Isn't that rather a wild guess?'

'You get a feeling about these things after quarter of a century. Anyway, it ties in with the guy's silence.'

'You reckon he may have had a heavy accent?'

'Or his English wasn't so good. Either way, he couldn't sound like a New York cop and your man would have smelled a rat if he'd said more than a couple of sentences.'

Tim made an effort to drag his mind away from Mike Thomson. 'I've certainly been involved with a number of robberies and attempted robberies. It's part of my job to study changing criminal methods. I can't call to mind anything very similar at the moment. Imitating a policeman or some other authorised person isn't new, of course, and I've known thieves kill when they get in a panic. But unnecessary, cold-blooded murder?' He shook his head. 'I'll certainly check my files as soon as I get back to my office. What was it that was stolen – the Liège Bible?'

'No, not according to Mr Brand.' Freeman referred to his notebook. 'He says the only thing missing is . . .' He squinted at his scrawled handwriting '. . . the Dresden Text – is that right?'

'The Dresden Text?' Tim's brow crumpled into a frown.

'Surprised?'

'Yes, I am rather.'

'Why?'

'Well, Lieutenant, this is a very special exhibition of medieval illuminated manuscripts.'

'Sort of early picture books?'

'That's one way of describing them. They were hand-painted by monastic craftsmen in incredible detail – abstract designs, animals, mythical beasts, scenes from everyday life. They're superb works of art. Each one, each page, is unique. They are, of course, extremely rare.'

'And valuable?'

'Naturally. Only well-funded museums and a few rich connoisseurs can afford to own collections.'

'So what's surprising about someone arranging to add this Dresden Text to his collection?'

'Just that it was one of the least important items in this display. Look, let me show you.'

He led the way out into the gallery and took the lieutenant on a tour of the exhibits. 'A French book of hours – probably one of several commissioned by the Duc de Berry, a fourteenth/ fifteenth-century collector. The Harkville Psalter – Irish, tenth century. The Liège Bible – earliest complete text in French and stunningly illustrated. Made for Louis IX – Saint Louis. The Verona Vulgate – arguably the finest piece of pre-Renaissance Italian work-manship. Lieutenant, all these are priceless.'

'And the Dresden Text isn't?'

They stood before the empty niche with its glass door hanging open. The descriptive note, tastefully printed on cream card, read

THE DRESDEN TEXT

This fragment of a Bible or New Testament is some-thing of a mystery. It dates from the late fourteenth century and was probably made in the Abbey of St Wulfberga, near the modern city of Dresden. It contains the full biblical text from the *Epistle to the Romans* through the *Revelation of St John*. The illustrated capitals are remarkable, particularly those displaying horses – a constant theme throughout the fragment. Nothing is known of its history prior to its appearance in the library of an Austrian nobleman in the late nineteenth century.

Loan courtesy of the Manuscripts Dept, British Library, London.

Lieutenant Freeman stepped back from the empty case. 'Small beer, huh?'

Tim shrugged. 'A superb fragment, but only a fragment. Certainly not in the same league as most of the other exhibits.'

'What you're saying is, "Why'd our guy go to all that trouble for something worth relatively little, when he could just as easily have taken something worth a whole lot more?" '

'Exactly.'

'He looked like he knew what he was doing. He checked carefully. He went straight to that particular case. He read the description before setting the explosive.'

Tim had to agree, although it seemed to make little sense. Part of the pattern was familiar: a wealthy collector or a crime syndicate employing a skilled professional to acquire a specific item. It was the kind of crime that was becoming all too common. What was odd about it was the bad economics. Experts like Mike Thomson's killer don't come cheap. Tim knew the insurance value placed on the Dresden Text because he had had to cover it in transit.

Two hundred and fifty thousand pounds. On the black market it would be worth about half that. By the time the expenses of the operation had been paid the profit margin would be minimal.

Freeman broke in on his thoughts as they walked back to the office. 'Why do you have your own staff here, Mr Lacy? We do have experienced security guards in this ex-colony, you know.'

Tim smiled. 'There's nothing chauvinistic about it, Lieutenant. Our security systems have a few rather specialist elements. We insist on training the people who are going to operate them. The arrangement here was that my men would be in charge till after Christmas, then spend a couple of days training local staff hired by Mr Brand.'

'I see. What'll you do now?'

'That'll depend on Mr Brand.'

'Well, I'd be happier to see all this stuff put away in a bank vault somewhere until you and Mr Brand have finished talking it out. We'll be done with him in an hour or two. Then you're welcome to him. Meantime, I suggest you go get some coffee.'

'I want this bastard, Major.' George Martin stared down at the black liquid in his cup and expressed his anger in cool, controlled tones.

'Well, you can only have him if I don't get to him first.'

In a diner a few doors along from the Brand Gallery the two men sat morosely, each trying to come to terms with his loss.

The usually taciturn ex-sergeant found relief in talking. 'Sitting in there with the body last night and cops milling all over the place, I was remembering how Mike and I first met. Belfast 1972. Mike was seconded to our unit from

26

REME. He hadn't been there more than a week when the two of us got separated from our patrol and pinned down by sniper fire somewhere off the Falls Road. We've been in quite a few scrapes together since then and Mike never got so much as a scratch. Snipers, terrorists, guerrillas, bandits – he faced 'em all. And he ends up getting shot in the back, without a chance, by a hired killer – all for a few scraps of old parchment.'

'Don't worry, George. I'll make sure they nail the murderer.'

'I hope these Yanks know what they're doing.' George did not look very convinced.

'Freeman seems on the ball.'

The two men fell silent. At the next table a family party – Mum, Dad and two young girls – were enjoying a Christmas outing. Bags and packages were spread around them. The kids were demolishing multi-coloured ice creams in tall glasses. There was a lot of laughter.

Tim reflected that Lacy Security was more a family than a business. It was small. Everyone mucked in together. Most shared a military background and had never really grown out of the soldier's mentality. They enjoyed the unsocial hours, the uncertainty of being sent anywhere in the world, often at short notice. They were closer to each other than ordinary colleagues or workmates.

He looked at George Martin, officially designated 'Head of Operations'. 'I'm sorry, George. It must have been dreadful for you. Did you discover the body?'

'No, half the neighbourhood were there by the time I arrived. Busting the display case lock had set the alarm going and no one knew how to switch it off. There were police, local residents and late-night revellers all over the place. Major,' he changed the subject, 'what's the form with Madge Thomson, Mike's wife? We've never lost anyone on the job before. I don't know whether I . . .'

'No, it's not down to you, George. Madge will be officially informed through diplomatic channels. Freeman will get on to our embassy and they'll set the necessary wheels in motion. I'll go down and see Madge in a few days.'

'You're sure you wouldn't like me to . . .?'

'I'll need you to keep an eye on things here for a while. I shall have to face the museum and talk to the insurance people. God, this'll look bad for the firm.'

'Not your fault, Major. If that precious Brand fellow hadn't skimped on details . . . There should've been a double door. Then Mike could've taken a close look at that phoney copper.'

'I wonder if it would have made much difference. It was a clever idea – clever and simple. A solitary policeman. Even if Mike was suspicious he must have reckoned he was more than a match for one man.' He drained his cup. 'Another coffee?'

When the waitress had refilled their cups, Tim turned to the other aspect of the night's activities. 'Got any ideas about this burglary? It seems very odd to me. Hiring a top-notch professional to steal a medium-priced item. It's the sledgehammer and the walnut, George.'

The older man put on a disapproving frown. 'From what I've seen of rich collectors, you can't apply any ordinary rules to them. They're obsessed. Some of them would stop at nothing to get an item they've set their hearts on.'

Tim shook his head. 'But they don't like splashing money about unnecessarily. And there can't be many who'd actually sanction murder.'

George shrugged. 'He may not even know about it.

Someone in a plush office somewhere picks up a phone and says, "Get the Dresden Text for me. I don't care how you do it. Just get it." '

Tim pondered that analysis silently for several seconds and sipped the hot, strong coffee. He looked up. 'Well, you're right about one thing. Whoever ordered this job is just as guilty as the man who pulled the trigger. I'll do my damnedest to see them both behind bars.'

'Amen to that, Major.' One of the precocious little girls at the next table was making faces at him over her empty glass. George grimaced and stuck his tongue out at her. She went into uncontrollable giggles. 'Kids! Why do they have to grow up?'

Tim nodded.. 'Kids!' Then sat up suddenly. 'Oh my gosh, Catherine!' He looked at his watch. Well past noon. In Wiltshire it would be getting-Toot-ready-for-bed time and Catherine would be looking forward to her husband's imminent return. He stood up. 'George, I have to get to a phone and placate an angry wife.'

By the time Tim had made sketchy explanations to Catherine, called the airline office and spent an hour sorting out new arrangements with a still-smouldering Rob Brand, a drizzling light grey afternoon was giving way prematurely to a drizzling dark grey evening. He arrived at Kennedy Airport feeling as soggy as the city he had just left. Before him lay the prospect of a night flight. He hated night flights. He knew he would not sleep, would not be interested in any of the movies on offer and would not be able to concentrate on even a lightweight whodunit.

He was right. By the time he had collected his car from the long-stay car park at Heathrow and pointed it west-wards down the M4, he felt like a zombie and a potential menace to other road users. The holiday trek out of the capital had already begun and Tim needed all his concentration to manoeuvre his 31-year-old Porsche Roadster around family saloons with high-piled roof racks hogging the centre lane. It took forty-five minutes to reach his motorway exit, but at last he was crossing the chalk downs south of Hungerford and approaching, by ever-narrowing lanes, the hollow where Farrans Court lay hidden from the world.

It was a crisp December morning. The low sunlight had just begun to slew across the south front of the old house and glint on the first floor casements. As he brought the car to a halt on the gravel and uncreased himself wearily from the bucket seat, Catherine appeared in the arched porch. The roll-neck green jumper and matching check trousers enhanced her slim figure and fair colouring.

Wordlessly she wrapped herself round him in a long welcoming hug. Then she held him at arms' length and studied him – sympathetic and practical as ever. 'My poor Darling. It must have been awful. What you need right now is a shower, a brandy and a bed, in that order. I'll wake you for lunch and you can tell me all about it then.'

In fact, it was not till bedtime that they had a chance to talk without interruptions. Catherine's enthusiasm to 'do Christmas properly' saw to that. Her first English Christmas and her first in her own home had to be perfect. She had bought the biggest tree she could find. It dominated the great hall and reached right up to the gallery. It took the two of them plus the au pair most of the afternoon to decorate it. Then there were drinks and snacks to lay out in the hall. They scarcely had time to change before their guests began to arrive. Tim tried to be a sparkling, attentive host and was aware that he was not making a very good job of it. Three or four couples lingered on till gone 10.00 and soon after 11.00 Catherine propelled her drooping husband out into the frosty night for the short drive to Little Farrans church for midnight service.

When, at last, they had retreated to their snug flat in the east wing Tim walked straight through to the bedroom and threw himself down on the counterpane fully clothed. His body felt as though it was seeping into the mattress but his mind was suddenly wide awake. As Catherine undressed, he narrated the sequence of events at the Brand Gallery.

Before he had finished she came and sat beside him. She laid a cool hand on his brow. 'We'll all miss Mike badly.'

'He was always so cheerful; always looking on the bright side; the sort of man to have beside you in a crisis. Do you know, he gave me a Christmas present for Toot.'

'How sweet. And how typical. He and Madge didn't have any kids, did they?'

Tim was only half listening. 'Do you know what makes me so mad? The poor sod never had a chance. Never knew what hit him. One moment standing there in the gallery. The next – nothing, *finito*.'

Catherine lay down beside him. 'You're not blaming yourself, are you?'

'I've never lost anyone. In almost eight years we've had some nasty situations, some close calls, but I've never lost anyone.'

'Tim. Darling.' She propped herself on one elbow and looked down at him. 'You didn't *lose* Mike. He was a grown man, responsible for his own actions. With a hired assassin like that, he never stood a chance. It's the killer who's responsible; no one else.' She kissed him lightly.

'Well, I'm damned well going to make sure he pays for it – and whoever is behind him.'

'That's what the cops are for. You reckon this Lieutenant Freeman seemed on the ball?'

Tim rolled off the bed and slowly peeled off his clothes. 'I'd say he was pretty shrewd, but he doesn't have much to go on.'

'He knows what the murderer looks like.'

'Yes, but if the killer is as efficient as he seems, and if Freeman's right about him being a foreigner, he's probably disguised and out of the country on a false passport by now.'

'Well, there's nothing you can do about it.' She addressed the observation to Tim's back as he stood before the cheval mirror, brushing his dark hair. She noted the unyielding set of his shoulders. 'Tim, there really *is* nothing you can do.'

'And another thing,' he spoke to his reflection. 'I don't like objects going missing when I'm responsible for them.'

Catherine turned down the covers and slid between the sheets. 'Come to bed, Tim.'

He climbed in beside her and lay on his back, brow wrinkled. 'Why the Dresden Text? That's the key; I'm sure of it. Somebody wanted it – and wanted it so badly that they sent an armed killer to get it. But who?'

Catherine snuggled up to him. 'Whoever it is, getting the Dresden Text has probably made his Christmas.'

'Yeah.'

'Darling, let's try not to let it spoil ours.'

Chapter 3

'It really is too bad, Mr Lacy. I was due to stay in Scotland till after New Year. This means two whole days out of my leave. You realise I'll have hell's delight trying to claim another two days later, don't you?'

Dr Hesther Macready – five-foot-nothing of Highland indignation – led the way at a brisk pace past the museum showcases, flinging verbal grenades over her shoulder as she went. 'Heaven knows I don't get home very often, Mr Lacy, and to have this news landing like a bombshell on Christmas morning – *Christmas morning*, Mr Lacy. Well can you imagine the effect it had on my holiday?'

Tim tutted sympathetically as he hurried in her wake and resisted pointing out that for him, too, the season just past had been anything but festive.

'My boss couldn't come. He's in Salzburg. So he had to telephone me. Can you imagine how *shocked* I was, Mr Lacy?' She surprised him by stopping abruptly and turning to face him with thick eyebrows arched over searching green eyes.

'I realise how awful . . .'

'We were *both* deeply shocked. This way.' She was off again steering a tortuous path between the displays of autographed letters, exotic bindings and incunabula.

33

She came to rest, at last, before a door into which she inserted a key produced from the pocket of her culottes. They entered a corridor. Dr Macready unlocked another door and ushered Tim into a cubicle that would have been cramped had its contents not been arranged with mathematical precision.

Dr Macready seated herself primly behind the desk, motioned Tim to the only other chair, and moved her PC to one side so as not to impair her view of the man who had complicated her life. 'Well, what happens now?'

'Well, I . . .'

'Presumably there are procedures, but I'm not *au fait* with them. I've never faced this problem before. We don't make a habit of losing things at the British Library. In fact, nothing's gone missing from this department since I've been here. I mean – the very idea!'

She was shocked into a momentary pause by this near blasphemy and Tim grabbed his opportunity.

'The New York police will circulate full details in the States and to Interpol, international auction houses and other major outfits.'

'You will forgive me, Mr Lacy, if I find that assurance rather underwhelming.' Her frank stare had in it a trace of humour and Tim thought she could be quite an attractive woman. As if reading his mind, she scowled. 'Do you know what percentage of stolen art treasures are ever recovered?'

'The last published figure was twenty-two per cent.'

'So the odds on our getting the Dresden Text back are in the region of five to one against.'

'Looked at that way . . .'

'What other way do you suggest we look at it, Mr Lacy?' Tim tried a new tack. 'Any additional information we

34

can provide may help. That's one reason why I asked for this meeting and cut into your holiday so unforgivably.'

'I thought you were a security expert, Mr Lacy, not a detective.'

'In my job I have to be a bit of both. I know the world of dealers, experts, collectors, museums and – sad to say – specialist thieves rather better than the average policeman. So they often come to me for help.'

'So you have a good idea where our missing manuscript is?'

Tim laughed. 'Oh, I didn't say that. But perhaps with your help, I may be able to make some inspired guesses.'

'What can I tell you?'

'Perhaps, what it was that was special about the Dresden Text?'

'Special?'

'Someone wanted that manuscript very particularly. The thief deliberately ignored more valuable items in the exhibition and made a beeline for this fragment of a fourteenth-century Bible. I keep asking myself "Why?" Any ideas?'

'I must confess the same thought had occurred to me.' She opened a file on the desk in front of her. 'I anticipated your visit. This is all the information we have on the Dresden Text. It's been here in the museum since 1897, when it was bought from Count Conrad von Aufenberg.'

'Who's he?'

She shrugged. 'The record doesn't say. Perhaps some Austro-Hungarian nobleman fallen on hard times.'

'Has it often been loaned for exhibition?'

'Three times, including the current loan.'

'And the last was when?'

Dr Macready referred to her notes: '1933 – a big

exhibition at the Bibliothèque Nationale in Paris – *Les Arts Monastiques*.'

'Was it on regular, open display here?'

'No. Frankly, Mr Lacy, we have many more significant works of the period in our collection. I'm afraid the Dresden Text has languished in our vaults for the greater part of the last century.'

'So this has been the first opportunity anyone has really had to get hold of it?'

She fixed him with eyes still dark with disapproval. 'It's the first time since 1933 that this manuscript has been out of the museum. And inside the museum we have a very effective security system.'

Tim persevered from behind his defensive smile. 'But, of course, outsiders – scholars, students, experts – have studied it here?'

'That is what we exist for, Mr Lacy – to help *bona fide* researchers with their work.'

'So you would have a list of all the people who have handled the Dresden Text?'

'Thousands of people have temporary or long-term readers' tickets. Every one is thoroughly vetted. Scores of them use our reading room *every day*. Hundreds of manuscripts, documents and incunabula are accessed *every day*. There are very strict procedures governing the handling of items – especially those, like the Dresden Text, which call for particular care. So we have neither the time, nor the inclination – nor, indeed, the need to keep records of who's seen what.'

'Then, we have no means of knowing who has shown an interest in the Dresden Text in recent years?'

'Not unless they've published something significant and given the library an acknowledgement.'

Tim thought he saw the faintest glimmer of light at the end of the tunnel. 'And has anyone . . .'

Dr Macready was already holding out a slim pamphlet in a faded blue cover. Tim took it and read the legend, 'Offprint from the Journal of Ecclesiastical History', followed by a volume number in Roman numerals. The title of the article was inside: 'The Dresden Text and the Teutonic Knights, by Hans Fischer.'

'Professor Fischer's monograph sets out pretty well all that is known about the Dresden Text – or, at least, all that was known seven years ago, when he wrote it.'

'May I keep this?'

'I'll get you a photocopy.'

'And this Professor Fischer – do you know where I might find him?'

She referred to her files. 'Seven years ago he was at the University of Hamburg. If he isn't still there, they'll know where he's moved to.' She stood up. 'Well, if there's nothing else, Mr Lacy, I'll get your photocopy.'

Tim thought, 'Class dismissed!' He said, 'I'm very grateful to you for your time, Dr Macready. Perhaps you'd allow me to offer you some lunch.'

To his surprise she turned in the doorway and gave him a smile. 'Under the circumstances, that's the least you can do, Mr Lacy. Thank you.'

Over the next couple of hours Tim devoted all his energies to thawing the relationship between the British Library and Lacy Security. Not until his mid-afternoon train slid out of Paddington was he able to read Hans Fischer's learned treatise and to ponder on the connection – if any – between the Dresden Text, a medieval order of chivalry, and a murder in Manhattan.

★ ★ ★

There was no vision. Ulrich's young limbs, stretched out on the cold stone, ached for a while, then went numb. Yet, try as he might, the fair-haired novice had no sensation of his spirit, body-freed, soaring upwards through the carved stone vault – obscured now in thick shadow – across the greater void of infinity to the curtain wall of heaven. On this eve of his initiation as a knight of Christ, no angels rushed to fling wide the portals of the New Jerusalem to give him a glimpse of the splendours within.

For hours he fixed his gaze intently on the single candle set before the high altar. He willed its wavering flame to take on the shape of the Blessed Virgin or one of the saints who were the special protectors of the Order. He urged his ears to translate the chapel's wind-whispers into revelations of divine will. When he could no longer hold his head up and was forced to rest it on the hard granite of the choir floor he incanted countless *Paters* and *Aves*, hoping through repetition of the familiar to achieve a state of holy trance. When that failed, he lifted his eyes again. He could scarcely make out the figures on the carved and painted altarpiece. That did not matter: he knew the details by heart. Every day of his five-year novitiate – with the exception of periods spent on campaign with his uncle Sigmund – he had kept the canonical hours with this Marienburg chapter of the order. Had processed into this chapel eight times every day for prayer and chanted praise. He no longer needed to see the Virgin and Child flanked by St Elizabeth and St George, to know that they were there, looking down on him. He could sense the doleful crucifix in its muted polychrome. Yet neither the remembrance of the Saviour, nor anything else about this sacred place, enabled Ulrich to hold his thoughts on those holy topics which, according to novice-master Pieter, were appropriate to a man keeping his lonely vigil before being admitted as Knight of the Order of St Mary of Jerusalem.

There were too many other exciting and daunting thoughts scurrying about in his mind. The most powerful was pride. At last he was taking over the family tradition which had linked the von Walenrods with the Teutonic Knights for generations. Many younger sons of this great house had donned the black cross and served – some in the Levant and others on the northern crusade. Greatest of all had been his grandfather, Conrad von Walenrod who, as Grand Master, had steered the Order through one of its more critical phases. It was Conrad who was remembered in one of the Order's most treasured possessions. Though out of Ulrich's line of vision, it lay just a few feet from his outstretched body. Grand Master von Walenrod had presented, at his own expense, a magnificent Bible. It had pride of place on the altar at Marienburg. Passages from it were read on special occasions. Only senior members of the Order were allowed to handle it but Brother Pieter had, sometimes, obtained permission to show it to the novices. Ulrich remembered vividly the thick book with its golden clasp dotted with jewels and the gem-like quality of the pictures within – the glowing reds, blues and greens, the sinuous animals and plants which adorned the letters of the text, which only scholars like Brother Pieter could read. The Marienburg Bible gave Ulrich a very special link with the Knights of St Mary – almost a proprietorial link. And now he was to take his place among them.

What mission would the Grand Master have for his newest warrior? There were many trouble spots to which he might be sent. Never had the Teutonic Knights been more hard pressed. There were those among the older brothers who said that this year, 1454, was the worst the

Order had faced since their expulsion from the Holy Land two hundred years before. Well, difficulties meant opportunities for a young knight to prove himself. Perhaps he would be sent out with a force to break through the lines of the Polish army now encircling the city of Marienburg. He had heard talk in the frater of a major counter attack to open a supply route from the Vistula. Or he might lead a reconnaissance party to discover the weak points in the enemy's lines. Then again someone ought to be sent eastwards to the *Landmeister* in Livonia or westwards to the *Deutschmeister* in Swabia to hasten reinforcements from the other provinces of the Order. They must be told that Marienburg was in danger from the Grand Master's own rebellious Prussian subjects, in league with the King of Poland.

Ingrates! The Order brought the holy faith to these Baltic wastelands. The Order civilised its barbaric people. The Order established the rule of law. The Order made it possible for men to till the ground without fear of marauding hordes. The Order encouraged Hanse merchants from Lübeck . . . Bremen . . . set up new trading posts like . . . like Danzig . . . yes Danzig and . . . and Riga . . . The Order built . . . great . . . cities . . . like heroic . . . Marienburg . . . Marien . . .

Ulrich was woken by the great bell calling the brothers to prime. He suppressed a yawn as sandalled feet shuffled past him and the knights took up their positions for the first office of the day.

Ulrich remained prone, motionless before the altar as the familiar recitation of psalms and responses continued. But his heart beat faster as the short litany drew to its conclusion.

At last the moment came. The touch on the shoulder

and a knight brother on each side helping him to his feet.
The sub-prior stepped forward for the catechism.

'Ulrich von Walenrod, are you a member of any other
Christian order?'

'I am not.'

'Are you married?'

'I am not.'

'Are you suffering from any physical infirmity?'

'I am not.'

'Are you in debt?'

'I am not.'

'Are you a serf?'

'I am not.'

The young man felt a tremor all over his body as the
moment of his solemn vows arrived.

'Will you fight for the Christian faith against unbelievers
and heretics?'

'I will with God's help.'

'Will you go to any land where you are sent?'

'I will with God's help.'

'Will you care for the sick?'

'I will with God's help.'

'Will you practise any craft in which you are skilled as
ordered by your superiors?'

'I will with God's help.'

'Will you obey the Rule of our Order?'

'I will with God's help.'

'Then, Ulrich von Walenrod, I call upon you to make
your submission.'

The tall figure of the Grand Master moved to the space
before the high altar. Ulrich knelt. He held his hands
together before his face and they were clasped by the
larger hands of the old warrior. Ulrich concentrated hard,

determined not to stumble over his words.

'I, Ulrich von Walenrod, do profess and promise chastity, renunciation of property, and obedience, to God and to the Blessed Virgin Mary, and to you, Brother Ludwig von Erlichshausen, Master of the Order of St Mary of Jerusalem, and to your successors, according to the Rules and Institutions of the Order, and I will be obedient to you, and to your successors, even unto death.'

The Grand Master spoke the few words which irrevocably changed the young man's life. 'Ulrich von Walenrod, I welcome you to the brotherhood of the Order of St Mary of Jerusalem.'

He raised the new knight to his feet and clasped him in a brief embrace. Then he turned to receive the insignia brought by the sub-prior from the altar where it had lain overnight. Over Ulrich's shirt went the coarse, grey, knee-length habit, then the white surcoat with the long black cross front and back. The Grand Master settled around Ulrich's shoulders the white mantle with the black cross on the left shoulder. Finally he delivered into the young man's hand the strong sword, undecorated save for the image of the Virgin chased on the pommel.

There remained one final ceremony. Ludwig von Erlichshausen turned to the altar and lifted the great Marienburg Bible – Conrad's Bible; Ulrich's Bible. He brought it to where the new knight stood. Ulrich bent forward and kissed the polished calf skin just above the clasp with its globules of precious stones.

He raised his head. And at that moment he was, briefly, granted his vision. The first rays of the sun burst through the great east window in a blaze of multicoloured brilliance. They clothed the Grand Master's head with heavenly radiance and threw a halo around his close-cropped, iron-grey hair.

As the train gathered speed again after Newbury, Tim turned the last page of Professor Hans Fischer's scholarly exploration of the possible connection between the Dresden Text and the Teutonic Knights. He finished reading, sat back against the BR upholstery and felt little the wiser.

The manuscript, according to Fischer's hypothesis, had originated in the celebrated scriptorium of St Wulfberga's Benedictine Abbey near Dresden around the middle of the fourteenth century, at the time when the Latin Church was thrusting into the last wide tracts of heathendom to the north-east and hurrying to get there before rival missions despatched from Orthodox Byzantium. It was commissioned by or presented to the Teutonic Knights – a fact 'proved', in the professor's submission, by the frequent depiction of horses in borders and illuminated capitals and by the occasional appearance of the Order's device, a black cross on a white or silver ground. This occurred long after the Teutonic Knights' role in the Holy Land had come to an end and they had discovered a new one in the territories bordering the Baltic. These half-knights, half-monks were, for the most part, sons of German noble houses, members of an aristocratic élite who needed a reason for living and who found in the northern crusade a holy cause which sanctified their devotion to the military life.

Fischer believed that what was now called the Dresden Text was part of a collection of biblical material though whether of a complete Bible it was, of course, impossible to say. Nor could he cast much light on the book's subsequent fragmentation. The golden age of the Teutonic Order had lasted almost two hundred years, during which time they had converted and colonised tens of thousands of square miles comprising (in modern terms) northern Poland (Prussia), the greater part of Lithuania, Latvia (Livonia) and Estonia. During the course of the fifteenth century the power of the knights ebbed away rapidly, sapped by internal divisions and external pressures. The monastic ideal of Christian chivalry became an anachronism. It buckled under the forces of economic growth and political change. Much of its territory was incorporated into an expanding Polish state and thereafter the Teutonic Knights ceased to figure prominently in European history. Professor Fischer suggested that the volume of which the Dresden Text formed a part was probably carried off as booty during a Polish raid and subsequently broken up by ignorant troops interested only in the precious metal and perhaps jewels which, in all likelihood, adorned its cover.

Which all seemed to close the door quite firmly on one line of enquiry. People were driven to murder by all manner of bizarre motivations but surely not out of a passion for the artistic relics of a long-defunct band of pseudo-Christian bullyboys. Oh well, it had been an idea worth following up. Probably Catherine was right; these things were best left to the police. Tim slipped the monograph into his brief-case and reached down his overcoat from the rack as the train's intercom announced its imminent arrival at Pewsey.

When he reached Farrans after the short drive from the station, Catherine was out and there was a note on his desk. '*3.15 Gone over to Swindon to see Madge*

Thomson. Lieutenant Freeman phoned from New York. Wants you to call him back. Home by 6.00. Love you. C.' Tim dialled the number Catherine had jotted down for him.

Freeman's voice said, 'Mr Lacy, hi! I thought you'd want to be the first to know – we got the murderer.'

Chapter 4

The 18th September 1454 was one of the most memorable days in Ulrich's life, but it began with a shock. Restless with excitement over the coming battle, he slept fitfully and went early to the Church of Elizabeth, the Order's chapel in the garrison town of Choinitz. He let himself out of the house where he was billeted and climbed the narrow streets towards the church nestling against the massive castle wall. No one was about, but as he passed the licensed brothel its door opened. A man staggered out, fell to his knees, and pitched face forward into the mud. 'And don't come back till you've got money!' the *Wandelborefrower*, or 'woman of shame', shrieked as she slammed the thick oak back into place. Ulrich stared down in horror. It was not yet first light but there was no mistaking the white, though wine-stained, surcoat of a knight brother. Ulrich helped the man to his feet. For his pains he received a fist in the chest which threw him up against the wall. This was followed by a string of oaths before the stranger went reeling away up the street.

That was only the first part of the new knight's shock. Members of the Order were under oath to keep all the canonical hours whenever possible. Ulrich counted less than three dozen at prime. For the dedicatory mass that followed the church was scarcely half full. Of course, one did not expect great devotion from mercenaries, who now made up the larger part of the Order's armies, but if the knight brothers themselves were setting a bad example . . .

The sun was still streaking the underside of the clouds with pink and gold when Ulrich took his place at the top of one of the towers overlooking the plain to the west where King Casimir's army was camped. There were four knight brothers at this station. They shared the breakfast of coarse bread, salt herring and water brought by a servant. Ulrich said nothing about his encounter with the man in the street but he did raise with the others the question of why so many had absented themselves from divine office.

'Men have different ways of preparing themselves for death,' Hans, a bearded Saxon, muttered through a mouthful of bread.

Conrad, a dark-haired young man from one of the oldest families in Westphalia, nodded. 'For me it has to be silent prayer, as private as possible. For others . . .' He shrugged.

Otto von Stetten, an old companion of Ulrich's uncle, tested the edge of the sword he had been sharpening. 'On battle days this is my breviary. If I neglect it I don't deserve to survive. This is your first taste of the real thing, isn't it, Brother?'

Ulrich stiffened, feeling patronised. 'I often went on campaign with my uncle . . .'

'But when it came to the hand-to-hand stuff he made sure you were with the supply waggons or holding his spare horse. There's a first time for all of us, Brother. Nothing to be ashamed of.'

Hans was less charitable. 'I suppose you think . . .' he

belched loudly '. . . we ought all to meet our maker at the altar, then sally forth in brotherly harmony to meet him again, if need be, on the point of lance or sword?'

Conrad glared. 'Don't mock him, Hans. Just because you've lost all your ideals, that's no reason to disrespect those who haven't fallen into your cynicism.'

'It's not cynicism. I'm just trying to make him realise that if he comes safely through today – as, please God, he will – he'll see things very differently tomorrow.'

Ulrich shook his head. 'My family has served the Order for generations. I was brought up to serve it – to make my vows *and to keep them*. In my grandfather's day . . .'

Otto interrupted. 'When your grandfather was Grand Master, times were very different.'

'How different?'

'Simpler. It was just us and them. Christians versus pagans. Culture versus savagery. Now, we get more trouble from the Christians we've helped to establish here – farmers, tradespeople, fat Hanse merchants. Now they're all ganging up against the Christian knights and inviting Christian kings like Casimir to help them. So which side is God on, eh? And another thing – in the old days we used to fight our own battles. Now there aren't enough youngsters coming forward to take up the black cross. So we pay men who have no loyalty to any god but Mammon. And so do the enemy. So what it comes down to is mercenaries against mercenaries. What matters at the end of the day is not who has right on his side but who's got the better paymaster.'

Conrad laughed. 'It seems this cynicism is contagious.'

'Shut up the pair of you!' Hans was leaning over the low parapet, straining his eyes towards the enemy camp. 'Things are on the move. Casimir's coming out to play.'

Ulrich watched as the Polish cavalry formed up, armour glinting in the low sunlight. 'He has no choice.'

The watchers from the walls of Choinitz were ideally placed to realise the truth of that observation. There would be a battle and it would be on ground chosen by the military leadership of the Teutonic Order. To Ulrich it seemed that the coming gigantic clash would settle the complex political situation once and for all.

All summer there had existed a situation best described as animated stalemate. Large bodies of men had moved back and forth over a wide area of Prussia without basically altering the *status quo*. Casimir and his allies had invested the knights' capital at Marienburg but failed to break its resistance. The Grand Master had sent to Germany for massive reinforcements. In order to block their advance the Polish king had divided his force in a bid to take Choinitz, some seventy miles from Marienburg, which commanded the western route. With the end of the campaign season fast approaching, Casimir would soon have to withdraw to winter quarters. This prospect was of little comfort to the Grand Master. The enemy might retreat for the colder months but it would only be to reappear in the spring, when the financially wasteful sequence of events would begin all over again.

That was why Ludwig von Erlichshausen had decided on a bold, perhaps reckless, move. Letters carried by brave couriers to his principal subordinates established the details of the strategy. The Order was to throw every available knight and mercenary horseman it could muster into a pitched battle before Choinitz. Erlichshausen had sent all the men he could spare from Marienburg (including Ulrich and his three companions). The Grand Hospitaller, Heinrich von Plauen, had brought seven hundred troops from Elbing, at the mouth of the Vistula. His cousin Albrecht von Plauen, Master of Germany, arrived before Choinitz with the main contingent of eight thousand. Albrecht's men were now camped a mile to the south-east of the town. With the potential reinforcements within the walls, the Order had something over nine thousand fighting men to confront Casimir and the Prussian League. But the Polish king had forty thousand troops under his command. A third of them were deployed around Choinitz, keeping the defenders penned up. The remainder were encamped less than a mile to the west of the town.

This superiority in numbers should have been enough to ensure victory. But Albrecht was able to alter the odds somewhat by choosing his ground. His line of advance towards the encircling Poles took him across an area of marsh and small rivulets. As Ulrich said, Casimir had no alternative but to enter this boggy terrain to prevent the knights falling on the unprotected besiegers.

From their vantage point the defenders of Choinitz could watch the two armies.

'There goes our advance!' Ulrich pointed to the ridge away to the left where a white-coated mass of cavalry detached itself from von Plauen's main contingent. Like a shard of ice on a spring river it moved down the slope towards the swampy ground.

At the sound of a trumpet-call the watchers swung round to the right. Grimly they observed a huge mass of Polish horse circuiting the wet ground at full gallop.

'Casimir's leading the charge himself!' Hans pointed to the black and gold standard fluttering at the head of the enemy column. 'He'll reach our troops before they're into the marsh.'

Horrified, they followed the drama. Von Plauen's

advance guard spurred into a canter as they saw the danger of being caught in the flank. They had left it too late. The Poles would be upon them before the soft ground broke the impetus of their charge.

'Turn back!'

As though responding to Otto's growl, the white-clad horsemen wheeled away to the right, angling across the flank of the ridge. The spectators heard the triumphant whoops as the pursuers gave chase.

Then, as the enemy crossed the ground between the swamp and von Plauen's position, a second wave of Teutonic Knights detached themselves from the hilltop.

'That's Rudolf von Sagan and his Silesians. I'd recognise that great white stallion anywhere,' Hans shouted.

Now it was the Poles who were taken in the flank.

'They're faltering! They don't know which way to go!'

Casimir's pennant came to a halt. He tried to turn his men to face the new danger. But his contingent was too large and unwieldy. Some tried to retreat. Others swung to the right. The forward impetus of their own troops to the rear hampered these manoeuvres and created fresh confusion.

Meanwhile, the Order's advance guard had come to a halt at the crest of the ridge. In almost leisurely fashion they went about, formed up immaculately, then thundered down the slope, lances lowered. The two bodies of knights fell simultaneously on the superior force. The metallic clash echoed over the intervening ground. Ulrich and his companions felt the tower walls tremble at it.

The air rang to the crash and clang of hand-to-hand fighting and the cries of wounded men and horses. Many of the lightly-armed knight brothers leaped from their mounts to wield their swords with more deadly efficiency against enemy horses and riders. The more ponderously equipped Poles struggled to remain in the saddle, to avoid the marsh, to find room for manoeuvre. For almost an hour the turgid mass of men and animals swayed back and forth, neither side gaining any advantage.

Then came the sound of fresh, urgent trumpet-calls from the Polish camp.

A broad smile creased Hans's bearded features. 'Calling the reserves! This is our chance!'

From the lines of troops encircling the walls, small groups of horsemen separated themselves, cantering across the open ground to join the as yet uncommitted Polish force. This left the town gates poorly guarded.

A horn blared below. The knights rushed to their assembly points – some in the market square, some in the base court of the castle. In the square, Ulrich grabbed the reins from his servant and accepted a hoist into the saddle. He took the light lance and adjusted his helmet. Then he sat, alert, part of a strangely silent body of mounted men. A few yards away, the Grand Hospitaller, dressed no differently from the knights under his command, but accompanied by the black-on-white standard, waited while the contingent from the castle clattered down the short hill. When the troop was assembled he raised a mailed arm. He crossed himself. All the knight brothers crossed themselves. A horn sounded the advance. The main gates of Choinitz swung slowly, heavily open. And the Teutonic Order's last reserves moved forward to join the battle.

'Lieutenant, that's fantastic. You certainly don't let the grass grow under your feet.' Tim was genuinely surprised and relieved to learn of Freeman's success.

'Yeah, well, even the NYPD sometimes get things right.

But, I gotta tell you, we had a tip-off.'

The line fell silent. Obviously if Tim wanted more information he was going to have to ask for it.

'So, who was the killer? And who was behind the robbery? Have you got the manuscript? What did . . .'

'Hold on, Mr Lacy. I gave you the good news first. The bad news is that, no – we haven't recovered the stolen property. It must have been passed on already.'

'But surely you can make the murderer talk; find out who he gave the Dresden Text to?'

'We don't employ psychics, Mr Lacy. The murderer's dead.'

'Dead?'

'There was a shoot-out. At the end of it we had one extremely ex-public enemy. A shame, but it saves the city the expense of a trial. And it means I can stamp "closed" on the file.'

Closed be damned, Tim thought. 'But, Lieutenant . . .'

'Sorry, Mr Lacy, I don't have time to go into details. I just wanted you to know that justice has been done. Your colleague's death has been avenged.'

'Well, thanks. Naturally I'm glad you caught the bastard. Er . . . congratulations.'

'All in a day's work. Look, I guess you'll be back here soon.'

'Yes, I shall have to review the gallery's security with Mr Brand. Try to convince him that there's nothing wrong with our equipment.'

'Well, when you're here, if you'd like to call in at the precinct house I'd be happy to answer your questions. So long for now. Oh, by the way, I was right about the murderer not wanting to speak. One word and your man would really have – as you say – smelled a rat.'

The line went dead.

Over supper in their small kitchen Tim and Catherine caught up on each other's news.

'How's Madge?' Tim attacked his cold turkey without much enthusiasm.

'Still in shock, I think. Her sister-in-law is staying with her but I'm not sure she's much use. She keeps trying to jolly Madge along – "Get her out of herself" as she told me. Of course, what the poor woman needs to do is grieve and she won't be able to do that until she has Mike's body.'

'Any news of that?'

'The embassy rang her this morning. They're flying Mike home on Friday. I called in at the local undertakers and made the necessary arrangements for the casket to be collected from the airport.'

'*You* did.'

'Tim, if I hadn't those two women would still both be sitting there wondering what to do.'

'Poor Madge.' Tim went to the fridge and collected a can of beer. 'I don't know whether it will help her at all, but the New York police tracked down Mike's killer.' He reported his conversation with Freeman.

'Well, I'm glad that's all over.' Catherine collected up the plates and stacked them in the dishwasher. 'Mince pies or strawberry ice cream?'

'Just coffee, I think. I certainly couldn't face another mince pie until next December.' He stared at his wife. 'What do you mean, "over"?'

'Over, as in finished, ended, concluded, wound up.' Catherine spoke the words firmly, her back to him, her body language warding off any other point of view. 'Or, to use Freeman's words, "case closed".'

'But they haven't found the manuscript.'

'Did you ever seriously hope that they would? The Dresden Text is just one of thousands of art works that go missing every year – and thank God it's not an important one.' She filled the kettle and ladled a measure of coffee beans into the grinder – back still firmly turned. 'So, it's gone. Big deal. The insurance company will pay up. The library will buy something more interesting with the money. *Life will go on!*'

If Tim saw the storm cones he ignored them. 'That's just it; life will go on for everyone – including the perpetrator of this outrage. That means that next time he takes a fancy to some precious, rare object and a human life happens to stand in the way, there'll be another Madge Thomson waiting for a coffin delivery.'

Catherine poured boiling water into the cafetière. 'And having Tim Lacy worry about it won't make two cents' difference.'

'Yes, but . . .'

'But nothing!' Now she did turn to face him. 'Listen, Tim! We've had this business hanging over us all Christmas. Now I don't blame you for that. Of course you were angry and worried. I was, too, specially after seeing Madge. But the police have got a result. In a few days we'll be able to lay Mike to rest. In my book, that means the affair is O-V-E-R. Madge has to get on with her life. If she can do it so can we. So, could we, please, start the new year without you pursuing this Dresden Text as though it was the Holy Grail.'

Tim stood up and held out his arms. 'That bad, eh?' he observed as she came to him. 'I'm sorry it's made such a mess of our first Christmas at home. I guess you're right. The best thing we can do is forget about it.'

Catherine hugged him tight – and knew that she had lost

the argument. Oh, well, she had married an idealist, a dragon-slayer and, if she was honest with herself, she did not really want him to change. She drew back and gave him a quick kiss.

'Pour your coffee while it's hot. I'm just going to check on Toot.'

In the doorway she turned. 'By the way, I'm thinking of changing the name of this place.'

Tim looked up, cafetière in hand. 'Oh, really? What to?'

'Camelot.'

Tim had to wait a quarter of an hour in the general office of the East Manhattan precinct house because Lieutenant Freeman was interviewing a suspect. He tried to close his ears against the hubbub – the battering of telephones, shouted badinage, customers demanding attention and arrested suspects calling upon heaven to bear witness to their innocence – and wondered how any work ever got done in such an atmosphere. He had made this his first port of call on his arrival because he could not settle to anything else until he found out all there was to be found out about Mike's murderer and the manner of his arrest.

'Mr Lacy, hi!' When Freeman did arrive he was in shirtsleeves and braces and was sweating. 'I swear, it gets harder every year to put the fear of God into these kids. Round here a crook's a pro by age eight. C'mon in.'

He led the way into an untidy office and Tim was careful to close the door behind him, shutting out about eighty per cent of the din.

The lieutenant dropped into a chair that creaked its protest. 'You couldn't stay away, then, Mr Lacy?'

'You were very enigmatic on the phone.'

'I guess I just wanted to see your face when I told you

about our killer. Would you mind opening the door?'

Tim did so and the next instant felt the full force of a Freeman command issued in a voice that would have been the envy of any drill sergeant.

'Marie! Brand Gallery file! And two coffees!'

All three items were delivered with impressive alacrity by a mouse of a policewoman who, mercifully, closed the door behind her. Freeman opened the slim, buff file cover and extracted a photograph. 'That's the murderer.'

Tim's eyebrows rose as he gazed at the morgue shot. 'But it's . . .'

'A woman, yeah. Shook me, too, especially having seen the killing on your video. Didn't someone say the female of the species is deadlier than the male?'

'You're sure there's no mistake?' Tim looked closely at the features of a middle-aged female with close-cropped blonde hair.

'Uh-uh. She still had the police uniform and we even found the bottle of dye she'd used to colour her hair as part of the disguise.'

'Do you know anything about her?'

'Oh, we know a whole heap of things about her.' He read from a typed sheet of paper. 'Name: Emma Freundlich. I'm told that's German for "friendly" – jeez! Date of birth – seven, ten, forty-five. Wanted in West Germany, Holland, Belgium and France in connection with assassination, armed robbery, abduction and other terrorist offences. Former convictions: 1969, fifteen years for armed raid on the Hamburg Creditbank in Wiesbaden. Escaped jail, August 1973. Convicted *in absentia* of the bombing of the American Embassy in Paris, 1974; the abduction and murder of the Swiss businessman Otto Streicher, 1976; the shooting of three policemen in Bonn, 1977. Suspected of complicity in several other crimes. Known associates: the Baader-Meinhof gang; the Red Brigades. Last known whereabouts: Istanbul, 1984. Here, see for yourself.' He handed Tim the paper edged in crimson. 'That's an Interpol red notice, the category they keep for top international criminals.'

'I've sometimes wondered what happens to old terrorists when their confederates are dead or behind bars, and they've run out of causes or excuses for violence. It seems that some, at least, turn into hired assassins. You still reckon she was brought into the country to do this job?'

'There's nothing in her record to connect her with America. According to Interpol the only recent, unconfirmed sightings have been in Turkey, Hungary and Germany. There'll be several police forces in Europe glad to put Ms Freundlich's records away in the basement.'

'How did you find her?'

'Anonymous phone call directed us to a modest hotel only a few blocks from the Brand Gallery. I took a couple of men, found the number of the room, knocked on the door. The next moment something zips past my right ear and I'm staring at a bullet hole. Well, we took no chances. I told my men to draw their guns and go in shooting. Then, like I said, we found plenty of evidence to connect her with the gallery murder.'

'Did you manage to trace her movements, her connections?'

'The room was booked by phone in the name of Emma Braun and she registered as a Swiss citizen.'

'Credit card number?'

'It was prearranged for her to pay cash. She arrived two days before the murder and spent most of the time in her room. None of the staff recall speaking to her.'

'She probably had no English.'

'That's what I reckon.'

Tim sat silently for some moments, sipping aggressively strong coffee. Much of what he had just heard was puzzling. 'The more you look at it, the less sense it seems to make.'

'What do you mean?'

'I spent a few years in the SAS – that's a sort of band of paid military criminals. That gave me some experience of planning and carrying out small-scale, clandestine operations. Our rule number one was KISS – Keep It Simple, Stupid. Just enough men, just enough equipment to do the job with a reasonable chance of success. Don't overelaborate. If you use a small team, follow straightforward instructions. If you have the advantage of surprise, and if you have a little bit of luck, you'll probably get away with it. Now this robbery has all the basic elements of a good plan. Above all, it's simple: one man, dressed as a cop, fools the guard, gains access, deals with the guard, makes straight for his single targeted objective, steals it – and away. An expert could do it inside three minutes. He wouldn't need much facial disguise to fool the security camera or the guard. Do you see what I'm getting at?'

Freeman sat back in his chair. 'Carry on.'

'It's as near as dammit a perfect crime. *So why louse it up with unnecessary elaboration?* Why bring in a woman – a foreign woman who probably has little or no English? Why murder the guard when a tap on the head would be just as quick and effective – a trained man can gag and truss a victim in seconds? That only risks the involvement of homicide experts and a much closer enquiry.'

'I guess they all along intended to use this ex-terrorist female, so they had to accept her methods.'

'And she's now conveniently dead and can tell you nothing. What does that suggest to you, Lieutenant?'

Freeman put his hands on the desk and eased himself wearily to his feet. 'It suggests that I'm mighty grateful to our anonymous informant for lightening my work load.'

'But, Lieutenant . . .'

'No buts, Mr Lacy, sir.' Freeman's tone changed abruptly. 'Do you know how many unsolved crimes we have in this precinct alone?' He paused slightly after the rhetorical question. 'Neither do I. I stopped counting long ago. It used to depress me. Day after day, I have the press on my back, and the politicians, and the citizens' organisations. Why aren't we doing more to clean up the city? Why are we losing the war against crime? I tell you, that doesn't do much for morale around here. So when I get a chance to wrap up a case quickly and tell the loudmouth critics that we're not as dumb as they say, I grab it.' He pointed to the photograph of the dead woman. 'Emma Freundlich, a dangerous terrorist, commits a crime on my patch. I nail her. That pleases my boss. He gets his back thumped by the mayor. For a couple of days, the newspapers are on our side. The New York cops have succeeded where all the police forces of Europe have failed. For a couple of days, my team here feels pretty good. But what's best about it is, I can add another file to the "case closed" pile. OK, so there are a few ragged edges, a few unanswered questions. That's life, Mr Lacy. At least, that's a cop's life.'

Tim did his best to calm the atmosphere. 'I'm sorry. I obviously trampled on a sore foot. I wasn't intending to criticise you or your men. Thanks to you there's one less person in the world committed to violence. I'm sure it will help Mike's widow to know that his killer has paid the price for her crime.'

'I shouldn't have sounded off at you.' Freeman's affability returned as quickly as it had vanished. 'You're obviously concerned to trace your manuscript. Believe me, we're doing all we can. A stolen art notice has gone to all the usual outlets. You never know, we might get lucky.'

Tim stood up to take his leave. 'I'd like to see the Dresden Text back where it belongs, of course. But what worries me more is the growth of violence related to art theft. What used to be a specialist – almost gentlemanly – activity, is now just part of the muck heap of international crime. The Mafia, terrorists, drug runners, company fraudsters – they're all connected with stealing, smuggling and illicit dealing in stolen artefacts. It's a vicious trend and one I'd like to put a stop to.'

Freeman laughed. 'Well, don't go starting any one-man crusade.' He held out his hand.

'Sorry, that all sounded very pretentious. Goodbye, Lieutenant, and thanks for taking me into your confidence.'

Tim's restlessness went on nibbling away at him. He was uneasy about the contradictions and enigmas that bedevilled the whole Dresden Text affair. And he was uneasy about his own reaction. Freeman told him not to be a lone crusader. Catherine warned him against knight errantry. And they were right. Chasing evildoers was not his job. But if nobody else was doing that job or, at least, if nobody was doing it effectively . . .

His mind was not eased by his interview with Rob Brand. He had steeled himself to face an indignant and self-righteous client, only to be confronted by a man who could scarcely have been more pleasant. As they toured the empty gallery, Brand fell in happily with all Tim's suggestions for improving the security system. All that seemed to concern him was how quickly the new work could be done. He even came within a whisker of apologising.

'I realise I was somewhat abrupt with you, in the first shock of the burglary.' Brand fiddled nervously with his bow tie.

'It was a very upsetting thing to happen on your very first day.'

Brand shrugged. 'It was, but fortunately the police were able to tidy everything up very efficiently.'

'They haven't got the manuscript.'

'No, a sad loss – but I'm sure it was well insured. I shouldn't lose any sleep over it . . . er . . . Tom. Life's too short. The case is closed.'

'You certainly seem to be able to put the whole thing behind you quickly.'

'Behind me? Are you crazy? Look at these.' They had entered Brand's office and he gestured to the scattering of newspapers on his wide, Gothic revival desk. 'Front page in all the state papers and most of the nationals. Space on three TV news networks. I couldn't have *bought* that kind of publicity. And there's more to come. I've been called by every gossip columnist and arts page editor in town. When am I reopening? Can they come and do a feature? Just as soon as you can fix the new security I'm doing another launch party – only bigger. And I'm going to have blow-ups of these headlines all round the catalogue counter.'

Tim muttered something about it being an ill wind but Brand was too absorbed in his own plans to notice.

'You know you ought to be cashing in on this opportunity, too, Tom. I could put you in touch with some of the top editors. I'm sure they'd be interested in doing something on the problems of securing the premises of the world's leading art dealers. It could do a lot for your international profile.'

Tim said goodbye as politely as he could.

George Martin joined him at the St Regis for the evening. They had been sitting in the King Cole bar for half an hour and had exhausted every topic except the one that was uppermost in both their minds. It was Tim who eventually broached it.

'Had any bright ideas about this business, George?'

'Nothing that makes much sense, Major.'

'Well, let's have some nonsense, then.'

George ran his fingers through his grey-streaked short-back-and-sides. 'I've been going over that video tape – the first one – and it just doesn't seem to square with the Mike Thomson I knew.'

'I think I know what you mean – but go on.'

'Good relations with the local police – that's important. Sometimes we need them. Sometimes they need us. But the frontiers are very well marked. Outside, on the beat, that's Plod's domain. Inside is our territory and no one gets in without our say so – even the cops. And especially so in the wee small hours. You need a very good reason for letting *anyone* in then.' He paused to down half his glass of lager. 'And I look at that tape and I see Mike open up to a complete stranger and then turn his back on him.'

'We all have our off days.'

'Not Mike. He was a pro. Look, Major, supposing he'd just got a knock on the head – enough to put him out for a few minutes. Next morning you'd have had him on the carpet, wanting to know what the bloody hell he thought he was playing at. Am I right?'

Tim drained his Campari and soda. 'Yes, George, you're right. So what answer do you think I'd have got?'

'Well, the way I see it, there's only one explanation for Mike's behaviour but I don't see that it helps us at all.'

'Let's hear it, anyway.'

'It seems to me Mike must have been expecting a copper – perhaps that particular copper – to call.'

They went in to dinner and through most of the first course Tim laid out in his mind all the loose ends. He made a couple of tentative connections. At last he said, 'George, if your idea is right then the only person who can have told Mike to expect a visit from the police is Rob Brand.'

The ex-sergeant put down his soup spoon. 'What you're suggesting is an inside job. Pay someone to steal the manuscript, sell it privately and scoop a great deal of valuable publicity into the bargain? It's possible. Brand's been purring like the cat that got the cream these last couple of days. He's been holding court to a stream of visitors – journalists, high-class friends, and so on. He's been revelling in all the attention. But plan a murder? I don't reckon he's got the bottle.'

'They probably said the same of Crippen. Mike never mentioned anything, even in passing, about any special instructions from the client?'

'No. I'd have picked up on it – told him to check with you. There's nothing in Mike's diary, either. You know he kept a sort of journal? Said it gave him something to do on a job like this. He used to jot things down in note form then write them up fully later. Well, I've been getting his things together and I looked at his journal. He was obviously a couple of days behind, because there are no up to date entries. There were a few things in his pocket diary. Nothing out of the ordinary. A shopping list – you know, presents to take home from America. Then his wife phoned him sometime in the evening. I hope she reversed the charges. Apart from that, the poor sod's last hours were uneventful – no, dull. How are you going to test your theory about Brand, Major? You can't go up to him and challenge him point blank. Any chance of the cops pulling him in for questioning?'

Tim recalled Freeman's earlier outburst. 'I'm not exactly flavour of the month with the local constabulary.' He sat back as the waiter removed their empty plates. 'Of course, there's very little we can do. It really comes down to you, George. Keep your eyes and ears open in the gallery. Snoop around a bit.'

'I'd like to be back home for the funeral, Major.'

'Yes, of course, George. It's fixed for Wednesday. Well, that gives you a couple of days to see if you can find anything.'

'If there's anything to find.' George lifted his glass and sipped tentatively at the red wine. 'What do you think to this Californian stuff?'

Tim was deflected from his oenological observations by the appearance of a waiter at his elbow, holding a telephone. 'Call for you, Mr Lacy.'

Tim took the receiver and said 'Hello.' He said 'Yes' a couple of times, then 'OK. Give me about an hour.' He put the instrument down.

He looked thoughtful. 'Well, well, well. That was Lieutenant Freeman. This morning he virtually told me never to darken his doors again. Now he wants me to go and have a drink with him.'

But George was only half listening. Most of his attention was focused on the T-bone that had just been set before him and which virtually overflowed the plate it was served on. George's eyes gleamed. 'I'll say one thing for the Yanks; they do know how to cook a decent steak.'

Towards the end of the meal there was another phone call for Tim. It was Catherine.

Tim checked his watch. 'Hey, what are you doing awake at this hour?'

'You'd better ask your son and heir that question. He woke up soon after one o'clock, bright as a button, wanting to play. We've been through his entire picture book library three times and I've just got him off again. Since I'm now wide awake I thought I might as well give you a ring. How are you getting on?'

Tim gave her a résumé of the day's events. 'All quiet your end?'

'Yes – out of range of the nursery! I had a word with Hans Fischer this afternoon.'

'Fischer . . . Fischer? I don't recall . . .'

'He's the guy who wrote the monograph about the Dresden Text. The monograph you brought back from the British Library. The monograph I spent part of this morning reading.'

'What were you reading that for? I thought you wanted to forget the whole affair.'

'Absolutely right. But that didn't make a nickel's worth of difference to your determination to pursue it. Well, I'm not the sort of woman who waves a kerchief from the castle battlements while her knight errant rides off in search of dragons. So I called Hamburg University and they put me on to Professor Fischer and he turned out to be very charming and helpful – *and* he spoke impeccable English. I told him about the burglary and he said it was an outrage. Then I asked him if he could think of anyone who might want to own the Dresden Text. And he said, "Why don't you ask the Teutonic Knights?" '

'The Teutonic Knights! But I thought . . .'

'That they'd laid up their rusty swords several centuries ago? Well, it seems not. They were revived some time in the last century as a sort of charitable organisation for middle-aged romantics who like dressing up in funny clothes. The Teutonic Order, it seems, is very much alive and well, and living in Vienna.'

Chapter 5

Ulrich's first experience of battle was invigorating, bloody and brief.

The second Polish corps made straight for the fray to succour their hard-pressed comrades before the walls of Choinitz. That was their mistake. They too were obliged to fight on the edge of the soft ground.

The Grand Hospitaller led his troops out of the town at a brisk canter, in a wide arc, circling the marsh. The knights fell on the enemy's right and rear, jamming the new arrivals up against the heaving mass of men and horses already in combat.

Ulrich cast aside his lance and trotted back and forth along the edge of the Polish horde flailing his sword. Feeling it rebound off metal. Cut into flesh and bone. Dealing out death and injury was strangely impersonal. The objects he saw through his visor's slit were not men. They were faceless, steel-encased fighting machines. Hampered by their mounts, floundering in mud up to their fetlocks, more and more of the Poles slithered or fell from their horses. Some failed to get a footing and were trampled by the to and fro of battle. Others could do little more than sway unsteadily, and lunge at the horses of their attackers.

Ulrich's blood was up. 'For Christ and Mary!' he whooped, as he hacked at the enemy fringe. 'For Christ and Mary!' as he toppled riders from their steeds or forced others into the thick of the fray. 'Christermary!' he screamed as he found himself surrounded by a ring of Polish knights. 'Smary! Smary! Smary!' as he plunged through into a clear space, wheeled and charged back into the attack. He swung his sword in a wide arc against an advancing horseman. Too late the man's shield, emblazoned in red and black, came up to ward off the blow. Ulrich's blade bit through the gorget. A fountain of blood spurted through the gash and sprayed Ulrich's surcoat. Ulrich battered his shield against the horse's mail-covered neck. With a whinny, it veered away, carrying its slumped, lifeless burden.

Suddenly, he was aware of cheering all around him. Falling back a few yards, he lifted his visor and saw everywhere small groups of Polish troops fleeing from the battlefield.

Hans rode up, breathless and smiling. 'Casimir's killed and they've taken fright.'

A horn sounded away to the right and Ulrich joined the Grand Hospitaller's regrouping force.

That evening the market place of Choinitz, the surrounding houses and adjoining streets were crammed with citizens, mercenaries and knight brothers for a solemn *Te Deum* and mass. Still high with jubilation, Ulrich had to concentrate his mind to give God the glory for the victory.

And it was a great victory. No one could remember a bigger triumph and Georg, a non-combatant monk who helped keep the records at Marienburg, was sure that there was nothing to compare with it in the annals since the Order had left the Holy Land. Six thousand of the enemy were dead at the cost of three hundred and fifty-four knight brothers. Sixteen massive siege pieces that Casimir had brought up the Vistula and conveyed laboriously overland were now drawn up in the middle of the square. Draped across the two largest bronze cannon were the royal standards of Poland and Lithuania. As well as these trophies, Casimir's baggage train of four thousand waggons had been captured with their contents – food, military equipment and chests of coin. Some of the spoil would be shared among the mercenaries but, because personal booty was forbidden to members of the Order, the bulk of it would be put into the treasury and store rooms at Marienburg. It had been, Ulrich exulted, a glorious day. The only disappointment had been Casimir's escape. He had not, as his army believed, been killed. He had been unhorsed and his standard had been grabbed by one of von Plauen's men. In the ensuing cheering and confusion the king had been spirited away from the battlefield. 'Well,' Ulrich reflected, 'it matters little. After today's drubbing, he won't be back.'

Had he known Casimir then – as he later knew him – Ulrich would not have underestimated him so completely.

The bar a couple of blocks from Tim's hotel was crowded and fogged with tobacco smoke. He stood inside the door, peering around for the lieutenant.

'Mr Lacy! Over here!' Freeman was sitting at one end of the counter, a cigar in one hand and a whisky in the other. 'I saved you a stool. What'll you drink?' Freeman was slightly drunk – but only slightly.

Tim loosened his overcoat. The smoky heat was oppressive. He perched on the seat next to the policeman and asked for a brandy. 'Favourite haunt of yours?'

'I have to circulate, otherwise the bartender would think I was investigating him. Ain't that right, Mac?'

The burly man behind the counter winked as he set down the balloon glass. 'Al, I'd worry if you were in here every night, and I'd worry if I never saw your smiling face from one year's end to the next.'

Tim said 'Cheers!' and sipped the inferior spirit. He ventured no other conversational opening. If Freeman had something to say, he would let him get to it in his own way.

It took him some minutes. Only when Tim had ordered a return round did the lieutenant seem to find the words he wanted.

'Look, Mr Lacy . . .'

'Tim.'

'Tim, fine. I'm Al. Look, Tim, I don't rightly know why I suggested this meeting. It's nothing to do with conscience. Every New York cop hands in his conscience when he collects his badge.' He stared long and hard into his drink, then started again. 'Look, what I'm going to tell you is absolutely off the record. If you can make some use of it, that's OK, but if you ever quote me, I'll deny every word.'

'I understand. It's presumably about your arrest of Emma Freundlich,' Tim prompted.

'That's right. Everything I told you about it was true but there were a couple of things I didn't tell you. When I was standing outside the door of her hotel room, there was a shot – a loud shot – and inches from my nose there's this hole the size of a golfball!'

'That must have shaken you up a bit.'

'Well, I certainly didn't just stand there staring at it. I got out of the firing line and told my boys to shoot their way in. They did a good job. When I went in after them, the woman was sprawled on the floor and there wasn't any point trying mouth-to-mouth. She was lying there, wearing only a bath robe, with a gun in her hand.'

'So?'

'So, the gun she was holding was a Luger with an integral silencer. We later established that it was the gun that killed your friend. It's a neat weapon for close range work. Being a military man, I guess you know it's a small bore pistol which does its job with the minimum of mess.'

Tim nodded. 'It fires a cased bullet which goes very cleanly through most things and certainly doesn't tear big holes out of wooden doors. What you're saying is that she didn't fire the shot that nearly took your head off?'

'The shot – the only shot – that came from inside the room came from something powerful that fired a soft lead bullet.'

'A .45 Magnum or revolver of similar type?' Tim pondered the problem. 'And there was no trace of such a weapon?'

Freeman shook his head.

'And there was . . . Sorry, it sounds silly to ask . . . There was no one else in the room?'

'Not in the room, or the bathroom or the closet. But . . .'

'But?'

'The window was open and there was a fire escape outside. And before you ask, no, I didn't look out. Not straight away. I'd just made a forced entry and my men had shot an armed suspect. That suspect turned out to be a woman. Well, that shook me. It shook all of us. I had plenty to think about without searching the back alley. It was only later I started putting two and two together and realising they came to a hell of a lot more than four.'

Tim let out a long breath. 'This proves what I suspected – that the Freundlich woman was set up.'

Freeman shook his head. 'You haven't heard the half.' He held up his glass. 'I could use another. How about you?'

When the drinks were brought the lieutenant continued. 'There was one other disturbing fact about the body. It was lying face down, with its head towards the window. That means, when we went in the woman had her back to the door.'

'So she wasn't even pointing a gun at you when you went in?'

'That's right. One of my guys was kinda cut up about that. I had to give him a couple of days off to get himself together.'

Tim said nothing. For a full half minute he pondered the question that was confronting him and did not know whether to ask it. At last, he thought. 'What the heck!'

'Was it to protect your men that you . . . what shall we say . . . *simplified* your version of the incident?'

Freeman slammed his glass down on the bar, suddenly belligerent. 'Are you suggesting I put in a fake report?'

'Not fake, exactly . . .'

'Listen, Mister, I put in a full report. Full. And someone upstairs didn't like it. It came back with red ink all over it. I was told to rewrite it. So, just to please someone upstairs, I made a few changes. So, an unfortunate incident in which a woman got shot in the back was presented as a brave confrontation with a dangerous terrorist. The case was efficiently wrapped up in a couple of days. And everyone was happy.'

'Everyone except you.'

Freeman laughed. 'Hell, no! I'm happy. I got a

commendation out of it. Another couple of results like that and I'm in with a good chance of promotion. Why shouldn't I be happy?'

Tim wanted to say 'Because you care about the truth' but in Freeman's state that would probably have led to a long alcohol-induced, philosophical, speculation about the meaning of truth. Instead, he said, 'I think you handled the situation very well, Al.'

With some difficulty, the lieutenant lit another cigar, inhaled, blew out smoke and peered at Tim through the cloud. 'You know, you're not as dumb as you look. Perhaps you can make some sense of all this. You haven't got someone upstairs telling you what to think. Hey, Mac!' He waved his glass.

Tim calculated that Freeman was about one scotch away from being impossible to handle. He motioned to the barman to ignore the lieutenant's order. He gently but firmly took hold of the other man's left arm. 'Look, Al, I've got an idea. I've got an unopened bottle of duty free right here in my coat pocket. Why don't we go back to your place and drink it?'

The policeman allowed himself to be guided to the door. As they stood on the sidewalk waiting for a cab Tim got Freeman to give him the address of his apartment. The first taxi driver to pull up to the kerb took one look at the two men, arms round each other's shoulders, swaying slightly, and drove off. The second was either more tolerant or more in need of the fare. He let Tim manoeuvre the lieutenant onto the back seat, accepted the twenty dollar bill Tim held out, and steered his vehicle out into the almost deserted street.

After thirty yards the cab stopped with a squeal of brakes.

'Hey, Tim!' Freeman's head poked out of the window.

Tim ran up to the stationary vehicle.

'There was something else I had to tell you.' The lieutenant's face was screwed into a frown of concentration.

'Tell me tomorrow, Al.'

'Got it!' Freeman beamed triumphantly. 'The man who shopped that German bitch . . .'

'Yes?' Tim ignored the throbbing in his own head. 'You know who it was?'

Freeman grinned. 'Anonymous.'

Tim groaned his disappointment. 'Yes, well, goodnight, Al. Pleasant dreams.'

'Tell you this, though: he was a German. Sergeant who took the call said the man spoke with a heavy German accent.' Exhausted by the effort of memory, he slumped back against the upholstery.

Half an hour later Tim eased a tired body between crisp sheets and was quickly asleep. When he woke six hours later with hot eyeballs and a sandpaper tongue he had the distinct impression that he had spent most of the night clad in armour, riding up and down Fifth Avenue on a white horse, brandishing a silenced automatic, looking for 'someone upstairs'.

By the time he had showered and shaved and consumed the breakfast delivered by room service his mind was considerably clearer. He spent several minutes writing down all he could remember of the information Freeman had given him. He shuffled the facts around in his mind. It was like starting off a jigsaw puzzle. Tim reckoned that he had now found and put in place most of the edging pieces. But all they told him was the size and shape of the problem. They did not give any details of the picture. And yet there were now traces, hints about the overall design which had not been there before. He reached for the phone and called George Martin.

'Ah, George, I'm glad I caught you. I've had another idea that might be worth following up. While you're ferreting around at the gallery, see if you can find the guest list for Brand's launch party.'

The first time Ulrich saw Stephan Zerwonka the little Bohemian was cheating at cards. It was in Königsberg on a summer's morning in 1455 and he had come down from the conventual buildings in the castle to find the man appointed as his military aide in the new position as commander of the garrison at Memel.

Promotion had come rapidly because the human resources of the Order were severely stretched. And the human resources of the Order were severely stretched because it had discovered in Casimir a new kind of enemy.

Casimir IV Jagiello, King of Poland and Lithuania, had a young man's impatience, coupled with boundless self-confidence. Only seventeen when his elder brother had been cut down fighting the Turks at Varna on the distant Black Sea coast, it took Casimir three years to break free from the tutelage of temporising bishops and cautious scholars. As soon as he was master in his own house he made it clear that he intended to deal once and for all with the Teutonic Knights, who lorded it over territory in the north that was rightfully his and blocked his access to the sea. The policy of earlier rulers – the policy of treaties and truces and ineffectual campaigns – was at an end. He, Casimir IV, would make a reality of Greater Poland and he would not let a minor setback like the Battle of Choinitz deflect him from his mission. A year after that failure he was back with an even bigger army but was forced to retreat at the end of the campaign season with a remnant of stumbling cadavers – defeated, not by the military prowess of the knight brothers, but by disease and famine. Still, he promised to return.

This fanatical determination forced the Order into a debilitating cycle of cause and effect from which there was no escape. To control their restless subjects and defend their extensive territory called for enormous manpower. Manpower cost money. Money meant increased taxes. Increased taxes made subject peoples more disaffected and therefore more likely to look to Poland for deliverance. In times past the Grand Master had appealed to the pope at times of crisis and the pope had proclaimed a crusade, calling on the military leaders of the Latin West to take arms against the heathen. But the Muslim sack of Constantinople only two years before had focused the attention of Christendom on a much more pressing danger. Now the only soldiers prepared to offer their services in the northern lands were no longer pious volunteers, pledging their swords (theoretically, at least) for the extension of the Christian mission, but hard-nosed professionals who came for one reason only. Such a man was Zerwonka.

He was pointed out to Ulrich by the landlord of one of the waterside inns. The young knight saw a man of small stature probably in his late thirties. His dark hair was shoulder length and he wore a long leather jerkin. He was sitting at an outside table playing tarok with a portly Hanse merchant whose fur-rimmed hat was pushed to the back of his head. Ulrich stood watching the game for some time. Three times he saw the mercenary slide one of the highly-coloured trump cards into the top of one of his thigh-length boots while distracting his opponent with some comment on the play or about cargo being loaded on a large ship across the quay. Ulrich noticed that while Zerwonka kept up a non-stop flow of badinage and frequently broke into raucous laughter, his eyes never even smiled.

At the end of a game Ulrich went over and introduced himself.

'So you're the young lord and master.' Without rising, the mercenary appraised him long and hard, as he might a horse at market. 'Sit down, young sir, and tell us tales of knightly deeds and battles won.' He winked at his companion.

The other man introduced himself as Wilhelm Kaufmann of Bremen. 'Like you, I travel on the *Bear* of Lübeck.' He indicated the cog, whose loading was now almost complete. 'If God grant a good wind we should be away on the next tide.'

The merchant ordered another jug of ale and declined a further hand of cards. 'No, my friend, you've taken enough money off me for one day.'

'Then how about you, my lord? Fancy winning a few florins to spend in the market at Memel? Not that I imagine there's much worth buying there; a dismal backwater by all accounts.'

'You should know better than to ask a knight of the Teutonic Order to gamble.' Ulrich realised that it sounded pompous as soon as he had said it and was annoyed at himself for letting this man get under his skin so quickly.

Zerwonka roared with laughter. 'Do you hear that, friend? Don't ask a White Knight to gamble? That's rich. Why some of the knight brothers I've met were sharper at the card table than the edge of their swords.'

Ulrich choked back the response that leaped into his mouth. He was getting off on the wrong foot. Playing the mercenary's game. Zerwonka was trying to get the upper hand by asserting his age and experience against Ulrich's authority. Somehow, Ulrich had to counter this. Remind the older man that he was under his command – and try not to make an enemy of him while doing it. He tried a neutral tack. 'I hear you're from Bohemia. Are there no wars to fight there?'

'Several.' Zerwonka took a deep draught of ale and belched noisily.

' "Woe to the land whose king is a child and whose princes feast in the morning." That's what the Bible says. Well, there's a boy king in Prague and that means everyone's squabbling for power. Regent versus the Church. Nobles versus the regent. Burghers and landholders versus the nobles. And to make it worse, half the country follows the heretic Huss.'

'Plenty of work for a trained soldier, then?'

'Not for this one. I don't hold with fighting in your own country. As I see it, that presents a man with two problems. First of all, he has to *believe* in the cause he's fighting for. He really has to be convinced that the country should be run by the Hussites, or the Archbishop of Prague, or Regent George or the Black Beast of Glatz. Now, I don't give an empty wine jar which one of 'em is in power. Because I know it won't make any difference to the peasants and the farmers and the tradesmen of my home town.'

Wilhelm filled the soldier's tankard. 'And the second problem?'

Zerwonka laughed. 'Why, coming out on the winning side. If you don't, and if you manage to keep your head on your shoulders, your land is forfeit and you watch your family starve. Only fools and idealists take that sort of risk.

And I am neither – which is why I prefer other people's wars. It doesn't matter who wins or who loses. You take your booty and your pay and you walk away a free man.'

'That is not the way the Order sees things. We have a faith that is worth fighting for. Worth dying for, if the Lord so wills.'

'Then why aren't you down in Moldavia, driving out the Turks?'

'I am pledged to go anywhere I am sent. If the Grand Master orders me to fight against the infidel, then I shall.'

Zerwonka snorted. 'Oh, you're quite safe on that score. Your Grand Master is too busy hanging onto his lands to worry about what's happening hundreds of miles away.'

Ulrich half rose from the bench but whatever he was going to say or do was thwarted by the merchant. Wilhelm stood. He smiled across the table at Zerwonka. 'My friend, I thank you for an enjoyable game but I must ask you to excuse me now. Unlike fighting men, we mere merchants don't enjoy abundant leisure. Good day to you, Meinherr Stephan. And to you, Brother Ulrich – unless, that is, you would like to walk with me along to the Rathaus.'

Ulrich responded to the hint. He fell in beside the merchant. The two men turned into the *Böttcherstrasse*, one of the parallel streets linking the waterfront and the market square.

'He likes an argument, that one.' Herr Kaufmann raised his voice above the hammering of the coopers' workshops. 'Especially if it ends in a brawl.'

'Thank you for stopping me getting into a fight with him.'

'Never get into a fight with the likes of him. He knows every dirty trick there is to know.'

Ulrich felt that he was being gently patronised. He could

81

not help riposting. 'And the man cheats at cards.'

Wilhelm bellowed his laughter. 'But, of course!'

'You knew?'

'Wasn't it rather obvious?'

'Well . . . yes. But, in that case, why didn't you . . .'

'Challenge him? What would have happened? A fight. And who would have come off the worse?'

'So you sat there and let him swindle you?'

Again the merchant laughed. 'Good heavens, no! I met low cunning with high cunning.' Seeing the younger man's bewilderment, he explained. 'You saw our friend cheating?'

'Yes.'

'Did you see me cheating?'

'No.'

'Exactly.'

'But you let him win?'

'A few pennies; enough for several pots of ale. It kept him happy and it amused me. So where's the harm?'

They walked on in silence and emerged minutes later, into Königsberg's wide market square. The elaborate brick façades of houses built by merchants who could afford their own premises fringed a cobbled area scattered with stalls and bubbling with commerce and gossip. Animals in the butchers' pens squealed and grunted. Pot-sellers shouted the virtues of their wares. Water waggons clustered around the well house. Two small boys strutted self-importantly, wielding staves to ward off the curs that slunk among the crowds to steal from the skeins of offal or salt fish hanging from the tradesmen's poles. Overall guardians of this urban prosperity stood the two buildings which symbolised civic and religious authority – the Rathaus and the Peterskirche.

Wilhelm Kaufmann turned to the left to circuit the throng. He slackened his pace, seeming reluctant to end the conversation. 'The trouble is that much of what that odious fellow says is quite right.'

'Oh, surely . . .'

'No, don't protest, Brother Ulrich. Let me try to explain. I travel a great deal – Denmark, the Low Countries, France, England, the German lands, sometimes even Venice and Rome. And what I see is a world that is changing – changing fast. Young men crowding into the universities and schools, princes and dukes who like to think of themselves as enlightened surrounding themselves with philosophers and poets. Heretics popping up everywhere and causing mayhem. Everyone wants *new* ideas.'

'Don't you think that's always been the case?'

'I know there's a temptation to think of one's own age as different from all ages that have gone before, but there is something special happening now. Let me give you an example. People learn from books, don't they?'

'Yes.'

'And who can afford books?'

'Rich men.'

'That's right – kings, nobles, wealthy abbeys, a few merchants. By and large that means that study of new ideas is restricted to those who have the education and leisure to evaluate them properly. Would you agree that that is a highly desirable state of affairs?'

'Certainly.'

'Well, last year in Mainz I was shown a new machine called a printing press. Whereas a monk or a commercial copyist takes several months to make a book, this machine can produce hundreds of identical copies in a matter of days, and at a fraction of the cost.'

Ulrich shook his head sceptically. 'Who would want to buy such books? Why, there aren't enough people in Christendom who can read to make this new machine pay for itself.'

Kaufmann stopped in his tracks and wagged a finger to emphasise his point. 'Print shops are already springing up along the Rhine and in the Low Countries. And they are doing roaring business. The joke in Mainz is "Who makes more money than the Imperial Mint?" Answer, "Johann Fust, the printer." Now, if books spread, ideas spread – new ideas, old ideas, holy ideas, impious ideas, creative ideas, destructive ideas. And that means change.'

They resumed their walk. Ulrich rejected his companion's disturbing suggestion. 'I'm sure you exaggerate. And I don't see what it has to do with Meinherr Zerwonka.'

'He was telling us that in his country all authority is being challenged. That is true. I've seen it – and not only in Bohemia. Now, when *all* authority is challenged, who are men to follow? What are they to believe?'

They had reached the Rathaus, the impressive building which served as both a civic administrative centre and an assembly hall for the leading citizens of Königsberg.

Wilhelm stood back and pointed up at the façade. The original modest building had been fronted in recent years with a wall of patterned brickwork pierced by arched windows and crowned with decorated gables and tapering pinnacles. Adjoining this flight of fancy and forming an architectural foil there rose a massive square bell-tower.

'What does a building like this say? I'll tell you. It says, "How rich and powerful are the merchants of the mighty Hanseatic League." And your castle? What does it say? "How rich and powerful are the knights of the mighty Teutonic Order." Hand in hand we arrived in these lands –

you to conquer and we to establish the blessings of trade and civilisation. Throughout the Baltic lands we established supremacy, authority. Well, now that authority is being challenged. Merchants not of our fraternity say, "Why should the Hansa have a Baltic monopoly?" Princes and kings say, "Why should the League enjoy privileges not granted to our own subjects?" And men say of your Order, "By what right do the knights rule in this land now that all its people are Christian?" That's why Casimir is so persistent in his challenge. That's why the Grand Master is forced to rely on men like Meinherr Zerwonka, who don't believe in the Order and who will have no hesitation about changing sides if it suits them.'

'Are you suggesting that the League and the Order are doomed?'

'I'm suggesting that, if we want to survive, we'd better come up with a few new ideas of our own: ideas that will convince this generation – or at least fire its imagination.'

With those words Wilhelm Kaufmann took his leave and strode into the building.

Ulrich hurried back to the garrison to be in time for sext, seeking in the familiar Latin a balm that would soothe a disquieted mind.

Chapter 6

Tim looked around the bare crematorium chapel with a feeling of almost outraged anticlimax. Was this all a life amounted to – a handful of friends and relatives, self-consciously muttering their way through 'The Lord's my Shepherd' while the next hearse waited outside? After the brief service, Madge Thomson urged him and Catherine to 'come back to the house for a bite'. In the pleasant semi overlooking fields on the edge of Swindon Tim ate sausage rolls and slices of quiche and made inconsequential conversation but Catherine spent a long time side-by-side on the sofa with Mike's widow.

'How is she?' Tim asked, as he turned the Porsche onto the bypass and headed back towards Farrans Court.

'Bearing up, as you'd expect. She's very grateful for all you've done.'

'Including getting Mike killed?'

Catherine looked at him sharply. 'Tim, it's time this moral self-flagellation stopped. Madge doesn't blame you for Mike's death. Nor does anyone – except you.'

'You're right, of course. My head tells me that what you say is based on faultless logic. And yet I can't shake off a feeling of responsibility. The feeling's got worse since my heart-to-heart with the inebriated Freeman. This thing's a

87

hell of a lot bigger than we first thought. It's not just a question of robbery with violence now. We're dealing with two premeditated murders planned by someone powerful enough to get the police investigation closed down. Now, if Freeman and his team can't do anything, someone else has to. And, whatever way I look at it, I have to admit the buck stops here.'

'I know, Darling, and despite all my instincts I'm with you.'

Tim clenched his hands on the wheel. 'I just want to be able to put a name to this monster.'

'The dragon,' Catherine said, half to herself.

'Yes, if you like, the Dragon. It's as good a code name as any. Well, I think I'm beginning to understand something of what the Dragon is like and I seem to be the only one who's even interested in finding out. And that's why I have a sense of responsibility about this business – why I have to go on. If I don't, no one else will.'

'OK, let's say – just for the sake of argument – that I buy that. Tell me about the Dragon.'

Tim slowed for a roundabout. 'Let's go cross-country through Aldbourne. It's a quieter road. It'll help me to think. The Dragon? Well, he (or, I suppose, she – we must keep as open a mind as possible) is rich, clever, has influence in high places, and contacts in very low places. He – or she – is an obsessive, a fanatic.'

'A psychopath?'

'Not necessarily. In fact, almost certainly not. We're in danger of missing the point if we put this crime down to mental disorder. Our Dragon behaves very rationally, deliberately, with ruthless thought. Given his premises, everything he does is logical.'

'Why do you call him a fanatic?'

'A fanatic is someone who is so devoted to a cause that he can justify any means in pursuing his chosen ends. I don't know why the Dragon wanted the Dresden Text but, in order to get it, he was prepared to kill and kill again.'

They had driven through Aldbourne and turned onto a lane winding its way down to the River Kennet before Tim spoke again. 'Do you mind if we stop for a bit? I'd like you to help me sort out the bits and pieces of this business.' He pulled the car into a field gateway and cut the engine.

'Shall I take notes, sir?' Catherine asked the question in fun.

Tim was already sitting back, eyes closed in deep concentration. 'What? Oh yes, good idea. Now, we can start from the point that the Dragon wants the manuscript for some reason as yet unknown.'

Catherine fumbled in her handbag for an envelope and a biro. 'And the Dragon's lair is probably in Germany.'

'Yeah. Germany, Austria, Switzerland – somewhere round there. He hears the Dresden Text is going to leave the safety of the British Library's vaults for the first time in years, after which it will be going back into limbo. For a whole month it'll be in New York and that's his only chance to grab it.'

'So he hires Emma Freundlich to do the deed.'

'But why? Why her? She's been rusting away for years in some Levantine scrapyard for pensioned-off terrorists. If the Dragon's got fairly unlimited funds, why hire a has-been instead of a specialist at the peak of his career?' He gazed through the windscreen, spotted now with the first drops of a shower of sleety rain.

'Secrecy?' Catherine ventured.

'Go on.'

She put the ideas together slowly, thinking as she went.

'He doesn't use any recommended villain currently in circulation because no one else must ever know where the Dresden Text has gone. Instead, he brings Fräulein Freundlich out of enforced retirement. She's probably desperate for money and action.'

'And he plans all along that she will never live to tell the tale.'

'And no one will shed a tear at her passing. There'll be no colleagues out for revenge. Even the police aren't going to turn over too many stones looking for the murderer of a known assassin.'

'OK, so he gets her into the States. What then?'

'Somehow he sets up Mike to expect a nocturnal visitor.'

'No. We're missing a stage. He has to suss out the gallery and know exactly where the Dresden Text is being displayed. Now this is where I think we can narrow the field. The arrangement of the exhibits wasn't finalised until a few hours before the official opening. Rob Brand couldn't make up his mind exactly where to position everything. I wanted to get all the loan items safely stowed behind glass, the alarm system working. But Brand kept on shifting things around. He nearly drove me mad.'

'So, apart from you and George and Mike, who knew exactly where the Dresden Text was?'

'Just Brand and his party guests.'

'What about the caterers?'

Tim nodded reluctantly. 'Yes, I suppose we have to include them. Except that, if we're right about the Dragon, he was at pains to involve as few people as possible. I don't see him letting one of the waitresses in on his scheme. No, I believe our Dragon was at the party.'

'How long does that make the suspect list?'

'Seventy-four, if they all turned up. But we can eliminate

most of them if we're looking for someone with a German accent, domiciled in Europe.'

'Of course, we could be wrong about the German angle. The only piece of solid evidence we have is the telephone call to the police and anyone can fake a mid-European accent.'

'Point conceded, and we certainly can't rule Rob Brand out entirely. But there are so many German ingredients in this affair. I just can't see the mind behind it all belonging to some wealthy, art-crazed New Yorker.'

'So who is on your list?'

'Before we get to names, let's just follow the crime through and see if we have a viable working script. The Dragon talks with Mike and tells him to expect a visit from a cop in the middle of the night.'

'That's a weak link.'

'Don't I know it! It's totally out of character for Mike not to question such an instruction. That's still an argument for Brand being involved in some way, whether wittingly or not.'

'So, for whatever reason, Mike was persuaded to open up to the bogus cop.'

'And was immediately gunned down.' Tim clenched his teeth. 'Not out of panic. Not because something had gone wrong. But because he knew who had set the robbery up. There can't be any other reason – apart from sheer, bloody sadism – for Mike's premeditated, ruthless murder. It was planned to avoid any possibility that might provide evidence leading back to the Dragon.'

'And the Freundlich woman was shot for the same reason.'

'Yes. Of course, the Dragon also receives a bonus – he doesn't have to pay her. He ends up getting the Dresden

Text for a few hundred dollars – or Deutschmarks.'

'And the last act of this little drama?'

'Simplicity itself. The Dragon has carefully chosen the assassin's hotel room, he makes a phone call to the police and tells them where to find her. Then he calls on her – perhaps to collect the manuscript. As soon as he hears Freeman outside, he pulls a gun, fires a random shot through the door and makes a swift exit via the fire escape.'

'The woman must have been panic-stricken, confused.'

'I wonder whether, in those next few seconds, she realised she'd been double-crossed. Her first reaction was to grab up her own gun and go after the Dragon.'

'And it was at that moment . . .'

'Yes, and while Freeman is getting over his shock at shooting a woman, the Dragon walks calmly away.'

For a full minute Tim and Catherine were both busy with their own thoughts. The only sound was the drumming of rain on the car roof.

It was Catherine who broke the silence. 'Do you suppose the Dragon knew the police would hush up the details of the case for their own reasons?'

Tim shrugged. 'Could just be the devil's luck.'

'You said you'd made a short list of suspects.'

Tim reached into an inside jacket pocket and took out his notebook. 'There was a big Renaissance sale at Parke-Bernet just a couple of days before, which brought several top collectors and dealers over. That was one reason for the timing of Brand's opening. Several of them were at the party.' He referred to his notes. 'There was Hans Meyer from Hamburg, a politician and one of the richest men in Germany – collects early European ivories. Gerda and Walter Frankl. You remember visiting their ever-so-discreet shop in Geneva last spring?'

'Yes. She was very amusing. I liked her.' She wrinkled her nose. 'Don't remember him, though.'

'No, poor Walter is rather pushed into the shade by his ebullient wife. But he has one of the shrewdest brains in the business. Then there was Oscar König. He's top of my list at the moment. Heavily in with the Russian mafia. If he ever quits dealing in icons, he could set up in business as a corkscrew.'

The light was fading as the storm grew. Tim switched on the interior light. 'Next comes Arthur Meredith.'

Catherine laughed. 'Meredith? That doesn't sound very Teutonic.'

'He's an odd mixture. His father was a GI in the army of occupation after the war. He married a local girl and took her to live in Ohio. It didn't work out. Some time later, Mrs Meredith married an Englishman and settled in Surrey. That's where Arthur was brought up. But as soon as he got the chance he went to Germany and got his own business going. I don't know what to make of him. He gives the impression of being quietly dotty, but that hasn't stopped him building up one of the biggest air-freight firms operating between Europe and America.'

'He sounds like the sort of man who would have all the right contacts. What's his interest in the art market?'

'He collects medieval manuscripts and early printed books.'

'Well, I think he'd be my prime suspect. Any more candidates?'

'Hoffer, Frederick Hoffer.'

'Rings a faint bell.'

'I did some work at his Jermyn Street gallery a couple of years back. Fred specialises in marine paintings. He's naturalised now but he came from Germany originally – Bavaria, I think.'

'He sounds a bit out of place at the Brand shindig.'

'He has a financial stake in a very chic emporium on Madison Avenue. He teamed up with a bright young man who used to work at the Met. I gather it's more than just a business arrangement.'

'Is he a serious contender?'

'By himself, no. But I wouldn't trust young Siggy as far as I could throw him.'

'Siggy being Fred's inamorato?'

'Yes. Sigmund Beard or Bard or somesuch name.'

'You don't like him. Is that because he's gay?'

'Not at all. He's actually very knowledgeable as well as being quite amusing and extremely charming. Since he set up in partnership with Fred he's pulled off one or two remarkable coups. He discovered three Rubens drawings in a folio of miscellaneous rubbish in a sale in Antwerp last year. So he obviously has a sixth sense for quality.'

'So, why . . .'

'When he left the museum it was under something of a cloud. I don't know the details and nothing was ever proved but the Met was certainly glad to see him depart quietly. Siggy is the sort of fellow who could get away with . . .'

'Murder?'

Tim gave a wry smile. 'Well, yes, possibly even that. He could undoubtedly talk Fred into just about anything. The poor old boy's besotted with him.'

Catherine grimaced at the scribbled shorthand which now covered almost both sides of the envelope. 'This list of yours is getting to look like a telephone directory.'

'There's only a couple more and they're not really

serious suspects – Karl Hammel and Ernst Müller. They're both Austrian collectors. Hammel comes from an ancient Viennese family and has all the old-world courtesy to prove it. I'd find it very difficult to imagine him caught up in anything remotely shady.'

'Which leaves?'

'Ernst Müller. Strange man, a semi-recluse. Several people remarked how surprised they were to see him at the party. He didn't seem to speak to anyone – not to me, anyway. He has a dirty great schloss stuffed with antiques not far from Vienna and seems to spend all his time gloating over his collection.'

'An obsessive?'

'Certainly.'

'A fanatic, even?'

'You could say that. And he's mean into the bargain. He once asked me to look at his security. What I saw made my hair stand on end – not so much state of the art; more state of the Ark. When I told him what it would cost to provide adequate protection for his fabulous collection – the man's an absolute magpie – he went all the colours of the rainbow and accused me of being a racketeer.'

Catherine sat quietly thoughtful for a while, then said, 'Both Müller and Hammel live in or near Vienna. I wonder if either of them belongs to the Grand Imperial Teutonic Order.'

'Is that what they call themselves? Well, I can't imagine Ernst Müller, for one, being a member of anything.'

'But it's a possible lead, isn't it? I mean, if we found that someone on your list was connected with these tinselled knights that would provide a motive for stealing the Dresden Text, and motive is something we're short of at the moment.'

Tim looked doubtful. 'I'm inclined to think this Teutonic Knights business is a red herring.'

'So what are you going to do with all these suspects of yours?'

'Talk to them.'

'You mean walk in and say, "Excuse me, did you steal the Dresden Text and kill two people in New York?" '

'Well, that's not quite as crazy as you make it sound. I have a perfectly legitimate reason for wanting to get to the bottom of this affair, so it's reasonable to ask people who were in the Brand Gallery that evening if they saw or heard anything which might cast some light on the problem.'

'And if one of these people really is a ruthless killer, what then? He's sure as hell not going to own up.'

Tim ran a finger along the bridge of his nose. 'Agreed. But put yourself in his place. You're feeling very pleased with yourself. You've got the manuscript. The theft went like clockwork. You've disposed of Freundlich. No one can point the finger at you. You've made sure the police have dropped the case. You're home and dry. Then, suddenly, out of the blue, someone turns up asking questions. You're rattled, caught off guard and maybe – just maybe – you'll give yourself away. A careless word, a gesture or glance. That's all I'd need.'

'It's a long shot.'

'None longer. But, to coin a phrase, If you know of a better 'ole . . .'

Tim put his notebook away. He switched on the headlights and fired the engine. 'Time we were getting back to the funny farm.'

But Catherine's mind had turned back to the day's earlier events. 'I guess we owe it to Madge to try. Do you know what she said was the hardest thing to bear? Not being able to say goodbye. If Mike had gotten ill and they'd known the end was coming, they could have said all the things that needed to be said. Madge reckons she could have coped with that. But her final memory is of Mike waving cheerfully as he went off to Heathrow in George's car. That was the last she ever saw or heard of him. Hey!'

She was thrown violently forward as Tim, easing the Porsche out onto the road, suddenly pulled his foot off the clutch and stalled the engine.

He stared hard at his wife. 'What did you just say?'

Ulrich found his first command tedious. Memel was one of a series of lightly-manned fortresses along the border with Lithuania. Potentially this was a trouble spot but Lithuania had, in effect, been neutralised by a secret treaty with the Grand Master. Despite the union of the crowns, the northern state had been persuaded – for a substantial payment – not to aid Casimir in his war with the Order. This enabled the Grand Master to concentrate the bulk of his forces in the Prussian heartland to the west where they were needed to counter the Polish incursions which were now made with almost monotonous regularity.

Ulrich, therefore, found himself master of a skeleton garrison of bored, under-occupied troops. There were a dozen knight brothers, five non-combatant monks to ensure the continuity of liturgical life and two hundred and fifty German and Czech mercenaries under the command of Stephan Zerwonka. After their initial encounter, relations between Ulrich and the Bohemian were surprisingly untroubled. At Memel the two men had a common purpose. Their main concern during the autumn and winter of 1455–6 was keeping the men occupied, out of trouble and in fighting trim. Ulrich discovered that Zerwonka was good at planning and organising military exercises over the frozen marshes and among the clumps of sparse deciduous woodland which scattered the higher ground. He learned, also, that his second-in-command was a strict disciplinarian. One of his own countrymen and a comrade of many campaigns got drunk, broke into one of the houses in the town, half-killed the owner, raped his daughter and went off with the man's best horse. When the news reached Zerwonka he ordered an immediate parade of the whole garrison, had the offender dragged before him and personally decapitated him.

Boredom and cold were the bitter enemies that assailed everyone. Hard, sharp winds surged across the Baltic ice-floes. The wells froze. Any man foolish enough to pick up armour with bare hands was likely to tear the skin from his fingers. Sleeping under the single blanket prescribed by the rule was difficult. It was a relief to shuffle into chapel for the night offices. Yet, Ulrich found even the recitation of the hours with his small contingent of brothers was uninspiring, even boring. The summons to action, when it came at the end of February, was, therefore, a welcome deliverance, even though the news from Marienburg was grave.

Casimir had decided not to wait for the spring thaw which brought with it better conditions for setting up encampments and moving large bodies of men. Instead, he was forced into marching his troops northwards, hoping to catch the defenders of Marienburg unawares. Von Erlichshausen's spies informed him that the Polish levies and auxiliaries were making their way in three main contingents which were to rendezvous before the walls of Marienburg. Ulrich's orders were to take half his men and march southwards, linking up with contingents from other garrisons. Grand Hospitaller von Plauen was marching from Elbing to take command of the combined force which would assemble at Allenstein, some thirty miles from the Polish border, to intercept or, at least, harass one party of invaders.

Ulrich left Zerwonka in charge at Memel and set out with his brother knights and a hundred and ten fit men for the 250-mile march to Tannenberg. They travelled light, unencumbered with supply waggons. The land supplied their food. Ulrich always preferred to rely on the produce of forest and river. Every day he sent out hunting parties to bring down boar and deer with their crossbows. But the speed of their advance made it impossible to meet their needs entirely from the wild, so that Ulrich was obliged to requisition from peasants and farmers some of the supplies they had stored for the winter. He always disliked confiscating food that the people could hardly spare. It seemed to him, not only cruel, but politically ill-advised: it made already-reluctant subjects into potential rebels. Brother knights he noticed, were often less scrupulous. They would whip truculent householders or peasants who tried to hide their barrels of dried meat or salted fish.

It was slow, hard going. The snow concealed potholes and frozen ruts that caught horses unaware and sent them lame. Sometimes they were able to cut across the fringes of frozen lakes but there were places, usually discovered by trial and error, where the ice would not bear the weight of fully armed mounted men. Often the belts of forest which lay across their path were too dense to be penetrated. Circuiting such a barrier could cost a whole day's march. Snow fell almost constantly but Ulrich's troops stumbled on, only once sheltering in a village from a blizzard which raged for almost twenty-four hours. The first glimpse through the snow flurries of sheer brick walls rising from the plain always provoked a cheer from the men. It brought the prospect of new comrades, warm fires and the chance to dry out clothes soaked with melted snow. Their advance punctuated by brief rests at the Order's forts and their numbers gradually increasing, Ulrich's force reached Allenstein seventeen days after leaving Memel.

It was this impressive citadel, commanding the major routes from the east and south-east, that Heinrich von Plauen had elected as his operations centre. The Grand Hospitaller's troops had already arrived by the time the force from the Lithuanian border clattered wearily in through Allenstein's main gateway. With most of his slender army assembled, the hero of Choinitz called all his commanders together the following morning. After a solemn mass in the Marienkirche, they gathered in the castle's vaulted council chamber. Von Plauen placed his subordinates around a long trestle table and seated himself centrally on one of its sides.

Ulrich found himself sitting almost opposite. It was the closest he had ever been to a man he idolised as the greatest living military leader and tactician in the Order. He saw a stocky man of middle years with thick black hair and tired eyes. He was full-faced and high-coloured but anxiety showed in the lines around his mouth.

'Brothers.' Von Plauen called the meeting to order. 'I will be as brief as possible. We must be on the march again tomorrow for reasons which will soon become obvious. We have some three and a half thousand men here. Our task is to delay and inflict as much damage as possible on a Polish army reported to be a hundred thousand strong.'

The statement provoked a flutter of conversation

around the table which von Plauen quickly silenced with a raised hand.

'We do, God be praised, have some advantages on our side. Casimir's priority is to get his men, his waggons and his artillery through to the north, as quickly and with as few losses as possible, so that he can invest Marienburg and our other main towns in strength. In order to minimise any delay caused by our harassing tactics, he has split his force into three. Carl!'

A young page standing behind the Grand Hospitaller produced a small sack from which he spilled a pile of fine sand onto the table, then spread it out with his hand.

'Casimir will bring his siege pieces and heavy equipment down the Vistula. He has no choice. It would take weeks to get them across country, over the frozen ground.' He drew a wiggly line through the sand close to its left-hand edge. 'Now, young Casimir would like us to think that he is bringing his main force across the border up the best road available which comes to Tannenberg.' He inscribed a line in the centre of his improvised map. 'But our intelligence tells us that he's only bringing a quarter of his army by that route, although he is leading it himself in an attempt to fool us. In fact, the main thrust of the invasion will be across the lake area to the east of where we are now – the Masurian Lakes.' He cleared a row of circular holes in the sand. 'So, our enemy sets us an interesting problem. With the resources at our disposal we can only attempt one interception. Which is it to be? Block the Vistula and try to capture the Polish supplies? Attack the royal contingent, with at least the possibility of laying our hands on Casimir himself? Or try to slow down the main force?' Von Plauen looked along the table to left and right. 'Any suggestions, Brothers?'

'Surely there's only one possibility.' Almost without realising it, Ulrich blundered into the silence. As all eyes turned upon him he faltered.

Von Plauen smiled. 'Go on, Brother. It's von Walenrod's nephew, isn't it? Let's hear your suggestion.'

'Well, sir.' What had seemed obvious to Ulrich a few moments before now appeared to be subject to a host of possible objections. 'I just thought that if we attacked either the supplies or the smaller force we would only be tying ourselves up. The main Polish army could get round behind us or ignore us altogether and head straight for Marienburg.'

'So you advise pitting our tiny force against the main enemy host?' There was no mockery in von Plauen's voice.

'Well, sir, I may be wrong but it seems to me that in that kind of terrain,' he pointed to the Grand Hospitaller's row of blobs, 'numbers are less important. The only strips of dry ground between the lakes are narrow. We could keep the enemy penned up there for weeks, and all that time they would be running short of food.'

Von Plauen nodded. 'Wouldn't the king come to their aid before they got into serious trouble?'

'Exactly!' Ulrich was now warming to his theme. 'He must rescue his main force. He dare not move northwards without it and that means more delay. It also means he can't link up with his supply train. So surely *that* would be the moment for us to swing westwards to the Vistula.'

'Well done, young Walenrod.' The Grand Hospitaller looked around the table. 'Brothers, we have a new tactician in the Order. That analysis fits in with mine almost exactly. Tomorrow, then, we march eastwards. I shall want half a dozen scouting parties of twenty men each to go on ahead and discover the enemy's exact movements. Brother Michael . . .'

As the meeting went on to discuss the campaign plan in detail Ulrich was only half listening. He was basking in the warm glow of his hero's approval. 'A new tactician,' the Grand Hospitaller had called him. How proud his uncle would have been. He felt even more pleased with himself at dinner time in the frater. Several older knight brothers came up to congratulate him.

When, after nones, he received a summons to the Grand Hospitaller's quarters his heart raced in anticipation of some fresh accolade. Had von Plauen marked him out for some special mission, something calling for the special skills of a tactician? He knocked on the thick oak door. It was opened by a page and Ulrich stepped into the chamber.

Von Plauen was standing by a blazing fire in the hearth at the far end of the room. He was talking to someone and he was obviously very angry. As the door closed the other man turned to face Ulrich. It was Stephan Zerwonka.

Von Plauen nodded curtly. 'Come in, Brother Ulrich. Thank you, Herr Zerwonka. You may leave us now.'

When the Bohemian had withdrawn, the Grand Hospitaller stared hard at Ulrich. 'So, it seems that I was premature in the good opinion I formed of you earlier today.'

Tim switched off the ignition. 'Sorry to jolt you like that.' He faced his wife and spoke slowly and deliberately. 'Are you absolutely sure that Madge said she had no contact with Mike after he left for the States?'

'Absolutely sure. She made a point of it.'

'There's no possibility that you might have misheard?'

Catherine was getting exasperated. 'No! Tim, what is this – the Spanish Inquisition?'

Tim picked up the car phone. 'It's just something that doesn't tie up. Probably not important, but it'll nag at me if I don't sort it out. Have you got the Thomsons' number?'

Seconds later he made his connection and was speaking to Mike's widow. 'Tim Lacy here, Madge. Sorry to bother you but is George still there?'

'Yes. Hang on. I'll fetch him.'

When George came on the line Tim said, 'You remember telling me that according to Mike's diary he had a phone call from Madge on that last evening.'

'Yes, that's right.'

'Are you quite sure?'

'Quite sure.'

'Hm. Look, if you get a chance, could you have another peep at that diary?'

'No need. I can remember it pretty clearly. Like I told you, there was a shopping list and, in the middle of it, a separate note: "*9.35 M phoned.*" '

It had come on to rain, and Tim stared at the golden streaks slanting through the beam of the headlights.

'All the same, George, I'd like you to get hold of that diary if you can. I want a close look at it.'

PART II

THE RIDER ON A
PALE HORSE

I looked, and there was a pale horse. Its rider was named Death, and Hell followed close behind.
The Revelation of John the Divine 7:8

Chapter 7

The flaming logs crackled in the hearth. Ulrich stared at them for some seconds, then lifted his head to return the gaze of the Grand Hospitaller. 'I'm sorry if you have heard anything to my discredit but, since my conscience is clear . . .'

'Silence!' Von Plauen seated himself on a large chair over which several furs had been thrown. 'I hope for the sake of your family that what I hear is not true. It is because your name is an honourable one in the Order that I have taken the unusual step of seeing you in private. You know what the official procedure is in cases of treason.'

'Treason!' It was no more than a gasp. The accusation, like a physical blow to the stomach, drove the breath from Ulrich's body.

'As you can imagine, I have more than enough to think about at the moment.' He rubbed a hand over tired eyes. 'So you may consider this interview a privilege.'

'I'm grateful, sir. If you can just tell me what I'm supposed to have done . . .'

'Before leaving Memel you had a talk with the Lithuanian Duke, Vytautas?'

'Yes.'

'What was the purpose of this meeting?'

'Vytautas is the most powerful man on the other side of the border in that region. Our movements would be reported to him very quickly. I didn't want him to misunderstand the reason for the reduction of our garrison. I pointed out that it was only temporary and I reminded him of his treaty obligation of neutrality.'

Von Plauen spoke his next words slowly, his stern gaze directed from beneath overarching, dark eyebrows. 'Brother Ulrich, I remind you of your oath of obedience to the Grand Master and his representatives, and I charge you to answer me truthfully. Did any money change hands during your conversation with the Lithuanian?'

'Money!' Ulrich felt icy fingers gripping his stomach. He forced himself to say, as evenly as he could, 'No money passed between Vytautas and me at that meeting.'

'Pick up that purse on the table.' The Grand Hospitaller's voice registered neither belief nor doubt.

Ulrich felt the blood pounding in his temple as he walked to the centre of the room and picked up the leather pouch which lay beside von Plauen's gauntlets.

'Do you recognise it?'

Ulrich shook his head.

'Or the contents?'

Ulrich undid the draw string and peered inside. The bag was well filled with gold coins. Again he shook his head. 'It's more money than I have ever seen.'

'Fifty gold florins. It was found stitched into your saddle. I, myself, was present at the discovery not one hour since. Now, do you still wish – on your oath – to deny all knowledge of this gold?'

'Yes, sir. On my oath.' The young knight gazed levelly back at the man who was the second greatest figure in the

Order. 'Please, may I know exactly what I am charged with?'

'Two days after your departure, Duke Vytautas arrived at Memel with a hundred men and demanded the keys of the town. He claimed that you had sold it to him for fifty florins.'

'But that's a lie . . .!'

'Silence!' Von Plauen snapped the word. 'The garrison commander, of course, refused to yield. Vytautas claimed that Memel was his by right, that he had witnesses to the sale and that if our men did not withdraw, he would return and take the town by force. The man you had left in charge held on as long as he could but the force at his command was too small to defend Memel and any serious attempt to do so would have put the townspeople at unnecessary risk. After a further two days he yielded. He and his men have ridden hard to join us here and report the loss of our fortress.'

Ulrich opened his mouth to protest but restrained himself when he saw that von Plauen had not finished.

'You must hear the rest, Brother Ulrich. This man Zerwonka found it very difficult to believe in your treachery. He questioned other members of the garrison. Three of them said they recalled hearing you say that the Order was doomed to defeat and that anyone who was wise would make provision for the future. Was fifty florins your means of ensuring security for the years ahead, Brother Ulrich?'

Ulrich struggled to contain the welter of emotions which threatened to overwhelm him. It was anger that refused to be restrained.

'None of this is true, sir. And I trust you will believe me rather than a gang of unprincipled mercenaries.'

Von Plauen shook his head wearily. 'It isn't a matter of truth and falsehood.' He seemed about to go on but thought better of it. For some moments he sat silent, gazing into the fire. Then he stood abruptly. 'Well, Brother Ulrich, this matter must be tried when we get back to Marienburg. For the present, I cannot afford to be deprived of your services in the field. You will ride with us tomorrow, but as an auxiliary. You will not wear the insignia of the Order. You are stripped of command. In camp you will be under guard. You will be taken straight to the dungeons from here and you will remain there until we prepare to march. Now, go!' He called for the guard, who stood outside the door, handed Ulrich over and gave his instructions. Then he turned his broad back on the prisoner, forestalling any appeal.

'It's obvious once you've seen it, isn't it?'

Tim pointed to an entry in the small pocket diary that lay open on his desk. With Catherine and George he stood staring down at Mike's last scribbled, seemingly inconsequential words:

> Handbag
> Earrings
> Silk scarf – Macys
> 9.35 M. phoned
> Cap
> Shirts
> Toy

George shook his head. 'I just assumed . . .'

Tim sank back into the leather chair. 'Of course you did. What's more natural than that Madge should phone him? It

110

was the small hours of the morning in Swindon but she might well have had some urgent reason to speak to Mike, and she would realise that that was a good time to catch him alone. But we now know that Madge *didn't* call that night. Someone else did – presumably while Mike was in the middle of writing out his shopping list. So he noted the caller – and the message.'

George made a tutting noise. 'I should have seen it.'

'But you were conditioned not to see it. You read a list of clothes items and you looked at that word and your brain registered "cap" – probably envisaging a baseball cap that Mike might take home as a souvenir. But when you look closely at the word there's no doubt that it's "cop".'

The others nodded their agreement. Catherine said, 'Does that get us much further forward? Someone phoned Mike and told him to expect a visit from the police. That explains why he opened up so readily when the bogus cop appeared, but it still doesn't tell us who called Mike at 9.35.'

Tim tapped the piece of paper which lay beside the diary. 'It may narrow the field a bit. Look at our list of possible suspects.'

He turned the typed sheet so that the others could read it:

Hans Meyer
Gerda and Walter Frankl
Oscar König
Arthur Meredith
Frederick Hoffer
Karl Hammel
Ernst Müller

Catherine wrinkled her nose. 'You reckon the mysterious

"M" is one of the three men whose name happens to begin with that letter?'

Tim sat back. 'It's a link. The only one we've got. You don't look happy, George.'

The older man hunched his wide shoulders. 'Those blokes – Meyer, Meredith and Müller – they were complete strangers to Mike. I can't . . .'

'But do we know that?'

George snorted. 'Rich men like those don't have much to do with the likes of us.'

'Unless they want something. Don't forget we're talking about someone very clever. If he wanted to use Mike, he'd be sure to ingratiate himself first. Suppose you were sitting in that cramped little office all by yourself during the party. All the nobs are milling about in the gallery enjoying themselves. Brand hasn't offered you so much as a beer, and you're feeling pretty fed up. Then one of the guests wanders in with a glass of something strong and cheering. Wouldn't you be pleased that someone had noticed you? Wouldn't you happily spend a few minutes chatting with your benefactor?'

Catherine perched on the edge of the desk. 'If someone had gone in to talk to Mike wouldn't you have noticed?'

'In that crush? Pretty unlikely. Anyway, I left quite early.'

George was unconvinced. 'Even if this "M" character had struck up an acquaintance, I still can't see Mike agreeing to let an unknown cop onto the premises in the middle of the night.'

Tim scowled. 'George, do you want to find out who killed Mike or not?'

'Of course, but . . .'

'Then let's have a bit less of this negative thinking.'

George stood his ground. 'Is it negative thinking to be loyal to a friend's memory?'

The two men glared at each other. Catherine headed off the row. 'Hey, come on, guys. We're all emotionally screwed up about Mike's death. It's frustrating having so little to go on but if we're set on finding out what we can, I guess we have to follow up the only leads we have. Now, Tim, you've got this list of possible suspects. Three of them happen to have names beginning with "M". OK, so why not talk to them first.'

'That's what I was planning to do.'

'Fine. While you're doing that, I'll follow up my Teutonic Knights hunch.'

'But that's . . .'

Catherine ignored her husband's protest. 'Now this Ernst Müller character lives near Vienna – right?'

'Yes.'

'And that's where the Grand Order hangs out. So I suggest that's where we start – Vienna.'

The cold, the stone floor and the scuttling of rats had nothing to do with Ulrich's sleeplessness that night: it was misery that kept him awake. Through the barred window he heard the bell punctuating the dark hours with its summons to vespers, compline and matins. He even caught snatches of the brothers' chant. The feeling of exclusion from the familiar routine was too bitter to be borne. Frenziedly, he wrapped his single blanket round his head to cut out the sounds of the Order's life.

For hours he was unable to surmount the barrier of mental anguish. His world, his life lay in ruins. Five generations of distinguished service to Christ and Holy

Church were ending in shame and disgrace. Now there was nothing for him. The future was a black void. From childhood he had wanted only to be a knight brother. Women, lands, fortune and the preoccupations of his youthful colleagues had meant nothing to him. His dream had been to repeat the achievements of Conrad von Walenrod, the grandfather he had never known but whose exploits as one of the great conquering grand masters he knew by heart. Time and again, he pictured the great Bible on the altar at Marienburg – the Walenrod Bible, costly and magnificent – that symbolised his family's commitment to the Order. Now that great tradition was irrevocably stained and all because of the viciousness and greed of Stephan Zerwonka, and the blindness of Heinrich von Plauen who could not see or understand or believe that a Walenrod could never do what he had been accused of doing.

It was only in the long silence that fell over Allenstein after matins, the midnight office, that Ulrich's thoughts turned away from himself. Why, he asked himself, were Zerwonka and the Grand Hospitaller against him? The mercenary was only interested in money. Why, then, had he not taken the fifty florins – which obviously Vytautas had paid him – and disappeared? The answer was obvious: he was playing a deeper game, and one that would bring him greater financial reward. As he began to think more clearly, Ulrich understood, or thought he understood, the little Bohemian's cunning strategy. Exposing a 'traitor' was a way of worming his way into the confidence of the Order's high command. And he had done his work well. There was no way that Ulrich could establish his innocence in the face of perjured witnesses and the damning evidence of the money planted among his possessions.

But von Plauen? Why had such an experienced and devoted leader of the Order not seen through the stratagems of a mere mercenary? How could he so readily believe in the guilt of a knight brother? For hours Ulrich prodded these problems around his mind, sometimes pacing the blackness of the empty cell, sometimes crouching in a corner, the blanket hugged around him. At some point he recalled the words of the merchant he had met in Königsberg. Kaufmann had spoken of a changing world, challenging old ideas and thirsting for new ones, hinting – more than hinting – that the days of the Teutonic Order were numbered. In the months since then, Ulrich had heard faint echoes of the merchant's gloomy prophecy. In the frater, in camp, on the march – wherever knight brothers met, they talked. And sometimes their talk had interwoven threads of doubt, dissatisfaction, regret, questioning the very ethos of the Order.

Von Plauen, Ulrich now realised, must be well aware of the changing mood among the ranks. He would see that there was a canker attacking the very core of their common life. He would believe that there *were* brothers disillusioned with the Order, capable of submitting to temptation. Could it be that the Grand Hospitaller himself – and perhaps even the Grand Master – shared a fear for the future of the Order? No. Ulrich dismissed the thought as absurd. But one thing was clear: they would be compelled to suppress any sign of disaffection. They would be sure to make an example of a knight brother accused of betraying their trust. Whether or not they believed in Ulrich's guilt, they would see him condemned as a Judas as a warning to others who might otherwise put their own interests before those of the Order.

Once – and only once – Ulrich had witnessed the public

punishment of an apostate knight. The memory was vivid. The crowds in the square at Marienburg. The brother ceremonially stripped of all insignia until he stood in a plain grey shift. The climb to the scaffold. The stake. The last prayers. The rope around the neck, swiftly tightened. The croaking gasp and the body heaving for breath. The fire. The stench of burning flesh. Ulrich knew that, whatever else happened, he would not allow himself to become such a spectacle – not even for the good of the Order.

Then he knew what he must do. The answer, when it came to him, was dazzlingly obvious. There was only one way to restore his honour, protect the name of the Order – and dispose of the traitor Zerwonka.

'What time's your appointment?' Tim called from the bathroom and received no answer.

Moments later he emerged, wrapping a bathrobe round his steaming body. 'I said . . .'

'Ssh! I'm listening!' Catherine, already dressed in a close-fitting, pale-green jersey suit, flapped a hand at him. She was sitting in one of the room's two gilded, bergère-style armchairs and watching the morning TV news programme. On the screen groups of police and demonstrators grappled in the glare of arc-lamps directed from what seemed to be an armoured vehicle bearing the legend *Polizei*. Red swastikas were daubed on a building in the background.

'What do you mean, "listening"? You don't speak German.'

Catherine did not look up. 'If you have an ear for languages, you can learn a lot from watching television. Anyway, I'm interested in these Berlin riots. They're frightening.'

Tim walked over to the tall windows and gazed down into the Opernring. The tramlines seemed etched against the overnight fall of fresh snow. Beneath the laden trees, pavement cleaners were already at work, adding to the grey-white ridges deposited over the last month. As yet there were few people on the streets. Tim reflected that the Viennese – an admirably leisurely people – were not early risers.

As well as following up their inquiries, Tim and Catherine had decided to make their trip to Austria a brief winter holiday. By the time all their plans had been finalised, their three days' schedule had become very crowded. Last night they had watched a highly dramatic performance of *Don Giovanni* at the Staatsoper. Ahead lay dinner with old friends of Catherine's from the American Embassy, a skiing outing with those same friends, an exhibition of eighteenth-century portraiture at the Künsthistorisches Museum, and a concert in the Musikverein. But today, or a large part of it, was not devoted to pleasure.

'The answer to your question is 10.30.' Catherine switched off the television set which was now relaying news of a national skating competition. 'Herr Hoffmeister has asked me to be prompt. He sounds rather a stickler for punctuality.'

Albert Hoffmeister was the Grand Chamberlain of the Grand Imperial Order of Teutonic Knights and Catherine had obtained a personal audience by posing as a *Sunday Times* staff journalist writing a feature on orders of chivalry.

'After that I'm spending the afternoon shopping with Gloria. I guess you won't be back until late afternoon.'

'Probably not. Herr Müller may live like a hermit, but he certainly spoils himself – and his rare guests. Lunch at the schloss, as I recall, tends to be an elaborate, long-drawn-out ritual.'

An hour later, as he drove a hired car along the Vienna-Salzburg autobahn, Tim wondered whether he was wasting his time. Back home in cosy Wiltshire, following up the three 'M's on the suspect list had seemed to make good sense. He had managed to set up meetings with Meredith and Meyer as well as Müller. Now that it came down to actually putting the plan into action, he was not at all clear how he was going to bring up the business of the Dresden Text. He had managed to engineer an interview with the reluctant Müller on the pretext of talking about security, but, of course, if Müller was the Dragon, he would not be taken in by that.

After a hundred kilometres Tim turned off at the Ybbs intersection and took a road which climbed steadily, through banks of piled snow and picturesque villages of timbered and decoratively-gabled houses. Just past Gaming he reached a cleared, but unmarked track leading upwards through the forest. Three minutes later his way was barred by massive wrought-iron gates. Tim announced himself into the intercom attached to one of the stone pillars and the barrier swung open. It was another half mile before the car emerged suddenly onto a plateau-like drive. To the left, the ground dropped away precipitously, opening up a spectacular vista of ridge upon ridge of glistening, snow-mantled pines. To the right crouched the baroque absurdity of Schloss Turnitz.

A white-gloved butler escorted Tim to the library, poured drinks and withdrew. Tim looked around the oval, two-storey room whose walls were encased in shelves. Access to the upper racks of books was via a gallery from which descended, at regular intervals, curling staircases with gleaming brass handrails. Tim sipped the dry yet mellow Oloroso and gazed along the tooled leather backs of a section devoted to philosophy. He selected a volume at random and idly turned the pages.

'Saint-Simon, *De la Réorganisation de la Société Europ-éenne*, first edition, 1814.'

Tim turned, startled by the voice. Müller had entered through a concealed doorway in the wall of books and was standing just behind him. He was a tallish man in his seventies. Steel grey hair reached down both edges of his face in extravagant sideburns. Bright eyes were set either side of a pronounced beak-like nose. Over dark trousers and waistcoat he wore a long black velvet garment which was a cross between a frock coat and dressing gown.

Müller made no attempt at formal greeting. 'A man of interesting ideas, Saint-Simon. Of course, his followers twisted his philosophy into egalitarian socialism and other absurdities, but the man himself was really quite a prophet. He foresaw the emancipation of women, the United Nations, the European Community and other modern developments well over a century before there was any serious consideration of any of those things. Some of our present leaders might well benefit from reading some of his works, don't you think?'

Tim replaced the volume. 'From what little I know of Saint-Simon, he was an impractical visionary who was strong on theory and woefully weak on practice.'

A look of mild annoyance fluttered over the older man's face. 'Hm, a typically English remark.' His voice had a very nasal quality. 'You people have made such a virtue of pragmatism that you wouldn't now recognise a political ideal if you saw one.'

119

Tim attempted to brush aside the acerbic remark. 'Oh, we muddle through.'

'Aha!' Müller sounded like a jackdaw pouncing on a verbal treasure. 'The English motto – *Muddle through*.' He collected his sherry from a silver tray on a side table and seated himself on a leather chesterfield without inviting Tim to take a chair. 'You muddled yourselves in and out of empire. You muddled yourselves in and out of world economic leadership. Now you're trying to muddle yourselves into Europe. You won't succeed. You know why? Because in Europe people respect principles. They love ideals. They want to be led by men who have vision. They're not content, like the English, to muddle through from one economic crisis to the next. They want to be given a glimpse of a society worth working for, fighting for, dying for.'

Tim threw politeness overboard. 'In my experience men who talk about dying for society are usually nowhere to be seen when the bullets start flying.'

Müller gave no indication of having heard the riposte. 'Name one English man of vision – just one, who has given his people a dream, who has inspired them to strive for a new order. You can't do it. You can't produce a single British ruler or statesman worthy to be set beside Charlemagne or Frederick the Great or Napoleon or Cavour or Bismarck or Lenin or de Gaulle.'

As his host warmed to his theme, Tim relaxed into a cavernous armchair and determined not to let himself be provoked. It occurred to him that he could make Müller's abrasiveness work to his own advantage. Since the old man was set on argument and did not shrink from being rude, there was no reason for Tim to pull his punches. If he could steer the conversation the right way, he could slip in some very direct questions.

'On the whole, we tend not to like fanatics,' he offered.

'What you mean is you mistrust greatness and you don't understand people with new, challenging ideas.'

'No, what I mean is that we don't see much point in rushing headlong after a Hitler or a Stalin, regardless of what direction they happen to be going. We prefer to sit back and watch until we can see more clearly what they're up to. Usually, we don't much like the look of what we see. And usually we're right.'

The topic still had not been exhausted when the major-domo returned to announce lunch. Tim followed him into a room no less spectacular than the one he had just left. It was circular and, whereas the library had exuded an atmosphere of studious semi-gloom, this chamber was a bowl of dazzling light. Half its circumference was made of full length windows through which sunlight crashed into the room, reflected from the spectacular snowscape. The interior wall was faced with mirrors. The furniture – 1820s Biedermeyer-style tables and torchères, inlaid with fruit-wood – was splendid in its simplicity so as not to detract from the overall effect. The dining table, which was the same shape as the room, would have seated twenty people comfortably. It was laid for two. Tim and his host sat opposite each other, part of the space between them occupied by a low arrangement of flowers.

'So, Mr Lacy, you've come to make another sales pitch.' The subject changed but Müller's aggressive tone did not. 'Well, you're wasting your time. Anyway, I'm cutting down my collection.'

'Really?' Tim paused as the major-domo ladled an aromatic fish consommé into the Sèvres bowl before him.

'I thought I caught a glimpse of you in New York a few weeks back. I assumed you were there for the big Renaissance sale.'

'So I was. But selling, not buying.'

Tim sipped the rich, brittle, deep-chilled Auslese which made a surprising but perfect foil to the soup. 'I didn't realise. I haven't seen the catalogue. What were you disposing of?'

Müller waved a hand dismissively. 'A Cellini bronze and one or two other little pieces.'

'Not the Ferrara Cellini?' Tim vividly recalled the magnificent casting of a boar and hounds which, on his last visit, had formed the centrepiece of the very table at which they were sitting. Made by the superb sixteenth-century craftsman for one of the d'Este dukes, it had been among the few authenticated Cellinis still in private hands. 'Why on earth did you want to sell that?'

Müller shrugged. 'I'm getting old. When I'm gone the collection here will get split up. I might as well start the process off myself.'

'Where was it that I actually saw you?' Tim gave the appearance of engaging in a feat of memory. 'Wasn't it at the opening of Rob Brand's gallery?'

'Hm! Bumptious upstart!'

Tim laughed. 'He certainly seems to think that there's nothing anybody can teach him about early European antiquities. Still, even he didn't deserve that terrible piece of bad luck. You heard about it, I presume?'

Müller appeared to be concentrating hard on selecting foie gras and endives from the silver salver being presented to him by the butler. 'The burglary? Yes, I read something about it.'

'Odd thing to steal, wasn't it?'

'I really don't recall the details.'

'It was a fragment of an illuminated Bible. I can't think of anyone who would have gone to all that trouble for something so relatively unimportant – can you?' Tim watched closely for the other man's reaction.

Müller did not look up from his plate. 'There's altogether too much stealing and violence going on these days. It never used to be like this. Collecting was a gentlemanly business. The trouble is money has got into the wrong hands. Like power. Even after the war most politicians were men of education, culture, intelligence. Look at the ones we've got now – ill-bred boors who got where they are by playing to the gallery. The only talent most of them possess is how to project themselves on television.'

Tim ignored the attempted diversion. 'The man who was killed at the Brand Gallery – Mike Thomson – was a colleague and friend of mine. You may have met him when you were there.'

At last Müller looked up. 'That's very unlikely. I don't usually get into conversation with other people's staff. Naturally,' he added hastily, 'I'm sorry to hear that the man was a friend of yours.'

Tim decided to let the matter rest there for the time being. There was little point in prodding at an opponent whose guard was up. He concentrated on enjoying the guinea fowl and the hot cherry soufflé that followed the foie gras.

For coffee they adjourned to a small drawing room decorated in the French taste. Looking around the silk-panelled walls, Tim was sure that there were items missing that had been present when he had made an inventory of the premises for security purposes a couple of years before. Surely, there had been a small Boucher over the

123

fireplace, and a Fragonard on the opposite wall? Ernst Müller, it seemed, was feeling the pinch.

Tim made one more foray during the course of the after-lunch conversation. Having raised again the subject of the New York sale, he observed, 'It brought a lot of buyers over from Europe – people who usually bid by phone. Did you meet up with any fellow enthusiasts?'

'I am not a very gregarious person, Mr Lacy.'

'But you know Karl Hammel, don't you?'

'Hah! Sentimental old fool!'

'And the Frankls?'

'I've had some dealings with them in the past.'

'And Hans Meyer was there, too. Weren't you and he rivals for a Carolingian ivory triptych a couple of years ago?'

Müller was unable to suppress a triumphant chuckle. 'Yes, and I won.'

'Did you now?' That was not the version of the ill-tempered contest which had been current in art-world gossip at the time. 'I'd love to see the triptych.'

'Well you can't! I've sold it on.'

'To Herr Meyer?'

'Huh! That nouveau-riche Philistine! Certainly not! If you must know, it was acquired by a consortium for the cathedral treasury at Aachen. We felt that it should be on general display and that it ought to return to its original home.'

Tim restrained a laugh. The thought of Ernst Müller as a public-spirited philanthropist was bizarre in the extreme.

Shortly afterwards his host brought Tim's visit to a close by observing that more snow clouds were piling up and suggesting pointedly that Tim ought to be on the road back to Vienna.

As he turned the car on the wide forecourt and began the descent through the forest, Tim tried to decide whether the interview had left him enlightened or confused. Müller had not accounted very convincingly for his unexpected trip to New York and he certainly knew more about the affair at the Brand Gallery than he claimed to know. Yet the idea of this crotchety, eccentric, old-fashioned, refined, elderly Austrian consorting with the likes of Emma Freundlich and firing off a heavy handgun stretched imagination to breaking point.

Tim noted again, as he had noted on the way in, the cameras in trees along the drive. 'There's another thing,' he thought. 'Why does a man who is obliged to reduce the size of his collection pretty drastically suddenly go in for expensive increased security?' His professional eye had picked out signs in the castle of a fairly sophisticated new system, that was a distinct improvement on Müller's previous Heath Robinson anti-theft devices. 'So, why on earth, if he has all the security apparatus he needs and no intention of adding to it, did he agree to my visit?'

From a first-floor window of Schloss Turnitz, Ernst Müller watched the tail lights of his guest's car disappear round a bend in the drive. He thought, 'I wonder what I ought to do about that inquisitive young man?'

The headquarters of the Grand Imperial Teutonic Order are situated in a quiet back street behind the Belvedere Palace. Catherine emerged from the taxi, carefully negotiated the piled snow and gazed upwards. Beneath exuberant Baroque gables the façade of the corner building was remarkably plain. Like most of the other buildings in the street, which were occupied by lawyers, accountants and architects, it announced its purpose to the world by means of a discreet brass plaque. Catherine rang the bell, spoke her name into the intercom and was admitted. She found herself in a marble-floored hall from which a wide stone staircase wound impressively upwards to the first floor. Down it a rubicund figure was already hurrying. 'Ms Younger?' (Catherine had decided to use her maiden name.)

Catherine had envisaged that someone who bore the impressive title of Grand Chamberlain would be of mature years and grave demeanour, so Albert Hoffmeister took her by surprise. Mid-thirties, bespectacled and jaunty, he spoke English with a mixture of precision and slightly misplaced idiom.

'You are most punctual.' He shook her hand enthusiastically. 'The politeness of kings, is it not? We are most flattered that your august journal should want the low-down on our little organisation.'

'Thank you very much for allowing me to see your premises. I gather women are not normally allowed in here.'

He looked pained. 'It is only from our ceremonies that we exclude the distaff side.'

'Why, Herr Hoffmeister, what do you get up to in your gatherings – blood-curdling oaths and animal sacrifice?'

Hoffmeister looked genuinely horrified, then saw Catherine's smile. 'Ah, you are pulling one's leg, I see. But people do sometimes get the wrong idea about us. They think we are a branch of the Freemasons or the Rosicrucians. Nothing could be a greater distance from the truth. Perhaps you will permit me to show you around first. Afterwards I shall be delighted to answer any questions you may have. We'll commune in the Elisabethkirche.'

He led the way through two small, deserted offices to an

external door and across an alleyway inches deep in snow to a small, unprepossessing church. He fumbled a large key into the lock and swung the heavy door inwards. Muttering, 'One moment, please' he disappeared into the internal gloom. Seconds later there was a loud click and the lights came on. Catherine stepped across the threshold and was stunned by what she saw. The interior was a riot of Baroque overindulgence. Ornately carved walnut pews polished to a glassy finish formed three sides of a square facing an altar covered in silver cloth with the black cross of the Order surrounded by a golden nimbus. The carved and polychromed reredos displaying the figures of St Elizabeth and St George on either side of the Virgin and Child was of obvious early date but it had been set in a heavily-gilded framework which curved and spiralled its way towards the roof, almost completely obscuring the east window. On either side of the altar and facing inwards were two canopied thrones with flamboyant coats of arms worked into their padded backs. Catherine pointed to them.

'The honour seats of the Grand Master and the Grand Hospitaller,' her guide informed her in a whisper. 'Shall we?' He indicated a pew and Catherine slid into it. Hoffmeister entered the row in front and turned to speak to her over its back.

'I am certain that you will have done your homework, Ms Younger, but perhaps you will allow me briefly to sketch the history of our Order.'

He was an entertaining raconteur and, although Catherine had read up most of what he told her, she enjoyed the well-rehearsed performance. Hoffmeister described the beginnings in the Holy Land as an exclusive order confined to German knights of noble birth who dedicated themselves to the care and succour of crusaders and pilgrims. He told how in the thirteenth century it had, on the pope's orders, transferred its sphere of operation to the Baltic lands, conquering and converting the pagan Prussians and their neighbours and spreading Latin Christendom right up to the Russian border. Its glorious years lasted for two centuries during which the knight brothers presided over a unique form of Christian civilisation ruled from their massive fortress at Marienburg, the largest in Europe. Then in the decades preceding the Reformation and the disintegration of Christendom, heretics, ambitious Polish kings and rebellious subjects brought the rule of the Order to an end.

Catherine, scribbling shorthand and trying to look like an enthusiastic career journalist, glanced up from her notepad. 'What I don't understand is how the Teutonic Knights kept going after that. Surely, they had no *raison d'être*.'

A defensive note crept into Hoffmeister's voice. 'The principal *raison d'être* of the Order has always been works of charity. Even when they commanded large tracts of territory, the knights maintained hospitals, schools and homes for the elderly. When they were no longer encumbered with administration, they were able to concentrate on their primary function. So we have done ever since – that and keeping alive an important tradition of Christian service.'

'But surely there have been gaps. Didn't the French Revolution . . .?'

Hoffmeister nodded. 'That lamentable interlude destroyed much that was valuable in our common culture. Fortunately the Habsburg emperors took the Order underneath their wings and refounded it, here in Vienna, in 1840. They gave us this church and enabled us to acquire many valuable relics that had almost been given up for lost. The magnificent altarpiece, for example, comes from the great church at Marienburg.'

'But didn't the Order collapse again with the ending of the Imperial dynasty in the First World War?'

'There did, indeed, supervene another black era for the Order. However, in 1976, we rose once more like a phoenix from the embers. A group of leading politicians and businessmen – some of the sons or grandsons of former members – restored our fortunes. And so we soldier on – isn't that what you say?'

'That certainly is a magnificent reredos.' Catherine's notepad slipped from her lap and she bent to retrieve it as Hoffmeister launched into a descriptive paean of the Gothic miracle.

'And now, perhaps,' he concluded, rising, 'you will permit me to show you our little museum.'

As they retraced their steps to the neighbouring building Catherine cautiously began her probing about the current membership.

'Forgive my mentioning it, but you seem to be a little young for such an important post.'

'We are not all the old fogeys.' The chubby face assumed an indulgent smile. 'We are a very mixed brotherhood. Members are invited to join because they possess talents or attributes that can be useful to the Order. In my case, I was recommended by my professor – I'm at the university here. I studied the origins of the Order for my thesis. The previous Grand Chamberlain had died some months previously, and the Grand Chapter decided that I was well qualified to take charge of the Order's muniments. So here I am – after undergoing the usual initiation, of course.'

'I don't suppose you're prepared to tell me exactly what that initiation consists of?'

Hoffmeister held open a door and ushered her through into the vestibule from which they had started. 'Now you must permit us a few little secrets. If you follow me, I'll show you our modest museum.'

He threw open double doors beneath the staircase and Catherine entered a large chamber in which two lines of tall glass cases formed an aisle leading to another impressive portal at the far end. Each display was individually lit and comprised the robes worn by members of the Grand Chapter. Catherine could not help being impressed by the Order's sumptuous wardrobe. Over a silver silk tunic emblazoned with the black cross and girded by a gold sword belt each member of the Teutonic hierarchy wore a velvet cape, coloured according to rank – powder blue for the Grand Chamberlain, russet for the Master of Germany, and so on through the grades up to black for the Grand Hospitaller and white for the Grand Master.

Hoffmeister led her into an adjacent, smaller room, obviously the Order's library and archive. He waved a hand at the well-filled shelves. 'Here we have virtually everything ever written by or about the Teutonic Knights. I hope your article will make clear that the Teutonic Knights were not just soldiers. We have numbered many scholars of note among our number. Take for example the fourteenth-century Grand Master Luder. He wrote and commissioned several important works.' He opened a glass door and carefully lifted down a vellum-bound volume whose title was written along its fore edge – '*Von siben ingesigelen*'. He opened it to reveal pages of beautifully even hand written script. 'The Order played a leading role in the development of High German as a written language.'

'Do you have many original relics of the Order?'

It was an innocent question but Catherine was aware that her guide looked at her sharply before his face subsided into its habitual smile. 'Alas, much has been lost over the centuries. There are some interesting early documents here.' He turned back the cloth covering a long, glazed display table and gave her a commentary on the yellowed parchment and vellum of ancient charters, papal bulls and administrative orders bearing the big seal displaying the Virgin Mary.

Catherine thought that this was the obvious moment to go for the jugular. 'I was reading an interesting article recently by Professor Fischer of Hamburg . . .'

'Ah yes, that odd theory about the Dresden Text.'

A little bit too quick on that response, my chubby friend, Catherine thought. She said, 'You don't agree with Fischer's thesis?'

'I haven't seen the document, of course, but the connection he tries to make with our Order is not very convincing.'

'Still, it's a pity about the Dresden Text being stolen.'

'Stolen!' Grand Chamberlain Hoffmeister's face was a round O of shocked surprise. 'From the British Library?'

'No, it was on loan in America. You hadn't heard about it, then?'

'No, indeed. What a terrible world we live in, Ms Younger. One hardly likes to open the paper in the morning.'

The tour concluded in what Hoffmeister called the 'frater' but what most people would have described as a banqueting hall. It was entered by the double doors from the museum and its impact was immediate. Light entered the two-storeyed hall through coloured windows depicting the patron saints of the Order and the coats of arms of earlier Grand Masters. The panelling seemed to be genuinely medieval. Portraits of recent Grand Masters looked down from the wall behind the high table. Two other long tables extended the length of the hall, reflecting in their polished surfaces the sunlight tumbling through the stained glass above. Huge silver candelabra punctuated the gleaming boards but the high table was laden with the trophies of the Order – chalices, salvers, jugs and, in the centre, an elaborate silver-gilt casting of St George and the dragon.

'These premises were built in the 1970s?'

'Substantially, yes. The Order occupied this site from the middle of the last century but the building was severely damaged during World War II. Fortunately, plans and drawings existed of the original rooms and we were able to reconstruct them fairly faithfully.'

'That must have cost a packet!'

He looked puzzled. 'Packet?' The idiom was one not, as yet, added to his collection.

Catherine decided to change tack. 'I'd like to talk to one or two ordinary members of the Order. Get their impressions. Ask them what attracts them to it. That sort of thing. Would it be possible for me to have a list?'

Hoffmeister gazed up at the hammerbeam roof in indignation. 'Quite out of the question, Ms Younger! We have to respect the privacy of the brothers.'

Catherine smiled disarmingly. 'Oh well, it was worth a try. Look, let's compromise. I have my own list. It's names I've been given of people who might have some information. Now, I don't know if any of them is a member of the

Order. If I give you this list and if it does contain the name of a knight brother would you contact him and ask if he's willing to see me?'

Hoffmeister frowned dubiously but eventually said that he supposed there would be no harm in that. Catherine handed over a slip which she had typed before leaving Farrans. The names on it were:

> Ernst Müller
> Frederick Hoffer
> Walter Frankl
> Hans Meyer
> Karl Hammel
> Oscar König
> Arthur Meredith

She watched the Austrian carefully as he scanned the list. His face betrayed no emotion but a light dew of perspiration appeared on his brow. The frater was far from warm.

He stood up. 'It will be necessary for me to check these on the computer. Perhaps you would be good enough to accompany me to my office.'

They returned to the hallway and mounted the staircase to a suite of offices that contrasted totally with the rooms they had toured in being very modern and very comfortably appointed.

'If you wouldn't mind waiting a jiffy.' Her host settled Catherine in a leather swivel chair in what was obviously a secretary's room and went through to an adjoining office, closing the door behind him.

Seconds later Catherine saw a red light appear on the desk telephone console. 'What I'd give to know who's on the other end of that line,' she thought. She dismissed the idea of picking up the secretary's handset. It was too risky and, anyway, since the conversation would be in German she would not understand anything she overheard. She contented herself with examining the piece of paper she had noticed on the floor in the church and picked up while her guide's back was turned.

It was a letter on the thick, heavily-embossed paper of the Grand Imperial Order, and appeared to be nothing more exciting than the brief notice of a meeting. What was interesting, though, was the name of the addressee: '*O.R. König, 17 Goethestrasse, Berlin.*' The only words of the text that she could clearly understand were the first two: '*Bruder Oscar.*'

She folded the paper and slipped it back between the pages of her pad just as the telltale light went out. Catherine smiled to herself and began counting. She had got to 'four' when Hoffmeister reappeared.

He returned the list. 'I'm afraid I have to disappoint you, Ms Younger. None of these names corresponds to that of any of our members.'

Chapter 8

The dinner party that James and Gloria Homerton had arranged in the Lacys' honour at their house in the quiet suburb of Grinzing turned out to be quite a grand affair. Three other couples had been invited and Catherine found herself seated at table on her host's right with Jacob Windgren, Professor of Political Science at Vienna University, on her other side and Sandra Gibbs, a woman from California, whose husband was with Chase Manhattan, opposite. Conversation flowed easily across the gleaming mahogany and glittering crystal.

As the sole roulades were being served by staff borrowed from the embassy for the occasion, James said, 'Gloria tells me you were visiting with the Grand Imperial Order of Teutonic Knights this morning. I must say that's not on the usual tourist itinerary. Did you enjoy it?'

Catherine described her tour in general terms, omitting any reference to the Dresden Text and her grilling of Hoffmeister.

'Yeah, but just who are these "Grand Imperial Knights" or whatever they call themselves?' Sandra, a mid-forties bleach-blonde, wanted to know. 'I mean, we are living in the twentieth century, for heaven's sakes.'

Catherine smiled across the table. 'You know what men

are like; never happier than when they're in a gang – the more exclusive the better. I figure the Teutonic Knights for a bunch of wealthy Austrians who like to get away from their wives four times a year for a blow-out preceded by a load of semi-religious mumbo-jumbo.'

'More Chablis, ladies?' James beckoned the waiter to top up the glasses. 'I understand they're quite heavily into charity work.'

Catherine sipped the cool fragrant wine. 'I heard that, too, but when I asked this guy, Hoffmeister, he said he couldn't give me any details because the Order's money is always given anonymously.'

The university man had been listening in silence to the conversation. Now, he arranged his knife and fork with fastidious precision on the empty plate. When he spoke he appeared to be choosing his words with equal care. 'Here in Austria, not everyone regards this organisation with mild amusement.'

James looked at him over the rim of his glass. 'Are you hinting at something sinister, Jacob?'

The professor looked thoughtful. 'I certainly wouldn't want to be alarmist, but we are dealing here with a very old and emotionally powerful politico-religious tradition. The original Teutonic Knights had a Christianising, civilising mission. They were clad in white and went forth against the forces of heathen darkness. Later, in the popular imagination, their exploits got mixed up with the German equivalent of Arthurian legend – Parsifal, Lohengrin, the poems of Wolfram von Eschenbach and so on. The mythology became intertwined with German and, particularly, Prussian nationalism. The strength of that alliance is something foreigners always underestimate.'

'What you're saying,' James suggested, 'is that there is

something in the Germanic culture which sustains a sense of world mission?'

'Exactly!' Jacob's tone was that of a tutor with a group of bright students. 'Some people are apt to think that Hitler invented the master race concept – the sacred destiny of world leadership. In fact, of course, its roots are deeper and stronger.'

'My Gard!' Sandra threw up her hands in a theatrical gesture of horror. 'Does that mean that right here in Vienna we have a bunch of weirdos dressing up in Ruritanian costumes and planning the Fourth Reich?'

Everyone laughed but the professor quickly brought the class back to order. 'The juxtaposition seems absurd, does it not? In this instance I'm sure it is absurd. But, you know, when Himmler founded the SS he was trying to create a modern, politicised version of the Teutonic Knights. And the swastika drew its power from a race memory of the black cross on the white ground.'

Catherine broke the thoughtful silence that followed. 'This sense of destiny doesn't, I guess, have to be expressed militarily?'

Jacob turned and beamed at his 'star pupil'. 'Aha, I think you have grasped what I have been trying, very inadequately, to say. There are those who see in the signs of our own times the unfolding of an inevitable historic purpose. Germany is reunited. Slavic domination has been repulsed. Berlin is leading the eastward crusade of free market economics into the lands where Marxist darkness until recently held sway. Political leadership of the EC resides, to all intents and purposes, in Bonn. The Bundesbank dominates the financial markets. Who can doubt – so runs the argument – that, as American and Japanese economic empires crumble, a Germanicised Europe will emerge to lead the march of human progress?'

Catherine sat back and allowed herself to be served with *medaillons* of venison in a rich red sauce. When the waiter had moved on to Sandra, she asked, 'How organised are the people who think like this?'

'Oh, not at all.' The professor smiled reassuringly. 'Anyone who tried to erect a political programme on these emotional foundations would be doomed to failure. The German people have learned something from twentieth-century history.'

A period of silence followed while the diners applied themselves to their meat. When conversation resumed it was upon other topics.

Later Catherine lay awake in the enormous hotel bed. She looked up as Tim emerged from the shower, towelling himself down. 'Have we got time for a couple of days in Berlin? I've never been there.'

Tim shook his head emphatically. 'No way. We both have businesses to run, remember? And if you're thinking about Oscar König, forget it. It's a wild goose chase.'

'But why did Hoffmeister deny that König belonged to the Teutonic Order? You can't dismiss that as unimportant?' She was still annoyed because, earlier in the day, when she had triumphantly produced her 'clue', Tim had done just that.

He rubbed his hair briskly. 'Darling, look at it from Hoffmeister's point of view. Some journalist comes snooping around, probably intent on writing a lurid exposé of the "Secret World of the Teutonic Knights". He gives her the five-bob tour and hopes she'll be satisfied. She isn't. She tries to winkle out of him details about the membership. He doesn't quite know how to handle that, so he goes off and telephones the Great Panjandrum, or whatever he's called. Back comes the answer, "On no account tell her anything." It's deplorable but really, quite understandable.'

'And you don't think it's just the teeniest bit of a coincidence that König was in the Brand Gallery the night an old document which once belonged to the Teutonic Knights . . .'

'*Might* have once belonged to the Teutonic Knights!'

'OK, OK, *might* have belonged. As I was saying, König was there the night it went missing and you yourself said you didn't know why he was in New York. Now it turns out that this same König is also a member of the rejuvenated Order. None of that strikes you as odd?'

Tim slipped naked between the sheets and pressed himself against her.

Catherine poked him in the ribs. 'Your hair's still damp. And don't change the subject.'

With a sigh, Tim rolled onto his back. 'Oscar König is a devious bastard who would probably stop at nothing to turn a dishonest buck. If he's mixed up with the Teutonic Knights it'll be for his own good, not theirs.'

'So, if the Grand Chapter paid him to get hold of the Dresden Text . . .?'

'Yes, but why? What use could it possibly be to them? They couldn't display it among the sacred relics of the Order.'

'Suppose, as you suggested, they've come across the rest of the book, or even a part of it? That would make it more valuable.'

'Yes, but I come back to the same question – what would they do with it?'

'Use it in their arcane rituals?'

'Did they strike you as the sort of people who would go to vast expense – not to mention two murders – just to get a book to put on their altar?'

Catherine lay back with her hands behind her head. She thought hard, unwilling to relinquish her theory. 'They certainly have the money. No expense has been spared on their premises. And, yes, I think I can see how gang loyalty could lead in their case to fanaticism. The idea of the *Brüderbund* is a powerful one in most societies. When I worked in Japan it was perfectly easy to see how the medieval cult of the samurai had become the basis for the criminal clubs, the Yakuza. It's the same with the Triads in China, the Mafia in Sicily, even the Freemasons. Wherever men band together in exclusivist clubs they develop their own ethical codes and usually end up perverting common justice and decency.'

Tim propped himself on one elbow and looked down at his wife. 'That was quite a feminist speech. Have you been secretly reading *Cosmopolitan* again?' Then, as Catherine sat up, glaring, 'OK, OK. Point taken. Let's agree to put the mysterious Oscar König in the pending tray. I just think all this pseudo-medieval knight errantry is probably complicating things unnecessarily.'

'Well, at least my sleuthing turned up more than yours.'

'Oh, I don't know. I think my outing to Schloss Turnitz was very productive – in a negative sort of way. We can now eliminate one of the M's. Ernst Müller gets more and more eccentric as the years go by but I really can't see him hiring assassins. Anyway, at the moment he's reducing his art hoard, not adding to it.'

'So you'll concentrate on the other two M's, now?'

'Yes, I'll see if I can surprise something out of one of them when I meet them next month.'

'And if they turn out negative, too?'

He grinned up at her. 'Then I suppose it's back to Camelot, trailing my unused lance behind me. And now . . .' He reached up and pulled her on top of him.

This time Catherine was happy to let him change the subject.

Their love-making did not, as usual, lead easily to sound, satisfying sleep. For a long time Tim and Catherine lay in the darkness, alert minds grappling with different puzzles. Catherine was trying to square Hoffmeister and his boyish enthusiasm for 'old, unhappy far-off things and battles long ago' with Professor Windgren's warnings about advocates of a greater Germany. Tim was worrying about the lead to Oscar König. Hoping he had thrown Catherine off the scent. Of course she was right. König's name cropping up in the Teutonic Order's HQ could not possibly be a coincidence. That meant that someone, somehow, knew why he and Catherine were in Vienna.

It was on the fifth day out from Allenstein that von Plauen's force located the main Polish contingent. Scouts reported to the commander in the string of summer fishing huts where he had found meagre shelter for his men and horses. The simple, thatched sheds were perfectly adequate for the peasants who came here in the warmer months to work the lakes but in the March of 1456 when winter seemed more reluctant than usual to relinquish its grip on the land, icy winds poked through every chink in the mud walls and tore frenziedly at roofs making existing holes bigger and allowing fresh falls of snow to settle on the occupants.

The message that came to the Grand Hospitaller was that the enemy was fifteen miles to the east, making very slow progress along a corridor seldom more than a quarter of a mile wide twisting between expanses of semi-frozen water. From local guides pressed into service, von Plauen learned that the route of the invaders' advance would bring them onto ever narrower causeways where they would be forced to proceed at an even more sluggish pace or divide their host into smaller columns.

Von Plauen split his much smaller army into three mobile units which set out, by separate routes, to impede the Polish line of advance. Ulrich was assigned to the Grand Hospitaller's contingent. So was Stephan Zerwonka. The two men had not spoken during the march from Allenstein. Ulrich deliberately avoided his adversary, not out of sullen hostility – although his comrades probably attributed it to that – but because he wanted to keep the Bohemian guessing. As long as the man he had wronged was at liberty and studiously keeping his own counsel, Zerwonka would have to watch his back. Doubtless he had assumed that the Grand Hospitaller would keep the accused under lock and key at Allenstein. As things stood he had to be on his guard against Ulrich's vengeance at all hours of the day and night. It gave Ulrich grim satisfaction to note that the mercenary was always accompanied by three or four cronies and that he looked up warily whenever the young knight came anywhere near him. Ulrich noted these things, preserved an outward calm and kept his anger on a tight rein. He could wait.

The first encounter between the invaders and von Plauen's force was highly satisfactory. The Grand Hospitaller drew up his men in five ranks, plugging a causeway that was scarcely a hundred yards wide. He adopted an arrowhead formation. His best knights formed the narrow point. Each succeeding row of horsemen was wider than the one in front. The object was to break the force of the Polish charge. If the arrow's tip held firm it would cleave the enemy ranks, whose impetus would take them to right and left where the brittle ice of the marsh-fringed lakes awaited. The plan worked. Three frontal assaults of increasing ferocity were launched against the Order's position. The Teutonic Knights and their auxiliaries shuddered at each impact. Holes were cut in their ranks by the flailing swords of the Poles but they held their position. Dozens of enemy knights were brought crashing down. Others trusted to the ice in an attempt to outflank the defenders. The frozen surfaces gave way beneath thudding hooves. From his position at the rear, Ulrich watched several Polish horsemen struggling in the water, shrieking with terror as their plunging steeds threw them off, and sinking rapidly under the weight of their own armour. 'That,' he thought grimly, 'would be a fitting way for Zerwonka to die.'

His opportunity for revenge came sooner than he had dared hope. Dusk was falling by the time the Poles broke off the engagement and retreated. Von Plauen had no intention of pursuing them but he did despatch fifty men to follow the enemy and discover their movements. He placed Zerwonka in charge. In the gloom it was easy for Ulrich to attach himself to the reconnaissance party. Deprived as he was of his white surcoat and wrapped in a nondescript cloak with the hood over his head, he was indistinguishable from the mercenaries who made up Zerwonka's force. It had begun to snow again and every man rode with his head down against the wind, disinclined to talk. Undetected, Ulrich jogged along the iron-hard track only a few paces from the object of his hatred.

They had been travelling for less than half an hour when

Zerwonka ordered a halt. He called his men round him and pointed triumphantly along the trail. 'I smell booty, lads!'

They stood on a slight spur of higher ground. Beyond and beneath them, some two hundred yards ahead, they could just make out a small group of enemy stragglers. Ulrich knew that they would be men with bad injuries or lame horses and probably a few able-bodied comrades detailed to bring them safe back to camp. He could already see the fires of the Polish encampment, perhaps a couple of miles off. The etiquette of the Order forbade attacks on wounded enemies after a battle. But Zerwonka knew nothing of etiquette.

'Right, lads, they're all ours, but we must be quick before the Poles send out a relief force. No prisoners. Just take what you can, horses, weapons – armour if there's time. Let's go!' He threw back his hood and donned his helmet. He adjusted the shield over his left arm, drew his sword and dug his spurs into his mount's flanks.

As they thundered down the slope Ulrich pushed his way to the front. When they reached the enemy he was at the Bohemian's shoulder. He saw Zerwonka hack at a knight who rode slumped over his horse's mane. The vicious, cowardly act unleashed all Ulrich's anger. As the mercenary leaned forward to grab the reins of the now riderless horse, Ulrich swung his sword in a wide arc. It clanged against the back of Zerwonka's helmet and sent him sprawling from the saddle.

Ulrich hoped that the force of the blow had been enough to break the traitor's neck. He wheeled his mare away as three riders crashed across his line of vision to enter the fray. When they had passed he saw Zerwonka on his knees, shaking his head. He rode at the mercenary, raising his visor as he did so.

'Zerwonka!' he roared and saw a flash of recognition in the instant before his blade struck again. He aimed for a point just below the gorget, hoping to sever neck or shoulder. The mercenary ducked with surprising speed and the blow struck again on the helmet, sending him sprawling on his back.

Ulrich dismounted, detaching the long-handled mace from his saddle as he did so. He advanced on Zerwonka who was now on all fours, frantically scrabbling around for his sword. As his fingers closed over the hilt, the ridged iron of Ulrich's mace smashed down upon them. He staggered to his feet and took a step backwards as Ulrich's weapon swung at his chest. Ulrich lifted the vicious mace above his head. Again the Bohemian stumbled out of reach, throwing up his shield to ward off the blow. Again the young knight advanced, driving his adversary back towards the frozen fringe of the lake.

Ulrich was now totally oblivious of the skirmish going on around him. All his attention was concentrated on the gnarled metal fist at the end of its haft as it struck, over and again, on helmet, shield and breastplate. Zerwonka was on the ice now, his mailed feet slithering. Ulrich prodded and slashed, forcing his adversary further out, ears alert for the groan and creak of fracturing ice. The blood pounded in his head as he pursued the mercenary to the freezing death that should enwrap them both.

Suddenly, the Bohemian shouted something in his own language. Ulrich half turned but not quickly enough to avoid the sword of a pursuer. It slashed through his thigh above the greave. The strength went from his left leg. He fell and slithered forward over the frozen surface.

Zerwonka moved aside. At that moment Ulrich heard the crack. He rolled onto his back. He felt the ice yield beneath him. Felt the pain surge through his useless limb. Saw Zerwonka grinning arrogantly, an upraised sword now in his hand. Instinctively, he held the mace up to ward off the blow.

Then numbing, freezing water flowed around him. Over him. He saw no more.

Chapter 9

'Here's the Ernst Müller list you wanted.' Sally, Tim's secretary, placed a sheet of typed A4 on his desk and glanced pointedly at her wristwatch.

It was a couple of weeks since Tim and Catherine had returned to Farrans from Vienna and they had both been extremely busy. Matters had not been improved by a spell of bitter February weather which had played havoc with Farrans Court's ancient plumbing and put the central heating temporarily out of action.

Tim smiled at the attractive brunette whose shapely figure was padded out with a thick sweater and a cardigan. He took the hint. 'That's fine, Sally. Thanks very much. Why don't you get away a bit early. I know I've kept you after hours for the last few days. Tell Mary she can go, too.'

'Thanks, Tim. About that list – it's not complete, of course. Imelda of Amsterdam were very cagey and Galerie Charpentier said we should buy their back catalogues. Anyway, that list will give you a general idea.'

Tim ran his eyes over the catalogue of paintings, sculptures and *objets d'art*. He had been curious to know what Müller had been selling and had asked Sally to look out the inventory of the Austrian's collection and to make discreet enquiries through contacts in the auction houses and the trade about which items had been disposed of over the last couple of years.

'I'm sure this'll make interesting reading. Thanks again. Now, off you go – and have a good weekend.'

'OK. Don't burn the midnight oil, Tim.' She left the room.

Moments later she put her head back round the door. 'By the way, I take it you didn't want to know what Mr Müller's been buying.'

'Buying? I thought he'd been slimming down his collection, not adding to it.'

'Seems not. Corinne Noble at Christie's volunteered the information that Herr Müller has been pretty active in the rooms recently. She said to get in touch if you want any gen – strictly off the record, of course. I reckon she has a soft spot for you. Well, I'm off. Good night again.'

Tim studied the list. The Cellini bronze was there. So were several French and Italian paintings and some pieces of Renaissance bijouterie. Top quality items, every one. If the secretive Austrian was raising cash in such large quantities in order to reinvest he must be laying the foundation of a major new collection. That would certainly explain his elaborate security arrangements. He picked up the phone. When he got through to the appropriate department at Christie's, it was to be informed that Ms Noble was with clients in the country and would not be back in the office till Monday.

On Monday Tim would be in Germany. Well, probably Müller was not very important. Checking him out could wait. On the other hand . . . He scribbled a note on his pad: '*Please phone Corinne Noble and find out what you can about Ernst Müller's buying habits. I'll phone you mid-week from Bonn. T.L.*' He took the message through to the next room and taped it to Sally's word processor.

At his desk again, he sat back, closed tired eyes and thought about the days ahead. Officially – in other words, as far as Catherine and anyone else at Farrans knew – he was making a week's business trip round Europe, calling on various clients and contacts, among whom were Hans Meyer, member of the *Bundestag*, and Arthur Meredith the Frankfurt businessman. In fact, that was only partly true. He did not like deceiving Catherine but that was better than letting her worry about the possible danger he might be running into.

On Monday morning, at about the time that Sally was discovering his note, Tim was at the British Airways Club Class reservations desk at Heathrow's Terminal One, changing the Paris ticket his secretary had obtained for one which had the destination 'Berlin' printed on it.

From Tegel airport he phoned Oscar König.

'Tim! How delightful! Where are you speaking from?' Was Lacy imagining an apprehensive note underlying the German's habitual ebullience?

'I'm at the airport. Over here for a few days doing business in Berlin, Bonn and Frankfurt.'

'Oho! That sounds impressive. There must be more money in guarding art than in selling it.'

'I don't imagine you're on the breadline, Oscar. Listen, last time we met you offered me dinner. I'm here to claim it. How about tonight?'

A slight hesitation, then, 'Delighted, old friend.' He sounded as though he meant it.

When they met that evening, in a quiet first-floor restaurant overlooking the Tiergarten, the stout dealer was gracious, attentive, hospitality personified. Tim let him rumble on good humouredly about art world shop, and watched him shovel food industriously into the small orifice above his multiple chins. He wanted to relax the German and try to catch him off guard. Not until they had almost finished their *Bauernschmaus* did he twist the conversation quickly.

'Very tasty.' He prodded another forkful of pork, sauerkraut and dumpling. 'Of course, it's a Viennese dish, really, isn't it? Do you get to Vienna often?' Tim was gratified to see König choke slightly over his beer.

The German recovered quickly. 'No. There's not much call for my sort of thing over there. Anyway, the dealers there have their own contacts in Hungary.'

'You just go down for the meetings of the Order, do you?' Tim took a pull at his stein and pretended not to notice König's feigned bewilderment. 'I must say I was a bit surprised to hear that you were mixed up with a bunch of oddballs like the Grand Imperial Teutonic Order.'

'The Grand . . . what?' Oscar dabbed his napkin to his lips, and mopped his brow. 'Never heard of them. What made you think I had anything to do with them?'

'Oh, this.' Casually, Tim produced from an inside pocket a photostat of the letter he had borrowed from Catherine's desk drawer.

The German looked at the typed sheet and made a strange noise in his throat. His eyes bulged. His florid cheeks turned a glistening puce. For a startled moment Tim thought he was having a heart attack. König took a long gulp of beer and tried to recover himself. He laughed and returned the letter. 'The English sense of humour. I shall never understand it.'

Tim shrugged, folded the paper, but left it on the table beside his plate. 'You must do a lot of business in

Istanbul,' he remarked casually.

König shook his head and smiled, but his dark eyes were now focused intently on his guest's face. 'Not so much these days. Good-quality icons do, of course, still reach Turkey and Greece from Georgia and Bulgaria but the prices are exorbitant. Frankly, I do better business sitting here in Berlin waiting for merchandise to reach me over our no-longer-existing border.'

'Emma Freundlich spent a lot of time in Istanbul in recent years.'

This time König took refuge in a coughing fit, pulling the large silk handkerchief from his breast pocket and burying his face in it. 'Forgive me. A cold on the chest. I don't seem to be able to throw it off. Berlin has been very damp recently. What sort of a winter are you having in Britain?'

'I was mentioning Emma Freundlich, your compatriot, or more accurately, your late compatriot.'

'My friend, you seem intent on riddles this evening.'

'Surely, you haven't forgotten Emma so soon.'

König made a pretence of vain concentration. 'I'm sorry, but I don't think . . .'

'Emma Freundlich was the woman involved in that business at the Brand Gallery in New York, just before Christmas.'

'Ah, yes. I remember reading about it in the papers. I simply didn't register her name. I had no reason to.'

Tim stared at the corpulent figure opposite who was trying to regain his composure. If ever he was going to discover anything about Mike's death, it was now. König was shaken. The only thing to do was shake him some more – and hope that something would drop out.

'Come off it, Oscar. You know a hell of a lot more than

that. A good friend of mine was gunned down by an ex-terrorist, someone who lived in that old twilight zone between East and West, between Europe and the Middle East. That's your territory, Oscar. Don't tell me you've never heard of her. Someone smuggled her into America. Arranged passports. Provided cash. Fixed hotel reservations. Someone familiar with the criminal underworld of Europe. Someone who crosses the Atlantic frequently. Once again, Oscar, you fit the bill. The whole object of the operation was to steal an ancient manuscript which once belonged to the Teutonic Order. And in Vienna, at the headquarters of a bunch of nutters claiming to be the spiritual heirs of that Order, whose name do I find? Oscar König. Now, either you tell me all you know about this business or I go to the police with my suspicions. Whether or not they'll find enough to tie you into the New York murders I don't know, but I'm quite sure you don't want the *Polizei* ferreting around in your affairs, tracing your Russian mafia contacts, uncovering the lucrative line in looted church treasures that keeps you in silk shirts and *Bauernschmaus*.'

The fat Berliner lumbered to his feet with a poor attempt at dignity. He glowered down at Tim. 'I am not prepared to listen to any more of these ridiculous accusations and insults.'

'Please yourself, Oscar. But I'll be back – depend on it.'

Without another word, König turned and swerved his way among the tables to the exit. Tim watched the broad, retreating back. 'Now, Oscar, old chum, just who are you scared of? It sure as hell isn't me.'

The feeling he had had since Vienna had become a lot stronger during the evening. He gazed around the full restaurant. Any diners who had noticed the recent fracas were studiously ignoring it. They all seemed engrossed with their own meals and conversations. Yet that sense that he had developed in SAS days was now overwhelming. Being watched. No, that was not exactly right. What *was* it precisely that he felt?

Tim was aware of the head waiter hovering solicitously. Was the other gentleman all right? Tim explained that Herr König had been called away on unexpected business. And yes, in answer to the next question, he would certainly like to try the special house *Torte*.

Minutes later, as he prodded at the flakes of pastry, kirsch-laced fruit and piled cream, he decided his tactics. He would wait. Let König stew for a while. See if anything happened.

'Manipulated.' That was the word he wanted.

For the next couple of days Tim behaved like any other tourist returning to the once-and-future German capital, after an interval of several years, to see the 'changes'. He strolled the renamed streets of the old Eastern Sector and gazed at the empty graffiti-daubed plinths from which the heroes of Communism had once frowned upon a cowed citizenry. He looked at the scar of dreary wasteland where the wall had once gashed the city. He absorbed the self-conscious atmosphere of the Unter den Linden, trying to recapture the chic gaiety of a long-vanished epoch. He noticed the new lavishly-stocked shops, gleaming like capped teeth next to their drab neighbours. He went to view the mysterious cache of French masters – Corot, Delacroix, Courbet, Renoir, Seurat and others – recently put on display in the National Gallery. Part of a soldier's loot, they had lain in rough parcels and suitcases, in a succession of East German hiding places, since the last days of the Second World War. Now it was just one of many secrets to have come to light since the collapse of the Honecker regime. He obtained a seat for *Orfeo ed Euridice* at the Staatsoper. He was enthralled both by the glittering performance and the restored Baroque magnificence of the building – one of the few legacies of the old order of which Berliners were proud. The clear impression Tim gained of the once-closed city beyond the Brandenburg Gate was that of a poor relation, frantically seeking to better himself and turn his back on his shabby, Socialist past.

But there were other messages. They were not openly proclaimed. But in this city where all the incompatible elements of the new Germany were poured into a common pot, any visitor with open eyes and ears could sense the fears, uncertainties, contradictions, resentments and frustrations that were East Berlin. Tim was subjected to a private demonstration in the crowded opera-house bar during the interval of Gluck's masterpiece. He had found an untenanted corner and wedged himself into it when a young man with a Beethovenian aureole of red hair breasted the human sea and emerged into the tiny space. He licked the palm that had been protectively fastened over his whisky glass.

'English?' He scarcely looked up.

'Yes.'

'Speak no German?'

'I'm afraid not.'

The young man's nod and downturned mouth suggested a disapproval of all foreigners.

'Is it that obvious?' Tim asked, with a smile.

'You're not a Wessi.'

'Wessi?'

'West Berliner. If you're not a Wessi, you must be a tourist. East Germans can't afford the opera now.' He scowled at Tim truculently, inviting argument.

'Aren't you an East German?' Tim stared pointedly at the spirit the young man was sipping carefully.

'Oh, I don't count.' The German sneered. 'I'm a music critic. All this costs me nothing. It's the ordinary citizens who have been culturally deprived by unification. A few years ago a factory worker or an office clerk could afford to bring his wife here once – even twice – a month. Culture was for the people.' He sneered cynically. 'Now that we've been liberated from Marxist-Leninist bondage, the prices have shot up. Now only Wessies and foreigners can afford the Staatsoper. People like you come along and see a packed audience and you think, "What a blessing capitalism is for these downtrodden East Germans." Well, things aren't always what they seem.'

Tim was beginning to find this man a boor and a bore. 'So you're nostalgic for the good old days of apparatchiks, the Stasi and corrupt leaders with luxury dachas?'

The German prodded a nicotine-stained finger into Tim's chest. 'You western capitalists don't understand anything. Sure, there was a hell of a lot wrong under the old regime. But we had an identity, a public morality, a set of ideals.'

Tim firmly pushed aside the hand that was beating a tattoo on his lapel. He was torn between mounting anger and the desire not to create a scene. 'If the East was so marvellous, what was the Berlin Wall all about?'

'You weren't here when the Wall came down. You didn't see the people surging through the gaps like dazzled lemmings. Throwing away every last pfennig they had in the Kurfürstendamm shops. It was a mad, mad spending spree. And when it was over, what did they have to show for it? Most of them are now worse off than they were before. Goods may be plentiful but prices are higher. Lots of men have lost their jobs because their employers can't compete in the western capitalist bear ring. Now they want to bring the parliament back here – at a cost of eight billion marks – and make Berlin an even more glittering show-place. Unification means a bigger market for the West and nothing for the East.'

A dozen arguments sprang to Tim's mind but before he could select one the red-haired man drained his glass, surveyed its emptiness morosely, turned and plunged back into the human sea.

Burning. He was burning. He felt the flame. Smelt his own flesh. Wanted to scream but something filled his mouth. Then merciful nothingness. But it did not last. Pain, searing fever and blurred, bewildering images alternated with terror-haunted sleep. Ulrich was fitfully aware of a jolting motion unrelated to his own flaccid limbs. Then there was stillness, cool hands and dimly-perceived, half-familiar faces. Sometimes liquid was forced down his burning, protesting throat. Gradually, the intense desire to be parted from his quivering, sweating body subsided.

Full consciousness returned abruptly. Ulrich opened his eyes and saw a bearded man in a long red-brown mantle with one arm incongruously round the neck of a diminutive ox. Immediately he knew where he was. Often he had visited sick brothers in the Marienburg infirmary and been faintly amused by the long fresco depicting various saints, including Luke, the writer-physician. If he turned his head from side to side he would see the other dozen or so beds and, to the right, the archway which led to the rooms where Brother Christof kept his potions and washed his bandages. Ulrich rolled his head on the pillow – and wished that he had not.

He closed his eyes. Waited for the throbbing to subside. Tried to dredge some facts from the black deeps of memory.

When a cool hand on his brow brought him out of sleep the light in the room had changed and he realised that several hours must have passed. Brother Christof's white hair almost shone in the full sunlight from the window high above Ulrich's bed. The old man's smile was equally radiant.

'So, Brother Ulrich, you have returned to us.' He fussed with the furs covering the bed. 'You have been a sore test of my faith. I have seen many miracles within these walls but when they brought you in I said to myself, "Not even Mary and all the saints can save this one." You had the pallor of death upon you. Scarce a drop of blood left in your body and a wound that had more colours than a bank of wild flowers and smelled like a midden. Brother Ulrich, you are a miracle among miracles, God be praised.'

'Amen.' The response was something between a croak and a whisper.

'Well,' Christof folded his arms inside the wide sleeves of his grey habit, 'no doubt you'll be hungry. I'll fetch you some strong broth.'

'Wait, Brother Christof!' Ulrich lifted a hand a few inches above the bed. 'First, tell me how I came to be here. I've been trying to remember . . .'

The old man shook his head. 'Memory is often the last to heal and it's well beyond my skills. It's my job to get your body working. I'll fetch your broth and we can talk while you drink it.'

Ulrich gulped the soup greedily. He insisted on trying to hold the spoon himself and only after spilling much down his shirt did he permit the infirmarian to take over. The feeding process effectively prevented him interrupting Christof's narrative.

'Let me see now, it was eight – no, nine – days ago they brought you in here. They fetched you up by waggon with three other wounded men from Allenstein. The story, as I heard it from one of the Grand Hospitaller's force that got back yesterday, was that you'd been caught in an ambush. He said you fought like a cornered bear against a ring of Poles until one of them brought you down with a cut to the thigh that went right to the bone. They'd have finished you off if the mercenary captain Zerwonka hadn't come to your aid. He and his men got you back to the camp. The wound was cauterised in the field hospital – a rough and ready remedy. It saved your leg but it nearly killed you. It would have killed a less strong man. As it was, it brought on a near-fatal fever.'

As the old man prattled on Ulrich tried to fit the story with the scraps of information and the disjointed images suggested by his own brain. Water. He had a vivid picture of water. Zerwonka. The name stirred deep feelings. But not of gratitude. Anger. Contempt. Whenever he opened his mouth to question the infirmarian in went another spoonful of delicious, much-needed broth. But at last the bowl was empty.

'Where is this Zerwonka? I must talk with him.'

The old man nodded and smiled. 'You certainly have much to thank him for, but it will be some days yet before you can. You have a long journey back to health and strength. Your leg will be many weeks a-mending.'

'Could you possibly take a message to him? Ask him to come and see me?'

'I rather think he'll be too busy for that. He's a very important man, now.'

'Important?'

'He came back a hero from the western front. The Grand Master has promoted him to the highest military office which can be held by someone who is not a member of the Order. He is the new commander of the Marienburg garrison.'

On Thursday morning, Tim flew to Bonn for his meeting with Hans Meyer. It turned out to be not the leisurely opportunity for discussion that he had hoped for. The politician met him in the vestibule of the Bundeshaus, shaking him perfunctorily by the hand and leading him outside to a waiting limousine.

As Tim seated himself beside the German, Meyer treated him to what was a statement rather than an apology.

'Sorry about the change of plan, Tim. I have to deputise for my minister at a wretched diplomatic reception. Do you mind if we talk on the journey?'

The large Mercedes with the tinted, bullet-proof glass left the compound dominated by the ugly, towering Langer Eugen, negotiated the intersection with Adenauerallee and Reuterstrasse and headed southwards through the Bonn suburbs.

In its spacious interior Tim Lacy appraised the slim, immaculate German with the swept-back grey hair and practised smile for whom self-advertisement had become second nature.

'If only you'd given me more warning . . . Normally, I

can rearrange my schedule within limits, but they've made me chairman of this wretched committee which is arranging the move of the parliament to Berlin. With that and my other parliamentary responsibilities I have scarcely a moment to myself. We must fix up for you and your wife to visit us in Hamburg sometime in the summer. I've added one or two interesting pieces to the collection since you saw it last.' Hans Meyer spoke precise, well-practised, diplomatic English.

Tim had done some homework on his distinguished host. Meyer was the only son of an East German father and a Polish mother. The family had fled their Rostock home in 1963, escaping by sea, and eventually settling in Hamburg. Hans had been fifteen at the time, a difficult age to put down new roots. But he had flourished in the freer climate. Had become almost the epitome of the German economic miracle. A career in financial journalism, some clever stock exchange dealing and, by the age of thirty, he had been able to establish his own newspaper. That had been the first brick in the construction of an impressive media edifice which embraced radio and television companies as well as magazines and a leading Sunday paper. Within a few years, he was acknowledged to be one of the richest men in Germany. 1985 had been a star year for Hans Meyer. That was the year he married Elsa Christina who, as well as being an extremely beautiful international model, was also a member of an ancient and prestigious Prussian family. It was also the year that he was elected as a Christian Democrat to the *Bundestag*. He quickly made a name for himself as one of the more outspoken and ambitious younger politicians. All observers agreed that it was only a matter of time and electoral good fortune before he achieved high government office.

Tim was conscious that he had little time to probe Meyer. Bad Godesberg, Bonn's legation suburb, was a mere seven kilometres away. Yet, abrupt introduction of the real reason for this visit might well be counterproductive. He tried an oblique approach. 'I'm glad the collection goes from strength to strength. As a matter of fact your name cropped up in conversation with another connoisseur in Vienna a few weeks ago – Ernst Müller.'

'Ah, you must have been discussing the Aachen altarpiece. Beautiful, and remarkably well preserved. I was so glad we were able to restore it to its rightful home.'

'We?'

'Yes, surely Müller told you. He joined a consortium I set up to acquire the altarpiece for the cathedral treasury.'

Tim smiled, seeing the truth behind the conflicting stories told by the two collectors. Clearly, they had both wanted the ancient ivory. Neither had been prepared to yield and having bid each other into the stratosphere they had agreed a truce. Since neither could possess the altarpiece, they had bought kudos instead by jointly presenting it to the Aachen museum. He said, 'Müller seems to be making some radical changes to his collection. Branching out into new fields.'

'Really? I don't know the man well, you understand. I gather he's something of a recluse.'

'Yes. I was rather surprised to see him in New York before Christmas, at the Brand Gallery opening. Am I not right in thinking that you were there, too?'

'You're very observant.'

'As you know, one of my men was killed in that robbery. I'm trying to make some sense of the wretched business. Gathering information from people who were there that might throw some light on it.'

'You're a very tenacious and thorough man, Tim. Those are qualities we Germans understand. I only wish I could in some way reward your dedication to the task. I was at the gallery opening rather by chance. I was in New York for a conference at the UN and managed to snatch a couple of extra days for sniffing round the galleries. I was at Brand's quite by accident – a gatecrasher, really. I bumped into someone who told me that a prestigious new place was opening up. Naturally, I wanted to see it for myself.'

'Can you remember who told you about the opening?'

'Yes, it was Walter Frankl, the Genevan dealer.'

'One thing that puzzles me is why the thief singled out the Dresden Text when there were several more important and valuable items on display. Can you think of anyone – or perhaps a group of people – here in Germany for whom such a manuscript would have significance?' Tim watched the politician carefully as he posed the question.

'Why do you say "here in Germany"? The robbery occurred in America.' The question was posed casually – perhaps too casually?

'All the signs point in this direction. The manuscript was created here. The woman who took it was German, and a one-time member of a left-wing terrorist group operating here. There's a theory that the Dresden Text once belonged to the Teutonic Order. You know most of the leading collectors and dealers in medieval artefacts. Is there anyone for whom such a relic might be very important?'

Meyer seemed to give the question careful thought for several seconds. At last he shrugged. 'The art world is becoming a very violent place, as you know well, Tim. The lamentable affair in New York is far from unique. Nowadays, there seem to be armed thugs and ruthless entrepreneurs everywhere. I've every sympathy for your motives and I admire your determination to leave no stone unturned to avenge your friend's death. But I wonder if you're not making this crime more complex than it really is. It looks to me like a bungled burglary by a none-too-smart gang. They went to a lot of trouble but ended up with the wrong manuscript. It happens. I certainly have no knowledge of such gangs. The people I deal with are still reputable and law-abiding – well, reasonably law-abiding.' He laughed lightly.

'Do you know Oscar König?' Tim asked the question suddenly, hoping for unguarded reaction. He was disappointed.

'Vaguely. He is definitely not the sort of dealer I do business with. Why do you ask?'

'I was talking with him the other day in Berlin. He obviously knows something about this business. He looked very worried. I intend to arrange another interview. This time I'll be less gentle with him.'

'I hope you're not planning anything illegal. That would be taking loyalty to the memory of an old friend too far.'

'König is my only lead. And König is a crook. If I lean on him he's in no position to complain to the police.'

'Why don't you go to them yourself?'

'How much attention would they pay to an Englishman bringing unsubstantiated accusations against a German citizen about a crime committed in the USA?'

Meyer frowned. 'Well, I hope you'll be very, very careful. If you were to fall foul of the authorities I wouldn't be able to help you. In fact, I hope you wouldn't even mention my name.' The politician brushed at the worsted covering his right knee as though some impropriety had settled there and had to be removed.

'Don't worry, Hans.' Tim managed a smile at the ambitious Meyer's abhorrence of scandal. 'I won't embarrass you.'

The vehicle had now joined a convoy of look-alike limousines drawing up to an impressive porte-cochère over which a large flag hung limply in the still air.

Meyer ran a hand over his hair. 'I'm afraid this is where I must leave you, Tim. Albert, my chauffeur, will take you back into Bonn. Is there somewhere particular you'd like to be dropped?'

'The airport, please. I must get back to Berlin.'

The car came to a halt. Meyer unfolded himself elegantly and stepped through the opened door onto the red carpet laid over the broad steps leading to an impressive entrance hall. He leaned in to shake hands, renewed his vague invitation to his country estate, and was gone.

At Wahn, the airport shared by Bonn and Cologne, Tim had an hour's wait for the next Berlin shuttle. He phoned in to the office. Sally passed on a couple of important messages and then reported on her conversation with Corinne Noble.

'She was curious about your interest in Müller because she's become intrigued with him, herself.'

'Why's that?'

'According to Corinne, he's bidding for everything he can lay hands on by German national schools of the last two centuries – works by the Nazarenes, the Bauhaus and the like. She commented – for your ears only and repeat it at your peril – that he is buying with more enthusiasm than taste. Is that the sort of thing you wanted to know?'

'It certainly provides food for thought. Thanks, Sally. Unless anything crops up I should be flying back from

Frankfurt next Tuesday, straight after my meeting with Meredith.'

'OK. Where can I reach you in the meantime?'

'Difficult to say. I'll be on the move quite a bit. I'll give you a buzz on Friday. Is Catherine there?'

'No, up in town for the day. Shall I leave a message?'

'Just say I'll call this evening. One more thing, I need to have a word with George. Is he around?'

'No, he's still on the Edinburgh job.'

'Oh, yes, of course. When's he due back?'

'He's flying down tomorrow morning.'

'Right, well call him and tell him to go to the BA desk at Heathrow Terminal One and pick up a ticket I will have arranged for him. I need him over here for a few days.'

During the short flight to Berlin, Tim pondered the events of the morning. So Ernst Müller had decided to change the whole basis of his collection. He was selling some of his finest pieces in order to stock up with examples of Germanic art. Tim associated the Nazarenes with massive murals and huge canvases depicting heroic scenes from the Bible and German mythology. The Bauhaus was the inter-war school which emerged at Weimar, was banned as decadent by Hitler, and produced such masters as Klee, Kandinsky and the sculptor Gerhard Marks. At seventy-plus the cantankerous old man was breaking a lifetime habit of random collecting to specialize in purely Teutonic artists. Not only that, he was also making a hamfisted attempt to be secretive about it. Tim had seen no evidence of Müller's new craze when he was at Schloss Turnitz. Just what *was* the Austrian millionaire up to? Was he creating a secret hoard with a highly pan-German theme? Was he, with an old man's desperate haste, acquiring works with little or no regard to law or morals? Was the Dresden Text secreted away in a vault somewhere in Schloss Turnitz's palatial interior? Just when Tim had thought that he could safely eliminate Müller from any suggestion of complicity in the New York affair, it seemed he had reinstated himself in the list of suspects.

And what about Hans Meyer? Tim had not really expected to penetrate the politician's thick skin, and he had not done so. He had been treated to a highly professional performance: the right mix of courtesy and preoccupation; the skilful evasion of probing questions; the affectation of genuine concern; the media interviewee's knack of saying nothing and making it sound impressive. Meyer was a man unlikely to do anything to damage his own prospects – and a man prepared to do anything to enhance them. By the time his plane touched down at Tegel, Tim had a sackful of new questions. And no answers.

He was collecting his key at the Hotel Inter-Continental's reception desk when a voice behind him said, 'Hey, Tim Lacy. This is a pleasant coincidence – I hope.'

Standing there, looking dishevelled and weary, was Al Freeman.

Ulrich's memory returned by stages over the next few days with the help of friends and comrades who came to visit him in the infirmary. As the fog in his brain thinned and dispersed, the young knight's alarm grew. One fact above all became clear: Zerwonka must be stopped.

Ulrich's days were spent in rigid discipline of mind and body. Indifferent to Brother Christof's protestations and, at times, almost rude to the solicitous infirmarian, he imposed his own regime. On the third day after his return to full consciousness he got out of bed. As soon as he stood, his wounded leg gave way. The thigh muscles had no strength at all. Christof bustled up angrily, demanding to know whether Brother Ulrich was bent on undoing all his patient work.

When could he walk, Ulrich demanded. Christof did not know. Perhaps never. It was all in the hands of God. Ulrich retorted that he was not prepared to lie about awaiting the divine pleasure. He demanded a pair of crutches. Christof told him he was not yet strong enough. Then Ulrich lost his temper. He had to get well and mobile – quickly. There was important work to do. He must get to the Grand Master, or someone close to the Grand Master. It was a matter of urgency. Eventually, to keep his troublesome patient quiet, the infirmarian fetched crutches and stood beside Ulrich as he staggered and fell, and rose, sweating, balanced himself, then staggered and fell again, and again, and again. Every day Ulrich kept up the self-imposed torture. The pain in his leg echoed through every nerve in his body but he would not give up until he was too exhausted to leave his bed.

Then he would lie there, thinking. Always the object of his thoughts was the perfidious Stephan Zerwonka. The mental effort of trying to fathom the Bohemian's motives and tactics was even harder than the physical effort of forcing his damaged leg back into action. Ulrich had always been a man of action and not a man of reflection. His mental muscles were flabby. But at last he had answers to the questions he posed himself about Zerwonka – or at least answers that satisfied him.

Question: Why did Zerwonka betray the Memel garrison to the Lithuanians?

167

Answer:	Money.
Question:	Why did he not just disappear with his thirty pieces of silver?
Answer:	He saw the chance to make more money by further acts of treachery.
Question:	Why did he lay the blame on me?
Answer:	Sheer malice. I represented the traditional values of the Order – values Zerwonka loathed.
Question:	Why did Zerwonka not kill me when he had the opportunity?
Answer:	Because he is cunning as well as evil. He saw the opportunity to pose as a hero. By 'rescuing' the man who was his sworn enemy he could ingratiate himself with von Plauen.
Question:	What was he up to now?

The answer to that question really terrified Ulrich. He tried to find alternatives. There were none. Knowing what he now knew of the mercenary's record and character he could not doubt that Zerwonka had in mind the ultimate treachery. As captain of the Marienburg garrison he only had to wait for the right opportunity to sell the Order's capital to King Casimir.

He must be stopped, and Ulrich was the only one who could stop him. But could he? He was both crippled and disgraced. The only reason that the threat of a trial had been lifted was, as Ulrich learned, that Zerwonka had personally pleaded for him with the Grand Master. Any move he now made against the garrison commander would look like the worst possible kind of ingratitude.

Ulrich lay in his sweat-soaked shirt and recalled his first

sight of Zerwonka – at the card table. Well, the little Bohemian had dealt himself all the winning cards and ensured that Ulrich held only two taroks – the Fool and Death.

'Why, Lieutenant.' Tim held out his hand to the jet-lagged American. 'What brings you to the old world?'

The policeman yawned and pushed his hat to the back of his head. 'You really don't know?'

'No.'

'Well, that's a relief. I'm going to take a shower. Is there a quiet bar where we can meet in about an hour?'

'The rooftop bar won't be crowded yet.'

'See you there.' Freeman stepped up to the counter to check in.

An hour later they were sitting at a wide window watching the huge zoological gardens slide into shadow and the lights and illuminated fountains of Breitscheidplatz emerge in all their glaring brilliance.

'The last time we did this I guess I made a horse's ass of myself.' Freeman tilted his glass and sipped it cautiously.

Tim grinned. 'Forget it. I put it down to professional stress. So, tell me why you're here. You sounded very mysterious downstairs.'

The policeman smoothed his drooping moustache. 'Well, you don't get a prize for guessing that it's the Brand Gallery case.'

'I thought that file was officially dead.'

'Yeah, me too. Well, it suddenly got resurrected.'

'How?'

'Would you believe an anonymous tip-off? We got an overseas call to say that if we wanted to know more about Emma Freundlich and her circle we ought to talk to a guy by the name of Oscar König in Berlin.'

Tim nearly choked on his excellent Armagnac. 'When was this?' He tried to make the question sound casual.

'Coupla days ago – Tuesday. I ignored it. I've been told the case is closed. I'm not going to get my knuckles rapped by asking permission to discuss the case with the *Polizei*. Then, within the hour, I get a buzz from upstairs. It seems someone's put the finger on König to our Berlin colleagues. They've picked him up and are holding him for questioning. So I get to drop everything and jet myself over to the land of frankfurters and sauerkraut. So, here I am. How about you? I guess it's too much to hope that your being here has nothing to do with this König guy.'

Tim was only half listening. It was happening again – manipulation. He made his own moves, sought information, interviewed possible suspects – and got nowhere. Then, some unseen puppet master jerked a string and set him moving in a pre-ordained direction. Damn!

He was aware of Freeman looking at him strangely.

'Hey, I'm supposed to be the one with the jet-lag. So, tell me what you know about König.'

'Sorry, miles away. I had dinner – or rather, half a dinner – with him on Monday. He's a crook and he's up to his armpits in this business.'

Freeman nodded. 'So the local cops aren't sorry to have an excuse to bring him in? OK, better tell me about this "half-dinner".'

Tim gave a concise account of his meeting with König. 'I reckon your best bet is to press him on his connection with the Freundlich woman.'

Al nodded thoughtfully. 'Guess you're right. Thanks.'

'When are you going to interrogate him?'

'In the morning.'

'Any chance of my tagging along?'

Freeman shrugged. 'Not my ballgame. We're in Berlin police jurisdiction and I'll bet these guys play strictly by the book. Be my guest, by all means, but I can't guarantee they'll let you see König.'

The two men decided to walk to the *Polizei-Präsidium* on Wilhelmstrasse the following morning. Freeman said he needed exercise and fresh air but proceeded to negate the beneficial effects of both by smoking a large cigar all the way. When they arrived, Tim used his limited German to announce their business at the reception desk. The woman officer looked at them sharply, pressed a button on her console and spoke rapidly into her microphone. She frowned anxiously at the response, and motioned them to chairs in a corner of the foyer. They had scarcely sat down when an inner door banged open to admit a middle-aged officer who was dark-haired, solidly-built, bespectacled – and very angry.

'Lieutenant Freeman!' More an accusation than an enquiry.

The American stood and offered his hand. 'Al Freeman.'

'*Polizeiinspektor* Johann Steiger.' The man gave a perfunctory hand-shake and looked quizzically at Tim.

Freeman made introductions.

Steiger nodded, barked 'Come!' and turned back through the doorway.

When the three were alone in his office, Steiger glowered at his visitors. 'I left a message at your hotel half an hour ago, asking you to delay your visit.'

Al shrugged. 'We must have left already. We walked. Something wrong?'

'Oh yes, something is most certainly wrong, Lieutenant.'

'Trouble with König?'

'You could say that. Sometime between 7.55 and 8.30 this morning, Herr König committed suicide.'

Chapter 10

As soon as he was sufficiently mobile, Ulrich limped his
way to the great church at Marienburg. He was not strong
enough to attend the regular services, but at least he could
come here to pray and perhaps hear a mass. But on this
sunlit spring morning the church was empty. No priests
were offering sacrifice on any of the subsidiary altars. No
brothers were to be seen in the side chapels where they
customarily went to seek the aid of their favourite saints.

Ulrich had not come to gaze upon the painted, impassive visage of a statue or to light a candle to the Virgin. He
hobbled his way the length of the church until he stood
before the high altar. There he stopped, leaning his weight
on the ash sapling cut and shaped for him by his friend,
Conrad, and regained his breath. He looked up at the
elaborate painted crucifix and fixed his eyes on the
drooped head of the one who understood – who knew
about pain and betrayal and rejection and humiliation and
failure.

Now that he was in this sacred place – the very heart
of his beloved Order – he found he had no words. He
could only open his being, only share his suffering with
the suffering Saviour. Perhaps, like Christ, he would
experience a resurrection from failure to triumph, from

dishonour to glory. Perhaps, he would be given a chance to redress the great evil that had been perpetrated on him and the brotherhood. Perhaps, through divine intervention, the Grand Master's heart would be softened. Perhaps, with God's grace, he would be able to open von Erlichshausen's eyes to the truth.

Ulrich looked around him. Was it really less than two years since he had knelt on this very spot to make his vows? So much had happened it scarcely seemed possible that it could all have been contained within a few months. Well, one thing was certain: the time had come for a fresh vow, a new commitment.

He ascended the three steps until he stood where only priests and the senior officers of the Order were allowed to stand. He looked down on the plain cloth which covered the altar. At the great Bible with its jewelled clasp that glowed red, blue and green in the sunlight. He opened it. Turned the pages of mysterious, powerful Latin script. Gazed on the writhing, multi-coloured animals and flowers that wound round the capitals, and the pictures of angels and men that adorned every page. He turned leaf after leaf and beheld a fresh wonder on each.

Reluctantly, he closed the heavy cover and refastened the clasp. Then, with his right hand resting on the shiny leather, he swore an oath.

'I, Ulrich von Walenrod, solemnly dedicate myself to cleansing the Order of St Mary of Jerusalem from all and every evil that besets it and I call upon holy Mary, St George, St Elizabeth and all the angels of heaven to help me.'

After a moment of shocked silence, Freeman said, 'König committed suicide? *Here?*'

'Yes, here – in his cell.' Steiger stared back, defying the American to comment.

'But, in the name of . . . How?'

Steiger struggled to control his anger. 'How is not the question. What I want to know is why. To help our American friends, we pick up a German citizen, suspected of complicity in a robbery. The next thing we know, he's dead in custody. Now, that's something I have to answer for. My superiors will want to know what the hell's going on. So, would you mind telling me what this König has really done and why he decided to take his own life, rather than face the music?'

Freeman did not respond well to being shouted at. 'I faxed you the details. All we know for sure about König is that he was in New York at the time of the crime. On top of that, we have an anonymous report that he was in league with Emma Freundlich and that he set her up to be killed in a shoot-out. That's all we've got. König could have denied everything and that would really have put me on the spot. I wouldn't have had enough evidence to make an application for extradition. If there's a reason for his death, it's on your side of the pond, not mine.'

Steiger, who had been pacing the room, subsided into his swivel chair. His anger seemed to shrink also. 'Well, if that's what you say, I have to believe you. What makes it doubly bad for me is that König's death is a lost opportunity. We know he was involved with organised crime in Russia. The activities of Moscow-based gangs are becoming a hell of a problem in Germany. Since the collapse of the old regime there's political and economic chaos in the East. The police are underfunded and demoralised. Most government officials are corrupt. The emerging capitalist class is riddled with fraudsters and drug-traffickers. Moscow has become another Palermo or thirties Chicago – drugs, assassinations, gang wars, racketeering, white-collar crime. And it's coming westwards. Fast. The Russians and the Poles can't control their own borders. The disease is spreading, and bloated crooks like König are the carriers. Always he was very careful but we know he was a link between crime bosses in Europe and America. At last, you gave us an excuse to bring him in. I was looking forward to a long session with Herr König after you'd finished with him.'

Freeman nodded his sympathy. 'Surely, there's your reason for his suicide. König knew damn well what would happen to him if he was even suspected of blabbing to the cops. So he took the easy way out.'

Tim only half listened to this exchange. He was busy with his own thoughts. König sweating with fear across the dinner table. König who, beyond a shadow of doubt, knew Emma Freundlich. The trail leading to König. König, like Freundlich, conveniently dead. Manipulation. Powerful, influential forces at work. Russian mafia?

He said, 'Did König hang himself? I gather that's the commonest form of suicide in custody.'

Tim expected the badly-shaken Steiger to erupt in self-righteous wrath at the merest suggestion that the vigilance of his officers was being questioned. In fact, the German relaxed slightly. 'Oh, no. We take all the normal precautions – remove the detainee's belt, shoe laces, personal belongings and so forth. But this one came prepared. He had sachets of cyanide sewn into one of his trouser turnups.'

'Cyanide?'

'Well, the pathologist is still examining the body, but

you can take it from me that it was cyanide. The symptoms are unmistakable.'

'And you're equally sure about the time of death?' Tim ignored Freeman's disapproving frown as he continued his questioning.

'At approximately 7.55 one of the duty officers took breakfast to the cells. We had three detainees over night – two drunks and König. At 8.30 the breakfast trays were collected up.'

'By the same officer?'

'Yes. He discovered the body. He was, as you can imagine, badly shaken. But he acted very correctly. After checking that König was dead, he locked the cell, disturbing nothing, and reported to me. I examined the body and satisfied myself about the cause of death. I called in the pathologist and I tried to get you at your hotel.'

Al Freeman sat back in his chair. 'Well, Inspector, I'm sorry things have turned out like this – for both our sakes. It's certainly been a waste of my time coming all the way over here. I guess there's nothing more to say. With your permission, I ought to have a look at the body – just for the record.'

'Of course. Follow me, please.'

Steiger led the way from his office. In the corridor they met the pathologist. In a quick exchange with Steiger, he confirmed that death was by hydrocyanic poisoning. The duty officer unlocked the door of Cell 4.

The convulsed body of Oscar König occupied most of the meagre floor space between a bench-bed and a table. The fat man lay on his side, legs drawn up to his chest, arms flung wide. The flabby features had a livid, purplish tinge. The wide eyes stared. The lips were drawn back from clenched teeth. A faint odour of almonds pervaded the tiny room. As Steiger said, there could be no doubt about the cause of death. During his army years Tim had seen more than his fair share of cadavers, many mutilated by the violence of man to man. Yet there was something particularly repellent about this corpse and its almost clinical surroundings.

He forced himself to examine the body and the cell with dispassionate concentration. On the table a tray of food lay untouched – bread, cheese, salami. Beside it there was a small, square, white sachet with one corner torn off. A plastic beaker lay near König's head, its brown-black contents spattered over the stone floor.

Steiger knelt beside the body. He pointed to the left trouser leg, which had been rolled half way up the calf. The hem was torn. From the slit he removed a small, white packet and laid it beside the empty one on the table. They were identical. 'It doesn't need a detective to work it out, does it? He emptied one of these into his coffee and . . .' Steiger snapped his fingers.

Tim frowned. 'I thought that sort of thing went out with the Nazi high command.'

Steiger shuddered and turned his back on the body. 'Some of the terrorist groups in the seventies and eighties carried poison so that they couldn't be forced to incriminate their comrades under interrogation. When we've analysed these sachets, I'll have the records checked. See if there's any connection.'

'But why would an antique dealer – albeit a crooked antique dealer – carry poison around with him? Did he have any warning of his impending arrest?'

'None whatsoever. I picked him up myself at his shop on Wednesday afternoon. You've never seen anyone more surprised and indignant. Shall we?' Steiger ushered them from the cell.

Back in Steiger's office, Freeman said, 'I'd be grateful if we could have a word with the officer who discovered the body. Sorry to be a nuisance, but my boss will want a full report. They don't like paying out for trips to Europe and having nothing to show for it.'

The German sighed. 'Oh, very well.' He picked up the phone and gave some order. 'Please don't upset him any more than he already is. He's a young lad, still learning the ropes. He was seconded to us only a few days ago from Hamburg.'

Karl Pressner turned out to be a dark-haired young man of athletic build who looked very impressive in his green *Ordnungspolizei* uniform. If he was badly shaken by his recent experience, Tim thought, he concealed it well. They learned little from him. With Steiger acting as interpreter, he told them that he had collected the breakfast trays from the canteen and used a trolley to convey them to the cell area. All three detainees had identical food. The coffee came from the same pot. The trays never left his sight until he delivered them. König had been very agitated and became even more so when Pressner informed him that an American detective would be here soon to interview him. No one had reported any disturbance from König's cell, so that the discovery of the body had been a total shock.

There was nothing else to be done. Freeman agreed to be available for a couple of days in case Steiger's *Kriminalpolizei* bosses wanted to talk to him. Then everyone shook hands and the visitors left. Outside the building they turned right towards Unter den Linden and walked for a while without conversation.

Freeman eventually broke the silence. 'Time for a beer?'

Tim looked at his watch. 'Afraid not. I have to get out to the airport to meet a colleague.'

'What do you reckon to all that?' The American did a backward nod with his head.

'I think it stinks.'

'You don't figure König as the suicide type?'

Tim shook his head emphatically. 'Oscar König was the original born survivor, the first rat off the sinking ship, a squirmer, a dealer, who'd wriggle his way out of any hole. He'd go to the gallows protesting his innocence – and expecting an eleventh-hour reprieve. Even if I could see him topping himself in a sudden blind panic – and, frankly, the imagination boggles at that – the idea of him carrying cyanide around for use in emergencies – huh!'

'If you're right, you realise what that means?'

'Oh, yes.'

They walked in silence for another block. Tim was experimenting with various connections. Hamburg? Pressner had been sent urgently from Hamburg. One of the most powerful and influential men in Hamburg was Hans Meyer. Could it be that the prim, ambitious politician was also involved in this shady world of crooked art deals?

Once again it was Freeman who spoke first. 'There's damn all that I can do about it.'

'I know.'

'I mean, I can't tell *Polizeiinspektor* Steiger that he doesn't know his job.'

'Of course not.'

'I can't tell him to clean out his own closet before he starts taking on the mafia.'

'Right.'

'For one thing I'm a guest, an ambassador, supposedly here to demonstrate the friendly co-operation existing between our two forces.'

'Certainly.'

'And, for another, I don't have a shred of evidence.'

'No.'

He stopped and stared at the Englishman. 'There's not a damn thing I can do. My hands are tied.'

Tim replied quietly, unemotionally. 'I know, Al. But mine aren't.'

There were twenty-three of them, mostly younger men, though a few grey heads gave the group an appearance of greater stability. They had left Marienburg in twos and threes so as not to attract attention. They had arrived by different routes at the battered, abandoned village of Östering, five miles upriver. Now they sat in a circle on blocks of stone, upturned, broken-lidded coffers and piles of rubble in the ruined church. Solemn-faced, dedicated knight brothers, who knew they were putting their lives and honour at risk by attending this meeting but who felt compelled by a higher loyalty to be present.

Ulrich had not intended to form a faction. Yet the emergence of one had been inevitable, given the circumstances. As soon as he could hobble on one crutch he had sought – and been denied – an interview with the Grand Master. Instead, he had confided in a senior member of the Order whom he believed he could trust. As a result he had been summoned before the sub-prior, who reminded him that he was an inexperienced young man who was still under a cloud. He advised Ulrich to concentrate on his prayers – thanking God for his recovery and the magnanimity of the Grand Master who had overlooked his treason – and he ordered him to keep his subversive ideas to himself.

That had been in April. Now it was midsummer. By this time, Ulrich knew that his leg had recovered as much as it was ever going to. He walked with a bad limp and some movements, such as mounting a horse, were agony. Sometimes his head throbbed for days on end. But the worst pain of all was inflicted by his rejection. Counted unfit for military service, he missed the comradeship of the camp and the sense of purpose of being on campaign. Ulrich devoted himself with more diligence than most to the religious duties of a knight brother. He was always in his stall for the canonical hours. Faithfully he kept all the appointed fasts and stringently observed the four meatless days every week – even though, as a convalescent, he was excused the dietary rigours of the Order. He was appointed to assist in the town hospital run by the brothers. He subjected himself to the hours of penetrating self-examination enjoined by his confessor. Day after day he agonised in prayer. Why was he being punished? His conscience was clear; he had bent all his efforts to serving God and Church faithfully as a knight brother. So why this injustice? Why this suffering? Why was he repudiated by superiors and friends alike? The isolation was almost unbearable – the empty places next to his own in the frater; the eyes averted at his approach; the laughing groups of former comrades which dispersed when he tried to join them.

Thus it was inevitable that when, one by one, a few members of the Marienburg convent sought out the ostracised brother to express their support and sympathy Ulrich should have felt a particularly strong bond with these friends in adversity. It was also inevitable that this score or so of individuals should have cohered into a group. From the beginning there was something clandestine about their activities. It was not just that they rallied to the support of a wronged brother; they also, to a large extent, shared his convictions and concerns. Some of them had fallen foul of Zerwonka and his cronies. Others had overheard conversations or witnessed events which aroused their suspicions about the little Bohemian. Three, like Ulrich, had been disciplined for making their views known.

So the meetings had begun. At first, it was just a matter of four or six men gathering in a corner of the cloister or in a town tavern and grumbling about the conduct of the Order's affairs. But, bit by bit, numbers grew and expressions of discontent gave way to discussions of how things might be changed. The 'true knights', as the cabal members began to call themselves, became more organised and more secretive. They planned their meetings carefully, and they located them in places where they were unlikely to be discovered.

The meeting at Östering began, as had become the custom, with a general absolution by Father Sebastian, one of the Order's priest brothers. He proclaimed in advance forgiveness for all words spoken with the interests of the Order at heart. Then Ulrich pulled himself to his feet with the aid of his ash stake. He gazed around the circle of men whose white cloaks gleamed in the sunlight shafting through glassless windows. Were they, in fact, the last honest, uncompromised knight brothers in Marienburg?

'Has anyone anything new to report?'

'It's said that Casimir's lost another four hundred men at Thorn.'

'I heard that he's preparing to lift the siege.'

'Someone told me that Casimir offered ten thousand

florins to the governor of Thorn.'

'I heard that, too. Fortunately, Governor von Kleist is unshakably loyal.'

'There are still messengers going back and forth between Zerwonka and the Polish camp.'

The information came in scraps and fragments from different members of the group. When everyone had been given a chance to contribute, Ulrich summed up.

'Casimir must know by now that he's never going to win by military force. He's been at Thorn for three months, but he can't break it because it's too well provisioned. It's the same everywhere he's been. He always runs out of food and supplies long before we do. If I were in his position, I would realise that there was only one weak point in the Order's defence. The mercenaries. Where steel fails gold may succeed. Once a few of our citadels begin to succumb to bribery, others will follow.'

'And if Marienburg falls?' It was thoughtful, dark-haired Brother Conrad who asked the question.

'Then that will be the death of the Order – at least, in Prussia. Casimir knows that. So does Zerwonka.'

'The only people who don't seem to know it are our leaders,' someone growled.

Another asked, 'Why hasn't the Bohemian bastard sold out already?'

'Knowing Zerwonka, I should think the answer's pretty obvious.'

'Haggling,' Conrad suggested.

'Precisely. My guess is that all these messengers rushing back and forth between Marienburg and Thorn are carrying Casimir's offers and Zerwonka's demands. I think the little man also wants to make sure of his position. He's won over the Grand Master. He's had most of the knight brothers taken off duty in the castle. But the Treasurer and the Vice-Master are far from convinced about him. If he declared his hand too soon, he could lose everything.'

'Well, as long as he hesitates we have a chance to act.' Father Sebastian, a tall, spare pine tree of a man, offered the observation.

Wilhelm von Hagen, one of the younger knights and the most headstrong, could not restrain his impatience. 'Then let's stop talking and do something.'

Ulrich allowed himself a faint smile. 'What do you suggest, Brother Wilhelm? The floor is yours. Let's hear your plan.'

The young man blushed. 'Well . . . er . . .' He glowered round the laughing circle. 'Well, I didn't say I had a plan. Just that we ought to have one and put it into operation quickly.'

Father Sebastian came to his rescue. 'Quite right, Brother. Couldn't we intercept one of Zerwonka's messengers and take him to the Vice-Master?'

There was a murmur of agreement but someone said, 'Suppose he won't talk.' Another voice commented, 'The little Bohemian only uses his most trusted henchman – a vicious, one-eyed thug who's been with him for years.'

Ulrich nodded. 'We'd certainly have a big problem if anything went wrong. We'd have revealed ourselves for nothing. At the moment Zerwonka knows nothing of our existence. So we have the advantage of surprise. We mustn't throw that away.'

There was a long silence broken only by the twittering of swallows swooping to nests in the broken vault above and dislodging dust specks which hovered in the sunbeams.

It was Conrad eventually who said quietly what many thought. 'As I see it, there's only one thing to be done.'

The true knights spent the rest of the meeting discussing the bringing of Stephan Zerwonka to justice and death.

Tim swore loudly and colourfully as a yellow bus pulled out without warning from the stop in front of the Spandauer Damm museum complex.

George Martin, in the passenger seat of the hired VW, raised a bushy eyebrow. 'Things are bad, are they, Major?'

Because Tim was still simmering with suppressed anger and, therefore, finding it difficult to organise his thoughts, he had given George only the tersest account of recent events then subsided into silence for most of the journey from the airport. Now he unburdened himself.

'I hate being manipulated.'

'How do you mean – manipulated?'

'This whole business has been like chasing someone through a maze. Someone who knows the way and has been playing with us. He lets us blunder around for a bit, then suddenly appears in a gap. Beckoning. We go rushing through after him. Nothing. Again we hare off along circling paths and blind alleys. Just as we've got thoroughly lost, there he is again. Smirking at us. Daring us to go on with the pursuit.'

'I don't know about mazes, Major, but you've certainly lost me.' George pinched the immaculate crease in his grey flannels.

Tim slowed for the heavy, late-morning traffic on Otto Suhr Allee. 'Well, look – there's a robbery with violence in New York. The police haven't a clue. Then someone phones up and says, "The person you want is in such-and-such hotel." Freeman and Co set off hot foot, hoping to catch the assassin and get to the bottom of things. What happens? Bang! Bang! Dead terrorist, dead end. We take

over from the cops. Start exploring a few avenues ourselves. Nothing. Then Catherine "accidentally" picks up a
letter in Vienna with Oscar König's name on it and König
is one of the names on our list of suspects. Coincidence?
No way. It's the beckoning finger again. I manage to
persuade Catherine that her clue is really a red herring and
come here without her knowing. I put the fear of God into
König. I let him sweat for a few days before I go back to
put real pressure on. But someone's ahead of me. There's
another police tip-off. The Berlin CID contact Freeman.
He comes out to interrogate König. Then – surprise,
surprise – our fat friend "commits suicide" in his cell. Now,
do you see what I mean about being manipulated?'

'If you reckon you're being given the run around – only
being allowed to see what someone wants you to see – you
might as well jack it in.'

'That, I presume, is precisely the conclusion someone
wants me to reach. What he doesn't realise is that every
dead end only makes me more determined to go on.'

George looked thoughtful. 'If what you say is right, we
must be up against more than just one man. Whoever is
behind this has got to have quite an organisation. That
means he's dangerous.'

'Which is precisely why I persuaded Catherine that
König was a red herring, and why I came here without her
knowing.'

'And why you want me here?'

'Right.'

'Well, I just hope we find whoever's behind it all in
Berlin. I'm ready for him. Oh, and I've got some news for
you on that score.'

'Oh yes. What's that?' Tim only half listened, most of
his attention being concentrated on negotiating the

swirling traffic of Ernst Reuter Platz.

'You're not going to like it.'

'Try me.'

'Well, I got Madge Thomson to lend me all Mike's journals and diaries. I felt a bit bad about it. He was always very secretive about his journals. But Madge didn't seem to mind and I thought I just might be able to find out something about this "M" character.'

'Aha.' Tim hit the horn as a taxi cut in front of him while he was trying to turn past the university.

'I was looking at them on the plane this morning. It's the first chance I've had. It didn't take me long to work out Mike's system. As you know, he made cryptic notes in a pocket diary and used them as the basis for his journal. Most of his diary jottings were in a kind of personal code.'

'So?'

Tim turned onto a quieter road running beside the Landwehrkanal.

'Well, I thought that if I went back through the diaries and journals I might just get a clue to the identity of "M". And I was right. I know who "M" is.'

'Come on then. Stop screwing up the suspense like an Australian soap opera.'

'OK. "M" is you, Major.'

'What!'

'No doubt about it. All the boys call you the "Major". Mike did, too. In his diary he abbreviated that to "M". I've checked a dozen or so diary entries with the corresponding journal references. "M" always stands for "Major".'

'And no one else?'

'Not that I could see.'

'But that's crazy. I didn't phone Mike that evening.' Tim

188

slowed for the hotel entrance. He parked the VW close to the Inter-Continental's opulently-functional portal.

'No, it's not at all crazy. Not when you think about it. What was the one thing we couldn't understand about Mike's behaviour?'

'Why he opened up so casually to an unknown cop.'

'That's right. And we assumed that someone must have warned him to expect a visit. Well, as you know, I was never a hundred per cent happy about that. If someone had called me and told me to admit an unknown policeman in the middle of the night, I'd have checked with you. So would Mike. But if the instruction had come from you in the first place, he'd have no need to check.'

'Yes, George, but I never . . .'

'No, Major. But Mike *thought* you did.'

The windows were steaming up. Tim opened his door. 'What you're suggesting is that someone phoned Mike, pretending to be me.'

'It's not all that difficult. You've got a pretty distinctive voice. A couple of the lads reckon they've got you to a "T".'

Tim smiled ruefully. 'Bloody hell! To think I've been wasting my time chasing all these other M's – Müller, Meyer, Meredith – and all the time it was M for me.'

'So what happens now? You still haven't said what you want me here for.'

'A little hedge-breaking.'

'Come again.'

'One way to get out of a maze is to smash a path through the hedges.'

'Sounds a bit drastic.'

'Drastic – but, I hope, effective. If nothing else, it should make whoever's behind all this realise that we're not prepared to play his way any longer. Come on. Let's get you checked in.'

Over lunch a little later Tim explained what he had in mind. George was far from happy about the plan but he contented himself with a shrug and the comment, 'You're the boss.'

The two Englishmen left the hotel at just after two-thirty the following morning. They did not have far to go but they took the car so as not to attract the attention of any passing police patrol. Tim parked just off the Savigny Platz in one of the arches under the S-Bahn, Berlin's elevated railway. Then he and George continued on foot.

König's shop was on one of the small streets running down to Kurfürstendamm. Beside it there was a double-door car entrance. The lock offered no problem and the two men found themselves in a wide courtyard enclosed by a square of shops, offices and apartments. They gazed up at three storeys of darkened windows. An iron ladder fixed to the wall provided a somewhat inadequate fire escape but seemed tailor-made for burglars.

Tim pointed to the first-floor window. 'There you are,' he said softly. 'A piece of cake.'

George looked doubtful. 'You're quite sure there's no one else living here?'

'As I said, König's wife left him years ago. I've been here a couple of times when we were installing the security system. It's a very comfortable and well-appointed bachelor pad.'

'And definitely no alarms?'

'Only in the shop. Upstairs it's clean. Come on.'

He led the way up the ladder. He used a suction clamp and a glass cutter to make a hole in the window. He passed the tools and the loosened circle of glass back to George, reached in his hand and unfastened the catch.

Inside, with the window closed behind them and a curtain drawn across it, Tim risked a torch. They were on a narrow landing. 'Over there,' he whispered, pointing to the furthest of three doors.

It led into a sitting room which, even in the darkness, breathed opulence. The torchlight reflected from polished wood, gilded icons and glazed cabinets. In one corner stood a harpsichord, a painted landscape gleaming from its open lid.

'He was quite a musician,' Tim recalled. 'Strange that someone so crass should have such a sensitive streak. Through here.' He opened a door in the far wall.

It led to a small study. Street lighting shone in through one floor-length window. Tim stepped across and closed the shutters. For good measure he also pulled the heavy velvet drapes across. 'OK, we can have the light on now.'

George found the switch and flicked it. He pushed the door to. Though lightly furnished, the room reflected its late owner's voluptuous taste. The desk was a magnificent eighteenth-century creation of sinuous curves, crisp ormolu and riotous boule inlay of coloured woods, tortoiseshell and brass. On one corner stood a tall, ivory statuette of the Virgin and Child, at least seven centuries old. Facing the desk was a large, framed Byzantine mosaic of an early emperor, glittering in gold, blue and green.

'If I remember rightly, George, you should find a filing cabinet in that corner, behind a false book stack.'

The door wall of the study was lined with shelves. George explored it, found the catch and pulled open a concealed door. The cupboard behind contained nothing but a very functional steel filing cabinet.

'Got it.'

'Good. See what you can find. I'll concentrate on the safe.'

Tim swung back the mosaic panel. From the bag of tricks George had brought from England he took what looked like a pocket calculator with two wires attached. At the end of each was a small suction pad. He fixed them either side of the safe's dial. Slowly he turned the outer ring, concentrating on the display panel of the safe-breaker. It showed blank as the dial revolved. Then, suddenly, it threw up the number 32. Tim turned his attention to the next ring.

'*Keine Bewegung!*'

Tim spun round. In the doorway stood a woman of twenty or twenty-one with luxuriant, shoulder-length auburn hair. But there were two things more striking about her than that. The first was that she was pointing a gun at him, professionally, with two very steady hands. The second was that she was stark naked.

PART III

THE RIDER ON A BLACK HORSE

I looked and there was a black horse. Its rider held a pair of scales in his hand.

The Revelation of John the Divine 6:5

Chapter 11

'*Ich sagte: keine Bewegung!*'

Obeying rules of combat absorbed long ago, Tim fixed his gaze, not on the gun, but on the woman's dark eyes. What he read there was determination and contempt. There was no sign of fear or uncertainty. '*Ich spreche nicht Deutsch,*' he said as calmly and levelly as he could.

'English?' She took a couple of paces forward, never relaxing her concentration from the spot between Tim's eyes. 'What the hell do you think you're doing?'

Behind her, George Martin's solid frame moved noiselessly.

Tim held the woman's attention. 'Despite what it may look like, I'm not a burglar. And I'm not armed. Do you think you could point that thing somewhere else? Neither of us would want it to go off.'

'Speak for yourself.' The smirk gave her pleasant features an ugly twist. 'I'd drill you with the greatest of . . .'

'Excuse me, miss.' George spoke from right behind her.

The girl half turned. Tim ducked behind the desk. With a single movement, George's large hand clamped on the woman's wrist, forcing her to drop the gun, and twisted her arm behind her. She kicked back with her right foot. Then yelped with pain as her captor increased the pressure.

'Please don't make me hurt you any more, miss.' George sounded as apologetic and embarrassed as he felt.

Tim picked up the pistol, a Walther P38, removed the clip and applied the magazine safety lock. 'OK, George, let the lady go. And perhaps you could find her something to wear.'

'You needn't bother.' She pouted and sank, deflated but still defiant, onto a Russian, Louis XV-style fauteuil.

'Well, if you wouldn't mind . . . It would certainly make us feel more comfortable.'

The woman said nothing and remained glowering until George returned with a bathrobe which she draped round herself. 'So what happens now? Gang rape, or are you just going to knock me about?'

Tim had no idea what he was going to do. He surveyed the strange, composed young woman and tried to form a quick assessment. Tough. Unfeminine. Brash. A prostitute or stripper, perhaps. Yet there was nothing vulgar about her and she seemed very intelligent. Her English was very good, particularly the pronunciation. And she certainly knew how to handle a gun. The fact that she was here alone presumably meant that she was König's lover – hard though that was to imagine.

'Perhaps we could start with introductions. My name is Tim Lacy and this is my colleague, George Martin. I was a friend of Oscar König. You've presumably heard . . .'

'Yes I've heard.' She showed no emotion. 'So what are Oscar's "friends" doing, breaking into his apartment at dead of night?'

Tim perched himself on the edge of the desk. 'I've told you who we are. Now, just who are you?'

The girl was not to be intimidated. 'It's not for me to explain myself. I have every right to be here.'

Tim looked at her and wondered whether to take the gamble. At last, he said, 'OK. We're looking for an item of stolen property that just might have come into Oscar's hands and we're also trying to find out who killed him.'

That *did* shake her. 'Killed! . . . But the cops . . .'

'Told you that he committed suicide in his cell.'

'Yes. So why should I believe you and not them? What makes you think someone killed him?'

'It's a long story and it can only distress you further. I'd rather not go into details just now.'

'Well, I'd rather you did. I've a right to know what's going on. Oscar was a shit. But he was my father.'

It was Tim's turn to be taken aback. 'You're . . .'

'Maria König.'

'I'm sorry. I had no idea Oscar had a daughter.'

'Not many people did. I certainly didn't advertise the connection. I live in Frankfurt. Came to see him a couple of times a year. But he was generous. Sent me to schools in Paris and London to improve my foreign languages and set me up in my own business. In every other respect he was a lousy father. Still, I owe him something. So, unless this talk of him being murdered is a load of bullshit, I want to know the details.'

'OK. I'll trade information with you.'

Tim gave a potted version of everything that had happened since Mike's death. Maria listened attentively, sometimes asking questions. She relaxed visibly and, after a while, she suggested that they make themselves more comfortable in the sitting room. They sat in deep easy chairs enjoying drinks from Oscar's well-stocked cupboard.

When the story was over Maria stared at the two men over the rim of her glass. 'Why should I believe you?'

Tim said, quietly, 'If you want reasons, try these for size! Number one: what else are we doing here? If we were burglars, we'd have made a beeline for the goodies downstairs. I installed your father's alarm system. That means I know how to get round it. Number two: why are we talking? George and I could have tied you up – or worse – and got clean away. As it is, we're in your hands. You can report us to the police if you want to.'

'I still might do just that.'

'Then you'll never know how your father died. And, as you said, you owe him something. I think you felt more for him than you're ready to admit.'

'What exactly did you hope to find?' She refused to let the conversation take a personal turn.

Tim shrugged. 'The Dresden Text or something, anything that would explain Oscar's link with it. I'm sure that he was involved in some way. He probably organised the burglary. Even if he didn't, he negotiated the disposal of the manuscript. I'm hoping against hope that I can find documentary proof of who wanted the Dresden Text and where it is now, if it isn't here.'

'And if you do?'

'Then, the rest is up to the police. I've already spent longer on this business than I should have. May we have your permission to continue our search? If you want to go back to bed . . .'

'You won't find anything.'

'Really?' Tim regarded her suspiciously. 'You sound very sure about that.'

Maria got up and busied herself refilling glasses. She sighed deeply as she handed Tim a cut glass tumbler with a generous measure of brandy.

'I wish I could be sure I could trust you. Oscar had so

many "associates" – most of them crooked.' She picked up a framed photograph standing on the harpsichord. 'I hated coming to see him here in Berlin. He led a secret, shady life in a sordid, walled-in city. But every year, without fail, he used to take me skiing.'

She held out the picture of a laughing girl in pigtails and a smiling Oscar König in a red ski-suit against a snowy background. 'Those were good times. Fun times. I only discovered a couple of days ago that there were business reasons for our special holidays together in Switzerland.'

'What happened?'

'He phoned me at the office on Tuesday. He said it was vitally important that I come to see him. It wasn't very convenient but he sounded so desperate that I came that evening. He gave me an envelope. It contained a letter of authorisation to a Genevan bank and an account number. He told me that if anything happened to him, the contents were mine. There was a large sum of money and various papers. He said I would have to decide whether to destroy the papers or hand them to the authorities. As for the cash . . .' Her voice began to falter. To maintain her composure she took a long gulp from her glass of hock. '. . . he hoped it would bring me happiness. If there are any documents of interest to you, that's where they'll be.'

Tim smiled at her. 'Thank you for being so open with us, and I'm sorry we startled you by coming in as we did. If I'd known you were here, or even that you existed, I'd have made contact in a more orthodox way.'

Maria laughed suddenly – a deep, warm throaty laugh. 'Well, you came within an ace of getting a bullet between the eyes. I would have fired, you know – if you'd tried anything.'

Tim nodded gravely. 'Oh, yes, I know you would.'

She laughed, then yawned. 'I'm going back to bed. There's not much of the night left. Do you guys want to come back in the morning and search in a less clandestine way?'

Tim shook his head. 'Since we're here . . .'

Maria tossed her magnificent, shining mane of hair. 'Please yourselves, but you won't find anything. Well, goodnight. Let yourselves out quietly. I'm a light sleeper.' She moved slowly towards the door.

'About that Swiss account – would you be prepared to have a look for anything that might help us? We're at the Inter-Continental. If you think of . . .'

Maria turned briefly. 'Let me sleep on it.' She disappeared into the corridor.

The twelve horsemen under the command of Brother Conrad waited in a strip of sparse forest some fifty yards from the highway, glad of the shade in the hot August afternoon. They wore plain ragged tunics over shirts of mail, and carried battered helmets. They sat quietly, well practised at being relaxed in the saddle. Yet every man gazed frequently down the road, watching for the telltale swirl of dust. Each knew how much depended on the success or failure of this mission.

The most difficult part of the plan was to lure Zerwonka out of Marienburg. Ulrich and his friends had considered and rejected several possible ways of getting at the mercenary chief inside his garrison. Past grand masters had made the Hochschloss – the innermost citadel – impregnable, and Zerwonka now occupied the Hochschloss with his own troops. With its walls, layers deep in brick, its narrow windows and few doors, it was a castle within a castle. Every portal was guarded by members of an élite

Bohemian corps, who admitted only people they recognised and trusted. Since this excluded virtually all knight
brothers Zerwonka had effectively ousted the Teutonic
Order from its own citadel. The knights were housed in the
Mittelschloss which comprised the church, the conventual
buildings and the elegant palace of the Grand Master. No
less well fortified than the Hochschloss, it was separated
from it. The two complexes, in fact, formed self-contained
units. They were distinct again from the town whose
narrow streets radiated out to the perimeter wall, the
towered gatehouses and the bridges which crossed the
moat or the River Nogat, one of the Vistula's sluggish
effluents. Triple-locked within mighty Marienburg,
Stephan Zerwonka was secure against all potential
enemies. Ulrich had calculated that there was only one
man for whom the Bohemian would leave this position of
safety – King Casimir of Poland. That was why Conrad and
his men were now lying in wait for Zerwonka's emissary,
returning from the Polish camp.

Someone shouted. Conrad looked up and saw the white
dust plume over a mile along the road. He gave his orders
quietly. Half his force moved off through the trees to a
point a hundred yards away. The remaining seven men
donned helmets, drew swords and took up the slack in
their reins.

Now the travellers were clearly visible. The messenger
and a four-man escort. They came at a steady trot. They
would be hot and dusty, looking forward to a rest and cool
ale at Marienburg within the hour.

Conrad waited until they were abreast of his position,
then led the charge.

The mercenaries were shaken but recovered quickly.
Their orders were to get their messages safely back. They

spurred their horses to a gallop.

And ran straight into the other 'brigands' who emerged from the trees to block their path.

The skirmish was short. Three of the Bohemians were cut down. Conrad personally felled Zerwonka's one-eyed emissary. The other two mercenaries fled. Three of Conrad's men made a pretence at pursuit, then broke off the chase.

The dead men were stripped of weapons, helmets and any items of value. Conrad unfastened the messenger's saddle bag. Inside there was a weighty leather purse and a single letter, bearing Casimir's impressive seal. Conrad took both. Back into the bag he thrust the other paper that looked identical. The one that had been written by Father Sebastian and sealed with a fair imitation of the Polish king's device.

Maria König called Tim the evening of the following day, Saturday, and suggested dinner. He found the meeting disturbing. Tim's first encounter had been with a brash, deliberately unconventional girl who apparently thought nothing of confronting a strange intruder in a state of nature. Now he found himself sitting opposite a sophisticated woman who could have been that girl's responsible elder sister. She was certainly older than he had first thought – mid-twenties, probably. Her hair was drawn back and caught at the neck with a large bow. She wore an immaculately-tailored pin stripe suit of darkest green over a cream silk shirt. Her make-up was light but flawless. Her perfume subtle yet compelling. Her behaviour correct to the point of being prim. The transformation was so complete as to be unnerving.

Throughout most of the meal they talked like business

acquaintances getting to know each other for the first time. Neither alluded to the bizarre events of the previous night. They might have been incidents from a movie known to both of them, though neither realised the other had seen it. Their conversation was a journey of mutual exploration. Tim discovered that Maria had lived with her mother since the age of five, when her parents had divorced. Most of her childhood had been spent in smart boarding schools and a finishing academy. Oscar had spoiled his only daughter appallingly and that daughter had instinctively taken full advantage of his generosity and his sense of guilt. There had been wonderful holidays, expensive toys, charge accounts at stores and fashion houses in Frankfurt, Paris and London. Two years ago, again with Daddy's help, she had bought a small wine-exporting business. She had no close relatives, her mother having died some five years before, and she was – or so she claimed – too busy for emotional entanglements. Her hobbies were judo and small arms shooting.

So much she told him. More interesting was what she did not. What he deduced. The two Maria Königs were so different, yet each in its way was wholly convincing. The woman was such an accomplished actress that she set a swarm of questions buzzing around in his brain. How many transmutations was this chameleon capable of? Which was the real Maria? Was there a real Maria? How much of what she told him could be taken at face value?

Then he told himself not to be so critical – so unsympathetic. Was it not inevitable that someone in Maria's position should have problems with self-identity? No stable family background. A father she half loved, half despised, who only related to her through an open cheque book. An education that had taken her to various schools and countries. An almost unlimited supply of cash. With such a start in life how could she be expected to form values, establish genuine relationships?

Tim gazed into the dark eyes behind the mask of self-assurance and, for the first time, questioned the rightness of what he was doing. He had set out to try to discover who was behind Mike's murder and, if possible, to bring the culprit to justice. He had hoped to locate the Dresden Text and restore it to its rightful owner. Both worthy motives. Yet his enquiries had almost certainly caused another death. Oscar König, for all his faults, had been Maria's father. Now she had lost, in tragic circumstances, her life's main prop. She did not know how to come to terms with it; how to grieve. And here he was making things more difficult for her. He could not go through with it. He reached a sudden decision. Whatever the results for his own investigation, he would forget about Oscar's private papers; tell Maria he had been mistaken about her father's role in the affair. Then he would pay the bill, put her into a taxi and walk quietly, quickly, away.

That was the moment that Maria said, 'By the way, I've decided to go to Geneva on Monday to get Oscar's papers. If you want to look through them, you'd better come with me.'

Stephan Zerwonka was annoyed by the summons to a meeting with King Casimir, but he could not afford to ignore it. The fortune he stood to make from the surrender of the Teutonic Order's magnificent citadel would set him up with all the splendour of a *Graf* in his own country. The vision of wealth and status which had sustained his hazardous mercenary career was about to become reality. It was worth the small risk of leaving the security of his stronghold to travel the hundred miles to the Polish camp near Thorn. However, he minimised the risk as much as possible. He set out before dawn from Marienburg with a corps of two hundred mounted men. He intended to ride hard and reach his destination before nightfall. The only point of possible danger was the Order's fortress at Graudenz, about halfway between the two larger towns, and this he intended to skirt well to the east.

By the time the Bohemian's troop left, Ulrich and his contingent of twenty renegade knights were half way to Graudenz. They had left by one of the smaller gateways in the town wall thanks to an accomplice in charge of the guard. Attired now, not as anonymous brigands, but in the simple panoply of the Order, they carried sealed instructions from the Grand Master to the commander of Graudenz. The instructions bore further testimony to Father Sebastian's skill as a forger. They reached the fortress before the sun was half way to its zenith. Ulrich was careful to keep in the background in case any member of the garrison should recognise a disgraced brother. It was Conrad who gained access to the commander and delivered the message. Commander Gerhardt von Freilingen was an uncomplicated, unlettered soldier. Time was lost while he sent for one of the priest brothers to read the letter from Marienburg.

But once he understood his instructions, he acted. He ordered his full strength of five hundred men to be saddled and ready within the hour. When they were assembled in the town square, he explained their mission to them. Reinforcements from Danzig were on their way to support Casimir's army at Thorn. They were to be intercepted at all costs and destroyed. Von Freilingen despatched scouts ahead and led his troop out through the main gate. Ulrich rode with his friends at the rear of the contingent. As they crossed the Vistula by the wooden bridge and struck out across the wide water meadows, he stifled his impatience with difficulty. It was irksome keeping a low profile. He wanted to be in control – leading the men he had persuaded to risk everything. He trusted Conrad, of course, but the manoeuvring which lay ahead would be tricky. Ulrich wanted to be in charge of the moment-by-moment decisions, the sudden changes of plan which might become necessary. As it was, all he could do was hope and pray that their desperate scheme would come off.

On Monday morning George Martin, Al Freeman and Tim Lacy all flew out of Berlin; the first two were homeward bound. Tim was accompanying Maria to Geneva. From Cointrin airport they drove straight to the tinted-glass cube of the Société de Banque Suisse de Commerce, which jostles coyly with other financial institutions on the Rue de la Croix d'Or and neighbouring streets like girls at a dance trying to attract attention without appearing to do so.

Maria was conducted to an office by a deferential attendant to complete the necessary formalities, then escorted by another to the deposit-box vault. Tim waited in deep-cushioned comfort in an area provided with armchairs, marble-topped low tables and morning editions of all the leading European newspapers. He flipped through *The Times* without taking much in. He gazed out at the rose-coloured street scene. Mercedes, motor bikes and scooters glided silently past the bank's double-glazed frontage, without disturbing the vital transactions and negotiations proceeding within. Then he turned away to gaze at the door through which Maria had disappeared. Every few minutes he looked at his watch.

She had been gone over half an hour. What was she up to? All she had to do was bring any papers out. Was she going back on her word? Checking everything before letting him see it? Was there anything significant to see? Did Oscar's secret cache contain the explanation Tim had been seeking for weeks? Or was it yet another false trail? The final red herring? Tim knew that he could take this business no further. He had already spent too much time on it – as Catherine and Sally had both intimated in different ways when he had called home from Geneva airport. He picked up a copy of *Die Welt* and tested his meagre German on the headlines and photo captions. Race riots and anti-neo-Nazi protest rallies still seemed to be dominating the national news, he noticed.

'OK, where to now?'

Maria was suddenly beside him. She was carrying a large manila envelope.

'What kept you?'

'Swiss red tape – what else? Where do you want to go to look through this stuff?'

They emerged into the winter sunshine and the sudden noise of traffic. Tim had already thought out the answer to that question. 'Well, we could check into a hotel. I need a room for tonight, anyway. But I know somewhere else where we can be quiet and undisturbed. And it's only a stone's throw away.'

He took her by the elbow and guided her into the tangle of narrow streets that make up old Geneva and climb steeply to the cathedral. They were lined with small, exceedingly expensive shops – couturiers, jewellers, art galleries, and purveyors of stylish bathrooms, hand-made furniture, oriental carpets and other items selected to tempt Geneva's wealthy international élite.

Before one glass door Tim stopped. The small square window beside it presented a chaste display. An early sixteenth-century Italian painted terracotta statuette of St Catherine, complete with wheel, stood before a Franco-Flemish *mille-fleur* tapestry of the same period, depicting mythical beasts amidst a 'jungle' of radiant blooms and intertwining plant fronds. The age-muted greens, blues and pinks of the two very different pieces tastefully complemented each other, suggesting that some well-heeled client might like to spend a quarter of a million on the whole ensemble to grace his opulent lakeside villa. Tim rang the bell.

Moments later the door was flung wide with an expansive gesture. 'Tim Lacy, what a delicious surprise!' Gerda Frankl stood before them swathed in a flowing, burnous-like garment of floral silk.

Zerwonka's force was located around midday on the far side of a wooded ridge five miles due east of Graudenz. Von Freilingen charged down on their flank from the cover of the trees. Ulrich's party held back. They kept to the higher ground, to watch the outcome of the skirmish. It was a hand-to-hand mêlée which the superior force was sure to win. In the confusion of upraised shields, rearing horses, hacking swords and falling bodies Ulrich could not recognise Zerwonka. Yet he knew precisely where the traitor was. A knot of Bohemian soldiers at the centre of the fray formed a deliberate barrier round the rider of a powerful bay. As the carnage drew closer to this inner circle its members tried desperately to cut their way out. Swords flashing indiscriminately, Zerwonka's guards sliced down even their own men in their efforts to force a path through the press.

At last they succeeded. Conrad, beside Ulrich among the sparse trees, pointed as Zerwonka, with a handful of companions, broke free of the fracas and streaked up the slope towards the cover of the wood. Ulrich signalled and his men drew further back into cover.

Ulrich briefly removed his helm. 'Brother Conrad, take six men the other side of the copse in case he breaks over westwards. We'll work our way through and flush him out.'

Ulrich spread his men into a line abreast and they moved forward at walking pace, raking trees, shrubs and ferns like a comb drawn through thick hair. Occasionally, he called a halt and listened for the sounds of hooves and harness ahead. But the din of battle behind them drowned out other noises. He peered through the shifting pattern of sunlight and shadow.

Suddenly something crashed out of a thicket fifty yards ahead. Ulrich spurred his horse forward – and caught a glimpse of a roe deer breaking cover. He strained his eyes, willing them to see something else moving among the trees.

'Holy Mary, don't let me lose him, now.'

Three sharp notes on a horn sounded away to his left. A signal from Conrad. He turned the mare's head, at the same time shouting to his men. Ducking under low branches and avoiding sudden hollows they emerged on the other side of the wood. Fifty yards ahead Conrad's posse was in full gallop after the retreating Bohemians. Ulrich sank spurs into his horse's flanks. With a startled whinny, she leapt forward. Ulrich heard himself screaming but knew not what he said.

Through his visor he saw the mercenaries suddenly rein in. For a moment he thought they were going to stand and fight. Then, on an order from Zerwonka, they turned, once more, into the wood – and scattered.

Ulrich cursed as his own followers plunged in pursuit. In the confusion of trees and undergrowth some of the Bohemians would be caught but others would probably slip away or hide. The air filled with shouts and cries, with the sound of horses crashing through thickets and metal striking metal. Every man marked down his own quarry. There was no way of controlling the action.

He emerged into a wide glade. Away to his right he caught a glimpse of a bay horse cantering into the cover of a hawthorn brake. Ulrich pulled the mare's head round. She turned quickly. Too quickly. She stumbled, went down on her knees and struggled to recover. Ulrich twisted in the saddle. Pain lanced through his thigh. As he was thrown forward, there was no strength in his left leg to brace himself. He fell heavily over the horse's head. Struck the ground with a crash that forced the breath from his body.

For a few moments he lay still, gulping air. Then he threw off his helm and looked around. Ten yards away he saw a strong slender pine sapling. Ignoring the pain, he dragged himself towards it. Grasped it. Pulled himself to his feet. He whistled up the mare and when she came he tried to wriggle his way back into the saddle. It was no use. The weight of his armour, the weakness of his leg and the unevenness of the ground made remounting impossible. He let the horse graze and sat down with his back against a tree.

Wilhelm von Hagen found him there twenty minutes later. It was the young knight brother who rallied his comrades and brought them to the glade. One by one they emerged from the screen of trees. Some were leading prisoners. Ulrich studied them urgently. Zerwonka was not among them. Then Conrad rode up, holding in his left hand the reins of a powerful bay. Stephan Zerwonka, seemingly unhurt, sat limply in the saddle. Conrad brought him across the clearing.

The little Bohemian looked down with a nod and a slight smile. 'I might have guessed. I should have finished you off when I had the chance.'

'Yes, you should.' Ulrich summoned Wilhelm to help him to his feet. 'Now I'm going to put a stop to your treachery.'

Zerwonka seemed unmoved. He looked around the sunlit glade. 'This is as good a place as any to die. Let's get it over quickly.'

Ulrich shook his head. 'We're not going to kill you. Not yet. That would be barbaric. You must be made to face up to your crimes. Before a Vehmic court.'

Chapter 12

The large buff envelope lay between them on the green, tooled-leather surface of the partner's desk in the Frankls' back office. Maria and Tim stared at it as bomb disposal experts might look warily at a suspect device.

The ebullient Gerda had been marvellously understanding and helpful. After introductions, she had taken them up to the flat above the shop. Over coffee Tim had told her only that he and Maria had some important papers to go through and needed a quiet room for an hour or so.

'How mysterious!' Gerda had raised an elegantly plucked eyebrow. 'I'm not sure I should be a party to all this, Tim Lacy. You turn up here with a beautiful young woman, asking for a private room. Well, what's a girl to think?' Though fizzing with curiosity, she had not pressed her guests. 'Well, OK, I'll join your little conspiracy, but only on one condition – that you both have dinner with us this evening.'

That agreed, Gerda had cleared her desk for them and left them alone.

'Well, here goes.' Maria drew the envelope towards her. Tim noticed that her hand was trembling.

She extracted a slim black notebook and a sheaf of papers, some typed, some handwritten. Silently, Maria glanced through the loose notes. Then she extracted some sheets and studied them for several minutes, brow furrowed. At last she looked up. 'No wonder he kept them well hidden.'

'What are they?' Tim's impatience could not be restrained any longer.

'Transaction details. They describe objects Oscar acquired from the East. How they were smuggled to Berlin. How he sold them. Here's an example.' She extracted a sheet from the pile. 'It describes four items brought in on 23rd September 1990. For instance, "Saints George and Dimitri, tempera on panel, 42.1 centimetres by 28.7 centimetres, School of Kiev, c.1400." They arrived on a train from Warsaw. Oscar paid the courier, a train guard called Jan Potocki, DM127,000 for the consignment. Oscar disposed of them separately. The panel alone was sold through Christie's in London for £48,000.'

Tim whistled. 'Some profit margin.'

Maria was engrossed. 'All these pages have a letter in the top right-hand corner. This one has a "K". And this one. The next has an "R". It's some sort of code.'

Tim picked up the notebook. He opened it and smiled. 'And here's the key. It's a list of names and numbers. Phone numbers, perhaps. Each entry has its own identifying letter. "K" is Alexei Karapov.'

'The suppliers of the consignments?'

'Must be. A pound to a penny they're all Russian gang bosses.'

Maria sat back. 'This is . . .'

'Dynamite.'

'Poor Oscar.' She closed her eyes and bit her lip, fighting back tears.

Tim thought, but did not say, that 'poor Oscar' had

obviously made a sizable fortune out of his contacts with organised crime. He reached across the desk and laid a hand on Maria's. 'This little cache must have been his insurance policy. If ever his Russian mafia associates came on heavy, he could threaten them with exposure.'

Maria sniffed and took a couple of deep breaths. She blew her nose, surreptitiously dabbing her moist eyes. 'It didn't do him much good, did it?'

Tim squeezed her hand. 'Oscar gave this stuff to you so that you could pull the plug on the whole operation. It's your chance to avenge him.'

'You think I should turn this over to the police?'

Tim nodded. 'But first, let's go through all this scientifically. If it's about stuff coming out of Russia, I suppose there's no mention of the Dresden Text?'

But there was.

By carefully arranging Oscar König's papers chronologically they were able to chart the development of his illicit East-West trade. It had begun in 1989 when the rust patches on the Iron Curtain began to grow into holes. König already had some contact with crime bosses in the Soviet Union, and they were quick to see the potential of easier access to Western markets. Oscar's first consignment had reached him in Vienna, ferried by one of the refugees pouring across the Hungarian border. The collapse of the Berlin Wall had removed the need for such circuitous routes. Precious artefacts were soon flooding into the city by road, rail, air and sea. The dealer's papers showed a rapid increase in the illicit trade. The independence era was an entrepreneur's dream. There was an almost inexhaustible supply of valuable antiquities and a voracious demand. People with hoarded family treasures were eager for US dollars or West German Deutschmarks.

Long boarded-up churches were easy prey for looters. Regional museums with antediluvian security systems simply invited the attention of Moscow-based gangs.

The transactions reached a peak in the middle of 1991. König was receiving consignments two or three times a month. The couriers were railway and airline officials, Baltic ships' captains, long-distance lorry drivers, diplomats, businessmen, politicians, even policemen. With contacts like those, Tim reflected, it was hardly surprising that Oscar was not even safe in a prison cell. From the summer of 1991 a marked change had come over the business, presumably at Oscar's instigation. The quantity of artefacts coming through from the East decreased. The quality improved.

'I reckon your father started supplying goods to order,' Tim said. 'Things were coming through too fast. That meant handling difficulties and the risk of flooding the market. By now Oscar had a number of clients with very specific requirements. To a certain extent he could call the shots. My guess is that he sent "K", "R" and the others detailed lists of high-value items.

'It was a year later that the next development occurred. A reverse process was set up. Oscar had begun supplying antiquities acquired in Western Europe and America to his Russian confederates.'

Maria frowned. 'How do you explain that?'

'The emergence of a new wealthy élite. Capitalism spreads in the old Warsaw Pact countries. A new millionaire class emerges. People with money want luxuries and status symbols. Most of them have to be imported. Enter "K", "R" and Co – and their agent Oscar König. He has criminal contacts on this side of the fence as well as the other. There's already an efficient courier service in place.

What could be easier than to double profits by establishing a two-way system?'

'Well, here's what you're looking for.' Maria read from a handwritten sheet. 'On 3 January last, he supplied two items to "S".' She referred to the notebook. 'That's Feodr Sukalov – a bronze Bacchus, "School of Bernini", and a fourteenth-century illuminated biblical fragment, known as the Dresden Text. The agreed price for the two was DM500,000.'

'Bingo!' Tim breathed a long sigh. He felt not triumph but relief. He had emerged from the maze. He was, probably, no nearer to retrieving the Dresden Text or seeing the principal culprit brought to justice. But now everything made sense. He knew why Mike had been killed and the manuscript stolen. There was in the knowledge itself a feeling of achievement. Now he could go home, without unanswered questions and nagging misgivings haunting him. The rest could be left to the police.

Maria stared at him. 'That bit of paper solves your problems, does it? Well, it creates mine.'

'How so?'

Her head drooped. 'Do you think I can just trip happily along to the police and hand all this over to them and say, "There you are. That proves, not only that my father was fencing stolen art works on an international scale, but also that he was involved in a double murder." '

'But he wasn't.'

'What?'

'I mean, I'm sure he wasn't involved in murder. As I see it, Oscar had to be in New York to identify the Dresden Text and to get it safely back to Berlin. The actual burglary must have been organised by some local crime boss.'

'You really think so?'

'Maria, your father was an out-and-out rogue. There's no way of denying that. But I'm sure he would never commit a murder, or even plan one. These documents show quite clearly that he was just the middle man. He was increasingly caught between two major crime syndicates. That was a hell of a dangerous place to be. Towards the end I guess he felt trapped. You know how agitated he was last week.'

For a long time neither of them spoke.

Then Maria said, 'It's only just beginning to hit me that my father's not going to be around any more.'

Tim tapped the pile of papers. 'He would have wanted you to make use of these. That's why he told you about them. You have to take them to Steiger – and, for heaven's sake, warn him about that new man of his, Karl Pressner.'

She nodded. 'I'm glad you were here.'

'This *Stillding** of the Prussian *Vehmgericht*** is now in session before me, Georg von Minden, and six *Schöffen* appointed by me.'

The speaker – an impressive figure, tall and broad, with a luxuriant black and grey-speckled beard – stood before the altar of the ruined church at Östering, flanked on each side by three other knight brothers. Von Minden was the most senior of the 'true knights', a Saxon count in his own right before he joined the Order, and a close confidant of Ludwig von Erlichshausen. He was a *Freigraf*, one of the judges appointed by the Grand Master to administer local justice and preside over courts within the Order's jurisdiction.

* secret tribunal
** criminal court

'I remind the *Schöffen* of their sworn oath to hear evidence impartially, to judge truly, to see the sentence of the court carried out and to maintain the secrecy of the court's proceedings.'

He seated himself on the rough bench which had been set up for the tribunal. The only other people present were the accused, Stephan Zerwonka, who stood between two guards with his hands bound, and the witnesses – Ulrich von Walenrod and two other ex-members of the Memel garrison. Others of the dissident faction stood sentinel outside the church.

Zerwonka looked more ragged and uncouth than usual, after his six-day confinement. But his defiance had not been dulled.

'I protest against this play-acting!' he shouted. 'You do not have the sanction of the Grand Master for these proceedings.'

Von Minden glowered. 'The prisoner will be silent, or he will be removed and forfeit the right to speak in his own defence. This is a properly-constituted Vehmic court under my commission from the Grand Master to hold criminal tribunals as and where necessary.'

The Bohemian was not to be cowed. 'The Vehmic courts have been outlawed throughout Prussia! They were symbols of the Teutonic Order's tyranny!'

'Silence!' The massive Saxon's roar echoed round the ruined walls. 'The charge against the prisoner is treason. He is accused of conspiring with enemies of the Grand Master of the Order of St Mary of Jerusalem, lawful sovereign of these lands. The tribunal will now hear the evidence.'

It took less than half an hour for the witnesses to tell what they knew. One had heard two of Zerwonka's men laughing at the way Ulrich had been tricked. Another had seen the Bohemian holding negotiations with Vytautas's agent. Ulrich affirmed his loyalty to the Order and his innocence of any treachery. It was scarcely conclusive.

Zerwonka disdained defence. Von Minden deliberated with his colleagues. Then he announced, 'Stephan Zerwonka, we find you guilty of treason against your lawful lord, Ludwig von Erlichshausen, Grand Master of the Order of St Mary of Jerusalem. The sentence passed on you, according to custom, is death by hanging. That sentence will now be carried out.'

The place of execution had already been decided – a copse some two hundred yards from the village. The knight brothers mounted and formed up in two files with the prisoner between them.

They were halfway across the open ground when someone shouted, 'Polish troops!' Half a mile along the road to the south a contingent of a hundred or more cavalry were approaching at the trot.

Ulrich shouted, 'Quick, into the trees!' He spurred his horse forward.

The party hurried to reach cover. There was a brief moment of confusion. It was enough for Zerwonka. Turning in the saddle, Ulrich saw the traitor galloping away towards the road, his arms still pinioned behind him.

The glass-encased terrace of the Frankls' villa at Chambésy, just outside Geneva, offered a spectacular panorama of lake, south shore lights reflected in the water, and a skyline of white peaks frosted by moonlight. Gerda replenished the coffee cups and Walter followed her with the brandy decanter.

'This has been a wonderful evening.' Maria sank into the

deep cushions of a sofa that seemed to be made of clouds and sighed her contentment.

Walter – a slim, greying, patrician figure – smiled down at her. 'My dear, after all you've been through, you need a rest. Stay as long as you like. You too, Tim.'

It had been established earlier that they were to spend the night at the Frankls' home. Gerda refused to countenance the idea of their booking into a hotel.

Tim shook his head. 'Tempting, Walter. Terribly tempting. But I have a business to run. This affair has taken up time that I really can't afford. Anyway, I have an appointment in Frankfurt tomorrow.'

'Well, I think your tenacity does you great credit.' Gerda perched on a high-backed upright chair and managed to look both comfortable and elegant. 'You have done us all a favour, Tim. It's outrageous the way these crime syndicates have taken to targeting the antiques world. The police are worse than useless. If the crooks realise that some of us are going to fight back, perhaps they'll think twice about whom they hit.'

Over an excellent dinner, Tim and Maria had told their story. Each of them had found it a relief to talk through the recent experiences.

Walter settled back into his armchair. 'So it's over to the Berlin police, now, eh? Let's hope they don't make a mess of things after all your hard work.'

Tim warmed the cognac and inhaled its fumes. 'It's hard to see how they can go wrong. With the names and addresses in Oscar's book, and all the evidence that Maria will be handing to Inspector Steiger, there should be no difficulty in getting extradition orders.'

Walter was sceptical. 'But the Russians have to arrest them, and Russians are congenitally incompetent!'

The others laughed and Tim said, 'That's a bit strong, isn't it?'

The older man frowned at their levity. 'Not at all. Efficiency simply isn't their strong suit. Look at their history. Who ever managed to rule that vast empire? Ivan the Terrible, Peter the Great, Stalin the Unspeakable. All the rest were bunglers, unable to control troublesome dissidents and a corrupt, top-heavy bureaucracy. All other world empires – Egypt, Rome, China, Spain, Britain – did at least have periods of peace, stability and economic development. But Russia? Ungoverned and ungovernable. A disastrous catalogue of wasted resources and misdirected energies. It was the same whoever was in the Kremlin – tsars or commissars. Now, since Gorbachev, of course everything's collapsed into total chaos: president and parliament at each other's throats; squabbling over the pace of reform. Oh, no, I wouldn't be too sanguine about bringing this bunch of art thieves to book. The syndicates are being run by ex-KGB agents and sacked army generals, so it's not surprising that they're so powerful. Many of the top police are in their pocket. It certainly doesn't pay to get in their way. Do you know how many honest cops were assassinated in Russia last year? Two hundred and sixty! One poor devil went from police HQ to Sigorsk to investigate a cache of stolen antiquities. He was too successful. On his way back to Moscow he "fell from the train". They obviously had no difficulty about getting to poor Oscar inside a Berlin jail. Thanks to *détente*, we're opening our arms to all this Slavonic garbage – corruption, crime, atheism, fallout from crumbling atomic reactors. Europe stood a better chance of surviving the Black Death! Do you realise . . .'

'Darling,' Gerda intervened gently. 'You're preaching.'

There was a moment's embarrassed pause, then Walter laughed. 'Quite right, sweetheart. Change of subject called for, most decidedly. Maria, tell us about your business.'

The conversation drifted and eddied and, for a time, Tim took no part in it. He watched the others and wondered how much one ever knew about people. Gerda, flamboyant and "up front", always gave the impression of being the dominant member of the Frankl partnership but, in fact, she constantly deferred to her husband's knowledge in matters professional and, when they were together in public, she always allowed Walter the floor. As for Walter, he was certainly no moon to Gerda's sun, as people tended to think when they first met the couple. Nor did Tim find himself altogether convinced by the pose of right-wing drawing-room orator. Walter Frankl might hold extreme opinions, but he had thought them through intelligently and he possessed a greater depth than he allowed people easily to see. And Maria? She sat demurely, basking in the Frankls' warm sympathy, but was she really just the little girl lost, courageously covering her vulnerability with the tough shell of a mature career woman? Tim watched the others talking, laughing, watching each other. Actors on a stage concentrating on their parts and aware of their audience. Then, he put the idea from his head. It was fanciful. And, anyway, he reflected, aren't we all guilty of assuming roles?

It was past midnight when the party broke up and they all dispersed to their rooms. Twenty minutes later Tim had showered, wrapped himself in his dressing gown and was sitting by the window, staring at the lights of Geneva with an open book on his lap. There was a tap at the door and Maria slipped in. She was wearing a green silk wrap lent by Gerda. She had loosened and brushed her hair. It glowed copper and gold in the soft light. Her perfume filled the room before she had advanced a couple of paces.

She seated herself opposite Tim and smiled sheepishly. 'I'm afraid to go to sleep.'

'Why's that?'

'I've been having bad dreams these last few nights.'

'That's understandable.' Tim was determined to keep their conversation at a low emotional level. 'You've had some nasty shocks and you've still got a lot of grieving to do. It'll pass – especially when you've handed the papers to Steiger. You'll find that will be a kind of purging of Oscar's memory.'

'You think so?' She slipped from the chair and curled herself at his feet.

'I'm sure of it. Once you've washed your hands of your father's seamy activities you'll be able to concentrate on the happy memories – the skiing trips, the outings to the zoo, other special, very personal little things.' He stroked her hair to comfort her but knew that there was nothing fraternal or avuncular about the gesture.

She looked up at him appealingly. 'I'm all alone now. There's nobody. It's odd being without a family at my age. I feel like a forgotten old spinster. Do I look like an old spinster, Tim?'

'I can't think of anyone right now who looks less like an old maid.' He looked down into eyes moistening with tears.

'Oh, Tim, you're wonderful. I don't know what I'd have done without you. Say you'll stay on in Frankfurt a few days – please!'

'The first time we met, you wanted to put a bullet through me.'

Her eyes opened wide. 'Oh, I could never have done

that. I've never even pointed a gun at a real person before.'

'Well, you had me convinced – and scared.'

She grinned sheepishly. 'Sorry. I behaved terribly. You must have thought me the most awful brazen creature. I can't imagine . . . At the time it seemed like just another nightmare. Let me make it up to you. Come and stay for a few days.'

He ruffled her hair. 'Out of the question, I'm afraid. I'll be flying straight back to London after my appointment with Mr Meredith.'

Tim thought he felt her stiffen. But her voice sounded casual when she asked, 'This Meredith, has he got something to do with your enquiries about the Dresden Text?'

'No. He's just an old client: a rich, whacky collector.' The lie sprang automatically to his lips – as a reflex action to some stimulus in his unconscious. Not that it really was a lie, Tim reflected. Now that the business of the Dresden Text was cleared up, and particularly now that the mystery of Mike's diary entry had been solved, the list of suspect "M"s could be consigned to the wastebin, where it had always belonged. His meeting with Arthur Meredith would be just a routine business appointment.

'And, now, I reckon we both could do with some sleep . . .'

He stood up but Maria grabbed at his hand imploringly. 'The loneliness gets to me at night. It's almost like a physical pain. Couldn't I . . . Couldn't we . . .?'

Tim took both her hands and drew her to her feet. She was lovely. The wrap was falling open. The body beneath was lithe and well moulded. The perfume filled his head with drowsying sweetness. He pulled her to him and said very gently and firmly, 'My wife is American and we have a sort of understanding: she doesn't fry my bacon to a crisp, and I don't go to bed with other women.' He felt her stiffen with embarrassed resentment but he continued to hold her close. 'Now I have an infallible cure for insomnia and bad nights. Why don't we go down to the kitchen and I'll whip you up a Lacy special?'

They walked hand-in-hand from the room.

Tim and Maria flew together to Frankfurt, but took separate taxis from the airport.

The Meredith Corporation occupied three floors of one of the city's most impressive commercial buildings. Tim followed a secretary through acres of open-plan office space, past cohorts of employees sitting at computer terminals, along miles of glass-lined walkways bordered with hanging gardens of greenery. At last they reached the double doors screening the chairman's sanctum. Inside the prospect changed completely.

Arthur Meredith's office was lined with oak panelling inlaid with other-coloured woods in formalised floral patterns – unquestionably Renaissance workmanship created originally for some Italian palazzo. Inset into the walls, and subtly lit, were three exquisite fifteenth- or sixteenth-century portraits on panel by north Italian masters. The furniture was modern but clearly designed for the room. The total effect was discreetly opulent, tastefully impressive.

Meredith rose from behind the desk, smiling at Tim's reaction. He wore his habitual black, but today sported a flamboyant polychrome bow-tie. 'Like it? Most people get a bit of a jolt when they walk in here.'

'Well, it's not quite what you expect to find at the heart

of a very modern business empire.' Tim shook the prof-
fered hand.

'That's precisely the point. It's my small attempt to
make a personal statement. I want to remind people of
their great heritage. Coffee?'

Tim nodded and his host used the desk intercom to
instruct a minion to bring refreshments. He indicated a
cluster of armchairs in a window corner, and continued
talking as they sat.

'Do you realise that our schools are now deliberately
rearing the first generation of European children who are
historically illiterate?'

'Surely, that's a bit strong, Arthur?'

'Not at all. Today's educational experts have systemati-
cally trashed the past. History, religion, literature, art,
music – they're being steadily squeezed out of school
timetables. Computer science, technology, math, psychol-
ogy, "social studies" . . .' He wrinkled his nose. 'They're
the "in" subjects. We're in danger of breeding a race of
monsters, Tim – people who know how to live but have
never even asked the question "Why?" We're losing our
cultural identity. They don't make the same mistake in
other parts of the world. Even the poor Americans treasure the little history they have. But in Europe, which has
given the planet its finest . . .'

The coffee arrived in elegant bone china on a silver tray.
Tim took the opportunity to divert the flow of Meredith's
eloquence. 'Are you still organising exhibitions?'

'Yes, there are three on tour at the moment.' He walked
over to the desk with the angular movements reminiscent of a
stiff-jointed marionette and returned with a glossy pamphlet.
Even Tim's limited German could cope with the headlines
detailing the programme of the National Heritage Society.

'There's an excellent programme on Teutonic myths and legends for *Grundschülen* – primary schools. We have a splendid company of actors doing "German Romanticism" – readings, dramatic excerpts, that sort of thing. And the latest innovation is a standing exhibition, with lectures entitled "The Truth About Nazism".'

'That's brave.'

'It's certainly raised a few eyebrows, but we think it's vital in view of the resurgence of racism and neo-Nazism and the reluctance of many teachers to grasp the nettle. Of course, in the East the kids have been brainwashed about what happened fifty years ago.'

Tim sipped the excellent coffee.

'And how's your own collection? If I remember rightly, the last time we met was in New York – the Brand Gallery. Did you buy anything?'

Meredith laughed. 'What, at Robin Brand's prices!'

Tim grinned. 'Strictly for the Manhattan smart set. Still, it was a good exhibition and a chance to see some fine examples of illuminated texts.'

'Agreed. That theft was a shocking thing.'

'Yes. Despite cultural deprivation, there still appear to be enough people about who appreciate art sufficiently to commission burglaries. Who do you reckon was behind that one, Arthur?'

Meredith shrugged. 'It had all the hallmarks of a Mafia heist. Not that the word "Mafia" means much nowadays. Every country has its own version of syndicated crime – China, Japan, Russia and all the bits of its former empire. We've certainly got them here in Germany.'

A new thought struck Tim. 'I suppose you've had direct experience of the mobs on both sides of the Atlantic. Knowing how they've penetrated big business,

I can imagine that they'd love to get their hands on a major air freight concern.'

'I've had the occasional brush with unsavoury characters, but since I'm the major shareholder in the Meredith Corporation, there's no back door way in for them. And since my holding will go to a charitable trust after my death, they have nothing to gain from bumping me off.'

'Did you get a close look at the stolen work, the Dresden Text?'

'Obviously not as close as I should have done.'

'Pity. I think it would have appealed to your interest in German history. According to one theory, it has a connection with the Teutonic Knights.'

Meredith's eyebrows rose in mild interest. 'Really! How intriguing. There aren't many surviving relics of the Teutonic Order. I'm surprised I hadn't heard of that one. More coffee?'

Tim watched him as he reached for the pot. Was he being a mite too casual? He said, 'For my part, I can't imagine why anyone should want to commemorate a gang of armoured thugs!'

Meredith's involuntary jerk sent coffee all over the tray. He set the pot down angrily. 'Damn! I'll ring for some more.' He covered his confusion by going over to the desk and using the intercom again.

He returned and relaxed back into the armchair. 'What was it you were saying – "armoured thugs"? No, that's a bit OTT. There was a strong strand of religious idealism in the movement.'

'Religion at swordpoint?'

Meredith nodded. 'Religion and civilisation at swordpoint. In those days there was no other way of bringing about beneficial change. They certainly developed the

Baltic region quickly and effectively.'

Fresh coffee arrived and Meredith busied himself filling cups. 'Now, Tim, fascinating though all this is, I'm sure it's not what you've come to talk about.'

'True. It's just that I like to drop in on old clients from time to time to make sure that there are no hiccups in their security systems.'

The conversation drifted onto other topics.

Twelve hours later, Tim rolled over and lay back content-edly on his pillow. In the darkness beside him Catherine said, 'Wow!'

'Good?'

'This Maria must be some woman.'

'Meaning?'

'She certainly stoked your boiler.'

Tim leaned over and kissed her. 'You're the only woman who gets me up to white heat.'

Catherine giggled. 'Bullshit! Charming bullshit, but bullshit, nevertheless.'

'Do I detect the green-eyed monster?'

'Of course. Tell me more about this Maria.'

During the course of the evening, Tim had given his wife a fairly complete report of the events of the last few days. Now that the Dresden Text business was over, there was no reason not to come clean about his trip to Berlin. If she resented his deception in following the König trail without saying what he was doing, she said nothing. Like Tim, her overwhelming feeling was one of relief that the affair was over – at least as far as they were concerned.

'There's not much more to tell. She's attractive, intelli-gent. She's trying to build some sort of a life on pretty shaky foundations.'

'I assume she's also rich and spoilt, and used to getting her own way.'

'Certainly.'

'What intrigues me is why she tried to seduce you.'

'I'm irresistible to women. Hadn't you noticed?'

Catherine jabbed a pointed fingernail into his stomach. 'Sorry to deflate your masculine ego, but there must have been more to it than your fatal allure.'

Tim groaned. 'If you're going to conduct an inquest, I shall regret being open with you. The girl was emotionally upset, lonely, confused. She wanted to be comforted, loved, made to feel special – if only for a night. That's all there was to it, OK? Goodnight!' He turned emphatically on his side.

Catherine leaned across and kissed his cheek. 'Night, superstud!'

She lay awake for a while longer wondering what it really was that a determined and probably ruthless woman like Maria König had wanted from her husband.

Seventeen days later, a Polish railway worker was checking the track of the Warsaw-Berlin line close to the German border. It was a grey morning of intermittent showers. He was damp even inside his regulation waterproof jacket and overtrousers but he trudged on, eyes fixed on sleepers, rails and junctions, because he wanted to finish his allotted section quickly and reach the heated signal-box where he could stop for lunch and a chat with old Barti, who manned it. It took a particularly heavy cloudburst to send him slithering down a steep embankment towards a clump of dripping pines. Just twenty yards short of the shelter, he spotted the spreadeagled body of a man in a rain-darkened suit lying amidst the shale and ferns.

Foreman Lengthman Braniski was badly shaken, but not too shaken to examine the corpse carefully. The railway authorities were sticklers for detail. He calculated the man's height and age. He turned him over, the better to assess his appearance. But the neat bullet hole in the stranger's forehead deterred him from further investigation.

When the information reached the railway police at Poznan, they made a tentative identification based on a report about a traveller who had gone missing from the night express to Berlin, three days previously. That identification was later confirmed. The body was that of *Polizeiinspektor* Johann Steiger.

Chapter 13

One of the priest brothers hammered on the suspended
iron bar in the middle of the compound. Work ceased for
the day. The brick-makers stopped making bricks. The
cooks left their cauldrons. The carpenters wiped over their
saws and adzes. The tilers descended their ladders. All the
members of the community, except those guarding the
stockade wall, made their way through the lengthening
shadows to the half-finished church. Vespers was observed
as late as possible each day to allow the maximum time for
work.

At one of the long tables in the frater, Ulrich rolled up
the plans for the third extension to the Marienkirche and
allowed the draughtsman, Knight Brother Helmut, to help
him to his feet. In the ten months since he and his
companions had arrived at this lonely spot on the forested
banks of the Niemen they had constantly had to plan for
expansion. Scarcely a week passed without another group
of brothers seeking out the 'true knights' and asking to join
the community. Now, in June 1457, there were 256 members of the Order living and worshipping together in this
settlement called Elisabethenburg. Some came because
their garrison had been overthrown by or betrayed to the
Poles. Others were simply disillusioned by the weak

leadership or the poor morale of the Order and had come in search of a place where the spirit of the Teutonic Knights was preserved.

It would not be correct to call Ulrich's band outlaws. The Grand Chapter disowned them but made no attempt to track them down or disperse them. Von Erlichshausen and his senior command were far too busy with their war of attrition against Casimir to bother with a small group of dissidents. Nor did the Poles pay any attention to a disgraced bunch of knights hiding in the forest on the Lithuanian border. They posed no threat and could be dealt with once the Order had been expelled from Prussia. So Elisabethenburg was left alone. News of its existence as a worshipping community pledged to preserving the ancient ideals and rule of life of the Order spread rapidly and Ulrich found himself heading an ever-increasing body of radicals and idealists.

Ulrich staggered to the door refusing Helmut's arm. His leg was always painful, unreliable until he could get it moving. Thereafter, the limp was not too noticeable – or so he liked to think. He made his uneven way across the courtyard. Clearing this ground to make room for a few tents had, he recalled, seemed hard labour. But already the original space had been widened and much of it filled with buildings for which the felled trees had provided the framework.

There was a sudden commotion away to the left, by the main gate. The heavy portal swung open and half a dozen armed horsemen clattered through the opening, their surcoats dusty, their mounts in a lather.

Ulrich shook his head. 'More and more, Brother Helmut. Where shall we find room for them all!'

The newcomers dismounted and one of them looked

across at Ulrich, following the direction of a groom's pointing finger. He hurried across the intervening space.

'Brother Ulrich von Walenrod? We must talk.'

Ulrich smiled at the panting young man, who was little more than a boy. 'No, Brother, we must worship.'

'But . . .'

'After Vespers you can tell me all about yourself and your companions.'

The young man's agitation would not be calmed. 'We come from Marienburg. The Grand Master . . .'

'Then you will want to thank God for a safe journey. Brother Helmut, look after our new friends.' Ulrich hobbled into the church and made his way to his stall on the right of the altar.

After the office, while the rest of the community went to the frater, Ulrich received the newcomer, whose name was Hermann, in his simple one-roomed quarters.

'So, what is the news from Marienburg that is more important to you than supper?'

'Marienburg has fallen.' The young man almost sobbed the words, as he slumped in the chair.

Ulrich was unmoved. He thought of the massive castle – the strongest in Europe, unconquered in two hundred years. He pictured the confident townsfolk, who for generations had enjoyed the Order's protection. He saw in his mind drunken Polish troops surging through the streets, smashing in doors, dragging women out screaming, gorging themselves on food and wine, squabbling over valuables, rampaging through the knights' quarters smashing and burning, defiling the great church. And he was unmoved. 'We have expected that news for many months.'

'It was terrible. There wasn't even a battle. It happened at . . . at night . . . we woke . . .' Hermann choked.

'Let me spare you the agony of telling the story. I can probably relate it fairly accurately myself.' Ulrich stood by the window watching the lights of the frater grow in intensity as the sky and forest beyond were absorbed by night. He spent most of his waking hours on his feet to prevent his leg stiffening up. 'You were woken by members of the garrison – Zerwonka's men – who took your weapons and told you that you had minutes to get your horses and leave Marienburg. By that time the traitors had already moved all the garrison artillery into the Hochschloss and had it trained on the town. The knight brothers were herded into the square like sheep, while Zerwonka's men jeered and the people looked on in helpless disbelief. You were forced to mount your horses. The bridge gate was opened. You rode out into the night and somehow had to get through the encircling Polish lines. Some of you made it. Others didn't.'

Hermann nodded. 'Yes, but it was worse than that. They waited till we rose for Matins and fell on us actually in the church. They stripped us and beat us and chased us naked round the cloisters. Two of the priests were hacked to death in front of the high altar when they tried to stop Zerwonka's men taking the holy relics, statues and gold plate. Brothers were cut down in corners, unable to defend themselves. Some were forced at swordpoint to jump out of windows. It was cowardly! Bestial!'

'What happened to the Grand Master?'

'He was confined to his quarters and no one knows what they did to him there. I learned later that he was taken to the Vistula, put on board a fishing boat and left to fend for himself. He managed to get to Königsberg and has made his headquarters there.'

'So, why haven't you gone to Königsberg to join him, Brother Hermann?'

'Everyone knows now that you were right. The Grand Master – all the leaders of the Order – were wrong. Von Erlichshausen is weak. Everyone can see that now. He can't save the Order. But you can. That's why hundreds of brothers are on their way here . . .'

'What!' Ulrich stared at him in alarm.

'We're just the first. There are scores of other groups making their way to Elisabethenburg. Within a week you'll have an army at your disposal.'

Ulrich leaned back against the wall to take some of the weight from his left leg, to ease the pain so that he could think. After a long silence he said, 'And what am I supposed to do with this army?'

Hermann leaped to his feet and the light from the hanging lamp was reflected in eyes wide with adoration. 'Save the Order!'

Ulrich walked forward to the table. Rested his weight upon it and gazed angrily into those glittering eyes. 'Have you taken leave of your senses? Lead an army? How could that possibly save the Order? It would be an act of rank rebellion. It would split the Order, irrevocably. I have taken an oath of obedience to the Grand Master. So have you. So have we all.'

Hermann stood his ground and returned Ulrich's gaze. 'The Grand Master has forfeited our allegiance.'

'That decision is not yours to make!' He thumped his fist on the table. 'Nor mine!'

Hermann was not to be cowed. 'There's no time for niceties of protocol.'

'Protocol!' Ulrich shouted. 'We're not talking about protocol! We're talking about a solemn oath, made before God!'

The young man raised his voice to match Ulrich's. 'While you're examining your conscience, the whole country's falling into Casimir's hands. There are scores of garrisons that want to remain loyal to the Order. They've seen Marienburg surrender to the Poles and they're looking for leadership. It isn't coming from Königsberg. If it doesn't come from you, they'll decide that the only thing they can do is get the best terms they can from Casimir. If that happens the Order is finished.'

'And if the Order is divided against itself it's finished. Brother Hermann, those of us who came here did not do so to set up a rival body. Every one of us has renewed his vows. We live a life of prayer and work, and we remain under the Grand Master's authority. When he summons us to the fray we shall be ready. If you are looking for someone to lead a revolt you must search elsewhere. I advise you to sleep on that thought.'

Ulrich himself spent a sleepless night. Matins provided a welcome interlude of common purpose and devotion but he returned to his bed to pass the remaining dark hours in renewed wrestling with complex and frightening thoughts. After Prime he summoned to the frater Conrad, Father Sebastian and young Wilhelm von Hagen. He had come to rely increasingly on this unofficial 'council', with its combination of wisdom, holiness and exuberant enthusiasm. As the other three sat together at one of the long tables, Ulrich paced the room and told them the news from Marienburg.

Wilhelm fidgeted and plucked stable-strands from his unkempt bush of hair. (He was in charge of the horses.) 'I said we should have finished the little Bohemian off while we had the chance.'

Conrad gazed into space, his words a private reflection rather than a statement. 'It isn't Zerwonka that's the real problem. The heart has gone out of the Order.'

Sebastian looked up sharply. 'We mustn't give way to the sin of despair, Brother.'

'Is it despair to acknowledge the truth?' Conrad's eyes were dark in his deceptively impassive face. 'I don't think so. We've lost our vision. Our leaders have become politicians, negotiating for land and power, instead of standard bearers of a holy mission.'

Ulrich turned from the window. 'But is our task to put heart back into the Order?'

Sebastian provided the answer. 'Whether we like it or not, we're becoming the rallying point for those who still carry some of the fire of your mission, Ulrich. I believe that gives us a measure of influence, even authority.'

'Does it? Don't we run the risk of being forced into ill-considered action by disgruntled brothers frustrated by defeat, who simply want to hit back at the invaders?'

No one ventured a reply. Ulrich knew that they were looking to him for leadership. 'I think perhaps I should go to Königsberg and ask for a meeting with the Grand Master.'

Conrad shook his head. 'If you show your face there, they'll put you under guard.'

Wilhelm jumped up. 'Not if he has an army at his back! With a few hundred men behind him, the Grand Master will have to listen . . .'

'No!' Ulrich had gone over all these arguments during the long dark hours. 'No, Wilhelm, we can't be seen to threaten the Grand Chapter. If I go alone – put myself at risk – they'll see that I'm sincere. They'll have to listen to me.'

'Madness!' Wilhelm shouted and Sebastian muttered his agreement.

Conrad shook his head again, wearily. 'Brother Ulrich, are you still so naive? These men are politicians. They have reputations, status to maintain. Although they would deny it, that is more important to them than preventing the disintegration of the Order. They can't be seen to be taking advice from a disgraced, junior knight brother. I agree that we must make contact with Königsberg, but we must do so in strength – not to threaten, but to make them see we cannot be ignored.'

After a further half hour's discussion it was agreed that Ulrich would be accompanied to the new capital by a force of fifty, hand-picked knights. Wilhelm would wait at Elisabethenburg. If the deputation failed to return within a week, he would follow with a larger force.

May began warm. Maria König, dressed in a light flowered frock, relished the feel of the sun on her bare arms as she emerged from her office building and walked with easy, swinging strides across Frankfurt's Domplatz. She avoided the shadow of the cathedral although that meant taking a more circuitous route to her favourite café. She left the elaborate sandstone west front behind her and was passing the Römerberg U-Bahn entrance, when a voice behind her said, 'Maria, on your way to lunch? May I join you or would you prefer not to be seen in public with a middle-aged roué?'

Maria laughed. 'Don't be a fool, Arthur. Of course you may.' She looked up at the tall man with the muttonchop whiskers that made him look like something out of a Feydeau farce. 'Where have you been? I haven't seen you since the last meeting.'

'Oh, travelling. To and fro, back and forth, up and down. It's so hard to turn an honest mark these days.'

'Don't try to tell me business is bad. I simply shan't believe you. If I had your sort of money, I'd have retired long ago.'

He sighed theatrically. 'Oh, but commerce is such a treadmill, don't you find? Once you get on, it's so hard to get off.'

'Only if you're a workaholic by the name of Arthur Meredith.'

'And what of you, my dear? Still doing your bit to keep the alcoholics of the western world afloat?'

She smiled sweetly up at him. 'I'm still trying to sell quality German wines to discerning foreign customers, if that's what you mean.'

'Good, good. Tell me, have you cracked the American market yet?'

'I'm following up those New York and Boston leads you gave me, but there's a certain amount of resistance. The California growers are pushing their stuff like mad and making their countrymen feel like traitors if they drink imported wines.'

'I'm afraid that's typical of the Americans, my dear. You'll never convince them that something like making fine wine takes centuries of skill and experience. "Anything you can do, we can do better" – that's their motto.' His voice had taken on a harder edge, as it often did when he talked about the USA.

They were strolling along one side of the wide Römerberg, with its cordon of medieval buildings – most of them reconstructed since the devastating Allied bombing of 1944. Meredith stopped and grabbed Maria's arm. 'Can you spare a few minutes for a slight detour? There's a wonderful new exhibit in the museum that I simply must show you.' He steered her to the left, in the direction of the river.

'You still find time to be a trustee, then.'

'I'm passionate about it.' He waved his arms expansively. 'Heritage is so important, especially for Germans. If we can't come to terms with our past, how shall we prepare for our future? The tragedy is that the schools are teaching less and less of it. Someone has to try and fill in the gaps.'

They crossed Saalgasse and entered the Frankfurt Historical Museum by the modern extension, welded, not altogether happily, to the neighbouring eighteenth-century buildings. In the wide foyer Meredith strode towards the staircase but Maria paused beside the table-display of the city centre as it had appeared immediately after the Second World War. On her rare visits to the museum she was never able to pass this heart-rending exhibit. It showed Frankfurt almost totally flattened. The streets were ravines among hills of rubble accentuated here and there by a church tower or some other edifice which had escaped total destruction. It always amazed Maria that the spirit of a people could survive such devastation.

It was because she paused that Maria saw the two men. There was nothing remarkable about them. They wore dark suits and looked like youngish executives on the way to a business lunch. But Maria had noticed them walking behind her and Meredith in the Römerberg, and now here they were coming through the museum's glass doors. They paused momentarily, and Maria caught the surprised double take of the taller of the pair as he glanced swiftly from her to Meredith, standing at the bottom of the staircase.

She tensed, heart pounding. For a split second she thought of rushing for the door. She abandoned the idea. The two men, now showing an intense interest in a display of postcards and guidebooks, were between her and the exit. She stood looking down at the model. Took several deep breaths. Then turned and walked across to Meredith with a smile. 'Sorry, Arthur. I can never resist that display.'

He nodded, muttered something about the 'horrors of war' and took her arm as they ascended the stairs. They climbed to the second floor. Meredith strode briskly through several galleries, leading the way past cases filled with glittering imperial insignia and designs for the city's nineteenth-century sewers. The two followers were a dozen paces behind.

Maria tried to remain calm and to appear completely relaxed while she forced her brain into overdrive. Where were they taking her? Probably to some office with a rear exit. At this pace they would very soon reach the end of the gallery complex. She noted that there seemed to be about half a dozen members of the museum staff on this floor, and only a thin scattering of visitors. They entered the section devoted to civic plate. A heavyweight guard sat at the entrance. A party of schoolchildren were standing in front of a display of chalices and heavy gilt dishes. Meredith was leading the way along the right-hand side of an island unit in the centre of the room. Maria decided that it was now or never.

She stopped suddenly.

Meredith turned with a disarming smile. 'It's just along . . .'

'Arthur, what's all this really about?'

He looked back quickly. Saw that the followers were in

place, cutting off the only line of retreat. He nodded and gave a little sigh. 'I should have known you were too intelligent to be taken in by my little ruse. The fact is I've received orders from the Grand Hospitaller. He is convening a Vehmic court and I am to take you to appear before it.'

'Vehmic court!' The air temperature seemed to plummet. Maria shivered. 'On what charge?'

'You know the accused is not allowed advance notice of the charges.' He stooped towards her, speaking quietly, one hand on her shoulder. 'I'm genuinely sorry, Maria, but I have my orders.'

She nodded, eyes downcast. Her body went limp.

The next second she screamed at the top of her voice, swung her right fist against Meredith's cheek and followed it up with a hefty kick.

Meredith yelped and collapsed against the glass case.

Maria ran round the end of it. Momentarily the two followers were stranded on the wrong side of the display.

'Help! Rape!' Maria bisected the posse of wide-eyed children and rushed for the gallery entrance. She heard squeals and confusion behind her but dared not turn. The guard lumbered to his feet as she passed.

'That man assaulted me!' she shouted at him, and ran on.

She sped past display units and staring visitors. She reached the top of the staircase and heard the sounds of pursuit. Lift doors stood open. She ran over. Reached inside. Pressed the first button her fingers could find on the panel. Jumped back again as the shining metal slid across. In the corner was a door marked *Privat*. She darted inside. Staff washroom. Empty. She leaned against the wall, heart thumping.

Through the crack of the slightly-open door she saw Meredith's accomplices emerge onto the landing, followed by a panting Meredith. They hesitated. One gestured towards the elevator. Then they all clattered down the stairs.

Maria forced herself to stay where she was for three minutes. Then she went out and slowly descended the staircase. There was no sign of her pursuers in the foyer but Maria took no chances. She turned left and walked through the ground floor galleries until she found an emergency exit.

She came out onto Mainkai. She turned left and walked swiftly along the sunlit street beside the glistening river.

Britain did not share the anticyclonic good fortune of her continental neighbours. On a mid-May morning, Catherine Lacy sat on a broad window seat at Farrans, legs drawn up beneath her, hands wrapped round a mug of coffee, glowering at the translucent curtain of rain hanging across the valley.

'As I came back through Little Farrans yesterday I saw one of the farmers building a thing like an ark. Do you think he knows something we don't?'

Tim, sprawling in an armchair, grinned. 'That was George Toft and he's putting up a new barn. If this weather keeps up I doubt that he'll have much to put in it.'

They did not usually manage to take a mid-morning break together but Tim had had a London meeting cancelled and Catherine, who had been hanging a new exhibition since eight o'clock, needed a rest.

The phone rang. Catherine picked it up from the seat behind her. Tim listened to the one-sided conversation.

'Who? Oh, *really*! OK, Sally, put her through. Good

morning. This is *Mrs* Lacy speaking. No, we haven't. It's something I look forward to. Yes, of course you can. He's right here. I'll hand you over.' She held out the instrument with her finger on the hold button and a sickly sweet smile. 'It's your German Fraülein.'

Tim went over to her. 'Are you feeling all right, Darling? You look a little green.' He took the phone. 'Maria? How are you?'

As soon as she answered he could hear the tension in her voice. 'Oh, Tim, I need your help. There's no one else I can turn to.'

'What's up?' He tried to sound casual as Catherine looked daggers at him.

'Tim, it's the people who killed my father. They're after me. I've been on the run for days.'

'Where are you now?'

'Rouen.'

'Rouen? Why Rouen?'

'I don't know. I can't think straight. I got a train to Paris. I thought I'd try to get to England. So I set out for Dieppe. Then I realised I couldn't get across and I stopped here.'

'But why can't you come over?'

'I've left my passport in Frankfurt. I can get over land frontiers but the immigration people always want to see your passport if you travel by ferry or airline. Oh, Tim, please come over and help me.'

'Look, Maria, your best bet is to go to the police.'

'But you don't understand. I *can't* go to the police.' It was a desperate wail.

'Well, I really don't see what I can do.'

'Oh, Tim, if you knew what was really going on I'm sure you could think of some way out.'

'I'm sorry.' He shrugged helplessly at Catherine. 'Even if there was anything I could usefully do, I really can't get away from here. We're very busy at the moment.'

'Tim, please don't let me down.' The pitch of her voice rose a couple of tones. 'Look, I can help you discover the truth about your friend's death.'

'But that's all sorted out. We . . .'

'No! Tim, you've got it wrong! You think the murder was all tied up with international art smugglers. I made you think that. I had to. It's not true.'

He did not respond.

After several seconds of silence, Maria said, 'Tim, are you still there?'

'Yes. OK, I'll come. I'll fly to Le Havre in the morning. Can you get a train from Rouen?'

'Oh, yes, Tim. Oh, thank you . . .'

He clicked the off switch and sat back.

'Well?' Catherine swung her legs off the seat and faced him squarely.

Tim told her the gist of the conversation.

Catherine shrugged. 'And you're going to dance to her tune?'

'Meaning?'

'Well, she's not very subtle, is she? She wants you over there to hold her hand. So she's produced a cock-and-bull story to grab your sympathy.'

'And suppose she's telling the truth?'

'How can she be? That Dresden Text business is all sorted out.'

He went over and sat in the oriel window beside her. 'I wonder.'

'But you said it all fitted together once you'd found those papers in Geneva.'

'Yes I did. That's what I wanted to believe. There were still one or two ragged ends sticking out but I ignored them. I wanted it all to be over, to let the police get on with it. But, deep down, I always knew . . .'

'So what happens now?'

'I'll go and find out whether Maria is telling the truth. If she is I'll get her to tell me what she really knows. It'll only take a few hours. That's why I suggested Le Havre. It's a short flight from Gatwick. You can come as well if you like.'

'No. That would make it look as though I don't trust you.'

'And do you?'

She swung her legs over until she was sitting on his lap. 'I'm not sure I'd trust the pope with brazen young ladies who flaunt their charms.'

He kissed her. 'But for all you know, I've got more willpower than the pope.'

She kissed him back. 'You'd better have, buster. If I find out this German creature has had her wicked way with you, I won't just tear her eyes out; I'll start with yours.'

PART IV

THE RIDER ON A RED HORSE

Another horse came forth, a red one. Its rider was given the power to bring war on the earth, so that men should kill each other.

The Revelation of John the Divine 6:4

Chapter 14

'Well, Brother Ulrich, we can dispense with any preliminaries. You are here because I have persuaded the Grand Master, much against his will, to allow me to talk with you. There is only one subject for discussion – whether you and all those who have joined you intend to return to full allegiance.'

Heinrich von Plauen received Ulrich, accompanied by Father Sebastian, in the high-vaulted council chamber of Königsberg castle. They stood before the Grand Hospitaller who sat in a large chair spread with furs and seemed to Ulrich to have somehow shrivelled since their last meeting sixteen months before. He was flanked by his chaplain, a cadaverous individual who looked at Ulrich with mingled contempt and disdain, and a military aide who seemed bored with the whole proceedings. It was clearly von Plauen's intention to make his visitors feel that they were supplicants before some kind of unofficial tribunal.

Once Ulrich would have felt cowed by the presence of these senior members of the Order, but too much had happened to him over the last year to make him give unquestioning respect to any man. 'Sir, we thank you for receiving us, although we regret not being able to present

DEREK WILSON

our case to the Grand Master. As you say, there is no point
in tedious preliminaries. But neither is there any need for
us to discuss a return to our allegiance, since we have not
deviated from it.'

This was too much for the little chaplain. 'How dare you
speak to the Grand Hospitaller like . . .?'

Von Plauen waved him to silence. 'The Order is in crisis,
Father. It doesn't behove us to stand on our dignity.
Brother Ulrich, in the past your judgement has been called
in question – by me, among others. We were wrong to
doubt you, as events have proved. But that does not mean
that you are correct in all matters and that your superiors
are in error.'

'I admit it freely, sir.'

'Good. Then what I propose is that you bring all your
following to Königsberg. In return, we will restore you to
all your former privileges.'

The chaplain vigorously nodded his skull-like head. 'The
Grand Hospitaller is being exceedingly generous.'

Sebastian demurred. 'I must point out, Father, that
since Brother Ulrich has done nothing deserving of punishment, there is nothing generous in revoking such
punishment.'

His opposite number snorted. 'Forging the Grand Master's signature? Issuing instructions to a garrison commander without authority? These are "nothing"?'

'Those offences were mine – if offences they were. My
conscience is quite—'

'Silence!' Von Plauen brought a heavy fist down on the
table. 'Brother Ulrich, are we to understand that you want
a public apology?'

'No, sir.'

'Then it is as I said; the only matter to be discussed is the transfer of you and your men to Königsberg.'

'Not quite, sir.'

'Then, in God's name, Brother Ulrich, what *do* you want!' Von Plauen's bushy eyebrows met above his angry glare.

Ulrich took a step forward, grasped a bench, pulled it away from the table and sat down. He motioned Sebastian to the place beside him. 'All we seek is a voice in the counsels of the Order.'

'No!' Von Plauen roared. 'By Mary and all the saints, this is too much!'

Ulrich waited for the shout to stop reverberating around the chamber. Then he said, with a calmness he did not feel, 'Those who have joined us at Elisabethenburg have limited confidence in the present leadership of the Order . . .'

'Outrageous!' The chaplain bounced in his seat like an impatient hound on a leash.

Ulrich ignored him. 'I make no comment on their attitude. It is merely a fact. They require simply that their voice be heard at this table. I have come to ask for three places – for myself, Father Sebastian and Brother Conrad von Fürth.'

The thick eyebrows rose almost to meet the black hair-line. 'And that's *all* you want, is it? You wouldn't, perhaps, like the Grand Mastership for yourself.'

'That is a burden to be borne only by the man of God's choice, who has his grace to bear it.'

'Hmm. And just what contribution do you suppose that three inexperienced brothers can possibly make to the running of the Order?'

'Sir, as a pledge of our loyalty, we offer you a plan for the recapture of Marienburg.'

The Grand Hospitaller laughed. 'Do you imagine that

we haven't gone over all possible schemes for retaking Marienburg?'

'I doubt whether our strategy has occurred to you, sir.'

'So? What is this wonderful strategy?'

'First, sir, do you agree to our request?'

'That's not a decision for me to make. It would have to be discussed by the Grand Chapter.'

'Then, by your leave, sir, we will await the result of your deliberations.'

While the three men at the table stared in disbelief, Ulrich and Sebastian walked slowly to the door.

The waiter set down two beers, and sauntered back towards the café, flicking his cloth at the other pavement tables as he passed. At mid-morning on a coolish day he did not have many customers. In a couple of hours he would be rushed off his feet. Meanwhile, he conserved his energy.

'Well, I'm catching the afternoon plane back so, whatever your problems are, we've got five hours to sort them out. But first you have some hard explaining – not to say apologising – to do.' Tim looked at the young woman opposite, trying not to be moved either by the animal appeal she exuded or by her apparent distress.

Maria looked frightened, nervous. But how genuine was her appearance of helplessness? She was a creature of quick-change moods, but were her metamorphoses just the products of an unstable personality? He recalled Catherine's simple but pointed parting message as he left Farrans after a very early, rushed breakfast – *caveat emptor*. Maria's greeting at Le Havre airport had been effusive. She had seemed genuinely overcome with relief and gratitude. But she had said nothing during the brief cab ride into the town centre.

She stared miserably down into her glass. 'Now you're here, I don't know what to say, where to begin.'

'Try the truth. That would make a refreshing change.'

She shook back her tumble of chestnut hair. 'Oh, Tim, don't make it harder for me.'

'Is there any reason why I should make it easier?'

'Look, I know I lied to you, but I really had no choice.'

'Convince me.'

Maria sighed deeply. She gulped at her beer. Then she began her story.

'It's about Arthur Meredith.'

'What about him? In Vienna you gave me the impression you'd never heard of him.'

'I know.'

'Another lie?'

'Tim, Meredith is fanatical, insane, evil. He tried to kill me. He's the man you're looking for. He was in New York last December. He organised the theft of the Dresden Text, and had your friend killed.'

'Why?' Tim did not mention that he had met Meredith at the Brand Gallery and knew that that part of her story was true.

Maria shrugged. 'As I said, he's a fanatic. He wanted that particular manuscript. I don't know why. I do know that what Arthur Meredith wants Arthur Meredith gets.'

'Suddenly, it seems, you're very well acquainted with him.'

'He was a business associate of my father's. When I went to live in Frankfurt with my mother, he appointed himself a sort of unofficial uncle. But I never really liked him. When I was a little girl he used to tell me the most terrifying stories – old German myths and legends. I think he enjoyed frightening me. Anyway, it was Meredith who got Oscar mixed up in that New York business. He knew that my father had certain underworld connections and he needed a professional to carry out his plan. My father didn't want anything to do with it but Meredith knew too much about his activities, so he had no choice but to co-operate. Even so, I'm sure he would have resisted if he'd known that it involved murder.'

She drank some more beer and Tim knew she was watching him, trying to gauge his reaction.

'Oscar was in a terrible state when he got back from the USA. I spent New Year with him and he was very jumpy. But the days passed and nothing happened. He relaxed and thought everything was OK. Then you turned up. That really shook him. He phoned Meredith in a panic. Meredith said not to worry; he'd take care of everything. Well, he certainly did, didn't he? It must have been him who called the police and then . . .' Her voice faltered. She fumbled in her bag for a handkerchief.

'And Oscar told you all this when you went to see him in February?' Tim deliberately kept his voice matter-of-fact, emotionless.

She nodded. 'He sent for me to explain about the Swiss account. Everything I told you about that was true. He also warned me to keep away from Meredith. He told me what kind of a man he really was and explained to me about New York.'

'So when George and I dropped in at your father's flat . . .'

'I naturally assumed you'd been sent by Meredith.'

Tim sat back, running a finger along the bridge of his nose. He tried to remember all the details of his nocturnal visit to König's apartment. 'When I told you that I thought your father had been murdered, you must have suspected Meredith immediately. Yet you didn't say anything.'

'My God, Tim! What did you expect! I was upset. Confused. I didn't know who I could trust. I needed time to think.'

'So why all that charade about your father's papers? I assume they *were* fakes?'

Maria lowered her head and muttered something.

'What was that!' Tim responded sharply, stinging her into a riposte.

'Yes!' she almost shouted. 'Yes, they were fakes. There were – are – some of Oscar's important papers in the bank deposit but I haven't looked at them, so I don't know what's in them. The batch I showed you were given me by Meredith.'

'Meredith!'

'He phoned me the morning after you broke into the flat. He said that someone called Tim Lacy was nosing around in things that didn't concern him. He said I must tell him if you made contact with me and that he would know if I lied about it.'

'So you told him about our conversation?'

'I was frightened of him. He made threats.'

'What sort of threats?'

'He said that my business had been started with crooked money – money that Oscar was laundering for a crime syndicate. He said that if the police ever found out they would confiscate all my assets and close me down. What I had to do to avoid that was throw you off the scent. He had some of Oscar's papers – old letters and accounts. He used them to make the forgeries. On the next day – Sunday – he brought them to Berlin. He said that all I had to do was

257

"discover" them among my father's effects. He promised that once you'd disappeared from the scene I wouldn't be bothered any more. I didn't tell him about the Geneva account, but it all seemed to dovetail in with Meredith's plan. All I wanted was to get the whole thing over and put my life back together again.'

'Did you give the fake papers to Steiger?'

'Oh, no. That would have been asking for trouble.'

'So what's your problem, now? What are you running away from?'

'Meredith and a couple of thugs tried to kidnap me in Frankfurt last week.'

'Why? You had obeyed his instructions. Why didn't he keep his side of the bargain?'

'I don't know! I didn't stop to ask. I ran like hell and managed to get away from them. Now, I just don't know what to do. I can't keep on running. I've nowhere to run to. Oh, Tim, you must help me!'

He sat back in his chair and gazed idly at the passers by. Elegant women shoppers – why were most French women better dressed than their English counterparts? A knot of Gauloise-smoking teenagers standing around a friend with a motor-scooter. An elderly man with an outrageously-coiffed poodle. Maria watched him anxiously but said nothing.

At last Tim shook his head. 'No. I don't buy it.'

Maria sagged. 'You still think I'm lying? Well, I don't blame you. I was afraid I'd exhausted my credit with you.'

'It's not a very convincing picture, is it? The crazy collector who will stop at nothing – including multiple murder – to acquire another trophy? However rich Meredith is, he just doesn't have the resources for what's been going on the last few months. I was deliberately led to

Oscar. That takes organisation. Oscar was killed by a policeman. That suggests power in high places. No, Maria, you should have stuck to your Russian Mafia story. It was much more credible.'

'But, Tim, I swear it's true!' She looked desperate. She was obviously genuinely afraid.

'OK, I'll accept that you've got yourself into a mess; that you're running away from someone – perhaps even Meredith. Give me the simple facts and I might be prepared to help, but don't try to trap me with this elaborate net.'

She put her elbows on the table and held her head in her hands. 'Oh, how can I convince you?'

Tim treated it as a rhetorical question and the silence between them lengthened into minutes.

Eventually Maria stood up. 'There could be an explanation.' She spoke hesitantly, reluctantly. 'Meredith sometimes spoke about belonging to some powerful organisation. He . . . hinted at having political influence . . . friends in high places – that sort of thing.'

Tim laughed. 'That's the best you can do on the spur of the moment, is it? Having come all this way I really deserve a better standard of entertainment than that.'

That stung her. 'I didn't ask you here to entertain you!'

'Just why did you ask me? What do you want me to do?'

'It's nothing much – not for a man with your skills. I need my passport. I daren't go back to my apartment to get it. Meredith is sure to be having it watched. But you could break in.' She fumbled with her handbag and pulled out a piece of paper. 'Look, I've written the address, and even done a drawing showing you exactly how to do it.'

'Where will you go?'

'As far away as possible.'

'What about your business?'

She shrugged. 'Get my solicitors to wind it up, I suppose. Fortunately, with the money in Geneva I can start again somewhere.'

Tim studied her. She really seemed serious. She was as frightened as her father had been. But of one man – albeit a man of dubious sanity? While he pushed his thoughts around, searching for a pattern, Tim ordered another beer. Maria's glass was still half full.

When the waiter had gone, he said, 'Do you really expect me to believe that you have no idea why Meredith suddenly decided to kidnap you? Supposing what you tell me is even half true, you must have given him a pretty good reason for wanting to grab you.'

Suddenly Maria jumped up. 'I've had enough of this cross-examination. I thought you were a friend. I thought you'd help me. Obviously, I was wrong.' Her eyes filled with petulant tears. 'Oh, go to hell!' She turned and walked briskly down the street.

The waiter, leaning in the café doorway, smiled sympathetically. '*Les femmes, hein!*'

Tim spent an hour or so wandering around the town, deep in thought. It was hard work pulling apart an elaborate mental edifice and trying to build something else with the bricks. After lunch, which he ate distractedly in a restaurant overlooking the gardens in the Place de l'Hôtel de Ville, he could not even be sure he had got the foundations right. He checked his watch and decided to see if Al Freeman was at his desk yet. Perhaps the American would have some new information. He was in luck. The switchboard put him straight through.

'Al, glad I caught you. I thought I might be too early.'

'Hell, I live here! What are you doing with yourself,

Tim? Not still sniffing around after your precious medieval picture book, I hope?'

'Sort of. Look, I've come up with a lead. It might be nothing but I thought I'd pass it on. You could suggest to Steiger that he hauls in Arthur Meredith for questioning. He lives in Frankfurt. He's on Robin Brand's address list.'

There was a brief silence at the other end of the line. Then Freeman said, 'I guess you haven't heard, but there's no reason why you should.'

'Heard what?'

'Steiger was following up that information your girl friend gave him about Russian Mafia connections. He went to Poland to compare notes with the police in Warsaw. He never made it back. Someone put a bullet in him, and threw him from the night train to Berlin.'

'Bloody hell!'

'You can say that again. You sure got a crime syndicate problem on your hands over there in Europe.'

Tim hired a car and drove along the coast as far as Deauville. Then he walked. The town's over-the-top 1920s grandeur appealed to him, as did the memory of a couple of idyllic, summer days spent there half a dozen years ago with a banker's daughter called Nicole. But on a windswept May afternoon the resort looked very different and his thoughts were far removed from amorous reminiscences. The wide flat beach was empty save for a couple of small bulldozers, levelling and cleaning the sand. Painters were tarting up the long row of beach huts for the coming season. Otherwise Tim had the level seascape to himself. He paced the water's edge with long strides and patiently cleared the building site in his mind.

He collected materials – some were items he had used

before; some he had previously discarded; some were fresh. He laid them out in order: conversations in New York with an odd collection of Europeans, strangely brought together; a scholar's dry description of black-crossed crusaders; a frustrated NYPD cop balked by his own superiors; TV news items in Vienna; an old man's reactionary politics; the babbling of a drunken Berlin journalist; an eccentric millionaire with a passion for old myths; a police inspector killed – but not by antiquities smugglers; the lies and half-truths of a frightened girl; and, dominating the building site, a six-hundred-year-old manuscript and a series of ruthless killings.

He began to fit them together. The structure that emerged was larger than he had expected – and a thousand times more sinister. There were gaps, missing supports which made the edifice dangerously unstable. Yet Tim had a feeling that what he was looking at was substantially the temple of truth. There was one way to test it. Maria had the answers and Tim was pretty sure he knew where she would be. If she thought he had been hard on her before, she had a surprise coming to her.

Tim retraced his steps. He found a telephone and left a message with Sally to say that his plans had changed and that he would be in touch as soon as they became clear. Then he got back in the car and drove to Octeville airport on the edge of Le Havre.

He had just cancelled his ticket when he saw Maria looking up at the main departures screen. He came up behind her.

'I thought you'd show up here.'

She spun round, startled at first, then contrite. 'Oh, Tim, thank God I found you. I just wanted to apologise.

I'm really sorry about the way I behaved earlier. It was unforgivable. It's just that I'm absolutely desperate and you're my only hope.'

Tim smiled affably. 'That's very understandable. I forgive you.' He took her arm. 'Let's go, shall we?'

'Go where?'

'I thought you wanted me to collect a passport.'

'Oh, Tim!' She hugged his arm. 'Will you? Will you, really? Oh, that's absolutely wonderful of you.' She almost skipped to the car park.

Tim allowed her to enjoy her triumph while he circuited the town and steered the small, turbo-charged Renault onto the fast, three-lane N15, signposted to Rouen. The road passed through half a dozen villages before settling to the excellent practice adopted by French highways of tracing the shortest distance between two points. He eased the car up to 130kph then broke the silence.

'Tell me about Johann Steiger!'

He heard a sharp intake of breath. But when Maria spoke it was with a well-managed casualness. 'You mean Inspector Steiger?'

'To be precise, the late Inspector Steiger.'

'Late? You don't mean . . .'

'Cut the crap, Maria! No more lies! No more playacting! I want the truth. Now, there are two ways I can get it. You can tell me. In which case, I'll fetch your passport and you can take off into the wide blue yonder. Or I'll bring you and Arthur Meredith face to face.'

'You wouldn't!'

'Don't bet on it. Now, I'll ask again. Tell me about Johann Steiger.'

'Stop the car!' Maria's voice shifted into a higher pitch.

Tim laughed.

'I said, stop the car.'

He felt something digging him in the ribs. He glanced down and saw the Walther P38.

Chapter 15

A light flashed twice at the base of the black mass of Marienburg's outer wall.

'That's the signal.' Ulrich stood up and stepped from the simple field shelter of branches and loose thatch in which they had lain throughout the day. He walked a few paces up the track and back again to ease his left leg into action. Then he called softly to the twenty companions who were no more than dark shapes in the moonless night. They set off to walk the last half mile to the city.

The key to the plan was Conrad's close friendship with Gottlieb Blumen, the leader of the citizens' council. Ulrich's friend had entered Marienburg in disguise and sought out the old man. Within minutes he was pouring out a catalogue of complaints about Zerwonka's regime. The people were being brutalised by the mercenaries and Blumen assured Conrad of support for any attempt by the Order to gain control – as long as it was likely to succeed. He was naturally fearful of the savage reprisals which would inevitably follow failure. Conrad had had to go over the details of the plan several times and refine a number of details before his old friend was prepared to bring together a secret committee of collaborators to help the knight brothers regain their citadel. Further long discussions had

265

followed but finally everyone had agreed that the attack would begin on the night of 27–28 September. There would be no moon and there was time to make all the necessary arrangements. The intricacies then had to be discussed by the Grand Chapter of which Ulrich, Conrad and Sebastian were now members. That meant more argument and delay. Some of the Order's leaders made no secret of their resentment at having to share power with the 'rebels' of Elisabethenburg. They opposed the whole plan as risky and quibbled over every detail. They made it clear that they expected the attempt to fail, and that they would hold Ulrich responsible for the humiliation.

As the small party drew silently near the towering walls, Ulrich felt the full weight of his responsibility. He had to succeed. Not just for the sake of recapturing Marienburg. Not just for his own sake. For the sake of the Order. If the 'true knights' could restore the Grand Master to his capital, the leadership would have to take them seriously. Open their ears and their minds to new ideas. And through new ideas be led back to the old vision. The Teutonic Knights would really be an army under the Cross. Ruling their own lands in such a way as to be an example to the rest of Christendom. Ready to lead the Catholic world against pagans, Muslims, heretics and all enemies of the faith.

The single file of men felt their way along the wall, Conrad leading. They reached a patch where the darkness was of a different texture. The postern gate yielded to pressure and the knight brothers slipped through, one at a time. The acrid smell told them that they were in the tanners' quarter. It was to Martin the leather-dresser's workshop that they were quickly admitted. They crowded into the space between tool-littered benches, acid vats and racks of hanging skins. Blumen and three of his accomplices welcomed them with mingled enthusiasm and wariness. Then the members of the party were led, in twos and threes, to their various hiding places.

Conrad and Ulrich were lodged with Blumen at his house in the fishmarket. They were up early the next morning to oversee the next stage of the plan. Wilhelm von Hagen and two other young men, picked for their strength and agility, arrived at Blumen's premises while the streets were still quiet. Theirs was the most dangerous and unpleasant part of the operation. On the ground floor, which served as shop and store room, boxes and barrels of fish were stacked. Three barrels were empty. Into these Wilhelm and his companions climbed, curling themselves into as small a space as possible. Holes had been cut in the bases to allow fresh air into the barrels which reeked of brine and stale fish. Ulrich went in turn to clasp the warriors' hands and wish them God's blessing. A false ledge was fitted into each barrel. The top third of the space was filled with salt herring and the lid nailed on. Blumen and his apprentices wheeled the casks out to the street where a cart waited. They piled the vehicle with other produce. Then a sweating and trembling Blumen climbed up on the waggon with one of his men, whipped the horse and drove it towards the Hochschloss.

There was little for Ulrich and Conrad to do now but wait and pray that their friends would get safely into Zerwonka's stronghold and remain undetected. They donned disguises and, later in the morning, mingled with the crowds in the market square. In a beggar's rags and with a crutch under his arm, Ulrich took up a position close to the Bridge Gate and watched the guards. He noted their routine and the way the massive doors were fastened.

When he had seen all he wanted, he limped back to Blumen's. The fishmonger had not yet returned. His wife was agitated. Something must have gone wrong.

Conrad came in shortly before noon.

As soon as he had climbed to the Blumens' living chamber Ulrich rose from his seat by the door. 'Any news of Wilhelm and the others?'

Conrad sat at the table and tore himself a hunk of bread. He was, as usual, very calm and self-contained. 'No, but there's nothing to worry about. There were several waggons going up to the Hochschloss this morning. They all have to be checked. It takes time.' He chewed the dark bread and poured ale from a jug into pottery beakers. 'That will work in our favour. The busier the guards are, the less thorough they'll be. I've planned out exactly what we do at the Mittelschloss gate.'

'You're sure it will work?'

Conrad's narrow face broadened into a smile. 'You've asked me that a dozen times. If you had ever seen a cannon explode because of a fault in the metal or a too-heavy charge, you'd realise that the principle is very simple. We can't get an artillery piece trained on the gate but I assure you this will be just as effective.'

'What about the guards?'

'They're pretty slack. That's what comes of having three rings of defence. They concentrate on the outer wall and the Hochschloss ramparts. After all, what can an enemy do if he gets into the Mittelschloss? He still has to breach the inner citadel. And, as everyone knows, that has never been done. Once it's dark, I think I can get right up to the gate undetected. But even if anyone spots me, by the time they investigate it will be too late.'

There was a noise on the stairs and Blumen appeared,

pressing a rag to his large, red face. He crossed to the table, took a long draught of beer straight from the jug and sank down on a bench with a long exhalation of breath.

'Well?' Ulrich stared at him anxiously.

The old fishmonger nodded. 'All safe. But there were some dreadful moments. The guards had been told to be extra vigilant. They were taking so long that the whole street between the high and middle gates was clogged with carts. Then, just as we reached the checkpoint, an officer came along and told them to get rid of the congestion. We were waved straight through. Then, when we reached the warehouse, the quartermaster started making trouble. He wanted everything opened for inspection. He said he didn't like the look of the herrings. He told me he didn't want them and I must bring them back.'

'Bring them back!' Ulrich gasped.

Blumen drank more ale. 'It was only a ruse to get the price down, of course. I had to haggle. If I hadn't he might have been suspicious. We were standing right by the barrels, bargaining, and all I could think was, "supposing one of the young knights makes a noise". Oh, Brother Ulrich, it was terrible. I've aged five years in as many hours this morning.'

'But you saw the barrels safely stored?'

'That was the next problem. We were shown where to put them and we got everything off the waggon. Then along came an officious stockman and told us we hadn't stacked everything tidily enough. He wanted us to pile some of the boxes on top of the barrels. I had to do some quick thinking. I told him that that was the best way to make sure the herring went sour but if he wanted to upset the quartermaster that was his problem. Eventually he left us alone to get on with the job.'

Conrad smiled. 'Well done, friend. You managed to loosen the lids?'

'I never fastened them back properly after the inspection. They'll come off with a firm push.'

'Excellent, Gottlieb.' Ulrich clapped him on the shoulder. 'Now it's up to Brother Wilhelm.'

Conrad laughed lightly. 'Knowing him, he will find it much harder to wait around all day, doing nothing and smelling of fish, than fighting Bohemians tonight.'

The afternoon passed interminably slowly but gradually the light faded and the shadows in the streets gathered together into larger patches. In the Blumens' unlit chamber Ulrich paced restlessly, ears straining for the sound that would signal action.

At last, the Vespers bells rang out over the city. It was the signal. He threw a dark cloak over his upper body armour and headed for the staircase. Conrad, who had seemed to be sleeping in a corner, stood quickly. From the table he took an hourglass and inverted it. The two men made their way to the tanner's shop where the rest of the company were quickly assembled.

Three miles away, Heinrich von Plauen's thousand-strong force emerged from the cover of a forest at the sound of the distant bell. At walking pace and with their horses' hooves muffled, they moved across the meadows towards the city.

The noise that reached into a corner of the garrison's storehouse was dulled but the three concealed men heard it. They stretched their stiff and aching limbs and scrambled out of the barrels in a cascade of salted fish. Stealthily, they moved to the door. Wilhelm put his ear to it and listened for any sound. When he was sure that the street outside was empty, he stuck the point of his sword between the steel lockplate and the door's planking. He applied pressure until his muscles were aching. Then felt the nails yield. He slid the bolt back and pulled the box over to hold the door in place. Now there was nothing to do but wait.

The men at the tanner's stood or sat in tense silence. They were all lightly armoured and armed and wore nondescript cloaks to cover their accoutrements. The only light came from a close lamp which Conrad held. It illuminated the hourglass at which everyone gazed time and again.

Two-thirds of the sand had run through when Conrad nodded. He closed the lamp's shutter. Someone opened the door. The knight brothers moved out into the dark street in two groups. Ulrich turned to the right and led his force in the direction of the Bridge Gate. Conrad's party started towards the Mittelschloss, one of them carrying a large keg in a rope cradle. They climbed the narrow street until they could see the gate. A light shone in the narrow guardhouse window but there was no sign of life either there or on the wall above.

Conrad and his men slipped into the side street that ran beside the wall. Conrad measured thirty paces and stopped. He took the keg and removed the bung. Peering closely he saw the trickle of black powder spill onto the cobbles. He walked slowly and alone with the barrel back to the gate. He set it down against the oak at the point where the two halves met.

'Hey, who's that down there?' The challenge came from above.

'Just on my way home, sir,' Conrad called hoarsely with what he hoped was the right mixture of fear and respect.

'Get back to your kennel and be quick about it, cur!'

'Yes, sir. Of course.' Conrad shuffled back along the

street to where his companions waited.

'Lamp!'

Someone handed it to him. He opened the shutter and removed the candle. He knelt down searching for the end of the gunpowder trail. He found it and touched the flame to it. There was a sputtering and a flash as the fire caught. The flame ran swiftly forward. Conrad silently prayed that he had left no gaps in the trail. Breathless, they all watched the retreating flicker. It reached the gateway and vanished.

The next instant the keg exploded in a roar that echoed over the city.

Tim looked at the pistol and then, briefly, at Maria. 'You want to watch out; this could become a habit.'

'Pull over!' Her voice was sharp and brittle.

Tim pushed harder on the accelerator, eyes fixed on the traffic ahead. 'What we seem to have here is a stalemate.'

'I've got the gun . . .'

'Yes. And I've got the car. And they're both lethal weapons.'

Maria stared at the speedometer and saw the needle pass the 150kph mark – too fast for this busy stretch of *route nationale*. She shrieked at him. 'Stop it! You'll kill us both!'

Tim watched the vehicle on which they were rapidly closing and did some calculations. 'If I'm going to die anyway I may as well take you with me.'

'Stop this crazy bluffing!'

'No, you stop. Drop the gun.'

Her answer was to jab the barrel harder into his ribs.

The engine whined as the car hit 160kph. They flashed past a Mercedes. It blared its horn. Road empty now for a couple of miles. Tim thought coolly. Only one thing to do.

Get it wrong and the gun could go off. It was still making a dint in his flesh.

Maria screamed more in rage than fear. '*Stop the car!*'

Tim braced his neck against the headrest. 'OK!'

He jammed his foot on the brake pedal. He wrestled with the wheel as the Renault went into a skid. He listened for a gunshot over the screech of tyres.

What he heard was a grunt from Maria as she was thrown forward against the seatbelt. The pistol clattered to the floor.

He transferred his foot back to the gas pedal. The car stopped slewing across the road and came back under control. He eased the speed down. He let out a long breath and looked at his passenger. She was slumped in her seat. Momentarily, Tim panicked. 'God, I wonder if I've broken her neck!' Then he saw her move. He leaned forward, picked up the Walther and pocketed it. He brought the Renault back to a sedate 100kph. Seconds later, the Mercedes roared past, horn blaring, driver mouthing what were doubtless extremely colourful Gallic imprecations.

Maria groaned. She rubbed her neck. Then her stomach. 'Oh, my God. I feel sick. For God's sake, stop. I'm going to throw up.'

Tim shrugged. 'That's OK. It's not my car.' He opened the passenger window electronically. 'Take some deep breaths.'

He took the by-pass round Yvetot, then swung left onto the N29 for Amiens. When they were in open country again, he said, 'Better?'

'Bastard!'

'Ah, you *are* feeling better. Right, let's try again, and this time I want the truth.'

'I can't!' A whispered wail. 'I daren't!'

'As I see it, you daren't go on telling me lies. I can turn you over to Meredith or to the police. Alternatively, I can get that passport you want so badly and you can vanish with all of Daddy's ill-gotten gains. That looks to me like a pretty classic case of Hobson's Choice.'

'You really would let me go?'

'When I'm sure you've told me everything.'

'But you don't know . . . about me . . .'

'I've worked out quite a bit and guessed most of the rest.'

She slumped in the seat and sobs shook her body. Tim thought that this time her emotion was probably genuine. He let her take her time.

At last she let out a long, shuddering sigh. 'I don't know where to start.'

'How about last December? You were in New York, weren't you?'

'It goes way back beyond that.'

Bit by bit, as they drove round Amiens, picked up the autoroute at St Quentin and headed onwards into the night, the story came out. Detail after staggering, appalling detail.

And Tim had to admit that he had been wrong. Most of the details of his mental edifice were correct but he had not allowed his imagination enough free rein. The building was nothing like big enough.

The explosion was the second signal to all four attack groups. Everything now depended on timing, co-ordination and speed. For a few minutes the Teutonic Knights had the advantage of surprise. If the garrison recovered sufficiently to plug one of the holes in their defensive rings Ulrich's plan would fail.

The three gates were attacked simultaneously.

Ulrich and ten knight brothers fell on the six mercenaries in the outer guardhouse and despatched them before they had even drawn weapons. They dragged the Bridge Gate open and von Plauen's white-clad cohort cantered through.

Conrad and his companions rushed through the shattered Mittelschloss gate. Four men were left to hold it while Conrad led the others along the narrow street which lay like a sheer canyon of brick between the middle and inner gates. Soldiers spilled out from side doorways to see what was going on. Several were cut down in their bewilderment. Conrad's party ran on towards the Hochschloss. Their advance was slowed by the growing number of the enemy. Twenty yards from the gate they came to a halt, clogged in a morass of hand-to-hand fighting.

Inside the citadel the three infiltrators sprinted the fifty yards to the gate. Wilhelm struggled with the massive bar that secured it. The others guarded his back. Mercenaries were running everywhere, some buckling on swords as they ran. The air was filled with the confused sounds of shouts and scurrying feet. Several defenders rushed to the gate as a matter of course. They could not make out the three knight brothers in the darkness until they were upon them. Then they threw themselves forward frenziedly. Wilhelm could not budge the beam from its iron slots. He heaved at it desperately. His companions formed a shield and fended off a hail of blows. Then one buckled and fell with blood gushing from a wound which ran from his forehead to his stomach.

Von Plauen's mounted warriors swept up through the

narrow streets towards the garrison. They spilled in narrow file through the Mittelschloss gate, now thrown wide by Conrad's men. They came up to the knot of men fighting before the upper gate. Conrad and his friends fell back. The mounted knights trampled and thrust their way over the opposition. Foot soldiers stood no chance in the narrow defile. Now the Grand Hospitaller was on the threshold of the inner citadel.

On the other side of the gate Wilhelm still struggled with the thick balk of timber that held it shut. He was bleeding now from a glancing blow to the shoulder. His solitary protector was taking some punishment but stayed on his feet.

There was a sudden crash as the first mounted knight reached the gate and struck at it with his mace. The oak shivered. It was enough to loosen the beam. It came free in Wilhelm's hands. As it clattered to the ground, he just had time to leap aside. The gates shuddered open to admit the full tide of the returning Order.

Ulrich's limping run took him frustratingly slowly through narrow streets clogged with dead and wounded to the Hochschloss. There were groups of fighting men everywhere. Ulrich ignored them. He went straight to the great church. It was dark inside; not a single lamp lit. Familiarity enabled him to make his way unerringly to the high altar. Reaching the steps he halted briefly, bowed and crossed himself. Then he advanced into the sanctuary, eyes becoming accustomed to the gloom. He explored the altar itself, the retable, the surrounding area of the predella, the side tables, the wall niches. With mounting anger he confirmed his worst fears. It was as Brother Hermann had said. Every ornament, statue, crucifix, reliquary, monstrance, chalice and pix was gone. But this was no simple act of looting. The stench of stale urine confirmed as much. The church, the Order, had been deliberately desecrated. Desperately Ulrich probed the darkness with straining eyes and fumbling fingers. There was no sign of the Great Bible. He felt jagged edges on the reredos where gilded decoration had been ripped away. Had the same fate befallen his grandfather's book – torn to pieces for the sake of the gold and jewels which adorned it? Fury choked him as he blundered from the building. He had only one thought. Find Zerwonka. Make him pay.

The search lasted over an hour. It took Ulrich through the cloisters and conventual buildings and into the castle. He surveyed the herded mass of prisoners in the courtyard. His quarry was not among them. He turned over bodies sprawled on spiral staircases. He threw open the doors of a hundred disordered chambers. He strode corridors. He climbed from floor to floor. With every step the fear grew that his enemy might have escaped.

It was when he reached the north-west tower that Ulrich sensed that Zerwonka was within his grasp. The staircase was clogged with bodies. He recognised some members of the commander's bodyguard. The clash and clang of fighting sounded from above. Ulrich scrambled over the fallen. He reached a landing where two wounded knight brothers were being tended by a third.

Ulrich shouted, 'Zerwonka?'

One of the men pointed up the winding stair. Ulrich climbed as rapidly as his throbbing thigh would allow. He passed more recumbent figures. Some groaning their pain. Others still and soundless. His feet slipped on blood-smeared steps. He reached the topmost chamber and shouldered open the door.

The light from a single hanging lamp showed Ulrich two men. Zerwonka, weaponless, face streaked with blood, was perched on the sill of a narrow window embrasure, clinging desperately to the stonework. Brother Hermann stood before him, prodding the mercenary with his sword and screaming, 'Jump, pig! Jump!'

'No! Stop!' Ulrich rushed forward.

Zerwonka, face twitching with terror, stared at him. 'Ulrich, is that you? Thank God. In God's name, call off this angry dog.'

Hermann half turned. 'He's going to die as he made others die!'

'Wait!' Ulrich laid a hand on the young man's arm. 'He must be taken to the Grand Master.'

'No!' Hermann glowered, wide-eyed with rage.

'Put up your sword!' Ulrich snapped the order. 'There are things we need to know first.' He turned to the Bohemian. 'Where is the Order's treasure? Where are the things you've stolen from the church?'

Zerwonka edged forward from the empty space behind him. 'If I tell will you let me get down?'

'Yes.'

'On your oath?' Even at the extremity of fear the trembling schemer retained some of his cunning. He knew his enemy.

'On my oath.'

'There's a concealed chamber in my quarters.' Zerwonka jabbered the information, watching Hermann's still unsheathed sword. 'There's a large tapestry. The door's behind.' He stretched a foot tentatively forward.

That was the moment Hermann lunged. '*Now* jump!' he roared.

Zerwonka fell backwards into the blackness of the night. Ulrich heard the beginnings of a scream. Then there was silence.

Hermann turned truculently. '*I* didn't give my oath.' He strode from the room.

Chapter 16

Ulrich was oblivious to the pain in his leg and the exhaustion which tried to claim his whole body. He stumbled down staircases, through debris-strewn chambers, over fallen bodies. There was something he had to do – and quickly. The sounds of conflict had died away. There were a few hiding traitors still to be flushed out but, for all practical purposes, Marienburg had been re-taken. Soon von Plauen would be inspecting the fortress. He would have groups of men out to assess the damage, to attend to the wounded, to seek out and secure the property of the Order. There was one piece of property Ulrich was determined to secure first.

The entrance to the Grand Master's palace was open and unguarded. Ulrich had never been inside the building but, fortunately, torches burned in many of the sconces, illuminating corridors and stairways. He entered room after room, oblivious to the splendid furniture and hangings. He was looking for the main bedchamber. He guessed that was where Zerwonka's hidden hoard lay. If he was wrong, he would have to start on a more extensive search and he knew there would not be time.

Ulrich pushed open another door and encountered total darkness. He grabbed a torch from its bracket and thrust it inside the room. Nothing. The chamber was completely empty. He cursed Hermann's impatient lust for revenge. A few seconds more and he would have forced Zerwonka to tell him precisely where his personal loot was stored. He stumbled on and began climbing a winding stair with strength that was now ebbing rapidly.

On the first floor he found, at last, what must be the Grand Master's suite of private rooms, the quarters that, beyond a doubt, the usurping Bohemians would have appropriated. The last of a series of three interconnecting chambers was a lofty bedroom. It was lined on three sides with enormous tapestries. Ulrich's torchlight played on allegorical scenes in which larger-than-life figures were frozen in acts of high drama.

Clumsily, hastily, impatiently, Ulrich wrenched them away from the wall, thrusting his guttering flame behind. Time after time the flickering light reflected from bare stone. At last, beside the bed he discovered a small door. He grabbed the iron handle, twisted it, pulled. The oak did not yield. The door was locked.

Ulrich screamed and almost wept with frustration. He stood in the centre of the room and forced himself to be calm, to think. Should he search the chamber. No. Useless. He knew Zerwonka too well. The avaricious little thief would never have let the key out of his sight. It would almost certainly be on the mercenary's crumpled and bloody body, in some alleyway or courtyard.

Ulrich heard the sound of distant steps and voices. Von Plauen's men? The Grand Hospitaller himself? Ulrich drew his sword and rushed back to the concealed door. Summoning up reserves of power from deep in his being, he hacked at the frame by the lock. Splinters flew. A gash was carved along the edge. It was enough to force his blade in. Ulrich leaned all his weight against it. He felt the sweat running into his eyes as he strained every muscle. The next moment he was sprawling on the rush-strewn floor as the door opened with a crash.

Now he heard running footsteps. The sound had attracted the attention of the approaching knights. Ulrich barely had time to grab up the torch and hobble into the secret chamber before three men came into the room behind him.

A gruff voice demanded, 'Who are you and what are you doing here?'

Ulrich identified himself and held his torch aloft. 'Checking the safety of the Order's treasures.'

The soldiers gazed, speechless, at the open chests filled with coin and plate that gleamed in the light.

'Stay here and guard it,' Ulrich ordered. 'I will report to the Grand Hospitaller that it is safe.'

He sidled past them, one hand holding the torch, the other grasping the Marienburg Bible, concealed beneath his cloak.

Catherine was working late on the exhibition layout when the phone rang.

'Hello,' she observed distractedly.

'Hello, Darling.'

'Tim? Where the hell have you been? Where are you?' She had sudden total concentration.

'I know, I know, I should have phoned but things began happening rather quickly.'

'Well, you'd better have an A1 excuse ready to hand. You go chasing off with a *femme fatale* and all I get is a message left with Sally saying you'll be in touch.'

'Darling, you've every right to be angry and I'm sorry.

But I can do better than give you an excuse. I want you to come and join me.'

'Where?'

'Gdansk.'

'Gdansk!'

'Yes, in Poland.'

'I know where it is. What I don't know is what you're doing there.'

'It's a long story but . . . well . . . I've got to the bottom of this whole business. I'd like you to be here to see it all wound up. You deserve that after all you've had to put up with over the last few months.'

'Oh yeah? And where's the König woman?'

'Maria? I've sorted her problem out and packed her off.'

'She's not still with you?'

'Absolutely not. It'll be just you and me, I promise. As soon as we've finished in Gdansk we'll take a few days' break and visit some of the places you've always wanted to see – Warsaw, Prague, Berlin.'

'I've been to Prague.'

'Well, it's very different now. Throw some things in a bag and get yourself to the airport, first thing in the morning.'

'What! That's absolutely crazy. I can't . . .'

'OK, so let's be crazy. There's a flight to Gdansk via Warsaw that leaves at 11.40. I've already booked you on it.'

'Tim!'

'Please, Darling. Let's put this wretched Dresden Text business right behind us and get on with our lives.'

'Oh, talking about the Dresden Text reminds me. One of your other girl friends was on the phone today. It was that woman in Geneva, Gerda Frankl. She said she had some urgent information for you. *Unfortunately*, I couldn't tell her where to contact you, only that you'd gone to meet Maria.'

'I'll call her first thing. And I'll see you tomorrow afternoon.'

'I didn't say . . .'

'Please! I miss you. I need you here.'

'In the Dragon's lair? I thought you wanted me to stay cooped up in Camelot?'

'What?'

'Skip it. You're quite mad, you know. However, if I've got to change all my plans, I guess I'd better make a start.'

'Great, Darling! See you soon. Love you.' The line went dead.

Two weeks after the reconquest of Marienburg, von Erlichshausen summoned a Grand Chapter to meet at Königsberg. Ulrich, who rode the eighty miles with Conrad and Father Sebastian, could not understand why the Grand Master had not returned to his capital for the meeting. He soon grasped the political realities of the situation all too clearly.

'We thank God for your success and your safe return, Heinrich.' Von Erlichshausen smiled at the Grand Hospitaller, who sat at the other end of the long council table.

'Amen, sir. We must also show our gratitude to Brother Ulrich von Walenrod and his companions. It was their brilliant plan and their bravery in executing it . . .'

'Quite so.' The Grand Master waved his hand in Ulrich's direction. 'Very commendable. I shall have something to say about that later. First, we have a more urgent matter to discuss. Regaining Marienburg has given us a very strong negotiating position and Casimir has been forced to agree to a truce.'

A truce? Ulrich opened his mouth to shout a protest, but Sebastian, seated opposite, frowned and shook his head.

Von Erlichshausen continued. 'The Vice-Master has just returned from the Polish camp where he has been discussing preliminary terms. We must now consider those terms. Vice-Master?' He indicated a small, bald man on his right. Reimar von Tiefen was nondescript. Few people outside the Order's inner circle knew much about him but everyone said that he exercised considerable influence over the Grand Master. Some believed that he was the real power in the Order.

He cleared his throat, then paused while he gazed self-importantly round the table. When he was satisfied that all eyes were on him, he made his report. 'The fall of Marienburg has greatly shaken King Casimir, and it has encouraged our own garrison commanders to stand firm. On the basis of this we have discussed truce terms which, God willing, will lead to a permanent settlement of hostilities. The principle points are as follows: Casimir will withdraw all his troops and dissolve his alliance with the Prussian dissidents. In return we will recognise Polish suzerainty over Prussia, pay a war indemnity of 100,000 florins, and agree to a Polish garrison in Marienburg.'

Ulrich could no longer keep silent. 'Those terms are not just impossible; they're an insult to the Order! As Christian knights, we acknowledge only the authority of the pope. We can never be Polish vassals!'

Von Tiefen was affronted at being opposed by such a young member of the Order. He smiled indulgently at Ulrich and looked around for support at some of the more staid members of the chapter. 'I applaud our young brother's military prowess, but he has not yet learned that the conduct of international affairs is more subtle and complex.'

Ulrich was not prepared to be patronised. 'If Rome heard these proposals, we should see a very speedy end to Casimir's ambition.'

The Vice-Master sighed. Slowly, as though speaking to a child, he explained. 'Casimir is in constant communication with his holiness. Pope Calixtus desperately needs men and money for his crusade against the Turk. In return for Casimir's help, he turns a blind eye to events in Prussia. We cannot match Casimir's bribes. Therefore, we are of no interest to Rome. We have few outside friends. So we must use our own slender resources and our wits to negotiate for the best terms we can get.'

Ulrich looked round at the nodding council members, seeking for someone who would support him. 'Then all that blood shed at Marienburg was wasted.'

'Not at all.' It was von Plauen who tried to relieve Ulrich's despondency. 'As the Grand Master has explained, your fine piece of work has enabled us to obtain better terms.'

'So it was never intended that we keep Marienburg, the Order's capital, our greatest stronghold? It was just something to bargain with.'

The Grand Master fixed him with a stern stare. 'Brother Ulrich, you cannot see the broad picture. You lack knowledge and experience. What I and the members of this chapter are concerned with is not individual garrisons, but the survival of the Order.'

Ulrich felt utterly miserable. He looked for support to Conrad and Sebastian and received nods and encouraging smiles from them. When he spoke it was in a soft voice that some round the table had to strain to hear. 'With respect, sir, the Order will not deserve to survive if it forsakes its principles and the heritage that our fathers fought and died for.'

The Vice-Master leaned across and whispered something to von Erlichshausen, who nodded. The Grand Master looked directly at Ulrich. 'Over these last months the name of Walenrod – a noble name in the annals of the Order – has been sullied. Your honour and dedication have been called in question. Some of us round this table have shared those doubts. We were wrong. You have not only cleared your own name. You have given all your brethren a lesson in patience under suffering and generosity towards those who may have given you cause for resentment. You have done more. By putting your talents at the disposal of the Order, in accordance with your oath, you have written an important chapter in the chronicle of the Knights of St Mary of Jerusalem. It is my decree that you be now fully restored to your rank and privileges, and that you be accepted by all in our brotherhood as an honoured and honourable knight brother.'

There was a murmur of assent round the table.

Ulrich allowed himself to be moved by the speech. The honeyed commendation, therefore, left him unprepared for the bitter words which followed.

'To show the faith which we have in you, Brother Ulrich, I am appointing you to command the garrison at Riga. Your colleagues, who have helped the Grand Chapter so much in our recent deliberations, are also rewarded with important positions. Father Sebastian will take over leadership of the monastic community at Elbing. Brother

Conrad, you are to be the new commander at Allenstein. You are to leave for your new assignments in a week. Go now, with my blessing and the profound thanks of the Grand Chapter.'

Minutes later, the three friends stood, still dazed, in the courtyard of Königsberg castle. They stared at each other unable to still and express their tumbling thoughts until Conrad muttered the one word, 'Tricked.'

They walked in silence down to the town. Only when they were seated in a tavern fronting the market square were they able to share their thoughts and feelings.

It was Conrad who analysed the Grand Master's verdict with uncharacteristic bitterness. 'Clever. My God, they've been clever. Banishment dressed up as promotion. The greybeards hate what we stand for. They've no intention of even listening to our point of view. So they're dispersing us. Riga in distant Livonia; Allenstein well to the south; Elbing, von Plauen's headquarters close to the coast – my God, they've put enough miles between us to make sure we never meet again.'

Sebastian agreed. 'Worse than that: if we obey, our followers will assume we have abandoned them in return for personal honours.'

Ulrich gloomily looked at the other side of the coin. 'And if we disobey, we effectively put ourselves outside the Order.'

Conrad nodded. 'Either way, they'll silence all criticism. They'll go on bargaining away the Order's citadels and sovereignty until there's nothing left.'

The three men sat for a long time drinking their ale in silence.

At last Ulrich said, 'I must talk with the Grand Master.'

Sebastian ran his finger through a pool of spilled ale.

289

'He won't see you. Von Tiefen will make sure of that. Anyway, what will you say?'

'I'll tell him that I'm not strong enough for such an important military command. I'll ask his permission to retire to Elisabethenburg to follow a life of prayer.'

'Elisabethenburg!' Conrad banged his empty tankard on the table. 'That is the one place he'll never allow any of us to go.'

'I must, at least, ask. To go without having sought permission would be open rebellion. It would mean breaking my oath to the Order.'

The three men gazed at each other in morose silence until Conrad voiced what they were all thinking. 'We are the Order – what remains of it. It is not we who have broken faith. We have not bartered away lands, towns and fortifications. We have not abandoned the thousands of people who look to the Order for protection. We haven't compromised our principles.'

'The faithful remnant.' Sebastian muttered the words almost to himself.

'What was that, Father?' Ulrich asked.

The old priest sighed deeply. 'A thought that comes either from the throne of God or the lake of fire. It has been haunting my prayers for some time past.' He paused, seeking the right words. 'We read in Scripture how God often works through a faithful remnant. Under the old dispensation the people worshipped idols and stoned the prophets. So God resigned them to their apostasy. Yet he always kept for himself a faithful remnant who did not bow the knee to foreign deities. When he came in the shape of man, born of woman, his people, the Jews, rejected him. He found only a remnant – twelve men – to follow him. Yet with that remnant he established his church.'

Conrad nodded solemnly. 'And now we are the remnant. The leaders of the Order have rejected us and God has rejected them.'

Ulrich felt the almost intolerable weight of his friend's words. 'Is it not a great presumption, Father?'

Sebastian nodded. 'Yes. Or a great destiny to be accepted humbly.'

Conrad said, 'It is not something we have sought. We called ourselves the true knights. We prayed for the Order and we tried to be a reforming influence within it. We subdued the rebellious spirits who demanded change and wanted to challenge the leadership. At Marienburg, God vindicated us. We behaved honourably, obediently at all times. If we now walk a different path, men may call it rebellion but our consciences will be clear.'

The next few days were the most difficult Ulrich had ever had to face. At the same time as he was trying to sort right from wrong, truth from falsehood in his own mind, brother knights were resorting to him, singly and in small groups. What was Brother Ulrich going to do now? What advice did he have for them?

At the last, it was the Grand Master who unwittingly resolved the dilemma. He issued an order authorising Ulrich to hand-pick thirty men who were to be his escort to Riga and a reinforcement of the garrison. He even provided a room for the new commander to assemble his retinue.

With the aid of Conrad and Sebastian, Ulrich selected thirty of the most trustworthy and dependable members of their Elisabethenburg community. Ulrich explained to them the course of action he had, at length, decided to take. He gave them the opportunity to withdraw if they wanted to remain loyal to the official leadership of the Order. No man moved.

They stood, packed quite tightly in a small tower room and waited for their instructions. There was little light from the single, narrow window. A sudden squall had blown in from the Baltic sending grey thunder clouds rumbling over the town. Only those in the front rank saw Ulrich stoop to lift from the corner of the room something wrapped in cloth.

Ulrich removed the covering, turned and held up to them the Marienburg Bible. 'My brothers, I call on you to renew your vows to the Order of St Mary of Jerusalem as now reconstituted.'

He embarked on the familiar litany of initiation and every man present quietly and firmly made the responses.

'Will you fight for the Christian faith against unbelievers and heretics?'

'We will with God's help.'

'Will you go to any land where you are sent?'

'We will with God's help.'

'Will you care for the sick?'

'We will with God's help.'

'Will you practise any craft in which you are skilled as ordered by your superiors?'

'We will with God's help.'

'Will you obey the Rule of our Order?'

'We will with God's help.'

'Then, brothers, I call upon you to make your submission.'

One by one, the knights came forward and kissed the book in Ulrich's outstretched arms.

Two days later, after a special mass, Ulrich led his mounted contingent out of Königsberg. At a prearranged spot they were joined by Conrad and Sebastian. Then they turned southwards and made their way rapidly across country in the direction of distant Elisabethenburg.

It was soon after 5.00 am that the Renault emerged from the all-but-deserted autobahn system onto the lead road into the centre of Frankfurt. Following Maria's instructions, Tim drove the length of Theodor Heuss Allee, circuited the Ludwig Erhard public gardens and turned onto Westendstrasse.

'Pull into that side road and park.' Maria was looking extremely nervous. A pedestrian coming round a corner sent her ducking down out of sight.

'For heaven's sake, relax. Meredith hasn't got agents scouring the streets for you at this hour.' Tim was tired and not in the best of moods. 'Now, let's get this over with. Where's your apartment?'

'It's three blocks away. You take the first left. Just past the school, you'll come to a brick wall. Climb that and you're in the car park of the apartment block. There's a back door. It will be locked, but that won't be a problem. You go up the service stairs. Number 17 is on the third floor. Here's my kitchen door key. If there's no one watching, use it. But if you're in any doubt, carry on up to the roof and come down the fire escape. Once you're inside . . .'

'OK, OK. We've been over the details. I still think you're panicking unnecessarily. The chances of your place being indefinitely staked out are remote.'

'You don't know Meredith. Now go. And please, be careful.'

Tim got out of the car, stretched, yawned and set off on his quest for Maria König's passport.

293

Walking briskly through empty streets, he reached the gymnasium, passed it, came to the wall, and swore. Maria had neglected to mention that it was ten feet high. He explored its smooth brick surface. There was no suggestion of a foothold. Access to the school compound was easier. He prowled the yard in search of a ladder, a dustbin, anything that could provide a platform. What he found was the school minibus, parked at the rear of the building. In seconds he had forced the lock and released the handbrake. He rolled the vehicle backwards until it was resting against the wall of the adjoining property. From the top of the bus he peered into the car park. There wasn't so much as a prowling cat. He dropped onto the roof of a BMW and jumped lightly to the ground. The lock of the building's rear door indeed posed no problem, as Maria had suggested. Tim allowed his eyes to grow accustomed to the darkness within, then he went quietly up the stone staircase. The third floor landing was deserted but Tim climbed another flight to make sure that no one was watching from above. Satisfied, he let himself into Maria's flat, took out a pocket torch and steered his way across the small kitchen. The far door led him into a hallway. He ran the torch beam along the wall opposite. Door, small table, chair, another door, man in a leather jacket. Tim stiffened, then stepped back inside the kitchen. He was too slow. A blow from some soft, heavy object caught him on the side of the head.

Chapter 17

Tim did not black out. He just lay on the cushioned vinyl and watched the kitchen cabinets perform an aerial ballet.

Someone had switched the light on. As the room stopped spinning, he saw his assailant, a heavily built, fair-haired youth, grinning down at him from behind a hand gun. Then a taller man came in, pushing the thug aside, a man Tim had no difficulty, even in his dazed state, in recognising.

Meredith rubbed his eyes and straightened his tie, obviously emerging from sleep. He leaned forward, offering Tim his hand, and helped him to his feet. 'Oh dear. I feared our resourceful Miss König would get you to do her dirty work. I'm genuinely sorry, Tim. Her selfishness is involving you in more unpleasantness. I'm afraid we shall have to restrict your movements slightly.'

Meredith took the gun while his accomplice bound Tim's hands behind him. He gave the pistol back and smiled apologetically at his captive. 'Now, will you please tell us where we can find Maria?'

Tim glared back angrily. 'You'll have to get a hell of a lot tougher to force anything out of me. Doubtless you have an extensive repertoire of tortures.'

Meredith stroked his luxuriant whiskers. 'Now, I wonder

what makes you think that? I don't know what Maria has told you, but I do really have a very good reason for wanting to see her urgently. I can't explain now. Time is short. She'll doubtless be expecting you back and if you're much later she will probably do another disappearing trick. It could take weeks or months to find her again. I'll ask you once more – where is Maria?'

Tim shook his head.

'Then I must reluctantly resort to threats. *Kurt, der Klebestreifen.*'

The other man tore a strip from a roll of thick brown sticky tape and fastened it over Tim's mouth.

'Come with me, please.' Meredith led the way across the hall to a sitting room. He motioned Tim to an armchair. 'What I am going to do is barter your wife's safety for Maria.'

Tim felt suddenly sick. Helpless, bewildered and fearful, he could only glare up at Meredith. He couldn't have got to Catherine. Yet somehow Tim knew that he had. He tried to jump up but a firm hand on his shoulder restrained him.

Meredith continued. 'Please don't waste time. When you hear what I have to say, you will realise how important it is to co-operate. Now your wife . . . Catherine will, in a few hours, be setting out for a destination I have given her – or, as she thinks, which *you* have given her. You will, I suppose, require proof of that?'

Tim nodded vigorously.

'Very well.' Meredith picked up the telephone from the table beside Tim's chair. He held the receiver so that Tim could see the numbers. 'I'm calling your home.'

Tim heard the dialling tone ring for a long time. Then, unmistakably Catherine's sleepy 'Hello.' Meredith spoke into the receiver – only it was not Meredith's voice but Tim's own which he heard. 'Hello, Darling, it's me again. Sorry to wake you at this ungodly hour. I've just realised I forgot to give you the flight number.'

Tim stared, horrified. Bloody hell, the man was an incredible mimic. No wonder Mike had been taken in by him. As Meredith held the phone between them, he heard Catherine reply, 'That's OK. I phoned Heathrow and got the details. This is all very mysterious, Tim.'

'I'll explain everything later. Have a good journey and go carefully. Leave yourself plenty of time to get to the airport.'

'I'll be setting off at about 8.30.'

'See you later, then. Goodbye, Darling.'

'Goodbye.'

Meredith replaced the receiver. 'Now, the kind of welcome Catherine receives depends entirely on your behaviour in the next few seconds. Are you going to tell me where I can find Maria?'

Tim nodded.

Meredith motioned to his sidekick who ripped off the gag. Tim gave precise directions to the parked Renault. Meredith picked up the phone again and relayed the information to an accomplice.

He subsided into an armchair, sighing his relief. 'Let's hope we're in time.'

Tim sat dazed. His head still throbbed and his thoughts and feelings were a jumbled mess. He stared at the slumped, weary-looking figure opposite. 'Maria told me about you, but I thought she was exaggerating. I was obviously wrong. When was it that you parted company with reality, Meredith? There must have been a time when you weren't a fanatic. When did you decide that the cause was all important; that ends justify means; that you can go round murdering and kidnapping people with impunity?'

Meredith just sat staring into space.

Looking at him, Tim felt his fear, even his anger, being overlaid by an insistent curiosity. He really did want to know whether this man was just sick or whether, somewhere behind his bizarre, ruthless behaviour, there was some twisted logic. 'So what happens now? What are you going to do with Maria, Catherine and me? Three more murders? Three more steps along your own path to hell?'

Meredith motioned to his accomplice. '*Kurt, befreie ihn!*'

The young man pulled Tim to his feet and untied his hands.

Meredith stood also. 'I'm sorry I had to truss you up, but it was necessary to ensure that you didn't make trouble. There was no time to spare for coping with heroics. As it is, we may have delayed too long. Now, how about a drink while we wait? I noticed a rather good Moselle in the fridge.' He gave Kurt a brief order. The man went out and returned with a bottle and glasses.

Meredith poured the wine and raised his glass. 'To better times.'

Tim made no response to the toast but he drank gratefully. His throat felt as though it was lined with dusty bristles.

Meredith rubbed his tired eyes. 'It's been a long, unpleasant night for both of us.'

Tim glowered. 'Don't bracket us together. You and I have nothing in common.'

Again the tall German ignored the taunt. 'I'm sure you'd like to freshen up. The bathroom is through the bedroom over there.'

Tim grabbed the opportunity for a quick shower. While he was drying he heard the buzz of a telephone. Back in the sitting room minutes later he found Meredith standing by the door, looking much more relaxed.

He smiled at Tim. 'We can go now. My associates have picked up Maria. Kurt will have the car ready.'

As they descended in the lift, Tim asked, 'Where are we going? Is Catherine coming to Frankfurt?'

'Be patient a little longer, Tim.'

Outside, Kurt was standing at the open rear door of a Mercedes limousine. As Tim stooped to enter he noticed another car behind and thought he caught a glimpse of Maria on the back seat between two men. Meredith went over and spoke briefly to the driver. Then the vehicle – a white BMW – pulled away.

As Meredith settled himself on the leather upholstery, Tim asked, 'Where are they taking Maria?'

'We're all bound for the same destination. The others, however, will be travelling all the way by road. It would be too risky conveying her through the airport.'

'Airport! What exactly is going on? Where are you taking us?'

'We will be travelling by private jet to Gdansk . . .'

'Gdansk!'

'A Polish port on the Baltic—'

'I know where it is! Why the hell are we going there?'

'Well, for one thing, to meet your lovely wife.'

'And after we've done that?'

'I have been asked to extend an invitation to you to spend a day or two at a charming house not far from the airport.'

'An invitation which, I assume, we're in no position to decline.'

'Let us just say that the Grand Hospitaller is very anxious for you to accept. And I rather think that you would like to meet him.'

The nine years that Ulrich and his companions passed at Elisabethenburg were, on the surface, ordered and tranquil. Beneath, there was always tension and uncertainty. The knight brothers were in a state of perpetual preparedness – but for what? Ulrich, who allowed himself to be called 'Grand Master', insisted that his faithful remnant should be just that – faithful. Their task, as he defined it, was to maintain the life of prayer, ready to ride forth whenever the call to action came. For nine years it did not come. The daily and seasonal routine affected men in different ways. Some became impatient and left. Others were lulled into soporific contentment, desiring only rest after years of battle. The size of the community fluctuated but was usually around a hundred. For the first three years there was much hard work to be done. Ulrich and his friends finished the building. They cleared several acres of forest to create meadows where they could rear cattle and sheep. They dug their own pond and stocked it with fish from the river.

Father Sebastian became the religious head of the band – a sort of abbot, though he never assumed any such title. He maintained a firm but beneficent liturgical regime. He had a short way with any brother who became lax in chapel attendance but such was the love and respect felt for him that few did transgress. The saddest day in the young community's life occurred in the spring of 1463, when they laid Sebastian to rest in the small graveyard just outside the monastery wall.

Königsberg left the renegades alone. Von Erlichshausen

anathematised them. He branded them traitors and heretics. But he sent no force against them. He had much more pressing problems. The war was going badly, as the Elisabethenburg brothers knew only too well. Every piece of news brought by boatmen working up the Niemen or travellers enjoying a night's hospitality told of minor triumphs and major disasters. At Marienwerder the knights were forced to take refuge in the cathedral but mounted such a heavy counter-attack that the Poles were put to flight. Yet, weeks later in a riverain engagement at Mewe, the Order lost the bulk of their fleet. On land Casimir won few battles. He took few cities by force. It was his sheer determination that wore down his opponents. He came back year after year and never failed to return home leaving a few more Polish strongholds behind. Garrison commanders facing months of siege without succour, and without cash to pay their men, capitulated. The Grand Chapter, in repeated rounds of negotiation, made concession after concession, hoping that Casimir would be satisfied. But they were only staggering from humiliation to humiliation.

Ulrich received word of each catastrophe with sadness tinged with self-justification. It was as Sebastian had said; the Teutonic Order had forfeited divine favour. The remnant at Elisabethenburg were the sole heirs of the heroes who had fought in the Holy Land and launched the northern crusade. But, from time to time, news came that was more upsetting. One summer day in 1462 a message arrived from Ulrich's brother, denouncing him for bringing shame on the family and ordering him never to return to his home again. Conrad tried to comfort his friend by assuring him that time would bring vindication. Ulrich accepted that – with his head. Scarcely less worrying was the news of what people were saying about Elisabethen-burg in the outside world. Within a few years, Ulrich's little band was becoming the stuff of legend. Von Walenrod, a great hero, so the stories went, had retreated deep into the forest where he was accumulating a great army of men – and, some said, of angels – to fight against the Poles. The day was coming when this vast, white-clad host would sweep down like an avenging horde and drive the invader from the land. Ulrich, daily aware of the infirmity of his prematurely aged body, was wryly amused at the popular image of himself as a muscular, seven-foot hero with the most powerful sword arm in Christendom.

It was on a stormy day in late October 1466 that Ulrich received two items of news that made him summon his closest advisers immediately. They came to his quarters after Sext – Conrad, Wilhelm, Hermann and Father Otto, a thickset Pomeranian who had taken over as the community's spiritual leader.

They sat around the fire that Ulrich kept blazing most of the year. The pain in his thigh was now aggravated by the slightest damp. Ulrich looked round at their sombre faces. 'The war is over. Von Erlichshausen and Casimir have signed a treaty at Thorn.'

Conrad ran a hand over the beard, now streaked with grey. 'Do you know the terms?'

'Yes, they are worse than we could possibly have feared. The Order retains Königsberg and East Prussia – but as vassals! Von Erlichshausen and his successors have to do homage to the King of Poland every year for the privilege.'

Hermann stared at him. 'And the rest of the Order's territory?'

'Gone!'

There was a long silence. Then Conrad said, 'Then the

Grand Chapter have publicly forfeited all right to lead the Order.'

Hermann leaped to his feet. 'The time has come for us to act. We cannot stay here as subjects of King Casimir!'

Otto remonstrated. 'Brother, we are subjects of the King of Heaven. It matters not who rules our earthly bodies. Now, more than ever, we must maintain a strict regime of prayer.'

Ulrich rubbed his throbbing leg. 'No, Father, Hermann is right. We were chosen to accept the leadership of Christ's cause in these lands. Now that von Erlichshausen is discredited we must show that that cause is not lost. Besides, we have no choice. News has just reached me that a large Polish force is marching this way. Now that Casimir's army is free to move about the country, he is determined to stamp out all possible resistance. Elisabethenburg is his main target. I will speak to the community after Vespers and tell them that our time has come.'

The last echoes of the psalm faded among the deep shadows of the roof timbers. Ulrich limped from his place and stood before the altar. There was not one of the brothers who had not heard the news from Thorn and reflected on it during his afternoon labours. Now they looked to Ulrich, Grand Master von Walenrod, for leadership. They saw a man, not yet thirty, whose tall spare body, like a wind-blown tree, was twisted to one side. They saw a face lined with weariness and pain.

Ulrich took the heavy Bible from the altar and lifted it above his head. Candlelight caught the gem-studded cover and flashed a dozen reflected colours. He lowered it and held it, like a precious child, to his chest.

'My brothers, three times I have made solemn vows

upon this book. The first was when I was admitted to the Order. The second was a private moment of dedication of which I will not speak now. The third was when, in company with most of you, I made a solemn pledge to maintain our great Order, even though those appointed to command it might fail in their task.

'Today, we know that they have failed. Therefore, we must succeed. Our enemies are advancing upon us in their thousands. There are scarcely a hundred of us. Yet, within days we must face them. The odds are impossible – if we believe that we face the foe alone and in our own strength. We do not. God and his angels are on our side. He who has called us to the task will not allow us to be defeated. Does not this very book tell us that truth? We have all heard the stories – David and the giant Goliath; Daniel in the lions' lair; Samson and the hosts of Philistia.

'Therefore, be confident, and strong, and courageous and single-minded. Prepare yourselves tonight. Confess your sins. Sharpen your swords. Tomorrow, after dawn mass, we ride out once again under the black cross.'

Meredith and his prisoner were met on the tarmac at Rebiechowo by another large limousine. Airport authorities waved it through a security barrier after a cursory glimpse at a card Meredith produced.

Tim glowered at his companion. 'Right, Meredith, time for explanations.'

The German had maintained a truculent silence since leaving the apartment. During the short flight Tim had given up the struggle and allowed sleep to overtake him. Now, feeling fresher, he was determined not to be treated as a piece of hand luggage any longer. 'For starters, I want to know where we're going, why, and where Catherine is.'

Meredith nodded. 'Those questions I can answer. Your charming wife – we haven't met, of course, but she certainly sounds charming – will arrive here in Gdansk at about 15.30. She will be brought to the House. Since we have some time on our hands, I want to show you a small town called Malbork. It's one of the most remarkable sights in Europe.'

'I don't feel much like a tourist trip right now, especially with a guide who is a kidnapper, a thief and a murderer.'

Meredith sighed. 'Tim, there's a great deal you don't understand. Whatever I have done has been in response to instructions from a higher authority.'

Tim laughed. 'You're not going to give me the "just obeying orders" routine, are you? That's the oldest cop-out in the book. According to Maria, you enjoy power and violence. She really spilled the beans about you. What's going to happen to her now?'

'She will get to the House sometime this evening.'

'And where is this "House"?'

'It's a lovely old building, not far from here. Originally it was a royal hunting lodge. Now it belongs to a Polish export company which I helped local entrepreneurs to set up. It was one of the first capitalist enterprises to be established with the support of western money and expertise, after the collapse of the communist regime. The Poles need all the help they can get to build up a modern market economy.'

'And doubtless it also provides a nice, remote location for your arcane rituals. According to Maria, she was running away because you were going to subject her to some sort of bizarre trial.'

'Surely you know Maria well enough not to take everything she says at face value.'

'I believe that. She was terrified of you and your organisation – and not without cause.'

'Look, Tim, I'm in a very difficult situation. There are things that I'm not authorised to tell you. Maria has given you, I'm sure, a very garbled version of the truth – one that was intended to get you on her side. I can't correct the impression she has given you without betraying secrets I am sworn to keep. Tomorrow you will meet the Grand Hospitaller, and I'm sure he will answer all your questions. Now, shall we have some breakfast. You must be as famished as I am.'

Meredith opened a small cabinet set against the driver's partition. The top folded open to make a table. From insulated compartments inside he produced flasks of coffee, warm croissants and chilled grapefruit juice.

Tim watched this bizarre man performing simple domestic functions as casually as he planned bloody crimes. Meredith was a fanatic. Not of the wide-eyed, frenzied variety, but a fanatic nevertheless. Tim did not understand him. There was still much about this whole business that he did not understand. But that no longer mattered. All that did matter was waiting for Catherine and somehow getting both of them out of the clutches of Arthur Meredith and his insane crew.

Chapter 18

They had been driving about forty minutes when Meredith ordered the car to stop. The chauffeur jumped out smartly to open the door. They stepped out onto the roadside. It was a sunny morning, but the air had not yet lost its overnight bite.

'Malbork,' Meredith announced, waving his arm expansively. 'Or, as it used to be called, Marienburg.'

Tim was impressed despite himself. Beyond an expanse of slow-moving river there rose an agglomeration of massive walls, towers, pinnacles, a keep, and other buildings standing a solid six or seven storeys high, pierced with rows of narrow windows, topped with extravagant overhanging turrets and a roofscape of intricately patterned, coloured tiles.

'The biggest extant medieval fortification in Europe,' Meredith declared proprietorially. 'Headquarters of the Teutonic Order from 1309 to 1457. And home of the Dresden Text for much of that time.'

'Oh, yeah?' Tim frowned his scepticism. 'What makes you so sure about that?'

'I'll explain as we go round the castle.'

The car took them into Malbork, a jumble of old and modern buildings spreading outwards from the citadel.

They parked and climbed to the castle. Meredith flashed another pass at the ticket office and strode on through the main gate. 'I'm on an international committee for funding restoration work on Poland's historical sites.' Meredith easily assumed the role of a tour guide. He led Tim with confidence through a labyrinth of streets and alleys, scattering information like largesse. 'Marienburg was impregnable; built with three concentric defensive circles – low castle, middle castle and high castle. As far as we know, it never fell to a direct assault. Fourteenth-century barns – the town could withstand a siege virtually indefinitely . . . They were amazing military builders. Any invader fighting his way into the Mittelschloss could only reach the Hochschloss along this narrow defile – with the knights firing arrows and other missiles from the walls . . .'

Meredith showed him the knights' hall with its magnificent timber roof; the palace of the Grand Master with its vaulted ceilings and spacious chambers, once splendid with fine hangings and open cupboards loaded with plate; the chapels, cloisters and conventual buildings; the massive upper castle whose walls, several metres thick, encircled a veritable inner town of courtyards, passages, staircases and chambers.

He paused at last before the elaborate carved façade of the Marienkirche. 'One of the great treasures that the knights enjoyed when they lived here was a magnificent Bible. It was written and decorated by the finest monastic craftsmen and enclosed in a jewel-encrusted cover. We know about it from contemporary documents.' He led the way into the spacious church and advanced down the long nave. 'It must have been kept in the sanctuary – either on the altar or behind a gilded grille. Probably only taken out and used on special occasions. It was at the heart of the life of the Order. In 1456, at the height of what is called the Thirteen Years' War, the fortress was betrayed into the hands of Casimir Jagiellon, King of Poland. According to legend, to prevent the Marienburg Bible falling into the hands of the enemy, the Grand Master, Ludwig von Erlichshausen, had it broken into four parts and entrusted to four of the knights. They dispersed to different parts of the Order's territory. But it was as though the heart had been ripped out of the Order. From that time the Teutonic Knights declined. It was widely believed that their fortunes would only revive when the four segments of the Marienburg Bible were brought together again. When Christendom was in danger – so the story went – the four guardians would return, from North, South, East and West, and refound the Order.'

Tim smiled. 'A nice tale, and you tell it well. But it's only another version of a universal legend – Arthur and his Round Table companions sleeping in Avalon, Drake's Drum. Charlemagne waiting inside his mountain.'

'Ah, but this legend is true.' Meredith's eyes were wide with enthusiasm. 'Or, at least, it has a substantial kernel of truth . . .'

Suddenly Tim saw where this elaborate myth-spinning was leading. 'You don't mean . . . My God, you *do* mean . . .'

Meredith was oblivious to Tim's horrified reaction. 'Several years ago, in my early days as a collector, I bought a fragment of an illuminated bible, in the sale of a famous family library that had been built up over several centuries. Then, at the end of 1989, shortly after the collapse of the Berlin Wall, I was offered another manuscript by someone who had come over to the West and needed money. It was actually Oscar König who acted as intermediary. He knew my interest and he showed me the item. It was in a deplorable condition, but I realised immediately that it was identical in style to the fragment I already possessed. I had it restored and then I bound the two segments together. The more I studied it, the more intrigued I became by the depictions of armoured knights and crusading devices in the illustrations. I had already begun to take an interest in the Teutonic Knights – for other reasons – and it seemed to me quite certain that my book was connected with the Order. Then I came across Professor Fischer's monograph – I'm sure you've seen it. I dropped everything and went straight to London. Imagine my excitement when I realised that the Dresden Text was a third fragment of what I was now convinced was the Marienburg Bible and that I was the man chosen by destiny to fulfill the old prophecy – to bring the parts back together.'

'So you had to have the Dresden Text – at any cost.' Tim felt his whole body go cold and rigid with hate.

Meredith's expression changed as he sensed Tim's anger. ' "Any cost"? Hell, no. Tim, I did not murder your friend. I swear it.'

'You organised the robbery. It amounts to the same thing.'

'Tim, knowing what I did, what was I to do?'

'You could have sold your bits to the British Library.'

'I did consider that, very seriously. Then I heard that the Dresden Text was going on exhibition in New York. Fate was playing into my hands. The Marienburg Bible might still not be complete but it would be – it *is* – a work of the utmost importance, on a par with the Book of Kells and the Lindisfarne Gospels. And it has a significance even beyond that.'

Tim glared at him. At that moment there were several

rash things he might have said or done. But he thought of Catherine and the danger she was walking into, and decided to bide his time. 'I've seen all I want here. Can we go?'

They drove for about another half hour. A silent journey. Tim pointedly stared out of the window, ignoring the man beside him. He thought about the massive fortress of Marienburg and the power it symbolised. He looked out over the level landscape and envisaged the armoured knights who had lorded it over this territory and its people. Many of the small farms had tractors and silos and other aids to modern agriculture, but the car passed some fields which were being worked by horses as they had been since feudal times, and frequently it had to slow down for carts and waggons on the road. That seemed to telescope the centuries and bring closer the ancestors of these Polish people. What had they thought of the foreigners who demanded their labour and a share of their produce in exchange for an imposed religion and system of government? The Teutonic Knights had doubtless claimed that they were bringing the light of Christianity and civilisation to banish the darkness of heathendom. They presumably had no difficulty in justifying the use of force to spread the kingdom of the Prince of Peace. Did the Prussian peasants see it that way? Somehow, Tim doubted it.

Ends and means! That brought Tim's mind back to the present. To Meredith and his crew, who could justify the use of robbery, violence and murder in the pursuance of their 'higher' objectives. The implications of that were frightening. He and Catherine knew too much about Meredith and his organisation – or, at least, Tim did. There was no chance of their being allowed to walk away as though nothing had happened. Probably, they would just be another couple of tourists disappearing in mysterious circumstances. Two more digits in the statistics of unsolved crime. Well, not if Tim could help it!

The car turned onto a well-kept gravel drive, stopped briefly at a security checkpoint, and drove on through woods and parkland. It came to rest finally before a long rococo façade of tall windows interspersed with pilasters and plaster decoration.

Meredith led the way up the shallow flight of steps. 'Built by Augustus III between 1751 and 1755. An appalling king but a true son of the Enlightenment, and a patron of the arts.'

The door was opened by an elderly man in a dark suit. Meredith exchanged a few words with him in Polish as they stood in a marbled hallway from which a staircase curled upwards, bordered by an ornate wrought-iron balustrade.

Meredith turned to Tim. 'Stanislaus will show you to your room and he'll bring you up some lunch shortly. I'm afraid I have things to attend to. Please wander round at will. It's a splendid old house.'

Tim was escorted to a large, elegant chamber whose tall windows overlooked the formal gardens to the rear of the house. The room was furnished impeccably with period mahogany furniture, including a large bed, cornered by tall, fluted pillars tapering to a fringe of pink silk. The same silk was repeated in some of the gilded wall-panels. Others held romantic landscapes. The adjoining bathroom was scarcely less extravagant.

A quick tour of the house revealed that it had all been renovated and furnished to an equally magnificent standard. It also seemed to be virtually deserted. Tim came across two other indoor servants, both dark-suited like

Stanislaus. Of Meredith and his accomplices there was no sign.

The reason became obvious as soon as he explored the grounds. At one end of the rear terrace a low building ran at right angles to the main house. Its wide windows suggested that it had once been a conservatory or orangery. But it now served a different purpose. Tim could see several people moving about inside, but when he approached his way was barred by a large man who smiled but very firmly shook his head.

He set off across the wide lawn and walked briskly through the parkland beyond, taking a straight line from the house. His main intention was to find a way of reaching the road and the outside world. But half an hour's walking only landed him deep in a deciduous forest which had no discernible limits. Yet he quite failed to discover any sign of elaborate surveillance. There were, as far as his well-trained eye could see, no cameras or sensors. He went back to the house and subjected it to a close scrutiny. There was a good alarm system, probably three or four years old. Every door and window was wired. The ground floor and corridors had infra-red detectors linked to television cameras so that, when the system was operative, any movement about the house would be signalled to the control room along with a display of the relevant area.

Back in his room, Tim turned over a variety of plans and half-plans for escaping from what Catherine would probably call 'the Dragon's lair'. He lay on the bed gazing up at a painted ceiling oval depicting cavorting nymphs and shepherds. The only feasible scheme was crude in the extreme: to bypass the alarm on the bathroom window, which was on the side of the house, use knotted sheets to get down to the ground, then trust to luck that they could get off the estate without encountering patrols or concealed barriers. The odds were poor, but the alternative did not bear thinking about.

From a wooded hilltop Ulrich and Conrad watched rank upon rank of mounted knights advancing across the plain below.

'Two thousand?' Ulrich questioned.

'Nearer three. They're travelling fast for such a force.'

'Time isn't on their side. Winter's coming on. They want to finish us off and get back to their quarters. Look, they've even harnessed extra horses to their supply waggons.'

Conrad patted his restless gelding. 'Our best plan is to slow them down as much as possible. Harass their rearguard. Make repeated attacks on their baggage train.'

'Difficult in this terrain.'

'But soon they enter the forest. They can only travel two or three abreast there. Numbers count for little among trees and dense undergrowth.'

'But once they're in the forest they'll be dangerously close to Elisabethenburg. We'll have to do something before that.'

Conrad shook his head emphatically. 'I disagree. We can't afford casualties. Lightning raids in open country may irritate the Poles but we're bound to lose some men in the process.'

Ulrich tried to concentrate his mind on the problem, to keep at bay the relentless pressure of pain. Two days' riding in bitter cold had raised the agonising throbbing in his leg to an almost unbearable level.

'Don't contradict!' He glowered at his friend. 'We attack when I say!'

Conrad nodded silently. He had long ago discovered that argument only made Ulrich stubborn. For months he had watched as physical suffering and the pressures of command had eroded the leader's capacity for clear judgement. Often, he had been tempted to countermand orders, especially when other brothers grumbled about 'dictatorship' and 'stupid' decisions. But Ulrich was the leader and Conrad was wise enough to know that any sympathy for dissenters would split their little community into rival factions. So he supported his old friend and would go on supporting him – to the end. 'What are your orders?'

Ulrich's brow beneath the hood of his thick cloak was deeply scoured with concentration. 'What?'

Ulrich suddenly wheeled his horse around, his face now hidden from his companion. 'I should have thought that was obvious. Attack the enemy's baggage train. Destroy it. Without supplies they'll have to turn back. Work out the details yourself. By all the saints! Must I do everything?' He spurred back through the trees.

The knight brothers shadowed the Polish army until well into the winter's afternoon. As the sun dropped towards the edge of a clear sky they watched the enemy for signs of fatigue. Conrad had discussed tactics with Wilhelm and Hermann. They had agreed that dusk was the best time for their risky manoeuvre. After a long day's forced march the troops would have little in their minds but setting up camp for the night, filling their grumbling bellies, closing their tired eyes. That was the time for a surprise raid – when reflexes were dulled by fatigue.

Scouting ahead, Hermann found the best place for the ambush. Rising ground formed a shallow valley with outcrops of rock, affording some cover. Conrad divided his force into three. Wilhelm was to command the main assault. With fifty men, his task was to take the Poles in the flank and try to drive a wedge between the main army and the afterguard accompanying the supply train. As soon as a corridor had been opened up, Hermann would lead a dozen knights carrying torches to thrust into the waggons. Conrad himself was to command the reserve. He had to be ready to respond to whatever situation might arise – to ensure the success of the operation; to help as many of the attackers as possible to pull out of the mêlée; to ensure that Ulrich and all surviving brothers escaped into the gathering darkness.

From a safe vantage point Ulrich and Conrad watched the army approach the point where the knight brothers lay in wait.

Conrad pointed to the gap that had opened up between the main force and the rearguard. 'They're getting tired – and careless.'

The Polish host was moving slowly now.

Ulrich shivered as a biting wind from across the plain gathered strength. 'Pray God they don't stop and pitch camp before reaching our position.'

But even as he spoke the sound of a trumpet reached his ears and the vast mass of men and horses shuffled to a standstill. Soldiers began to dismount.

Ulrich groaned. 'Mother of God, could they not have gone another half mile?'

'Shall I send word to Hermann and Wilhelm to regroup here?'

'Yes, yes.'

Conrad beckoned one of the younger brothers and muttered a message to him.

But even as he put spurs to his grey and streaked away across the flank of the hill, Ulrich saw a sudden movement on the lower ground away to the left. Wilhelm and his men broke cover and charged across the level, frost-hardened ground at full gallop.

Ulrich turned to his friend. 'Stop the fool!' he shouted.

Conrad shook his head. 'Too late.'

'He'll never cover the ground in time. Look!' He pointed to the Polish rearguard, already closing the gap. Within minutes it would be at the centre of the Polish encampment, ready to unload tents and equipment from the covered carts.

'But Wilhelm might be right.' Conrad shielded his eyes against the setting sun. 'Look, he's made them panic!'

Most of the enemy troops had dismounted. Some had eased their saddle girths and were leading their horses away to find grazing. The sudden danger threw them into confusion. The watchers heard a bedlam of shouted orders. Saw men and animals wheeling around in disorganised groups.

Wilhelm's contingent gained the space between the Polish forces and went at the rearguard with swords and hand axes. The enemy fell back at the first impact but recovered quickly and formed a protective barrier between the attackers and the waggons. The air filled with the familiar clangour and shriek of battle.

The knight brothers gained ground slowly. By now the advantage of surprise had been used up. The army commander had got a body of troops into formation and was preparing to enter the fray. They would fall on Wilhelm's rear. He and his men would be surrounded, crushed.

Conrad shouted an order. Briefly he turned to Ulrich. 'Goodbye, Brother!' Then he was gone, galloping towards the battle at the head of the tiny reserve.

Ulrich was left with three companions. He saw Conrad

engage the approaching enemy. To his left he saw pin-points of light. Hermann and his men had lit their flambeaux of oily rags bound round branches.

Suddenly, he knew that this would be the Order's last battle. 'Come on!' he yelled. Someone shouted a protest but he ignored it. Drawing his sword as he went, he plunged towards the confused mass of men and horses.

Less than half an hour later, the survivors – many of them gashed and bleeding – slowly re-grouped at the prearranged spot. Behind them, the plain was lit by blazing waggons. In the lurid glow they could see groups of men desperately trying to douse the flames and drag casks and boxes clear.

But no one was thinking about the success or failure of the battle. Conrad, hood thrown back and a red-soaked rag tied round his head, gazed intently at each returning straggler. He was weak and exhausted but, for the moment, oblivious to his own feelings. All his attention was focused on searching for one face among all the familiar faces. When seventeen knight brothers had gathered, it was clear that no more would be returning. No one spoke the words, but all knew that Ulrich von Walenrod was among the slain.

'You've certainly made yourself comfortable.'

Tim woke with a start. Catherine was smiling down at him.

He jumped off the bed and held her close. 'I didn't mean to sleep. Are you all right?'

She eased herself out of his arms. 'Yes, of course. I can manage a simple air trip by myself – even one made at great inconvenience to please a demanding husband.'

'Sorry to be so fuzzy. It's just that I meant to be awake when you arrived. I guess I shouldn't have succumbed to the bed. I've missed out on sleep in the last . . . how many hours is it?'

'You left home yesterday morning for your assignation with the mysterious Maria.'

'Really? It feels like a week.'

'Boy, you're really in a bad way. What's going on?'

Suddenly Tim realised that he didn't know how to answer that question. He had not given any thought to exactly what he would tell Catherine. That he'd driven halfway across Europe with another woman? That he'd broken into her apartment? That he'd been shanghaied at gunpoint? That he had listened to another man imitating his voice to lure Catherine to Poland? That they were prisoners of a bunch of loonies who didn't think twice about killing people? He did not want to alarm her. At the same time he had to impress upon her how important it was to get away from this place.

He walked through to the bathroom and splashed cold water over his face. When he returned he found Stanislaus setting a tray of tea and small cakes on a table by the window.

Catherine poured as Tim sat down opposite. She gazed out over the sunlit flower beds arranged in geometrical pattern and guarded by sentinels of clipped yew. 'Well, whatever it is we're supposed to be doing here, it's a beautiful place. I could certainly get used to living like this. Oh, there's a letter for you.'

Tim picked up the crisp white envelope from the tray and unfolded the single sheet of expensive writing paper. It was stamped with the symbol of the Teutonic Order.

There was only a short, unsigned message.

> Dear Mr Lacy
>
> I am delighted to welcome you and Mrs Lacy to the House and I look forward to meeting you.
>
> 'I shall be delighted to receive you as my dinner guests this evening, at about 7.30.
>
> Stanislaus will escort you.
>
> > Yours sincerely
> > The Grand Hospitaller

Tim passed the letter over.

'No signature.' Catherine dropped it on the tray. ' "Grand Hospitaller"? Black cross? So this *has* got something to do with those cooky Teutonic Knights in Vienna.' Her expression said 'I told you so.'

Tim shook his head. 'No, this bunch are a very different proposition.'

'So just who are this bunch?'

'I think we'll let the Grand Hospitaller tell us that. I don't have all the answers. But, by God, I'll make sure I get them this evening.'

It was precisely seven-thirty when Stanislaus knocked at the door. He led the way to a suite of rooms at the other end of the first floor. The salon they entered seemed at first to be empty. It was a dazzling chamber of lemon yellow and lime green, decorated in the Chinese taste with gilded dragons and bamboo fronds rioting over the walls. There were mirrors in the shape of pagodas and cabinets rich in porcelain. When their eyes had recovered from the sudden spectacle they were aware of a small man standing by the velvet drapes at a far window. He turned, smiling, and advanced across the richly patterned carpet with hand outstretched.

When he was a few feet away Catherine stared hard, puzzled at first, then wide-eyed with recognition. 'But you're . . .'

Chapter 19

The midnight office was over. The brothers had retired to their beds. Conrad was left alone in the chapel. He knelt before the altar, wrestling with his thoughts and prayers as the hours of darkness slipped past.

The tiny community – reduced, now, to twenty-six knight brothers – had unanimously elected him as their new leader. That meant that he now had to decide the fate of Elisabethenburg. That, in turn, meant that he kept asking himself, 'What would Ulrich do?'

The monastery was safe – for the time being. The last battle – Ulrich's battle – had stopped the Poles' advance and sent them hurrying home to Marienburg. But they would be back. Back to raze Elisabethenburg to the ground and to obliterate its very memory. Meanwhile, von Erlichshausen continued as a puppet grand master of an organisation that still called itself the Order of St Mary of Jerusalem. Perhaps it would survive for a while – in name . . . But, eventually, it would either be extinguished by the king of greater Poland or it would decline into insignificance.

What then of the band of brothers who had followed Ulrich von Walenrod to this place to *be* the real Order? The sad truth was that the community was divided. Some, led by Father Otto, were all for remaining at Elisabethenburg to the end, if necessary giving their lives in its defence. Others spoke of moving on, to some more distant, safer location. No one voiced the fear that was in all hearts – that the great adventure, which had begun in the very land where Christ himself had walked and taught, was over.

Conrad could not bring himself to believe that. But nor could he see how the Order and what it stood for could survive. That mystery lay locked within the providence of God. All he could do was pray that God, in his own time and his own way, would revive the Teutonic Knights, or some other body pledged to spreading and maintaining the rule of Christ in the kingdoms of rebellious men.

That was why he had made the decision he had made – imploring heaven that it was the right one – and why he had shared it only with those he knew he could trust. More important to preserve an ideal than bricks and mortar. Elisabethenburg would die. The Order must not die with it.

Conrad heard a soft footfall behind him. He rose to his feet, made the sign of the cross, and turned.

Wilhelm stood by the door, wrapped in his thick, hooded travelling cloak. 'The horses are ready,' he said quietly.

Conrad nodded. 'I'll be there directly.'

As the door closed, he looked for the last time around the place that had been the centre of his life. Under Ulrich's supervision, he and the other members of their close-knit community had built it, plank by plank, brick by brick. It had become the expression of their shared vision. Now that vision must find some other way of manifesting itself to the world.

He advanced into the dimly-lit sanctuary. Only two things remained to be done. The light from the single hanging lamp fell upon the Great Bible and set its gem stones gleaming with light. Conrad unclasped the cover and opened the book upon the altar. He drew a sharp hunting knife and inserted it into the binding. Vellum and leather resisted the blade but Conrad continued with his task until he had severed the book into more-or-less equal sections. He put them back together and tucked them under his left arm.

Then he reached up to the hanging lamp. He detached it from its chain. He brought it crashing down on the altar. Rivulets of burning oil snaked across the cloth covering. Some found the carved wooden reredos. Conrad piled service books on to the blaze. He opened a chest of mass vestments, pulled out the garments and strewed some over the burning altar. Others he flung around the chapel. Only when he was satisfied with his handiwork did he turn and stride from the building.

His three confidants were in the courtyard with the horses. The first snow of winter was falling and the animals' hooves made little noise on the muffled ground. Conrad climbed into the saddle. Wilhelm walked his horse across to the outer gate. He drew back the bolts and pulled the heavy timber inwards. He mounted, and the four horsemen rode out of Elisabethenburg.

They cantered across the moonlit fields to the ridge where the forest began. There Conrad reined in. He took the four fragments of the Great Bible from beneath his cloak. He handed one to each of his companions.

'May God go with each of us and may he bring us together again – here or in paradise.'

He raised his hand in what might have been a blessing.

Then he turned his horse to the south and cantered into the night.

Catherine groped in her mind for the man's name. He was a leading member of the German government. He had been the chosen Bonn spokesman on the neo-Nazi disturbances back in the winter. Only a few days ago she had seen him interviewed on television in a programme from the EC headquarters in Brussels. At last it came to her. 'Ah yes, Herr Gerhardt . . .'

The man smiled and held a finger to his lips. 'No names, please. Here I am just the Grand Hospitaller. Now, let me arrange drinks for you.'

Tim had instantly recognised one of Europe's leading politicians. He was surprised to see how much smaller the man appeared in real life. A man in his early sixties, bespectacled and balding. Yet he exuded personality and authority. Tim's first thought was, *My God, if this man is the Grand Hospitaller, who is the Grand Master?* But he was determined not to be overawed. 'Before we get too pally, I want to know what your plans are for my wife and me. You've brought us here under duress. But why? If anything happens to us—'

The German stopped him with an abrupt wave of the hand. 'Mr Lacy, you have a military background. That makes you very direct. My training was in the diplomatic corps. I tend to approach things in a more roundabout way. But, I assure you, I do reach the same point in the end. I will deal with your questions, but we have the whole evening ahead of us. I think, if you let me handle things my way, you will understand what it is you have become so unfortunately involved in.'

He turned to Catherine. 'My dear Mrs Lacy, please

believe me when I say what a great pleasure it is to meet you and how very much I regret the – admittedly – underhand methods that were used to bring you here.'

Catherine felt the man's charm beginning to thaw her frosty suspicions. 'It was very cleverly done. Meredith fooled me completely.'

'Yes, he does have a remarkable talent – many remarkable talents. Not always very wisely directed, I fear. Now, how about that drink?'

While he busied himself with decanters and glasses, Catherine observed, 'This is a lovely house.'

'Yes, isn't it? It was built by a Polish king as a mere hunting lodge. I should point out that it's still used for that purpose from time to time. You mustn't be alarmed if you see men wandering round with rifles or shotguns.' He handed her a glass of sherry, and Tim a Campari with a bottle of soda. 'What I find so extraordinary about the place is that it was lovingly restored by the communist government.'

Tim stirred his drink. 'But it doesn't belong to the state now?'

'No, under the new regime, it was "privatised" and sold to us.'

'And just who is "us"?'

'A consortium of Polish and German businessmen with the help of some money put up by my government. We use it for a variety of purposes, but they're all directed towards achieving greater co-operation between our two countries.'

'I thought there was an ancient and deep-seated hatred between Germans and Poles.' Catherine seated herself on a canary-silk Louis XVI sofa.

'All the more reason for working hard to heal the wounds and trying to create a common future.'

The men seated themselves on matching fauteuils.

The Grand Hospitaller raised his glass of mineral water. 'To international understanding.' He sipped. 'That provides me with an excellent starting point.'

Tim grunted. 'You kidnapped us in the interests of the brotherhood of man?'

Their host ignored the taunt. 'Back in the late Eighties, three facts were becoming obvious to those of us at the centre of world politics. Number *one*: the Soviet empire was disintegrating fast. Number *two*: America was losing both the economic power and the will to continue her role as international policeman. Number *three*: as the EC grew in size it was becoming more fractious and disunited. Those three facts could only lead to that most dangerous of all phenomena in international affairs: a power vacuum. I think you'll agree that events have proved that analysis correct. Eastern Europe is ablaze with rival nationalisms from the Balkans to the Urals. Appeals to the UN or NATO to put a stop to these crises lead to political squabbling and inaction. Appeals for aid to Washington bring the wholly correct response that Europe must solve her own problems. The trouble is, we can't. We have crime, racism and nationalist tensions spilling across our newly-opened frontiers. We can't agree among ourselves what kind of a Europe we want. Every move towards greater integration sets politicians in London, Rome, Madrid, Lisbon and so on whining about lost sovereignty.

'Some of us, as I say, foresaw all this years ago. It was perfectly clear that the only way to overcome these problems was to provide Europe with a sense of purpose, with discipline, with leadership.'

Tim sneered: 'By which you mean German leadership.'

'We were the only people prepared and equipped to

take on the role. To a certain extent we already had. Our economy was the strongest on the Continent. European currency markets all revolved around the Deutschmark. We had the most powerful voice in Brussels and Strasbourg. Since 1945 we had proved yet again that the German people have a genius for leadership.'

Catherine wrinkled her nose. 'I seem to recall there was once a little man with a loud voice and a Charlie Chaplin moustache who said much the same sort of thing.'

The Grand Hospitaller did not rise to the jibe. 'Hitler was a shit of the first water. He will always be a warning to Germans not to get ideas above their station, but also a warning to other nations not to underestimate Germany. It was largely the abiding memory of Nazism that made us realise that any attempt to provide a new political, economic and ideological leadership for Europe would have to be covert, subtle. That's why we set up the Order.'

Catherine looked up sharply. 'The Teutonic Order?'

At that moment Stanislaus opened the double doors to an adjoining chamber and announced dinner. They all went through into a mahogany-panelled dining room. It was positively subdued by comparison with the salon they had just left, but even so, it was sumptuous. An immense crystal chandelier was reflected in a polished oval table laid with magnificent German porcelain and heavy silver.

Only after the soup had been served did their host take up the point Catherine had raised.

'We call our association "the Order" and its officers are known as "Grand Master", "Grand Hospitaller" and so on – largely because we have to call ourselves something. Our connection with the Teutonic Knights is otherwise rather tenuous.'

Tim gave a cynical laugh. 'Oh, come off it! You're just

as militant as they were. They made war on pagans and heretics. Your crusade is against socialists, nationalists and anyone else who opposes your particular gospel.'

Catherine asked, 'What's your connection with the Grand Imperial Order in Vienna?'

He laughed. 'Oh, we leave the dressing up to them, while we exercise influence – power, if you prefer the word. There *is* an ideological link with the medieval knights. Someone much cleverer than I once said, "Europe is a set of ideas and attitudes rooted in Christian values." The Teutonic Order represented those values. They gave cohesion, strong government and religion to northern Europe – to this very country where we are now, which used to be called Prussia. I won't bore you with a history lesson, but after the collapse of the Teutonic Order, northern and eastern Europe suffered centuries of recurrent chaos. Poland became a battleground for more powerful neighbouring states. We don't intend that to happen again.'

Catherine shivered, vividly remembering Professor Windgren's warnings about the Germans' sense of international destiny and his assurance that this crusading spirit could never be politically organised in the modern world.

Tim said, 'So you set up a secret society, accountable to nobody. And through it you manipulate people and events.'

There was another pause while Stanislaus served the fish course – a local version, their host explained, of Scandinavian gravadlax – and poured a dry but fruity Moselle to accompany it.

The Grand Hospitaller drank half his wine slowly, thoughtfully. 'You used the word "manipulate", Mr Lacy.

That suggests to me a certain political naiveté that I'm sure you cannot be guilty of.'

'I suppose you're going to tell me that we're all being manipulated all the time – by central government, local government, big business, the media, admen, bureaucrats . . .'

'Precisely. And every one of them has a vested interest. What we in the Order are doing is ensuring, to the best of our ability, that the moral and political values of the Western world are preserved. It's no use thinking that because those values are self-evident they will prevail. They have to be fought for against every insidious influence that seeks to undermine them – crime, communism, racism, drugs, nationalism. Believe me, we in reunified Germany know all about these influences.'

'I don't think . . .'

'Let me just make one more point, Mr Lacy. It's not merely a question of trying to conserve what we have created in the West. You may sneer at our "crusade", but we have to be aggressive with our culture – just as the Teutonic Knights were. Look at what's happening in Russia, Poland, Bulgaria, Romania – all the former communist countries. Governments are trying to introduce free-market economics. They're having a hell of a hard time. The transition is painful. Many people find themselves worse off than they were before. The reds start coming out of the woodwork and demanding a return to the bad old days. Sometimes they get elected back into office. Do we just sit back and let the rival ideologues slog it out? Do we really want to see a return to the fascist-versus-communist conflict of the Thirties? No. The new democrats are building very fragile structures in countries that have only ever known tyranny and totalitarianism.

They have got to be supported at every level – political, financial, commercial, educational. This is what the Order is about. We have members in most key areas – politics, police, armed forces, newspapers, banking, business, the churches. We are all using our influence to underpin a way of life you may take for granted.'

Catherine said, 'Surely that's the task of leading Western governments, using proper diplomatic channels.'

'Mrs Lacy, your faith in us statesmen is touching. But there's a limit to what we can do, and one reason for that is that we have to keep our hands clean. Governments of all complexions have always needed the support of hidden forces which don't have to be quite so scrupulous.'

Tim finished his salmon and laid down his fork. 'I might find your marvellous crusade convincing if it didn't involve the murder of innocent people – including a close friend of mine.'

For the first time their host looked less than fully self-assured. 'Ah, yes; Mr Thomson. An appalling mistake. I am truly sorry about that. Let me try to explain . . .'

'No.' Tim held up a hand. '*I'll* explain, and you can tell me if I've got it right. I've spent months piecing it all together – and being hindered by your people at every turn. Now you can damned well listen to my version.'

Chapter 20

Tim paused for a moment to collect his thoughts. Then he began.

'I reckon the trouble started when Meredith, who's one of your bigwigs . . .'

'He's commander of our Frankfurt chapter.'

'Right. He decided to steal the Dresden Text for the Order. He saw himself as a man of destiny, living out some old Germanic myth about reassembling the Teutonic Knights' Bible and bringing them back to life.'

'Would you like to see that Bible – the centrepiece of this whole lamentable affair?' Their host went through into the salon and returned almost immediately with a thick volume bound in plain vellum. He laid it on the polished mahogany. 'The Marienburg Bible – or all that remains of it.'

They gathered round and Catherine opened the cover. 'It's beautiful!' She slowly turned page after page, running her fingers lightly over the elegant script, the brilliant illustrations and illuminated capitals, glowing with reds, blues, greens and gold leaf. She noted the recurrent visual theme of mounted knights. 'But why on earth did the Order want it?'

The statesman sighed and shook his head. 'There's the

tragedy. We didn't really want it.'

'What!' Tim stared, open-mouthed. 'Are you saying that you didn't order . . .'

'Meredith, as I'm sure you know, is an impulsive romantic. He is obsessed with grand Wagnerian ideas that fit rather poorly with the very practical aims of the Order. However, when he told the Grand Chapter that he could obtain this wonderful book, and he suggested that it would be something to display here, as a kind of focus for members' loyalty, we – foolishly, as it turned out – let him go ahead.'

'But you must have sanctioned the details of his plan.'

'I'm afraid not. Regional chapters have a fair degree of autonomy. We encourage members to display initiative. We left the organisation to Meredith. Of course, had we known . . .'

'Yeah, yeah, just like President Nixon: "Nobody told me." '

Catherine was trying to follow the drift of the story. 'So Meredith stole the Dresden Text, and he killed Mike to get it.'

Tim grimaced. 'Yes and no.' He sat back as Stanislaus served the meat course.

The Grand Hospitaller said, 'I hope you enjoy this. It's wild boar from our own woods.'

Once their plates and glasses had been filled, Catherine's curiosity exploded. 'What do you mean, "Yes and no"?'

'According to Maria, who has no reason to defend Meredith, he never intended murder – not Mike's murder, anyway. He needed someone experienced to carry out the robbery. That's where Maria came into the picture.'

'Maria?'

'Meredith had recruited her. He mesmerised her – not very difficult. He made the Order sound glamorous and exciting. He made Maria feel that she had an important part to play in it. What he really wanted was to get a hold over her father. He needed underworld contacts. With Oscar's little girl under his influence, he could turn the screw whenever he wanted to.'

'And Maria fell for it. My God, she must be weak-minded.'

'She's very impressionable. Perhaps that's the same thing. She's always play-acting because she can't distinguish it from reality. Being a member of the Order was her biggest role yet. I guess she saw herself as a cross between Mata Hari and St Joan. Anyway, when Meredith wanted someone for the New York job, he activated the König connection and Oscar produced Emma Freundlich. It was when Meredith discovered who she was that he gave his plan a twist. He would steal a little-known medieval manuscript and, in return, he'd deliver a wanted terrorist to the police – dead. He really believed – probably still does believe – that he was performing a public service.'

Catherine sipped the smooth Aloxe-Corton. 'So it was Meredith who fired the shot through the hotel door?'

'No, that was Maria's job. She's a dab hand with guns. That was important to Meredith. The last thing he wanted was an accident which resulted in a dead or wounded policeman.'

Catherine frowned. 'The whole thing sounds a bit like a game.'

'I'm sure Meredith and Maria both hugely enjoyed their own cleverness. They were carrying out an audacious heist, which involved tricking other people. Meredith could show off his talent for mimicry, imitating my voice for Mike's benefit and then putting on a German accent to get the cops to the hotel. There Maria could display her fancy shooting. No one would get hurt except Emma Freundlich, and she didn't count. And it was all being done for a great cause.'

'But, how can you say no one was supposed to get hurt?' Catherine said angrily. 'What about poor Mike?'

Their host intervened. 'That was a mistake – a stupid blunder. Meredith hired someone he couldn't control.'

Tim nodded thoughtfully. 'Yes, by and large I'm prepared to accept that. Maria insists that it was Freundlich who blew the whole thing. She was meant to incapacitate Mike, not kill him. A blow on the head, or a quick injection – that was the plan. But Freundlich was either too vicious or too nervous. When it came to it, a bullet was easier and quicker.' Tim glowered at the German. 'A good man died. But not just because of Meredith's bungling incompetence or Freundlich's psychopathy. You're the real criminal – you and your inhuman "Order". In your grand schemes for the betterment of mankind, you take no account of real people.'

The other man returned Tim's gaze. 'I have already expressed my profound regret over your friend's death. I assure you that we have our ways of ensuring that such a mistake does not occur again.'

'Why didn't you just hand the culprits over to the police?'

'Oh, Mr Lacy, please be reasonable.' The German showed the first sign of annoyance.

'No, of course, you couldn't. In fact, all you could do after such a fiasco was organise a cover-up. That's what you've been doing ever since, and it's become more and more elaborate.'

The Grand Hospitaller nodded. 'And for that you must take your own share of the blame, Mr Lacy. The other deaths that have occurred have been as a direct result of your intervention.'

'Don't give me that crap!' Tim pushed his plate away, his appetite annihilated.

'It's absolutely true. Listen to me. After the "fiasco", as you rightly call it, the situation was reported to the Grand Master. He personally took care of the matter at the top diplomatic level.'

'Which is why the New York police were told to drop the case?'

'Precisely.'

Catherine stared at him. 'How come this "Order" of yours has influence in America?'

'Mrs Lacy, please try to grasp the importance of the Order and what we stand for. We are not a bunch of German political adventurers. We are a major force in international affairs. We have allies everywhere – including Washington. Perhaps I should say, *especially* Washington. The American government cannot and will not increase its direct involvement in Europe. But it is vital for them that Europe should remain stable and pro-American. They see us, rightly, as an association of influential men and women working for the same cause. In this particular case, as a result of certain talks initiated by the Grand Master, the unfortunate sequence of events in New York was brought to a rapid close. It would have been better for all concerned if things had stayed that way. Your activities led to further tragedy.'

'I still don't buy that. There had already been a falling out between König and Meredith. According to Maria, they had a furious row in New York.'

'Understandably.' The Grand Hospitaller drained his glass.

'When I persisted with my enquiries Meredith deliberately laid a trail leading to König. I guess Oscar had outlived his usefulness – except as bait.'

The German nodded. 'Correct, except that Meredith was now under much closer supervision. Your doggedness made things very difficult for us. If we put too many obstacles in your path, your suspicions would simply be confirmed. On the other hand, of course, we didn't want you to discover the truth.'

Catherine sat back in her chair. She, too, had lost interest in food. 'So that letter I found in Vienna was a plant?'

'We would have been delighted if you hadn't picked it up. We wanted the trail to run cold on you. But if you and your husband were going to persist, we had to know where you were.'

'Stop! Stop!' Catherine cried. 'My head is spinning. Are you trying to tell us that all the people we've been involved with – Hoffmeister, the Frankls, Müller and everybody – are all members of the Order?'

'Oh, good heavens, no.' The German seemed genuinely taken aback by the question. 'Our membership really isn't very large. We look for quality rather than quantity. But every one is a person with a wide circle of important contacts, friends and acquaintances – people they can ask favours of. You might be surprised at how much information you can gather simply by knowing the right people.'

'But someone was assigned to watch us in Vienna?'

'Yes.'

'Who?'

'The Grand Hospitaller smiled and shook his head.

'How about some dessert? No? Shall we adjourn for coffee, then?'

When they were seated in the salon, their host took up the story. 'You shook Oscar König very badly, Mr Lacy.'

'Which meant that you had to get rid of him to stop him blabbing.'

'It meant that we had to go along with Meredith's plan.'

'You also had to stop Maria knowing the truth.'

'Yes. It was necessary to make the "suicide" as convincing as possible.'

'You got a young policeman to administer the poison. I suppose he was another of your members.' Catherine was trying hard to keep up.

Tim cut in. 'No, I got that quite wrong. When Steiger told us that Pressner had just arrived on secondment, I assumed that he must have been sent to Berlin specifically to bump off König. Pressner came from Hamburg, which just happens to be Hans Meyer's home town. I put two and two together and made them add up to about a thousand. Of course, Pressner had nothing to do with König's death, did he?'

The German shook his head.

Catherine said, 'Then it must have been . . .'

'Steiger was the head of our Berlin chapter. We couldn't trust the task of silencing König to anyone else. He did his job well, and everything seemed to be working out satisfactorily. He even managed to persuade Fräulein König that her father had committed suicide out of fear of his gangland associates. Then, Mr Lacy, you upset the applecart again, although I'm not quite sure how. I need you to tell me about everything that happened afterwards. As you know, we've brought Maria here for investigation . . .'

'Your Vehmic court?'

'Yes. It would be very valuable if you could help us to get at the truth.'

'What's going to happen to her?'

'That will very much depend on what we discover.'

Catherine butted in. 'Hey, just a minute, what *is* this "court"?'

Tim grimaced. 'The Vehmic court is another quaint notion these jokers have picked up from those Teutonic Knights they apparently have no interest in. It's an *ad hoc* drumhead tribunal with life-and-death powers. Maria is terrified of it. That's why she went into hiding and came to me for help.'

'But what's she supposed to have done?'

There was a long silence during which two pairs of eyes were fixed on Tim. At last, the German said, 'Your husband won't answer that because he knows that he is largely responsible. He unwittingly goaded Maria König into a very grave offence. The day after her father's death, she contacted Meredith and told him that Mr Lacy had paid her a nocturnal visit. Two things alarmed Meredith about her report: it appeared that your husband still hadn't given up, and that he had also sown doubts in Maria's mind about her father's suicide. Meredith contacted us immediately, and we determined on one last stratagem to throw you off the scent. We had to work very hard and very fast.'

Tim explained. 'They cooked up some forged papers, rushed them to Berlin, and gave them to Maria. She was supposed to "find" them and show them to me. They tied the Dresden Text to Oscar's antiquities-smuggling activities. As you know, I was almost completely taken in. It seemed to wrap everything up so neatly. Ironical, isn't it: all that energetic laying of false trails had finally succeeded.'

The politician busied himself refilling the coffee cups. 'What else did you talk about with Maria during your time in Geneva?' The question was casual.

So was the answer. 'Oh, this and that.'

'I think you told her you were suspicious of Steiger. Is that correct?'

Tim shrugged. 'All you get out of me is name, rank and number.'

'Can you think of any other reason why Maria should have murdered him?'

Catherine yelped, 'Another murder!'

Tim said, 'Steiger was shot and thrown out of a train near the Polish-German border.' To the Grand Hospitaller, he said, 'Have you got proof?'

'Oh, I'm sure we shall have when we examine Maria and Meredith tomorrow.'

'Meredith? I thought you were only putting Maria on trial.'

'So did Meredith. That's why I wanted him to bring her here. Our *Vehmgericht*, of which you are so dismissive, is simply an internal tribunal. The Order has to exercise a degree of discipline, and these two both have a great deal to answer for.'

Catherine broke the silence that followed. Trying to keep a nervous quaver out of her voice. 'And what happens to *non*-members of the Order who cause you problems?'

The German raised an eyebrow. 'I don't quite understand . . .'

'Given all that we now know about your repulsive set-up, what are you going to do with us? An unfortunate accident? Or do we just disappear?'

He laughed. 'My dear Mrs Lacy, I can see that I still

341

haven't eradicated the Gestapo image you seem to have of us. Nothing will happen to you. Our aeroplane will be available to take you home tomorrow. As to what you know about us, what do you suppose you could do with the information?'

Tim grimaced and nodded. 'Clever.'

Catherine glowered. 'I don't see . . .'

Tim explained. 'Friends in high places. People with a vested interest in preserving the status-quo. Pro-Europeanism is in. If we went to the British police or the Foreign Office, our story would end up pigeonholed. I doubt whether even the more chauvinistic newspapers would touch it.'

Catherine was still doubtful. 'You're really letting us go?'

'Of course. Perhaps in return you'd do a small favour for me.' He went into the dining room and returned with the Marienburg Bible. 'We can never undo what is done, but we can make whatever restitution lies within our power. I'll arrange for you to go through Heathrow customs under diplomatic cover. Would you see that this reaches the British Library?'

When Stanislaus brought their breakfast tray in the morning, there was another message from the Grand Hospitaller.

Dear Mr and Mrs Lacy,

As you will realise, I am otherwise engaged this morning. Regrettably, I cannot, therefore, entertain you in person. It occurred to me that you might enjoy a ride around the estate. Stanislaus will see that you are kitted out, and the outside staff will have horses ready at the front of the house at about 10.00.

I will have a car sent to take you to the airport at 14.30.

I am sure that in the course of time you will come to see the events we discussed last night in a more favourable light.

Bon voyage!
The Grand Hospitaller

'It's all so nonchalant, isn't it? I think that's what sticks in my throat most. Our host behaves as if this was just a country house party. And all the time he and his cronies are . . . Bloody hell, it makes me sick to the stomach.' Tim had spent a bad night and had woken feeling black and uncommunicative.

Catherine passed him his coffee. 'Well, at least we'll be out of it soon. Then we can put the whole grisly business behind us.' She walked across to the window and the sunlight struck gold from her hair. She looked out at a party of men with guns strolling towards the trees away to the left, spilling long shadows on the dewy grass. 'And it is an absolutely gorgeous morning for a ride.'

It was. As he and Catherine followed their guides along the drive and then turned off onto a wide woodland track, Tim felt the warmth and the gentle motion ease away some of the tension. After an invigorating canter they emerged into a hollow with a stream running through it. They let the horses drink. Catherine looked at her husband and wondered if she could venture on some of the questions still fluttering around her brain like birds trying to roost.

'*Did* Maria kill that German policeman?'

'Yes.'

'You sound very sure.'

'She got stuck in her own honeycomb of lies. When I asked her if she had passed on her father's papers to Steiger she said she hadn't, because they were fakes. Now, if Steiger had no information about Oscar's supposed Russian and Polish contacts, he wouldn't have travelled to Warsaw. More to the point, there would have been no mob assassin hired to gun him down. Maria actually got the idea for the train murder from something Walter Frankl said when we were in Geneva. It was because I guessed the truth about Steiger's death that I was able to force the whole story out of Maria.'

'Presumably she killed out of revenge.'

They legged the horses on and walked them among the trees. Distant shooting broke the whispering stillness of the wood.

'Basically, yes. Her relationship with her father was ambiguous, but he was all she had by way of family. She'd also got disillusioned with the Order. She realised that Meredith had used her. She genuinely admired him once but then . . . I guess it was a case of "Hell hath no fury . . ." She decided to hit out and kill Steiger. When the hue and cry died down, she was going to disappear and make a new start, find a new role to play, using Daddy's money.'

'But how did she find out about Steiger? Was it you who put her on to him?'

'No, she worked it out for herself. At that time I still thought Pressner was our man. But Maria knew how devious Meredith was. When he came up with that desperate plan to turn attention to mythical Russian crooks, she realised he had something to hide. She probably put two and two together.'

'Did she really think she could get away with it?'

'Oh, yes. She's terribly mixed up but she's not stupid, and she has a lot of low cunning. Unfortunately, Meredith was too quick for her.'

'What a pair!'

'In a way, they deserve each other.'

'Meredith must be an incredibly twisted man.'

'He's the worst possible combination: devious and at the same time fanatically single-minded. Once he'd got it into his head that he had to have the Dresden Text, he just went on and on, using whatever stratagem, committing whatever crime seemed necessary, involving anyone else he needed without compunction. He has a mesmeric effect on people and enjoys manipulating them. You remember my telling you about Ernst Müller in Austria, and how he was selling off some of the best items in his collection? According to Maria, Meredith had been having some sessions with the old boy. Feeding him a lot of nationalist claptrap. Getting him to invest in second-rate German art.'

'And I suppose he must have got Gerda Frankl to phone me and ask where you were. He knew I wouldn't give any information to a complete stranger.'

'Oh, he's painstakingly thorough. I suppose that's the German strain in his ancestry. Do you know, I only realised, lying in bed last night, how he worked that trick in New York.'

'Imitating your voice and convincing Mike?'

'Yes. We conversed briefly at the party; just the usual sort of empty chit-chat one usually indulges in on such occasions – or so I thought. Now I realise that he was getting me to use certain words and phrases so that he could practise them. He must have had a hidden mike. We talked about the police. And he asked me to repeat a certain formula about the value of a manuscript – "You can expect to pay a million." I'll bet that when Meredith phoned Mike he used those very words – "You can expect the police to call" – something like that.'

'My God, what a creep! He must be a liability to this precious Order.'

'I'm sure they've realised that by now.'

'What do you think they'll do with him – and Maria?'

They had emerged from the trees on a rise about a mile away from the house. One of the guides pointed. It was an impressive sight: long, low and beautifully proportioned, sunlight glinting on its many windows.

Catherine suddenly shivered. 'I wish we were back at Farrans. I'm becoming decidedly unenthusiastic about foreign parts.'

'Come on!' Tim turned his grey's head. 'I'll race you down to the drive!'

They streaked across the flank of the hill at a fast canter. They reached the gravel, reined in and let the horses walk back to the house. The shooting party was returning as they reached it. Tim jumped down and held a hand up to help his wife.

But Catherine remained in the saddle, sitting very still.

'Tim,' she said, in a low hoarse voice, 'isn't this the *breeding* season for game?'

'It must be.'

'Then it's the closed season for shooting.'

'Yes.'

'Does that mean that the shooting we heard . . .?'

'Yes.'